FASTER
THAN
FALLING

THE SKYLIGHTER ADVENTURES

NATHAN VAN COOPS

Skylighter
Press

FASTER THAN FALLING

eBook ISBN: 978-0-9894755-6-3
Print ISBN: 978-0-989475570

Cover illustration by Merilliza Chan.
www.merilliza.com

Cover and interior design by Shayne Leighton and Parliament House Book Formatting and Design.
www.parliamenthousepress.com I www.shaynerocks.com

Custom map by Jared Blando.
www.TheRedEpic.com

Chapter illustrations by Julia Scheiber.

Author photo by Jennie Thunnell Photography.
www.jenniethunnell.com

"The Globe Mother" illustration by Nathan Van Coops.

Book edited by Emily Young and Ben Way.

Access free bonus content including more original
sketches by the author!

Get your free gift at
www.nathanvancoops.com/bonus

-NVC

THE GLOBE MOTHER

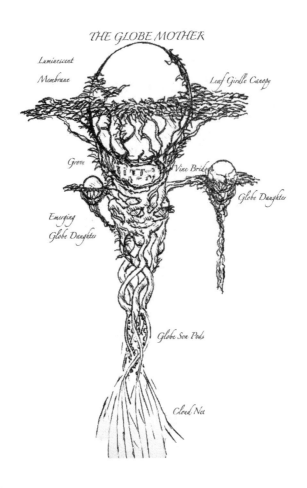

Luminescent
Membrane

Leaf Girdle Canopy

Grove

Vine Bridge

Globe Daughter

Emerging
Globe Daughter

Globe Son Pods

Cloud Net

For Horacio Garcia, Eddie Molina, Reed Skupny, Christy Meyer, Daniel Meyer, Marc Pipes, and all the other kids who shared my childhood adventures, real and imaginary.

And to my big sisters: Amy, Sarah, and Jenny. Because even though growing up was hard, I never had to do it alone.

-NVC

I

THE EXPRESS

Kipling was going to be the first to spot it. He just knew it.

Perched atop the most easterly of the globe daughters, he could scan the sky from Piper's Peak in the north, all the way to Southfang. The sight of the jagged mountaintops stabbing through the clouds usually brought delight and awe to all the patchlings—a deep wonder born of bedtime stories on cold nights, and mothers and fathers with a flair for the theatrical. Today those tales were a distraction good only for eight-year-olds. This season Kipling was twelve, and he was going to be the Watcher.

The sky revealed nothing so far, just puffy white clouds scattered below him and a twelve-thousand-foot drop to the surface of the ocean. In the distance, the sea foamed and frothed as it continued its relentless assault on the cliffs at the base of the Great Fanged Mountains.

The other boys and girls in Kipling's patch had mostly scrambled up Tamra Ohna, the floating globe just to the south of his position. Tamra Ohna was an older globe floating higher in the sky and presumably offering a better view, but Kipling had been watching this arm of the globe patch for the last two weeks and, as he predicted, this afternoon he was sitting nicely in Tamra Ohna's shadow. As his friends jostled for position atop his taller neighbor—squinting in the sunlight—he had a clear view from the shade, and he had this globe, Mona Leana, all to himself. Well . . . nearly.

"Why do you even want to be the Watcher?" Rufus yelled, still attempting to extract himself from the tangleweed at Mona Leana's base. "It's not like you get extra meals or anything."

Kipling, sitting cross-legged atop the leafy, floating sphere, leaned over to observe his friend, then went back to searching the sky. "People respect the Watcher. It means you're the best at spotting things. It makes you important."

"But we already have a Watcher." Something snapped as Rufus struggled out of the creepers and started to climb the globe.

Kipling frowned but kept his eyes on the horizon. "Don't break the vines. My dad will yell at us."

"Sorry," Rufus muttered. "It wouldn't let go." He huffed and puffed his way up the side of the globe, using whatever handholds he could find in the leaves and blooms on Mona Leana's surface. He finally gained the top, adjusted his buoyancy belt, and plopped down next to Kipling. "See anything yet?"

Kipling leaned forward and stuck his face out, knowing the few extra inches wouldn't make much difference, but wanting to at least clear Rufus from his peripheral vision. He sniffed the air, hoping to catch a whiff of the peculiar oily scent that always came with their annual visitor. "We have to watch for red. He told me that he was going to paint the nose this spring. He promised he'd make it red." Kipling grinned as he relayed this information to his companion. Rufus nodded but didn't seem especially overwhelmed by the news, a small disappointment for Kipling, who had kept the secret all year, gloating over this tidbit that would give him a slim advantage over his older and more seasoned competitors.

"What do you think he'll bring us this year?" Rufus asked. "I hope he brings more of the honey rocks. Those were the best. Also the toffee chews, and the gum whistles . . ."

"He can't just bring candy every year."

"Why not?"

"Because he's important. He's got a job to do," Kipling said.

"Father says he's just a crazy old Grounder and I'm not supposed to go chasing after him anymore. He says I need to stop acting like a patchling and start being a man." Rufus twiddled a piece of vine absentmindedly between his fingers until the tangleweed bloom came off in his hand. He realized too late what he'd done and tried to brush it off his fingertips discreetly.

Kipling just shook his head. "My dad says he's important because he brings us news and messages. He says without *The Sunshine Express*, we'd—" He stopped talking as the spot of red on the horizon caught his eye. "There he is! It's him! Where's my trumpet?" Kipling cast about in search of the star lily root he had carefully hollowed out and perfected playing in anticipation of this moment. The trumpet was nowhere to be seen. "Where did it go? I need to—" Kipling's heart sank as Rufus reached underneath himself and pulled out the twisted root. The delicate stem of the mouthpiece was dangling at an angle from a strand of bark. "Nooo!"

Rufus grimaced in shame as Kipling snatched the root from his hands. "Sorry. I didn't see it."

Spinning to search the horizon, Kipling tried desperately to coax a sound from the busted horn. A pitiful sputtering was the only result.

"Wait, you can use mine!" Rufus exclaimed. "I made one, too!" He patted the sides of his trousers and felt around under the buoyancy belt. "It was here just a minute ago." Kipling only had seconds at most to fulfill his dream, so he helped his friend search, then dropped his gaze to the patch of tangleweed Rufus had struggled through on the way up. Sure enough, the boy's trumpet was caught in the vines surrounding Mona Leana's main stalk. Kipling expelled his breath, shoved Rufus out of the way, and leapt.

The cluster of tangleweed around Mona Leana's globe was thick and sturdy this season. Kipling had been out to this end of the patch for years of pruning duty with his father and then more recently on his own as his father decided the chore was now his responsibility. While the plant was indeed a weed, and essentially a parasite on the floating globe patch, it served a purpose, binding the many globes of the patch together and granting handholds along an otherwise smooth stalk. As Kipling landed in the mess of vines, his hand immediately stretched for the trumpet, snatching it from the air just as the impact of his landing jolted it loose and sent it tumbling toward the sky below.

The thrill of his success wilted as a long tone blasted out from the top of Tamra Ohna. Kipling recognized the rich sound belonging to the horn of last year's Watcher, his older brother Kaleb. Kipling slumped into the vines and let the star lily trumpet fall from his fingertips. His piece of root danced its way into the blue below, disappearing completely into the void of sea and cloud. He stayed there, crestfallen, until he could hear the whirring and popping of the aircraft in the distance, even over the cheering from Tamra Ohna.

Observing the long drop below him didn't bring any particular emotion. Fear of heights was for Grounders. Kipling was a Skylighter, and Skylighters never fear a fall.

"Um, Kip? A little help?"

Kipling lifted his head as Rufus drifted by, his buoyancy belt keeping the boy from sinking or floating away but also hindering his ability to navigate his way back aboard the stalk. Rufus waved his arms a few times, trying to swim his way toward Kip, but to little avail. Kipling untangled a bit of creeper and tossed it to his friend, reeling him back in.

"I'm sorry I made you lose your chance at Watcher. I can tell them you saw it first if you want. I could tell them about—"

"It's okay." Kipling patted his friend on the shoulder and looked into his rotund face. "Sorry I shoved you so hard." He glanced up to where the other kids were celebrating his brother's victory. "You and I know. That's good enough, right? Come on. Let's go see what the *Express* brought."

2

THE GLOBE MOTHER

Corra Mara was the oldest globe mother aloft in the northern hemisphere. Nearly five hundred feet in diameter, its volume of internal gases could raise the entire globe patch to an altitude of twenty-five thousand feet in the peak of summer. It cruised the jet stream, riding the easterly winds and soaking up the sun. Corra Mara's long tendrils trailed through the clouds below, drinking them up into its core. Some claimed that over half the globe patches in the world were now its offspring. This year the giant globe was due to release two more of its daughters into the sky and it was a cause to celebrate. At least for everyone except Samra Rose.

Samra was still in her hammock when she heard the trumpet. Her father had given her permission to go with the other patchlings to watch for the *Express*, but this year her heart wasn't in it. How could it be, when this was her very last season on Corra Mara?

She rolled over in her hammock of colored silkbug ropes and tried to force herself to sleep. Perhaps if her parents found her asleep on this gorgeous, festive day, they'd finally realize the depths of her misery. So far her best efforts had proven ineffective. She'd tried arguing. She'd pouted. She'd even promised a hunger strike, only to have her own stomach betray her. Her stepmother had just laughed when she refused her greens for the second meal in a row. "Samra, you eat more than your father. Not that I know where any of it goes, skinny as a twig like you are." She'd been right. Samra had snuck down to the pantry that night and stuffed herself so full that she started floating out of her hammock in the morning.

Her father said being a Skylighter and refusing to eat the globe greens was like a fish trying to give up water. She supposed he had a point. The leaves of the globe patch were packed full of bollite and lumium—the same elements that got turned into bioluminescent, lifting gas in the center of the globes after being exposed to sunlight. It did the same thing to the Skylighters' anatomy on a smaller scale due to their high body heat, and the process physically changed the density of their bodies relative to the planet's denser atmosphere.

Samra was happy that at least she didn't have to balloon up like a globe in order to float. She didn't think she'd enjoy being the size of a globe daughter.

As it was, Samra was only okay at floating. She'd lost her chubby buoyancy weight early and was able to run and jump all over the patch by the time she was six. She'd learned to plummet earlier than any of her friends. While they were still drifting up into the catch nets of the nursery, she'd learned to expel her lifting gases and drop like a rock, enjoying the freedom of falling. She'd keep exhaling till she almost blacked out, relishing the rush of speed before finally having to breathe and arrest her momentum.

But the one thing Samra hadn't figured out was her glowing. The older kids all lit up on command and could use the extra heat to soar upward when they wanted to, or even lift things. Samra had no control. Some days she'd think she had it figured out only to have one of the other patchlings make her mad, and she'd darken completely, her pale yellow skin turning scarlet with emotion. She always claimed she did it on purpose to show how angry she was, but she wasn't sure anyone believed her anymore. Maybe Rufus. But then again, Rufus believed just about anybody.

The yelling from the top of the distant globe daughter was too loud, too many voices. It meant Kip and Rufus hadn't succeeded in their plan to be the Watcher. Samra frowned and parted the tendrils that formed the wall of her aerie. Making an opening large enough for her head, she peeked out to see the cause of the commotion. A big group of older boys was whooping and hollering on their way back across the thick stalk that linked Tamra Ohna to the Globe Mother. She recognized Darian and Tolmer and a few of the others gathered around the tall figure of Kaleb, who was, as usual, the center of attention.

Samra could admit that Kaleb was handsome. His hair had changed color early, transitioning from the light green of a patchling, straight through tawny adolescence, to an adult brown so dark it was nearly black. At almost seventeen, he didn't have much reason to spend time with the younger patchlings, but since she was a close friend of his brother, Kip, she saw more of him than other girls her age. Perhaps that was why she didn't get goo-goo-eyed over him and start giggling every time he walked by, the way the other girls seemed to.

Her closest neighbor, Khloe, used to stand near the edge of a platform and pretend to faint whenever Kaleb got near, hoping that he might rush to save her. It never worked anymore. Kaleb had caught on after the first few 'rescues' and tended to keep his eyes averted anytime Khloe looked in danger of wilting. Khloe was plenty buoyant anyway, so it's not like she was ever really in any danger. Rescues were all the rage with Khloe's crowd and they conspired daily to find new ways for boys to come to their aid. There was already a group of girls convening at the end of the stalk bridge, waiting to ambush the boys with compliments about their victory.

Samra turned her attention away from the Tamra Ohna stalk and instead concentrated on the two boys scrambling their way down the gangly and overgrown return route from Mona Leana. The lower-flying globe daughter saw much less traffic, as evidenced by the trouble the two boys were having getting back. Rufus was the most obvious. His additional width with his buoyancy belt on made him easy to spot. Kip, by contrast, seemed almost in danger of disappearing as he leapt and bounced over vines and roots thicker than he was. He had Kaleb's athletic frame, but somewhat in miniature, and his hair still had lingering bits of green, though he usually pretended they weren't there.

Samra was every bit as tall as Kip and just as good at jumping, but she did admire the way he could flit and tumble over things and climb his way around the patch. Samra could plummet faster than him, but there are only so many places you can get to by falling.

Samra looked around the cramped tendril pocket she called her room and realized her parents were unlikely to be back soon enough to make her sleeping protest worthwhile. She wasn't about to let them know that she had been secretly heeding their advice about attempting to enjoy her final days with friends before departure. She had too much invested in her protests now to let them off the hook completely, but she knew they were right.

In a few days it would be the spring festival and time for the mature globe daughters to detach and seek their own way in the winds. Her family would be founding members of the new colony, and it would mean a great deal of honor for her father. Her stepmother had reminded her that it didn't necessarily mean she would never see her friends again—you never knew when the winds might blow two colonies together for a time. Samra tried to imagine what it might be like to run into Kip and Rufus after years of being on her own colony. Would they still remember her? They'd better.

Samra swung herself out of her hammock, exhaled forcefully and dropped through the hole in the floor of her aerie. She climbed down the tendril ladder and swung out onto the walkway her family had woven to the main stalk. From there, she could just see Kip and Rufus climbing aboard the main mass of the Globe Mother. She hurried to catch up.

She found the boys on the landing platform, along with all the other patchlings who had come to meet the *Express*. There was Enzo, the wizened, silver-haired pilot, untying packages from the nose cargo hold. The littlest patchlings were tugging on the shirts and trousers of their elder siblings, trying to see what goodies the pilot may have brought this season. Enzo didn't disappoint.

The wiry old man seemed even thinner than last year, and he had always had a bony, birdlike frame to start—especially for a Grounder—but he lifted the heavy package from the hold with a noticeable twinkle in his eye. He unwrapped the crinkly paper packaging and revealed a wicker basket packed with sweets. The little green-haired patchlings squealed with joy as he began to hand out rock candy hammers and thick, chewy butter toffees.

Samra squeezed into the crowd behind Kip and poked him in the ribs. "What happened? I thought you said it was as good as yours this year."

Kip glanced back to see who was poking him, then faced forward again, trying to elbow past Finnigan Tundus, their patchmate from school. Finnigan wriggled under Kip's arm and held his ground. "It was my fault," Rufus explained. "I messed it up."

"It doesn't matter," Kipling replied. "Kaleb can keep the stupid Watcher prize. I didn't want it that much anyway."

Samra knew this was a lie, but she didn't say anything. Kipling had been ogling the carved wooden horn that Kaleb got to carry ever since he'd won it the year before. Unlike the star lily root trumpets the other patchlings made, the Watcher horn was carved from the sacred wood of the Globe Mother itself, dark heartwood from the core of the patch. Globe heartwood was in rare supply, durable and strong but lighter than any of the types of wood found on the surface. Grounders frequently envied the Skylighters' tools and belongings and traded eagerly whenever possible for items made of the stuff.

There was a rumor that the reason Enzo and *The Sunshine Express* came to the globe patch every year was to pay off a debt to the globe council for a bundle of heartwood from years before. As Samra scanned the fabric-wrapped frame of the yellow and red aircraft, she couldn't see any parts that looked like heartwood. The ribs and beams she could see mostly had a red hue, and some a caramel coloring. Nothing resembled the dark gloss of Kaleb's trumpet.

When the crowd of patchlings thinned to the last sticky-fingered boys and girls, Samra finally reached Enzo and his basket. The weathered old pilot looked up and grinned a patchwork smile at her. He had lost a tooth or two since last year, but his blue eyes still shone with the exuberance she remembered. "Ah, Samra. Let's see if I can remember what your favorite was."

Samra smiled, pleased that the old man had remembered her name. He plucked a paper-wrapped sucker from the basket and held it out to her. "Dazzleberry, if I recall."

Samra blushed and took the candy. "Thanks." She realized her hands were turning red and stuffed them in her pockets.

"Of course, my dear. Not every day I get to meet the bravest young colonist in the patch."

Samra cocked her head in surprise. "Me?"

"I heard you're departing on Cirra Sola this season. And what a beautiful new patch colony it will be."

Samra only nodded, surprised that this Grounder had taken the time to learn so much about their plans for after the festival.

Enzo took a quick draw from the mask that dangled from a cord around his neck. A flexible tube ran from the mask down to a little metal canister on his belt. Samra had once asked why he preferred the air in the canister to that of the patch. He'd said it was because he loved the way the ground smelled. Kipling had chastised her later for prying. Apparently all Grounders had trouble breathing for long in the Heights and it was rude to point it out. Enzo hadn't seemed to mind the question. He'd even let her smell the air from the can. To her it just smelled like him. Like cut grass and rainwater.

"I spoke to your father when I landed," Enzo said. "He's very proud of you." Enzo reached out and patted her on the shoulder.

She tried not to fault him for the lie. He was probably just trying to be kind. If her father really were proud of her, wouldn't he have told her and not a Grounder?

"And who have we got here? Kipling and Rufustus, yes?" Enzo glanced at Rufus's buoyancy belt. "Still healthy eaters in the family, I see. Very good. If I could float up into the sky just from eating breakfast, you'd bet I would, too."

Rufus had seemed slightly on guard, used to comments about his buoyancy belt not being nearly so complimentary, but as Enzo handed him a bright orange gum whistle, his trepidation faded away. "I've only drifted off twice this month. Mother says I'm likely to be able to lose the belt any day now."

Samra almost commented at this, knowing that Rufus's mother had been making this same claim for two years, but she opted to concentrate on her dazzleberry sucker instead. She looked over the aircraft and saw no sign of their other annual visitor. "Where's Fledge?"

"Being lazy," Enzo replied. He stepped onto the lower wing and climbed to the front of the cockpit, reaching down into the seat and extracting a brown and black ball of fur. "I swear all he does anymore is sleep." The animal in his arms opened its dark orb eyes and blinked a few times, letting out a yawn that revealed all of its pointed fangs. The big ears twitched and it stretched one leathery wing to full length before using its clawed end to scratch its neck.

Samra had rarely seen a cliff fox in the wild. The mammals were usually reclusive, inhabiting the clefts and hollows of the Miramoor Coast, feeding on insects, birds, and even small fish or crustaceans if they could catch them. They weren't really foxes, though their faces resembled one. They were actually part of the bat family, though the biggest of the species by far. Samra had heard stories of cliff foxes so large that they could carry off young patchlings who weren't paying attention. Her father said that was nonsense, but other parents in the patch loved to use the threat of cliff fox abduction to encourage obedience from their less than mindful offspring.

Fledge, the old aviator's companion, aided as much as the baskets of candy when it came to Enzo garnering awe from the youngest citizens of the patch. The cliff fox climbed his way up onto Enzo's shoulder, and after a flap of its wings, settled into a sleepy surveillance of its surroundings.

Enzo pulled another basket from the baggage hold of the aircraft. This one was filled with reed tubes, individually wrapped with colored ribbons. Samra knew that each one held messages — communications from other patches, and sometimes correspondence from Grounders hoping to reach the Skylighter High Council. Enzo tucked one of the tubes carefully inside his jacket pocket, then hoisted the basket on his hip and grinned at Kip. "I trust your family is keeping the patch in order. Your brother must be near to being a councilman by now, isn't he?"

Kipling frowned. "Yeah, I guess."

The old man straightened up and gave the formal Altirian sign for visitor. "May the north wind bring you vision to see paths that are clear."

Kipling held up his hand as well and dutifully responded. "May the west wind bring us calm to savor the company of friends."

"I come as invited guest of the globe council. Would you be so kind as to escort me safely to my destination?" Enzo smiled.

"The Globe Mother shines brighter because of your presence," Kipling replied. "You are welcome and received with joy. I will guide you safely to your destination." The last few words were more of a mumble, but Enzo didn't seem to mind.

They both performed the required bow and Enzo smiled again. He ruffled the boy's hair. "Council can't fault us for not following protocol. Let's go see them, shall we?"

Samra trailed behind the old man and the boys at first, shadowing their steps along the thick vine bridge that connected the landing platform to the main patch, but after a few minutes, she tired of walking. It wasn't something she did much, and she didn't care for it, except as a playful diversion when pretending to be a

Grounder. She preferred to float and bounce.

As soon as she was in range of the Globe Mother, Samra took a deep breath and sprang for the canopy of leaves that hung high above the vine bridge. She soared through the air and turned a flip just for the fun of it. When she landed in the greenery and tendrils high over the boys' heads, she looked back and saw the expression of jealousy on Rufus's face. His buoyancy belt kept him weighed down and, even if he didn't have it on, proper aim had never been one of his skills. Freely bounding about the patch was still beyond him.

She could tell that Kip was wishing he could spring after her, chase her up the outside of the stalks the way they'd loved to do since they were little. Most days Kip could keep up with her, sometimes even outrace her, but he was a councilwoman's son, and today, proper manners dictated that he escort their guest according to the dignity and limits of his species.

The old man didn't seem to mind Samra's lack of decorum. In fact, he was grinning up at her with a gleam in his eye that she couldn't help but interpret as envy. The wiry pilot didn't behave like the other Grounders she'd met at all. Other than needing his own special air on occasion, he seemed every bit as comfortable in the Heights as a Skylighter. With solid bones and no natural buoyancy cells built into their anatomy, most Grounders would panic and fret at being so high above the clouds, but she had never known the old man to so much as tremble at the drop-offs beneath him, even when the vine bridge narrowed or required him to cling to tendrils and handholds to keep his balance.

Samra leapt and climbed her way up the patch, taking her favorite paths as high as she could go. She jumped and scrambled onto the massive globe of the Mother herself, then around its circumference toward the grove of the councilors. The smooth membrane of the globe glowed warm under her touch.

The gigantic orb of the Mother was the primary source of lift for the patch. While the other globe daughters and sons provided added buoyancy, and even the bodies of the Skylighters themselves contributed in a small way to keeping the patch airborne, the Globe Mother's voluminous interior contained more hot lifting gases than any other object in the northern hemisphere. High above the rest of the patch, Samra felt like the Mother was pulsing with the same joy she felt.

The dozens of smaller globes attached to the Mother were spun out in a vast spiral today, like planets circling a star. The luminescent green spheres bobbed in the wind and occasionally bumped into one another, but the entire collection of them stretched for miles, leafy islands in a sea of blue.

Samra only perched on the side of the Globe Mother until she could make out Kip and Rufus far below, guiding the pilot toward the Gate of Thorns, the entrance to the council chambers. Forcing all the lift gases from her body and narrowing her eyes, she released her grip on the side of the globe and plummeted.

It was here that Samra felt most alive, watching the green of the patch blur by, refusing to breathe for as long as she could while she built up speed. Normally she could go faster, but the Gate of Thorns was rushing up to meet her. She flipped herself upright to position her feet below her, and slammed into the walkway just ahead of Kip with a satisfying thud, hard enough to send a tremor through the tendrils around the gate.

"Goodness!" the old pilot exclaimed, and Fledge flapped his wings to keep his balance on the old man's shoulder. Rufus had staggered back a step and had to find his equilibrium again as Samra straightened up in front of them. "Aren't you the acrobat," Enzo murmured.

Samra didn't know what an acro-bat was, but if it was a relative of the cliff fox, she took it to be a compliment. She smiled and moved out of the way for the old man. Kip frowned at her but she knew he would have been doing the same thing if he had the choice. The fact that she was free to do as she pleased and he wasn't was clearly irritating him, but she merely reveled in the glory of her position. Sadly this was as far as any of them could go.

The dark wooden door of the council chamber opened without them having to knock. Someone had no doubt heard her dramatic arrival on the walkway. Inside the doorway, Councilman Thur welcomed their guest. The old Skylighter was one of the seven councilors who ensured the welfare of the patch. His bold eyes were hazel and matched the threads of his councilor's tunic. His skin was a pale brown, so thin in places that Samra could see right through it. She could make out the outline of his teeth through his cheeks, even when his mouth was closed. It was a strange sensation to be seeing someone's insides. She wondered if other parts of him had become transparent, too. Could you look right into his stomach and see what he ate for breakfast? She shook off the thought in disgust. She was grateful that the council elders tended to stay covered in their ceremonial cloaks.

Enzo shook each of the patchlings' hands and he thanked Kip for guiding him, then stepped inside the council chamber. Councilman Thur nodded gravely to the three friends as proper manners dictated, but said nothing. He merely closed the door.

Samra frowned as the lock slid into place, disappointed not to know what messages might have come from the other colonies. Any private messages would be sorted by the council and delivered to the proper recipients, but she had little reason to expect any letters would be coming to her. Nearly all the people she knew still lived aboard the Globe Mother. Her patchmate, Racha, had flown away two seasons ago when her family colonized a new globe daughter, but she had only written once, and then never responded to the three or four notes Samra had sent. She didn't care. Racha had been a dull girl anyway. In fact, she hoped Racha's colony got blown into the North Fang Ridge or sunk by the long-taloned eagles over the misty forests of Gongarra.

She supposed that if Racha's patch had really gone missing, someone would have mentioned it, but she liked to imagine it anyway. It wasn't that she wished Racha or her family any harm. On the contrary, a good catastrophe would have served Racha well and livened up her otherwise humdrum existence.

The most interesting people all had harrowing stories to tell. Someday Samra was sure she'd be thought fascinating due to all the dangerous adventures she'd survived. Sadly, no one could think that yet, since nothing exciting ever seemed to happen aboard the Globe Mother—except perhaps the imagined adventures she shared with Kip and Rufus.

"So what do you want to do now?" Samra asked. "We could go jump off the skywalk. Want to see who can plummet the farthest?"

Kipling shook his head. "No. You always win that. And Rufus wouldn't be able to play. Plus it's broad daylight and someone is bound to catch us. You're lucky Thur didn't yell at us already for that landing you made."

"I didn't even fall that hard," Samra objected. "I can go way faster than that if I want to."

"Yeah, but you're not supposed to," Kipling said. "Nobody is, but you especially."

Samra frowned and glanced away.

Some days she regretted telling him. Other than Kip, only her parents knew what Doctor Kesh had said. Dangerous lack of air circulation. Prone to blackouts. Hereditary.

The patch all knew what had happened to her mother, but nobody talked about it anymore. Not even Samra.

"Okay. What do you want to do then?" Samra asked.

Kip stepped to the edge of the walkway that led back to the center stalk of the Globe Mother. Samra joined him in contemplating the view. Somewhere far below, a woman was laughing and the breeze carried the spicy scent of sun pepper stew simmering in someone's kitchen.

Rufus was still staring at the sturdy heartwood door to the council chambers, his hands resting on his hips. "What do you think they're talking about in there?"

Kipling plucked a tangleberry from one of the dangling tangleweed tendrils and started to suck on it. "Just council business. Nothing exciting."

"It could be exciting," Samra countered. "Maybe Enzo is coming to tell them that all the colonies have been blighted with horn worms and we're the only patch left. Could be he's in there delivering the terrible news right now."

"Horn worms can't bring down a whole colony," Kip replied. "You just dust them with sea salt powder and they shrivel right up."

Samra scowled. "Yeah, but these might have been giant horn worms that hatched after a plague of locusts ate all of the globe greens. Maybe the citizens of the patches were so weak and famished that they couldn't dust the globes with sea salt in time and then a swarm of flying sand lizards came to eat the worms and their talons punctured the globes. They all went down in a horrendous tangled mess."

Rufus went pale and his mouth hung open. "Could that happen?" he stammered. "Would they die?"

"It depends on if they went down in the water or over land," Samra explained. "If they went into the Western Ocean, they might have been attacked by dappled cape sharks. Out there I hear the sharks get so big that some can swallow a globe son whole. I heard one got ahold of a whole sack of globe sons before they'd spawned and it became so buoyant from eating them that it could fly through the air. It learned to swim through the sky and attack Grounders in their boats. Then it swam up even higher and sank its teeth into the Loma Dura globe daughter. That's why it went missing all those years ago. The flying cape shark ate it all up."

"Don't listen to her, Rufus," Kip said. "She's just trying to scare you."

"You can doubt me if you want," Samra said. "But you know as well as I do that no one has ever heard from Loma Dura again. I'm telling you, it was a flying shark."

She put on her most serious expression. "But that's not the most terrible fate. If your patch goes down over land, it can be even worse. I bet some of the patches got caught in a cyclone over the Sea of Sand. Down south, in the Somorian Desert, they have cyclones so big and so fast that they reach up into the sky and shred the globes with razor sand. Your patch gets sucked straight down into the desert and it doesn't stop there. The cyclones are so powerful that they even reach underground. They siphon you right into the sand. By the time anyone notices your patch is missing, the whole colony is a hundred feet deep, lost forever in the desert."

Rufus's eyes were as wide as they could open. He looked to Kip in horror. "Do you think we might be the last patch left?"

Kipling merely shook his head.

"Enzo had a special message tucked into his jacket," Samra said. "I bet it was from some lonely survivor of the disaster who used the last of his strength to nobly get word to us, just before he died of thirst in the desert. I bet if we climbed up onto the grove tendrils we might even be able to hear them read out his final warning."

Kipling frowned at this. "We're not allowed to climb the council grove."

"You really think they'll notice, when they're listening to Enzo tell the story of all those dead people?" Samra had gotten so into her story that she almost felt it was true. The line between her imagination and reality was blurring again. Even now her heart was racing, thinking that Enzo might really be detailing the end of their civilization somewhere on the other side of the tendril wall. "Let's go check it out."

She didn't wait for the boys. She leapt onto the wall and started to climb, looking for a cleft or hole in the tendrils that she might be able to see through. A moment later, Kipling flew up onto the wall beside her. "Not that way. There's a dead tendril bundle on the windward side. It's all shriveled and brittle now. We can listen there." He climbed left and started to circumnavigate the thick grove in that direction. Samra smiled and scrambled after him. There were benefits to hanging around the chief grower's son.

Rufus was still hanging onto the edge of the vine bridge, looking for a handhold or way to follow them. "What about me, guys?"

"We'll be right back," Samra replied. "Keep a lookout."

Rufus frowned but nodded and turned to watch the council door. He always took lookout duty seriously, and Samra had to admit he hadn't failed them yet. He was great at distractions and pretending to cry. If worst came to worst and he thought his friends were in danger of being caught, Rufus would 'lose' his buoyancy belt and float off the patch, yelling for a rescue. That was always good for a diversion. Watching the boy taking up his position in front of the council door, Samra paused. How many more times would he be a part of her adventures? Her family was leaving in a few days. Could this be the last time he'd cover for her?

Kip called for her. "Come on! I see it." Samra dragged her eyes from Rufus and turned to follow her friend. She wasn't leaving yet. And she still had to hear about the end of the world.

3

MR. AND MRS. ROOSE

There were only a handful of times Kipling had been caught doing something he shouldn't, but each one of those memories had one person in common—Samra Rose Coley. As he scaled the council grove, he hoped this excursion wouldn't be added to the list.

Kipling clung to the healthy vines at the lower hemisphere of the globe, and settled himself near the clump of desiccated leaves. From this position of security, he parted the dried-up tendrils as quietly as he could, making a hole to peer through. Samra was at his elbow, her head nearly touching his, curious to see what was going on inside. They kept their breaths shallow, ready to plunge away at the first sign of danger. Samra edged closer to the hole till their heads did touch. Kipling eased back the last deteriorated vine so she could see.

The interior of the council chamber was roughly a sphere—a pocket of space hollowed into the center of the council globe's main root system. Kipling had never been allowed inside during a session, but his mother came home each night with stories, so the room was constantly alive in his imagination.

The shape of the room was maintained by two wide horizontal discs made of latticed heartwood. One disc made up the floor, and the other the ceiling. Since both were porous in places, a few of the globe tendrils had sprouted down through the ceiling and out the bottom again, but these intrusions were symmetrically spaced, giving the illusion of support columns like one might find in a Grounder building.

"Looks crowded in there," Samra whispered.

In the center of the room, a table in the shape of a horseshoe was raised from the floor. Around this table, seven high-backed chairs made of plaited reeds faced the open space in the middle. All seven of the council chairs were occupied today. Old Mag, Doctor Kesh—Kipling knew each of the councilors well enough to greet them and engage in conversation when he encountered them about the patch, but he was most intimately acquainted with the occupant of the head chair, which sat at the apex of the table's curve. In that seat of honor sat his mother, Chief Councilor Katya Roose.

"Your mom looks worried," Samra said. Her breath tickled his nose.

Chief Roose, as she was commonly called, led the tribe on Corra Mara and, as a result, was the highest official in the Northern Sky, since all other northern colonies were now descendants of the Globe Mother. The title of chief councilor was somewhat of an anachronism, since there was no specific person the group was meant to advise—the globe council was simply required to reach a majority decision as a group when it came to issues affecting the various globe tribes—but his mother was chief nonetheless. She had her serious expression on today. At home, that look meant Kipling had better keep his mouth shut and steer clear till she finished whatever she was doing.

As Kipling scanned the room, he picked out the other occupants of the council chamber, some standing, some floating, and a few seated among the columns surrounding the council table. Kaleb looked smug, standing at his usual position, a few steps behind their mother's chair. Kip glared at the Watcher horn attached to his belt, then looked away. Surprisingly, his father was also in attendance, near the open end of the table. As master grower, his dad's knowledge of the patch and its health was occasionally made use of by the council, but he wasn't typically part of council meetings. Kipling wondered what news could have made his presence necessary today.

Enzo was in the center opening of the horseshoe table,

watching Chief Roose finish her analysis of the scroll in front of her. It seemed that everyone else was familiar with its contents and Kipling suspected that the messenger must have read it aloud during the time he and Samra were searching for a vantage point. The councilors' expressions were mostly grave, though Councilman Bottlebrock was merely picking at his teeth with a bit of twig.

"What we can be sure of, is that this issue is affecting us all," his mother said as she laid the scroll back on the table. "The health of this patch and all of our other colonies depends on our ability to get to the bottom of this mystery." She looked directly at Enzo. "Mr. Mooreside, you have done us a great service by bringing us this news. When you spoke with the smaller councils, did you perceive that some of the colonies are faring better than others in their spawning plans for next season?"

Enzo straightened up, his leather pilot's cap held in both hands. "Well, ma'am, it wasn't till about the third message came in with the same news that I put it together, so to speak. But from then on, whichever colony I intercepted, I did my best to ask for the master growers and tell them about the problems the others were having. I felt it would be in their best interest to know that they weren't the only ones having trouble."

"A wise decision," intoned Councilman Thur. "You've likely saved us a season's worth of confusion and unrest."

Enzo nodded. "Well, I can't say as I know all the ins and outs of pollinating a globe patch, but once I heard the severity of the issue and spread the news, each council had their master grower assess the situation and send you word." He rummaged in the basket and pulled another bundle of message tubes out. "Some of them have begun to inventory the globe sons they've still got on the vines. They wanted me to pass this information along to Master Roose for his advice."

Chief Roose signaled her husband and he stepped forward. Kipling's father accepted the messages from Enzo and bowed to the council.

Samra wiggled her body closer, pushing against him as she tried to see better, but Kipling stayed put, his eyes glued to his father.

"Master Roose," Chief Roose said, using her husband's formal title. "Please assess these messages posthaste, so that we can have time to pen appropriate responses to the colonies. We are counting on you to give us guidance on this issue. It would seem that resolving this threat must become our primary focus."

"I'll read the messages tonight and begin working on responses immediately," his father replied. "I should be able to leave instructions for the other colonies with Mr. Mooreside by the end of the festival."

"Globe pollination?" Samra whispered into Kipling's ear. "I thought for sure it was going to be something exciting."

Kipling shushed her and went back to watching. Whatever the issue was, it would certainly involve the growers.

His mom finished talking to his dad and had returned her attention to Enzo. "Mr. Mooreside, you can expect to hear from my husband when the patch descends. As I stated, we are grateful for your aid in this matter and hope that we may continue to engage your services. It would seem we will have many more messages with a pressing need for delivery."

Enzo bowed again. "My pleasure, ma'am. Always happy to be of service."

"And you will of course be paid for your haste. For now, please avail yourself of whatever hospitality we can show you until your return trip."

Enzo fiddled with his cap. "I think I'll be headed home straight away, while the winds are favorable. But I'll look forward to seeing you all when you land for the festival."

Samra elbowed Kip in the ribs. "What do you think is going on? Is the patch in trouble?"

Kip frowned and scooted away from the hole, not wanting his voice to carry inside the chamber. "Not sure. Something to do with breeding season. Sounds bad though."

"Will we still have the festival games?"

"I can't see why not. The patch has to—" He was cut off by a loud "Kacaw!" from near the Gate of Thorns. The signal from Rufus meant someone was coming. Kip released his grip on the vines and bounded upward, headed higher on the council globe. Samra launched herself after him, soaring past and leading the way. They perched high up in the globe's leaf girdle, hiding in a thick bunch of tangleweed that leaned far out over the patch. From there they could view the bridge to the Gate of Thorns. Rufus was in conversation with Kip's father and looked nervous. He glanced left, the way he saw his friends disappear, then returned his attention to Mr. Roose. Kip's father didn't linger, but seemed intent on shooing

Rufus in front of him. The rotund boy bounced along the vine bridge casting occasional glances behind and looking unhappy.

"Think your dad knows we're up here?" Samra asked.

"I'd better get home," Kip replied. "He might be looking for me."

"He has Enzo's basket," Samra noted as she watched Mr. Roose work his way along the bridge. "Try to see what's in those letters. I bet there's all kinds of interesting news from the other colonies."

Kipling crept along the rim of the globe till he was facing the direction of his family's aerie. "I'll see what I can find out. I'll meet you later. I'll get free after supper and find you."

"At the Starpark?"

"Yeah." He took aim, exhaled steadily, and leapt.

The fall down the main stalk of the Globe Mother was technically illegal. Plummeting was deemed unsafe, especially for patchlings. It was another one of the rules Kipling had seen fit to bend, largely because it was Samra's favorite method of navigating the patch. He had to admit, it beat walking the twisting trails and aerial bridges between globes.

Samra liked to plummet through the wide-open spaces between globes where she could get the fastest speeds, but Kip preferred a few obstacles. Also, a bit of cover. Samra wasn't the chief councilor's child and the consequences for breaking this particular rule never seemed to apply to her.

Kipling splayed his hands and feet out as he fell, dodging and ricocheting his way through the tendril clumps and creepers that clung to the side of the stalk, and relishing the wind on his skin. He whipped past other aeries occupied by families he knew. He spotted Mrs. Tundus washing out diapers from the latest of her green-faced babies.

He plummeted till he was below the level of the upper granaries and then took a deep breath, illuminating his skin to a warm yellow glow and arresting his fall. From there he stretched out and grabbed a tangleweed vine and swung himself into the heart of the main stalk. Kipling dimmed back down, then swung overhand below the deck of the granary till he reached the opening that ran up into the center of the main grove. He climbed inward, leaping when he could, over the thick clumps of vine and into the clearing that made up the core of Skylighter life on Corra Mara.

Kip moved slowly through the grove, trying not to attract

attention. He made sure his skin had properly darkened and he tried to look cool. It wouldn't do to come blazing into the grove white-hot. You were always watched here. If it wasn't by some well-meaning adult out to improve your character, it was nosy Mrs. Dinlas who seemed to do nothing but sit in her hammock near the window of her aerie, shouting at children to slow down and keep quiet. She never seemed to mind that she was louder than anyone else in the grove.

Kip climbed the vine bridge leading to a platform of stripped bark that made up the front porch of his family's aerie. He poked his head inside long enough to reassure himself that he had gotten there first, grabbed his school workbook, then took a seat in the chair on the porch, doing his best to pretend that he'd been there studying for a while.

Fortunately he didn't have to put on the act long enough that he was in danger of actually learning anything. His father arrived with the basket of reed message tubes and deposited them near the door. Rufus was nowhere in sight. Mr. Roose must have been reading some of the messages already on his way down to the grove because bits of ribbon and crumpled leaf paper protruded from the pocket of his trousers.

"Hey, Dad. What've you got there?" Kipling did his best to sound casual as he eyed the basket of messages.

"Kip, I need you to do something for me."

Kipling bounded to his feet. "You need help reading those messages?"

Mr. Roose shook his head. "No. I'll take care of the messages. I need you to head down to the seedpod cluster and start counting the globe sons we have stored in the nursery nests. Count every one that's ripe enough to fly and then count the ones still on the vines."

Kipling's heart sank. Doing inventory of the globe sons was nowhere near as interesting as reading the messages from other colonies. "Can't we get one of the pod tenders to do it? Dimli Bottlebrock is down there all the time. I'll bet he knows—"

"Kip, I want *you* to do it. This is important. The council has commissioned me to get to the bottom of a serious problem and I'm counting on you to help."

Kipling studied the stress ridges on his father's forehead. "What's the matter?"

"We're not certain just why yet, but there has been a severe shortage of globe sons in the slipstream this season. Without them the new globe daughters aren't getting pollinated. We're not sure what's happening to them, but we haven't seen many of last season's globes still aloft, and this season's early crop hasn't been doing well at reaching the other colonies."

"I thought it only takes one globe son to pollinate a globe daughter. Don't the patches germinate hundreds of globe sons per season?"

"And they still have been. But for some reason they haven't been reaching their targets. That's why the batch we've got growing may be more important than previous seasons. Might even be key to the survival of the northern colonies."

"Shouldn't I help you read the messages first, just in case there is more news? Maybe someone else fixed the problem already and—"

"If I need help with the messages, I'll drag Kaleb down from the council grove."

"I can do anything Kaleb can do," Kipling objected. "I know he's a council novice, but—"

"Kip. This is what I need. You're the grower apprentice, and you're my son, so it's your job to do what I say, understand?"

Kipling's mind wandered to Samra still bouncing around the globe tops. He was beginning to regret coming home early. "Do I have to do it right now?"

"Yes. Now. Get down there and get them counted for me. I'd like to have the numbers by supper." Mr. Roose turned his son toward the grove by the shoulders and pointed the way. "No dawdling."

"Yes, sir," Kipling mumbled.

Kipling trudged his way back through the central grove, suddenly envious of everyone milling around him that didn't have a boring chore to do. His plan had been foiled. Instead of having first knowledge of what the messages contained, and being the one to glory in sharing the latest news with his friends, Kaleb would probably get to. He'd probably be the last one to hear anything. All the messages about the goings on in other colonies would get delivered and he'd be stuck in the stupid pod grove.

Perhaps Samra would find him and want to help him count the globe sons. But why would she? She was free to roam the patch, race to the farthest outlying globes, or even stand watch with the patch guardians. She could do anything she pleased, really. The afternoon seemed suddenly full of tantalizing possibilities.

She was probably out on the upwind globes right now with Bronks, the guardian captain, saving nursery patchlings who'd gone overboard, or using his array of harpoons to defend the patch from a roving school of predatory wind eels. Maybe she'd save Bronks's life with a last-second harpoon throw and come home a decorated guardian hero. She'd join Kaleb tonight on the pedestal after he accepted the silly Watcher prize again, and the colony would cheer twice as loud for her. Kipling could see the envy in Kaleb's face. Only now it was him with the guardian medal around his neck and —

"Kip! Get moving!"

Kipling came unfrozen as his father's voice resounded across the grove. Passersby stopped to figure out the commotion, their eyes finding the grower's son as he jolted out of his reverie and sprinted toward the chute for the pod clusters.

4

SAMRA

The *Sunshine Express* vanished into the horizon below the jagged points of the Fanged Mountains. She couldn't spot it from here, but Samra knew the little aircraft was bouncing its way down the wind currents toward the Rift Valley hidden just this side of the farthest ridges. Samra sat atop Minda Dona, the newest globe that had spawned from the Mother. The bright green sphere tilted and bobbed in the slightest hint of a breeze, not yet stable enough or big enough for anyone to live on board.

Samra liked the new globes best. They were designated as dangerous and too turbulent for patchlings because you could be thrown off at a moment's notice. It was the kind of place anything could happen. If something ever would.

Laughter rang out from the nearby grove below Dimra Tasha, the closest globe to the west. Samra recognized the laugh as belonging to Khloe, her neighbor and soon-to-be fellow colonist on Cirra Sola. A gaggle of girls was clustered together in the sun at the edge of the grove. Khloe had taken advantage of every bit of attention that came with the honor of being a new colonist. She was currently surrounded by at least five other girls, giggling and whispering about their latest plans for the festival.

Khloe was a big topic of discussion at school because there was another colonist family leaving on Cirra Sola with Khloe's and Samra's—that of Jerem Stormblower. Jerem was sixteen and Khloe and her friends were intent on making sure that the new colony would be departing bright with the flame of new love.

Even from a distance, Samra could spot the rosy shade of pink that had recently begun to appear on Khloe's shoulders. All the girls in Khloe's year wanted to be old enough to be considered in bloom, but most of Khloe's friends were still using tangleberry juice to brighten their shoulders. Khloe's blushing skin was the real thing, a fact she was keen to show off with as many sleeveless outfits as she could conjure. Khloe's hair had lost all traces of green, and her long tresses had outdone the usual tawny brown of adolescence, instead turning a vibrant gold.

Khloe and her friends would no doubt be scouring the Grounder market for new fabrics and dresses when the patch landed. They would all want something new to wear for the festival ball. If ever there was a grand opportunity for Khloe to secure Jerem's love, it would be there.

Samra lowered her gaze to her own lap. Her rough trousers were decidedly worn, with rips at the knees and green streaks where she'd stained them climbing the globes with Kip. The skin of her arms was a pale yellow, bright and fresh, but nowhere near to turning pink. Not that she cared. The boys could ogle Khloe's shoulders all they wanted. She was glad that Khloe and Jerem would be distracted by each other on the new colony. She only regretted that she'd be stuck playing with Khloe's little brother, Willis. He was harmless enough for a patchling—if you could get past his tendency to drool on himself when his mind wandered—but she wasn't eager to be designated his babysitter while Khloe and Jerem were off canoodling.

A shadow passed over Samra and she looked up. The wide mechanical wings of a guardian were spread high above her. The sunlight blinded her temporarily, and she squinted, but then the guardian banked left and glided in a lazy circle down to a dozen feet above her. The wood-and-bone-framed wings tucked together and the guardian dropped, landing silently and surprisingly gently next to her.

From her seated position, Samra gazed up at the imposing form of Captain Bronks. Broad-shouldered and even wider due to his

27

mechanical wings, the guardian captain's expression was hard to read with the sun behind him. He certainly looked fierce with his harpoon in his left hand and his warhook dangling from his hip.

Some of the younger patchlings probably would have shrieked at his arrival, but Samra was not a little patchling anymore. She was due to be an Ascendare like Kipling this year—the age of transition. Even so, she waited quietly for Bronks to speak. It took a few moments, but finally he rested his free arm behind his back and addressed the horizon.

"Excellent view. I expect mist off the mountains tonight, but we'll be well above it till morning."

Samra stared stubbornly at the horizon, refusing to comment.

"I suspect one might have an even better view from Tamra Ohna or one of the more mature globes, don't you think?"

"Tamra Ohna is where Kaleb's friends hang out," Samra said.

"And you prefer the company of Kipling or Rufus instead."

"Kip is busy," she replied. She realized she didn't know where Rufus had gone. "Rufus wasn't feeling well. Had to go home."

"Must have gotten lost on the way," Bronks replied. "Might explain why I spotted him wandering around near the Gate of Thorns, calling your name."

Samra winced. She ought to have known better than to lie to a guardian, especially Bronks, who was rumored to have the best eyesight in the history of the patch. Her parents told stories about how he had been made Watcher every year he competed, before being appointed to the Guard. He'd made captain only three years after that. But all of it was before Samra was born, and keeping those sorts of stories fresh in her head took a great deal more effort than she was willing to give.

"Do you know why I dropped down?"

"I'm perfectly fine," Samra replied. "I'm not going to fall off. The restriction shouldn't be for all patchlings. Just people like Rufus who fall off everything. Doctor Kesh says I'll be able to glow soon. Then I can pass my Ascendare test and—"

"I wanted to be sure to say goodbye."

Samra sputtered to a stop. "You—you did?"

"It's a big responsibility leaving as a new colonist. It's going to be difficult." Bronks fixed his dark eyes on her face. "I'm glad Cirra Sola will have someone as brave as you aboard. There's no telling what dangers the patch might run into, and with only a second-year guardian on hand to defend it, you'll need to keep a sharp eye on things. Every person aboard a new colony is vital to its survival."

Samra stared at the guardian till she realized her mouth was open. She knew her patch had been assigned one of the newest guardians as its protector, but she still didn't consider that she might be as important as him to her colony. "*You* think I'm brave?"

"And you'll need to be. A colonist's job is a hard one. No telling where the winds might blow your patch at first. It will be a great adventure. Someday, when my duty to the Globe Mother is complete, I hope I'll have the opportunity to start a colony of my own."

"You want to be a colonist?" Samra couldn't believe what she was hearing. If you listened to Kip, guardian captain was the greatest job in the world. She hadn't ever thought of Bronks doing something as menial as manning a new globe daughter on its way into the winds.

"We all have our dreams. I think it would be marvelous."

Samra lapsed into silent awe, wondering what Kip would think when she told him that his hero wanted to drift away in the wind somewhere and live far from the glory of the Guard.

"I thought you were just coming down to kick me off this globe," she said.

"I'm certainly doing that as well. May I recommend taking the stalk back? You could use a handhold once or twice and really make me happy." The guardian pointed a muscular arm down the vine-covered stalk that led back to the Mother. A subtle smile played at the corner of his lips.

Samra frowned, but got to her feet. "You've never had to rescue me, you know. Not once."

"Let's see if we can preserve that record a few more days then, shall we?" Bronks smiled.

Samra climbed dutifully along the stalk and even stooped to brush her hand along the vines a few times as she walked. She didn't have to, but he *had* already admitted she was brave. You don't have to prove what's already a stated fact. She realized she'd never said thank you, and turned around, but Bronks was already airborne, launched back into the sky as quietly as he'd come — back to orbit the patch with silent, dutiful circles.

The girls on Tamra Ohna watched her pass. She couldn't hear their comments, but she knew what they'd be saying. She'd heard it all before. Red Sam. Samra the dim. Samra the faller.

She kept her hand on the vines. She would do it for Bronks —
do it his way for once — and prove that she could play by the rules
if she wanted to. She walked.

Dasha Cormunger said something that made the group of girls
titter and cover their mouths with their hands.

Samra was getting warm. Despite her determination to stay
calm, her hands were beginning to turn red and she could feel the
heat rising in her face.

She looked up to the figure of Bronks, high overhead, his silken
wings backlit by the afternoon sun. He disappeared beyond the
tallest globes, leaving her alone in her walk.

"Watch your step, Coley," Dasha shouted. "Nobody around to
save you."

Samra gritted her teeth and kept walking, trying to cool herself
down. Her skin only seemed to be getting redder.

"Not that anybody would!" Dasha added.

Samra broke into a run down the stalk as it curved away from
Tamra Ohna and branched back toward the Mother.

Laughter followed her retreat.

She didn't need saving. Not today. Not any day. And she would
prove it.

Samra sped to a sprint and launched herself off the vine bridge,
letting the wind lift her hair as she soared into the wide-open space
between globes. Then she plummeted.

The wind now tore at her hair as she fell, hands forward and
feet back, aiming for the central stalk of the Mother. Her vision
darkened as she fell, but she refused to breathe until the sound of
Dasha's laughter had vanished in the rush of the descent. She fell
three hundred feet before she finally inhaled, stretching for the last
thick tendrils above the wispy and fragile fronds of the Mother's
cloud net.

She grabbed hold of the tendrils and slid to a stop, now at the
very base of the patch. Samra clung to the vacant tendrils at the
bottom of her world and her body shook. After a while, her skin
finally cooled.

She had escaped the laughter from Tamra Ohna but now had a
long climb to get back home. Had Bronks seen her jump? Was he
disappointed? She scanned the sky but saw no sign of the winged
guardian.

The sea boomed as it crashed into the rocky barrier islands. The wind smelled of salt spray. They'd be over land soon, beginning the descent into the Rift Valley. It was still out of sight but the snow-capped peaks surrounding it were coming into view beyond the first row of mountains. She wondered briefly if any of the Grounders in those mountains were staring back in anticipation of their arrival. For now, all she saw were rocks, seabirds, and the long way down.

Samra lifted her eyes to Cirra Sola and slowly climbed for home.

5

ATLAS

Atlas squinted at the sky, studying the gaps between clouds for any sign of movement. So far, he'd only spotted a few birds and a slow-moving school of kettle rays. No airship.

The rickety fence along the west pasture smelled of wet goat. The rough-hewn rails made for an uncomfortable seat, likely as not to fill a tenant's rear end with splinters. This fact didn't deter him, but he was getting annoyed with the goat.

A tattered rag in his back pocket had attracted the attention of a grizzled, white billy goat a few feet behind him. It tugged at the rag, attempting to free the prize from his pocket.

"Cut it out, Murph," Atlas said, swatting at the animal's muzzle. The goat only chomped down harder and backed away. Atlas tried to yank the rag back, but Murph dug his hooves in and held on tighter. Atlas was about to hop down and continue the fight on the ground, but at that moment the sound of the airship's fans reached his ears. He spun around and sprang from the fence with a yell, launching himself into the tall grass beyond. The billy goat froze, the rag still dangling from its lips, but Atlas let him have it. He turned toward the sky instead and waved wildly as a yellow-winged aircraft danced its way over the treetops.

The Sunshine Express hadn't even rolled to a stop before Atlas was climbing aboard, his fingers clinging tight to the lateral fins.

"How'd it go? Did you see 'em? What did they give you this time? Was it something we can use for the *Dragon?*"

Enzo slid his goggles up onto his head and smiled at him. "Heavens alive, Atlas. You know we old folks have to breathe between sentences. Let me get my feet back on the ground and I'll tell you all about it."

Fledge, the cliff fox, let out a screech and climbed out of the front seat, perching on the edge of the cockpit and shaking out his wings. Atlas ruffled the fur atop his head, then hopped back into the grass, eager to see the day's treasures.

Atlas helped the old man float *The Sunshine Express* off the runway and stow it in the barn. The baggage compartment was significantly lighter than when the craft had taken off, but there were now bundles of blankets tied with string and a few reed baskets full of goods from the Skylighters. There would be more time for trading in the days to come. The festival always meant a bounty of good spirits and bartering for adults and kids alike. Last year, Atlas had been able to trade wool rope and a few bushels of wild apples for a genuine Skylighter star chart, and he had plans to double his haul this year. The nomad colonies had seen the entire northern hemisphere and some of the south in their travels, and their charts were the most accurate an aspiring aviator could hope for.

"When will the patch arrive?" Atlas asked.

Enzo took off his leather cap and hung it on a peg near the door. "I expect they'll be on the horizon by tomorrow night if these winds stay light. Sooner if we get a strong gust or two from the west. I'll be telling the mayor as soon as I get back to town."

The thin old man hefted the baskets out to Atlas, who attempted to see his way around them as he carried them to the table near the door. Once the cargo was unloaded, he unwrapped some of the parcels. Nothing interesting, just tubes of messages bound for other regions, baskets of dried herbs and spices, fresh sun peppers, strings of colorful eggshells, and bits of star lily root carved into jewelry or artwork. Enzo rummaged around and finally handed a package to Atlas that was about the width of his chest. "I think this might be the one you're looking for."

Atlas tore into the dried leaf wrappings impatiently, exposing bits of gnarled brown wood. He let out a gasp as he ripped the last of the scraps away. He held a smoothly polished half-wheel made of globe heartwood. It was a steering yoke. His fingers found the correct places at the sides of it and he grinned up at his grandfather. "It's the perfect size!"

He didn't wait for a response from the old man, but spun on his heel and sprinted for the back of the barn to the hulk of an aircraft waiting there under dusty blankets. He ran around the lateral fin and yanked away the section of canvas covering the cockpit, scrambling up the side of the fuselage using his free hand and then plopping himself down on the cushions he had stacked on the seat to give himself better visibility. He balanced the yoke in his palms, setting it gently atop the rod that would be rigged to his flight controls. The wheel was smooth and solid in his hands and it made it seem more real. Now he could feel it. He could picture the craft soaring through the air with clouds under its wings and him gliding high above the world. Now his *Dragon* would really fly.

Atlas waited as Enzo rounded the lower wing of the aircraft and studied his work on the side of the vertical tail fin. The faded letters that once read *Sunshine Express* were modified. Atlas had eliminated 'shine' with heavy brushstrokes of red paint turned somewhat orange by the yellow tail beneath. He had also painted over the faded black lettering of 'Express.' Thick lines scrawled overtop now spelled out the word *"Dragon"* in bold but slightly irregular letters. The result was a combination of the old print and freshly hand-painted scribble. *Sun Dragon.*

Enzo brushed some of the hay dust off the wing in a gesture Atlas recognized as affectionate. "You're almost there."

"Do you think we can put it on tonight? Will you help me make it work?"

Enzo smiled and mussed his hair. "Not tonight, but maybe tomorrow. I've got messages to deliver that need to get out right away. I'll be heading to town. You work on it tomorrow after school and I'll check your progress when I get back."

"Can't I skip school tomorrow and just come here? We never learn anything important anyway. All we ever talk about is which settlers dug which mines or built some village. Nobody cares. It's all stupid."

Enzo smiled at him. "I know it seems that way sometimes, but it adds up eventually. Schooling isn't about learning what's been done before, it's giving you the tools to figure out what hasn't been done. You'll see." He winked. "So, no skipping. Plus, your aunt would have my hide." He patted the side of the cockpit and moved away.

Atlas was a little disappointed, not just to be delaying his maiden voyage in the *Sun Dragon*. Time working with his grandfather had been scarce of late. When Enzo wasn't out flying, there was always the *Express* to work on, or leaks in the pressure machine that needed fixing. Atlas's *Sun Dragon* was tantalizingly close to being airworthy, but it still lacked a couple of vital parts. Occasionally he wondered if the omission was intentional by his grandfather, as they were essential enough to keep him from flying it—perhaps some plot by his aunt to keep him on the ground. But Atlas didn't think Enzo would fall for that, or betray his dreams that way. The old man was a hero and something of a legend—not just to Atlas, but to the whole village. If he could believe in anyone, it was Enzo.

Enzo wasn't anything like the other villagers. Most people in Womble had no desire to get more than a few feet off the ground. Out of all the adults in his village, Atlas could think of only one or two who had been more than a hundred miles from home in their lifetimes. A big outing would have been a trip to Kirkshire or the harbor villages along the white cliffs of Dunbery. Hardly anyone ever left Ridge Valley. The high mountains surrounding them may as well be a cage.

When it came to the other kids, few his age had even made it past the last hedgerows of Barrister Whicket's barley fields. Enzo, on the other hand, had flown the length and breadth of the entire valley, and even crossed the Strait of Gorra to explore the desert lands in the south. He'd navigated the Rift with *The Sunshine Express* and brought back stories of wild peoples he'd met and souvenirs from their various cultures to amaze and fascinate Atlas. It was those stories more than anything that fueled his desire to fly.

After Enzo finished unloading the wares and gifts from the Skylighters, he packed them into the three-wheeled motorcycle that he used to get about the village. The handlebars held the throttle and brake, and a single air-cylinder engine waited under the seat— mostly only good for coughing and banging when Enzo forced the contraption over especially rough country roads. Enzo had rigged the machine to use the same interchangeable compressed air charges that *The Sunshine Express* used in more plentiful numbers to power its thrust fan pistons.

"You have enough air?" Atlas asked, as he tapped on the canister affixed to the back fender.

"Grab me another," Enzo replied. "The *Express* can spare a few. I'll see about filling some more tomorrow."

Atlas trotted over to the rack of spherical air tanks stacked along the barn wall and selected one of the smaller ones suitable for the trike. He loved any excuse to linger inside this barn. The shining brass nozzles and intricate pipes of Enzo's air dispensing contraptions looked marvelously impressive arrayed across the barn wall, but the real power of Enzo's machine lay deep beneath his feet in the underground caverns, and the force of the fast-flowing river running through them. Atlas reverently placed a hand on the copper pipe that protruded from the ground and could feel the subtle vibrations of the river far below. He returned to the trike and secured the air tank carefully in the cargo area.

"Which pasture will the patch anchor to this year?" Atlas asked.

"Mayor Fillmore invited them to use his land again, as usual," Enzo replied.

"Why can't they use your pasture? We have enough room. They could anchor to the landing strip." Atlas followed Enzo around the *Express*, helping him secure the baggage holds and the fin locks for the night.

"It's not ours to decide, Atlas. The villagers make that decision."

"But you know the Skylighters better than anyone. You talk right to the high chief and—"

"Chief Councilor," Enzo corrected.

"Yeah, and she likes you best out of all of us settlers."

"I'm sure that the Skylighter High Council respects all of us equally."

"Did they sing for you when you were there and light up the way they do at the festival? Did they tell you all about the other skylands? Did they have any battles with lightning snakes?"

"The patch has just begun its descent from the Heights, Atlas. They're busy getting ready to spawn their latest colonies and release their globe sons. There wasn't time for all that. But don't worry. There will be plenty of stories shared during the festival." Enzo fixed the last strap to the cargo rack of the motortrike and closed the barn doors. "Now get home to Amelia. She'll be needing you and it's getting late."

"So, we can test fly the *Dragon* tomorrow?" Atlas asked.

"If you get your work done and we have time."

"I'll get it done," Atlas replied.

Enzo opened the air valve on the handlebars and the motortrike sputtered to life. "Then I'll see you tomorrow." He began to pedal and the trike lurched forward, bouncing and clattering its way down the lane toward town.

Atlas waited till his grandfather was out of sight before reentering the barn and stealing one more look at his new control wheel in the cockpit of the *Dragon*. He ran a hand along the seat and down to the fin controls. "Tomorrow. Tomorrow we'll really be flyers."

The dirt path through the hills to the home he shared with his aunt seemed to float beneath him as Atlas ran. He could already picture himself soaring above it — the *Sun Dragon*'s wings spread to catch the wind from the mountainside. He could feel it race along the valley, banking and gliding over the fields of his neighbors and friends from school. How envious they all would be. He would return to school a hero. He'd walk in with windblown hair and the smell of clouds about him. Perhaps he'd fly up to one of the floating kelp patches near the coast and bring down a bunch of star lilies for Heather Lanford. She wouldn't think he was such a little kid then. Cathy was on the porch lighting the lanterns when Atlas trotted into view. The lanterns gave an inviting glow to the sod-covered burrow nestled into the base of the cliffs. His aunt's partner was still in her work overalls but one shoulder strap dangled at her waist. Her sun-browned arms were sinewy and muscular, lifting the heavy steel lanterns with ease. Setting the most recently lit lantern on its hook, she used her other hand to brush away a moth and spotted Atlas. She raised her eyebrows and gestured for him to come to her.

"Hey, Cathy. Guess what Enzo—"

"Tell me later," Cathy interrupted, her voice firm and low. "You'd best hurry on in. Your aunt is . . . well, you'd just best get in there."

Atlas frowned and tried to recall what his aunt might be mad about. Then he remembered the goats. "Oh no! Did they not make it back in?" His heart sank as he imagined the worst. Had they been attacked by predators? He scanned the sky for any evidence of danger.

Cathy jabbed a thumb toward the front door and Atlas followed the gesture. The already heavy wooden door seemed weighted further by the dread of his impending fate. Atlas navigated the labyrinthine tunnels into the hillside home and followed the sound of running water to the kitchen. His aunt was at the sink, her back to him, with a stream of water exiting the copper pipe in front of her and trickling into a high-sided pot. Her back was taut, her thin frame a tensed coil he feared to release.

Atlas stalled at the threshold of the room and shifted uncomfortably as he attempted to think of an opening.

"I don't ask a lot, you know." Amelia set her hands on the edge of the sink. Her shoulder blades protruded sharply against the back of her shirt, her tight brown braid hanging between them.

"I'm sorry I forgot to pen the goats," Atlas muttered. "I meant to. I just got distracted because—"

"There's always an excuse, Atlas, but that doesn't fix the problem." Amelia turned around to face him and propped herself against the sink, crossing her arms. Her lean face looked tired. Her shirtsleeves were rolled up past her elbows and one of the buttons was misaligned on her shirt. Her dark brown eyes weren't angry, they were disappointed, and that was worse. Even Brody, Amelia's herding dog, had his head down on his paws and seemed afraid to look up. Atlas fixed his eyes on his shoes.

"I got most of the herd back inside but two are missing. I want you to get the pens clean and dry tonight before bed and in the morning you're going to find Tildy and Murph. If we're lucky, they just wandered into one of the gullies here in the canyon. They might hunker down for the night and stay safe that way. We've already suffered too many losses this year. You know how much Tildy matters to us right now."

Tildy the goat was pregnant for the first time in years, and Atlas knew that their herd numbers certainly needed the boost.

"I could go out now and look for them. Maybe they're close by and I could—"

"No." Amelia turned around and presented him with her back again as she scrubbed the pot. "It's getting too dark. Cathy will keep an eye out for them if they wander in. You'll do your chores and help me make up for the time I spent chasing them this afternoon. Then you'll do your schoolwork and get to bed." Atlas suspected that it was Brody that did most of the work this afternoon herding the goats, but the tone in her voice left no room for argument. "Tomorrow I'll need your help getting the weeds out of the vegetable garden. We'll add them to the goats' feed and maybe try to keep them off the willows for a bit. The saplings are getting bare and we'll need them healthy this summer."

"But tomorrow I'm supposed to meet Enzo and . . ."

Amelia twisted to look at Atlas and fixed him with a stare that made him trail off.

He scuffed his shoe on the floor and turned toward the tunnel that led to the goat pens.

"There will be a plate for you in the cupboard when you get back," Amelia said, returning her gaze to the sink. "You can eat when your chores are done."

The passage down to the pens sloped slightly and Atlas kicked a pebble ahead of him dejectedly as he walked. He passed through the two gates that kept the herd from wandering into the rest of the warren, then trudged into the pens.

Pens was a loose term. Caverns would be more apt, since the goats climbed the walls and wedged themselves high in the clefts of the underground cave, sometimes licking the minerals that seeped through the ceiling of the cavern and washed down the sides of the rocks.

The caverns were divided from one another by means of wooden gates affixed to the tunnel walls, although most of the goats were corralled in the center cavern where an underground stream had dug its way across the floor. This cavern also had a skylight—a section of the cave ceiling that had collapsed many years ago and been shored back up. One of his ancestors, likely his deceased grandfather, had been the one to block it off again. Iron bars now crisscrossed the opening, preventing access to all but the last glow of twilight and the checkered view of the sky.

Atlas stood in the circle of dim light on the cavern floor, surrounded by the smell of wet goats and their droppings. The bars may as well have been there to keep him in. The sky was never more out of reach than here. His thoughts wandered to the *Sun Dragon*, under wraps in his grandfather's barn, wings stowed and static. He ought to be out there, high in the evening clouds, looking down on the world. But that vision was fading. The sky was nearly dark now.

One of the goats tugged on his pant leg and bleated for his attention. He shoved her away and looked back to the skylight. A shadow passed overhead, flickering across the sky in silhouette, wings spread. His eyes strained to make out the shape, but it was gone.

Out in the darkness, some creature screamed.

6

THE STAR PARK

Kipling stared at the Watcher horn on the table and wished he could light it on fire with his mind. The fact that Kaleb seemed unable to keep his hands off it tonight had something to do with it. Kipling tried to look elsewhere, but his brother kept fidgeting with the prize, repositioning it on the table, always somewhere Kipling was sure to have a clear view.

"I really think it's best if we find a way to get the globes to the other colonies directly . . ." his father continued sharing his suggestions about the growth of the patch over dinner. "If we can find a way to transport them . . ."

The conversation around the table wasn't much of a distraction for Kipling. His mother and father had praised Kaleb again for his victory—a bit longer than he felt was necessary—and then launched straight into council business and the issue of the missing globe sons. While his parents seemed to welcome Kaleb's inclusion in the conversation about the best way to pollinate the colonies with their remaining supply, every solution Kipling suggested went largely ignored. He finally slumped in his chair and resigned himself to being irrelevant.

"Can I be excused?" He inserted the question into the first lull in the conversation he could find. "I told Samra I'd help her with her schoolwork tonight."

His mother arched an eyebrow in a skeptical appraisal of his request, but his father nodded vaguely and gestured toward the doorway. "Stay out of trouble, and be able to get inside at the warning signal. We're not in the Heights anymore."

The globes had already started to glow as Kipling ran through the grove and out the eastern tendril gate. He leapt into the canopy of leaves surrounding the Globe Mother and took a shortcut past the group of adults enjoying the view on the vine bridge. He swung overhand through the canopy till he could reach another less-used vine bridge and raced up it to the softly glowing sphere of Jana Luna on the far end. At roughly two hundred feet in diameter, the mid-sized globe was nearing full maturity, but in the last few years had become almost entirely covered in star lilies — more so than any other globe in the patch. As a patch buoyancy globe, Jana Luna had no one living aboard her, but had become a popular destination for loners, lovers, and those looking for an out of the way place for conversation.

For Kipling and Samra the 'Starpark' was for secret business, resolving mysteries, and making plans. He and Samra avoided the wide flowery top of the globe where couples did their stargazing among the night-blooming lilies. Instead, they had made their own more exciting hideout down amid the foliage at the equator. As Kipling climbed down the thick vines and tangles of umbrella leaves to the usual spot, he listened for any sign of movement ahead. He might be early. Maybe Samra hadn't finished dinner yet and he would have to wait. When Kip rounded the globe to the hideout they'd constructed in the creepers, he did spot someone sitting in it — but it wasn't Samra.

Rufus's legs swung beneath him as he sat perched on the bundle of roots at the doorway of their hideout. He'd changed his trousers and shirt and his tawny hair was combed back smoothly against his head. Between his clenched fingers he held a bunch of purple spring glories and a handbound journal made of paelae leaves. The flowers weren't wilting yet so Rufus must have picked them sometime today. Kip didn't have time to consider what he might be doing with them because Rufus spotted him and started.

"Oh! Hey, Kip!" Rufus floated off the vines and grabbed for the nearest root to steady himself. "Didn't see you there."

Rufus wasn't wearing his buoyancy belt and it took him a moment to settle back down.

"What are you doing out here, Rufe?"

"I finally found Samra after you guys left the council grove. She said she'd be meeting you here tonight. Thought I would come, too."

Kip swung into the hideout, glanced around the empty interior of the hollow, and took a seat next to Rufus. While Rufus occasionally tagged along to their hideaway, he had thought it would just be Samra he was meeting tonight. The intrusion wasn't unwelcome exactly, but he'd been looking forward to it being the two of them just the same. He studied the approaching horizon with his friend in silence.

The clouds were parting ahead of the patch and Domino, the smallest moon, was brightly reflected on the water tonight. The cliffs at the base of the mountains were definitely closer. The patch had also lost another thousand feet in altitude since the afternoon.

"Is it okay I came?"

Kipling turned back to his friend. "Yeah. Sure. What's with the flowers?"

Rufus's round cheeks began to glow faintly and he looked away again toward the horizon. "I was just thinking, you know. Thinking about the festival?"

Kipling studied his friend and tried to put the pieces of this puzzle together. "What about it?"

"I thought that maybe this year I would go to the festival ball."

"We never go to the ball. We always make fun of it and go out to the Grounder fields and go exploring."

"I know. But I thought that this year . . . maybe we would go."

Kipling stared at the flowers in Rufus's hand for another second before the situation finally dawned on him. "Wait, you want to ask Samra?"

"Well, I thought that—"

A keening wail came from the foliage along the vine path. Rufus jolted and scrabbled to find a handhold as Kipling leapt to his feet and spun to face the sound. In the shadow of the umbrella leaves, something was moving. The shape hissed in the darkness and shook the leaves. Next came a series of clicks and slurps.

"Is it a grim wailer?" Rufus exclaimed, backing against the tendril wall. "What do we do?"

Kipling looked around the hideout for anything that could be used as a weapon, but nothing was handy. As the foliage continued to shake, he balled his fists and concentrated. His skin warmed as he stared at the darkness. Heat radiated through his body and the light poured out of him, first from his hands then all through him, a faint glow that blazed rapidly to a brilliant yellow, illuminating the darkness.

The laughter from under the leaves preceded the face that emerged into the light.

"You're getting pretty good at that, Kip." Samra grinned in the glow and reveled in her success.

"Oh sweet mother!" Rufus exclaimed, and he drifted slowly toward the ceiling of the hideout as he got his breath back. He kept one hand on his chest as the other reached for a handhold.

Kip dimmed back down and finally let himself smile as Samra vaulted over to their position and dangled from the vines on the top of the hideout. "I got you guys good. If I was a real wailer I would have eaten you up." She contorted her hand into a claw and reached for Rufus. *"Beware the clatter of claws at night, what clicks and screeches outside the light —"*

"Don't," Kipling said. "You know he hates that rhyme."

Samra glanced at him, then back to Rufus, who was a bloodless shade of pale.

"Just joking around." Samra turned a flip and landed right side up in the doorway of the hideout. "What were you guys talking about?" She picked up one of her feet and noted the purple petals stuck to it. "Where'd all these come from?" The floor of the hideout was now littered with purple flowers, though the bulk of the bouquet had fallen out the door and into the sky below.

"I think . . . I think I'm going home," Rufus said, keeping his eyes off the petals. He maneuvered cautiously around the doorway and onto the vine path.

"Was I really that scary?" Samra asked. "I was just playing around."

"I've just got to go," Rufus mumbled. He extended a shaky hand toward Samra and offered her the little paper journal. "Here. I made you this." As soon as Samra took it, he retreated. "I'll see you guys later."

"But I just got here!" Samra called.

Kipling watched his friend pick his way up the vines and pulled

Samra back into the hideout. "Let him go."

She squirmed out of his grasp immediately and looked like she might attempt to argue, but finally just shrugged. "Okay, whatever. His loss." She exhaled heavily and plopped down on the floor of the hideout.

Kipling considered Samra for a moment, then eased himself down next to her, letting his legs dangle out the doorway. "He just doesn't do well talking about the nightbeasts."

"He's never even had a family member attacked, has he?" Samra said. "If anyone should be terrified of nightbeasts, it should be Cepil Mayer or Jojack Pento. They both had brothers get eaten. I heard a spotted skymander took Jojack's brother right in front of him. The venom from their fangs eats right through your—"

"It wasn't just the talk about nightbeasts. Rufus is . . . never mind it anyway. He'll be all right."

"Kind of being a baby, though." She picked the little journal back up. "What's this about?"

"I don't know. He just said he made it for you."

Samra flipped a few pages of the journal and paused. "It's . . . my stories."

Kipling leaned over and looked. Rufus had hand written some of their favorite imagined tales in the journal. He recognized character names from Samra's imagination. She was staring at the book with a confused expression on her face. A little flicker in Kipling made him want to distract her from it.

"What did you do this afternoon?" He shifted his hands to his sides and leaned back onto them.

Samra slowly closed the book and looked up. "Got kicked off Minda Dona. Did you know Captain Bronks wants to be a colonist?"

"Phssh. Yeah, right."

"I'm serious. He wants to fly off on his own colony. Just be on a little patch somewhere and not even be a guardian anymore."

Kipling shook his head. "No way. He'd never do that. He's captain of the Guard. He's the most decorated hero in guardian history. He has 120 saves and he's been awarded five patch defense horns. That's more than twice what anybody else in the guard has."

"Doesn't matter. He wants to go start a patch of his own."

"He was probably just saying that to make you feel better about having to leave." Kipling regretted the words as soon as they were out of his mouth. Samra was staring at him now in a way that meant she might believe him. "Not that leaving isn't . . . Look, never mind what I say. Bronks can do whatever he wants."

Samra frowned and looked away. "I don't care if you don't think being a colonist is important. Bronks said I'll have to keep an eye on things . . . It *will* be important and you never know what might . . ." She trailed off into nothing.

"Sam, I'm sorry. Don't listen to me. It is important. I don't know what I'm saying—I'll never get to be a colonist so what do I know? I'm going to be stuck as a patch gardener all my life."

"Yeah, but the growers really *are* important. Without a grower, the patch wouldn't have food. Or lift. Or anything to live on. Your dad is respected all over the colonies."

"My dad is. I'm not. Probably because all he ever lets me do is prune tangleweed. Any other job on the patch is better than what I've got."

Samra stared out at the distant mountains. "What if we floated away? Just you and me. We could go do anything we want. Nobody would ever hear from us for years and years until one day we came back, loaded with all the prizes from the adventures we've had. Everyone would love us and give us awards."

"They don't give out prizes to people for having adventures," Kipling replied. "And you don't get awards either. You only get awards for doing something great like rescuing someone or fighting off predators to save the patch."

"Or being the Watcher?" Samra asked.

Kip frowned and looked down toward the ocean surface where his own horn and his dream of being the Watcher had disappeared. "The Watcher horn is a dumb prize anyway." He lifted his eyes back to the horizon. "Maybe we *should* float away. We could be anyone we wanted out there." He let his mind relish the fantasy.

"Or we could just be us," Samra replied. "You really want to?" She had her eyes on his now, eager and ready. She would go. She really believed she could get away from the patch.

"We wouldn't even make it to the mountains," Kipling replied. "The guardians would pick us up and have us in the council grove in ten minutes. Kaleb would love it, though. He'd still be the perfect son and Dad would put me on pruning duty all day and night. You'd probably never see me again."

"But if we *did* make it to the mountains, think how jealous

Kaleb would be then. We'd be glorious adventurers and he'd still be a councilman novice."

Kipling allowed himself a smile. "We could bring home a bunch of Grounder treasures and impress the council. They'd be so amazed at our knowledge they'd want to make *us* councilors instead of him!"

Samra grinned back at him, but then let her eyes drift back to the horizon. "I'd say no."

"What?"

"I'd say no. If they wanted me to be on the globe council. I'd rather be off on an adventure with you any day, than be stuck in some boring council grove."

Kipling let the words linger in the air, considering her distant stare toward the horizon. The way she looked beyond the patch was optimistic longing, bold and unapologetic. He let his own gaze follow hers, out past the puffs of cumulus cloud glowing faintly in the starlight, to the dark ridge of slowly approaching mountains. Above the spine of the mountains, floating kelp towers blinked in the darkness.

Kipling tucked his legs up under him as the breeze sent more purple petals fluttering down into the sea. "I'd rather be on an adventure with you, too."

Samra stayed silent, but as she watched the horizon, her cheeks had the faintest hint of a glow.

7

AMELIA

Atlas had seen blood before. He'd certainly seen plenty of nightbeast tracks as well. Claw marks, acid burns, bits of teeth, and even the occasional carcass. But this was different. The gully between the rocks was littered with tufts of hair. There was no carcass. No remains. Just the bits of hair stuck to rocks, waving eerily in the morning fog—and one soaking wet red rag.

Atlas stared at the dripping rag for a long time.

There were no predators in the sky now. The rising sun had scattered all but the persistent fog. Atlas picked his way back through the gully, but paused when he heard the bleat. It was faint—timid—but there. He turned and followed the sound. The cleft between the boulders was nearly invisible in the mist, a switchback where sheets of rock had split and left a narrow gap at their base. Now the gap was jammed with the damp and ragged rear end of a goat.

"Tildy!"

Atlas wedged himself between the rocks and peered into the darkness of the cleft, letting his eyes adjust till he could make out the rest of Tildy. She'd wedged herself between the rocks as far as her fat belly would allow. Dried blood was caked on her rump and gashes marked her flanks, but whatever had been clawing at her couldn't reach her well enough to drag her out. Another faint bleat escaped the goat as Atlas approached. She squirmed in an attempt to flee but couldn't budge.

Atlas climbed up the cleft and over the goat to the narrow hollow beyond. The goat bleated louder.

"I'm trying to get you out. I'm going to save you." He braced himself against the rocks, pressed hard on the goat's shoulders, and grunted. "When my aunt sees you, maybe you can save me."

He wasn't completely grounded, but he might as well be. As Atlas stared out the window of the one-room schoolhouse, he couldn't help but think he'd never make it into the sky. Amelia had only watched quietly from the porch when he came home with Tildy. Cathy had set to work immediately on mending the goat's injuries. No one talked about Murph.

"Atlas, why don't you join the conversation?" Mr. Merritt observed him over the top of his half-moon spectacles. "You need to know this, too. Mayor Fillmore would like everyone on their best behavior during the festival."

Atlas pulled his eyes off the perfectly shaped clouds, leaned back in his chair and crossed his arms. Most of his classmates were slumped in their chairs as well. Heather Lanford had her chin propped in her palm, leaning on her desk and gazing out the window on the far side of the room. She looked as lovely as ever, but equally disinterested. The Skylighter Festival was exciting. Learning the history of human-Skylighter relations was far from it. Shirley Georgen was the only one with her attention on Mr. Merritt but that was nothing new.

"I don't know anything about it," Atlas said, letting his eyes drift to the window again.

"Of course you do," Mr. Merritt replied. "Your grandfather has been to the patch itself and seen them in their natural element. I know for a fact that he's told you a great deal." He scanned the class. "Who can tell me what the Skylighter homeland is called?"

"The Heights," Atlas muttered under his breath.

Shirley Georgen's hand shot into the air, but Mr. Merritt pointed to the back of the class. "Edison, how about you?"

Edison Froe looked like he was daydreaming as well, but jolted alert at the mention of his name. "Um, they live in the ... skylands?"

"Yes, but there are many skylands. More specifically?" Mr. Merritt questioned.

"They live in the Heights!" Shirley blurted out, no longer able to control herself.

Mr. Merritt surveyed the rest of the class and sighed before turning to address her. "Yes, Shirley. And why do we only get to visit with them once a year?"

"They usually live too high for us to see them."

She'd run out of air the fastest up there, the way she gasped when she talked. Atlas frowned at her and looked back out the window.

"Yes, that's true, but I meant why do they visit the village of Womble once a year?"

Sean Werthen, the boy seated in front of Atlas, cautiously raised a hand. "Because they like us?"

Mr. Merritt smiled and put his arms behind his back. "I certainly hope they do, but they also come to honor tradition. When our people first settled this valley, the Skylighters had been using this area as part of their patch breeding season for centuries. Our people had found shelter among the caves—safety from the nightbeasts. And when the Skylighters came, it was the first meeting of our peoples."

"I thought they were scared of us," Mindy Tandry said, piping up from the seat behind Atlas.

Mr. Merritt smiled. "Yes, Mindy. They were at first. They believed we had come up out of the ground itself. It's why they refer to us as 'Grounders' to this day. But your great-grandparents didn't mind. They adopted the name themselves over the years and it's even become a common term for humans in other Old World colonies."

"Do they know now that we really came from the Old World?" Maggie asked. "Or do they still think we came from underground?"

"We've learned much about each other's cultures over the years. But it's hard for us to teach them about the Old World since we don't know that much about it ourselves."

"But we have the earthen relic to teach us," Maggie said. "Can't we show them that?"

Mr. Merritt nodded. "The Skylighter High Council has come to visit the relic before, and they are very respectful of it. But our relic teaches us about growing plants that the Skylighters don't use, and many of the skills we've unlocked are only useful to humans: metallurgy, animal husbandry, architectural engineering. Not much use for people living in the sky.

"One day, if all the relic's secrets are unlocked, perhaps we will discover more information that the Skylighters would want. For now, they are happy just to visit us and trade. The relationship is important to both of our cultures. And everyone in the village has a responsibility to take care of that relationship."

"My older brother said Skylighters have a hundred mouths under their clothes and they can use them to suck the blood out of little kids," Sean said. "Is that true?"

Mr. Merritt frowned. "Your brother should spend more time here at school and less time making up stories to scare you." He turned to the rest of the class. "Since we'll be sharing a meal with the Skylighters again this year, we'd best get that sorted as well." He looked back to Sean. "The Skylighters have one mouth that they use for eating and also for breathing. What your brother may have been referring to is their lateral air vents. They have a variety of thin openings, mostly under their arms and down their sides that they use for inhaling oxygen and exhausting lifting gases. But it's a good idea not to bring up bodily orifices when dealing with a different culture. It's easy to offend someone." He put a hand to his hip. "That's why today we'll be working on our manners. Edison, come up here and show me how you bow."

Atlas slumped into his seat a little farther as Edison shuffled past. It was clear Mr. Merritt wouldn't be wandering into any topics Atlas found interesting today. Learning about the earthen relic was sometimes fascinating—especially the stories Mr. Merritt occasionally told about the olden days and the first colonists. They were real heroes—brave adventurers who'd journeyed across the stars to land here. Rune the Mighty, Garick the Bold. If there was anyone Atlas envied, it was them. Nobody would have made *them* sit around in school on a beautiful day like this.

When school let out, Atlas raced along the path for home, determined to resist temptation, but when he reached the turn-off for Enzo's farm, he paused anyway. Maybe he could see the *Dragon* for just a little while. Putting on the new control wheel wouldn't take long. He could do it in fifteen minutes if he had the right tools. Five minutes there, five minutes back. Amelia couldn't possibly miss him for twenty-five measly minutes, could she? He could say he was talking to his teacher after class. A special assignment? Staying after for a reprimand might be the most believable, but he didn't need more reasons to upset her. Maybe Mr. Merritt took a few extra minutes letting the class go . . . Before he knew it he was racing up to the barn. Enzo was out front, tinkering on the *Express*.

"Looks like someone's excited to get to work," Enzo said as Atlas struggled to catch his breath. The old man pointed a gnarled finger at the toolbox. "Use the joint pliers and a good solid pin. One of the big ones. A control wheel is one thing we never want coming apart in flight."

Atlas opened the drawer of the box eagerly and found pliers and a pin that would work for the wheel control, then raced inside with it to the cockpit. The control rod was a little undersized for the joint so he had to wrap it a few times with strips of canvas so it would be snug, then he fitted the control wheel over the joint and gently hammered the lock pin through. That in turn got some wire to keep it in place. When he was finished, he worked the control around, watching with satisfaction as the lateral fins responded. He craned his neck to check the tail and watched the pitch fins arch up and down, then used his foot controls to whip the entire tail section back and forth.

"Ready to roll her out and take her for a spin?" Enzo was smiling at him from the side of the fuselage.

"Doesn't it still need lift bags and new air charges for the fans?"

His grandfather smirked at him. "Got them all filled and installed this morning while you were at school. I had a feeling that you might want to take advantage of the sunshine, now that the mist has burned off. Good day for a maiden flight."

Atlas couldn't keep from grinning. His *Dragon* was ready. It was really ready.

"Come on. Help me pull it out of the barn," Enzo said.

Atlas hopped out of the cockpit and pushed on the root of

the lateral wing fin. The *Dragon* glided forward easily, perfectly balanced with buoyant air bags in the nose and tail. Enzo had already counterbalanced the craft with ballast and, once they were aboard, they'd pitch it over the side and be the ballast themselves.

It wasn't until Atlas was in the cockpit and strapping himself in that he remembered his aunt. "Um, Grandpa? Do you think we could fly southeast for today?"

"You want to overfly the schoolhouse, do you? The villagers will certainly get a kick out of seeing your *Sun Dragon* aloft. Thought you might want to fly over the farm first and let Amelia and Cathy have a look at your hard work. They sure know how much time you've put into it."

"I think maybe just the village would be good today," Atlas said, as his grandfather swung a leg over the side and climbed into the front seat. There was a knot in his stomach, but he tried to dismiss it. Amelia would eventually understand how hard he'd worked on this, but he could tell her another day. He checked the sun overhead. Just a quick flight, then he wouldn't mind being in the gardens the rest of the day. One flight would be enough. He could have it to remember and relive, and no chores would ever be as dull after.

"I thought I might find you here," Amelia's voice came from somewhere behind him, and Atlas swiveled in his seat, his heart suddenly in his throat. His aunt was sitting astride Destro, her speckled gelding.

"Amelia!" Enzo smiled. "Excellent timing. Just in time to witness Atlas's moment of glory."

"It's a moment of something, all right," Amelia replied.

Enzo turned around to face Atlas and muttered in an undertone. "Anything you forgot to mention?"

"I was on my way home," Atlas declared to his aunt. "I was just stopping in for a couple minutes to help put the control wheel on."

"And go for a joyride," Amelia said.

"It's not a joyride, it's a test flight."

"The only thing you're testing is my patience." She swung down from the saddle and stood at the horse's head. "Enzo, Atlas will be delaying his flight for a while because he failed to bring the herd in last night. I need him at home to get things sorted."

Enzo silently eased himself to his feet in the cockpit and put his leg back over the side.

"But we were just going to do one quick flight," Atlas sputtered. "It won't take long, and then I can do all my chores after. I promise I'll get them done. I'll weed and take care of the goats and do the dishes. I only want to do one flight."

Amelia stayed silent. Her horse whickered softly.

"I think you'd best leave the flight for another day, Atlas," Enzo said. "Best to do these things when you've got lots of time."

"But it's the maiden voyage," Atlas said.

"I used to tell your mother the same thing. A good pilot is never in a hurry," Enzo replied. The old man hopped down from the lateral fin into the tall grass and waited for Atlas to follow. Atlas gripped the control wheel again and his stomach burned. He was so close. The clouds were right there, waiting for him. He only needed to seize the controls, open the air valves, give a few good kicks to the pedals, and he'd be aloft.

He slowly unwrapped his fingers from the control wheel and stood.

"I'll put her away for you," Enzo offered. "Go get your chores done. She'll be waiting for you on another day."

Atlas refused to look his aunt in the eyes on the way home. He sat behind her on the ride back to the farm and, despite their proximity, he may as well have been a mile away. He avoided looking at her as she unsaddled Destro, instead making his way directly to the garden, tucked away in the canyon behind the warren.

He ripped up weeds and hurled them into the bin with as much ferocity as he could muster. Each twisted root that dared to cling to the soil was his enemy. He yanked and tore them from the dirt without mercy. When he finally wheeled the overloaded bin into the caverns to feed the goats, he ignored the playful tugs and bleats of the kids as they bounced and hopped around him. He would have laughed at their antics any other day as they careened into one another or attempted to head-butt his legs. Today there was no humor left in the world. He was a prisoner, and these were his tormentors—an underworld meant as punishment for those who dared to dream of the sky.

He didn't touch his dinner. Cathy made a few attempts to bridge the gulf of silence between him and his aunt, but her charm was wasted against their impassible walls. He scrubbed the dishes with the same ferocity he'd dealt to the weeds, and later he washed the dirt off himself with the same energy. It was only when he was in his room readying for bed that Amelia finally approached him.

She stood in the doorway, backlit by the hallway lantern. Atlas hadn't bothered to light the lamp in his room so her features remained shadowed as she spoke. "It's my job to raise you right, Atlas. It's my responsibility. We all have responsibilities."

"Nobody asked you to," Atlas replied. The words came out colder than he'd intended, but he couldn't stop them.

"That's true," Amelia replied. "They never got the chance. But I know what they wanted for you, and that's what I'm trying to give you."

"Mom flew. She flew every day. Grandpa said so."

Amelia crossed her arms and leaned against the doorpost. "And your dad worked this farm every day." She scuffed a worn boot across the doorjamb absentmindedly. "They both did."

Atlas flopped onto his bed and stared at the ceiling. The light from the open doorway cast a long triangular swath across it. He tried not to look at his aunt, but kept her in the corner of his eye.

"They worked this farm to give you the kind of life they thought you deserved. So you'd grow up to be the kind of person they knew you could be. They worked hard and they made a good life here. To keep you safe."

"And they flew," Atlas stabbed the words at the ceiling, as if to puncture it.

"Look where that got them!" Amelia blurted out.

She lifted her arms from her sides and raked her fingers through her hair with both hands before turning and facing the wall. "That's not what I wanted to say." With her hands still on the back of her head, she leaned her elbows against the wall of the hallway and stared down at her feet. "I know they loved to fly. And I know they wouldn't have kept you from it. I'm not keeping you from it either. I just need you to try, Atlas. You need to show me you care about this life we've made here."

Atlas couldn't tell if her eyes were open or closed. He studied her back—her shirt pulled tight against her spine. She was a coil again. A wound-up piece of clockwork tensed to spring apart.

Somewhere there was a sentence. Some assembly of words that could unwind that spring, release the stress between her shoulders.

There was something he could say that would ease the strain that permeated the space between his bed and her bent form in the doorway.

Atlas stayed quiet. He rolled over in bed and faced the wall.

He counted his breaths against the pillowcase. In. Out. In . . .

After a while the triangle of light on the ceiling narrowed to a line, then vanished as the door clicked shut behind her.

8

THE FESTIVAL

The mountains were teeth. Southfang was the most vicious, stabbing into the sky nearly twenty thousand feet, but for Samra, the whole Ridge Valley looked like a mouth opened to swallow the patch. Cutting loose from the weight of the rest of the patch was the only hope she had to save her globe. With knife poised over the tendril vine bridge, she waited for just the right moment, when the winds would be strong enough to lift her globe clear—up, up and away from the hungry gaping jaws—enough wind to send it soaring back to the Heights and the freedom of the open sky. The rest of the patch would crash into the vicious teeth of the mountains and get gnashed among the rocks. She would mourn them.

"Samra Rose, what are you doing out there?" Her stepmother's voice drifted from inside the globe tendrils. "These danion bulbs aren't going to chop themselves, you know."

Samra studied the blade of her cooking knife and sighed, then stood up. The patch continued its slow descent into the valley.

For the last few days everyone had been instructed to retain all of their water stores. They'd passed through a storm cloud overnight and the patch was now heavy with rainwater. With the added bulk of the globe sons that had not been released, the patch was losing altitude fast. Somewhere near the lead globes, the patch navigator would be giving orders to the ballast crews, reading the winds, adjusting altitudes accordingly, and keeping the patch headed for the valley.

Loara was working hard to assemble their family dishes for the arrival feast. She bustled around the aerie at high speed, whipping summer syrup and root sugar in bowls and occasionally stopping to sprinkle vegetables into her sun pepper stew. Samra's father had long ago finished his contribution to the feast, skewers of globe fruits with hearts of wind palms that she was pretty sure any patchling could have created, but she knew better than to suggest they were anything other than a complex delicacy.

As a soon-to-be globe chief, her father was intent on practicing his acceptance-of-duty speech, pacing from one side of the aerie to the other and gesturing to an imaginary crowd of no-doubt enthralled listeners.

"Why do we always serve the same food?" Samra asked. "Can't we just give the Grounders some globe green pudding and be done with it?"

Her stepmother whooshed past her to snatch up another mixing spoon from her arsenal. "Don't be silly, Samra. This is a feast to represent our culture. And it's an opportunity to demonstrate our good faith with the Grounders. You don't show good faith with globe green pudding."

By afternoon, her father was dressed in his ceremonial tunic and headdress, complete with reeds, feathers, and sea glass beads. Loara had decorated his face with the painted symbols of a first year chief, and Samra's cheeks and forehead now bore the painted lines of green and blue fit for a councilman's daughter. Her legs and wrists were wrapped in aged skyweed bands, and her tunic was bound at the waist with plaited vine tendrils. Her hair had the requisite headband adorned with star lilies, but she had also added a few personal touches: a row of black feathers from a storm crow, three pricklefish spines, and a necklace made of shark's teeth. She had attempted to attach a few poisonous eel skulls to the necklace but Loara vetoed the decision as soon as she was out of her tendril pocket.

Samra wanted to be in the landing party. What if when they reached land, the Grounders had all been mutated by an underground fungus and had gone raving mad? Or what if they appeared normal on the outside but were secretly plotting the ruin of the Skylighter High Council? Who would be there to notice and warn them? The council would be too intent on showing good manners. The whole patch might fall right into their trap.

Samra could only hope that Kipling would have his eyes open. She had made him promise to send up their war cry if he spotted anything suspicious. She didn't have much in the way of weapons, but she had smuggled her knife under her tunic, sheathed in a rootwood sleeve and dangling from her neck by a string. It was important to be prepared.

Her tunic also concealed the buoyancy belt. Though nowhere near as bulky as Rufus's contraption, all of the Skylighters would be wearing buoyancy belts tonight to compensate for the pressure changes. If they stayed down long enough, their bodies would acclimate to the lower altitude, but for now, every breath involved a struggle to keep from drifting to the ceiling. The belt took care of that. Tonight they would be servants of gravity, just like the Grounders.

When the globe patch touched down in the valley, she was still maddeningly high up in her aerie. Cirra Sola was a globe of honor this season, so unfortunately she would be one of the last families to descend. Khloe Mintz and her family were finished with preparations and enjoying rustleberry wine on the vine bridge. The Stormblower family was there, too, and Khloe and Jerem were positively gloating about being allowed to drink the festival wine this year. They'd both passed their Ascendare tests last autumn and seemed keen to show off their new privileges. Khloe's little brother, Willis, was racing up and down the bridge making a racket with the star lily root horn he'd attempted to make in school on the day of the Watcher prize. Samra was surprised he'd managed not to lose it yet, but wished he had. The horn didn't emit a blast so much as a sputter, and produced as much spit as it did noise.

The sight of Willis once again gave her that queasy feeling in the pit of her stomach. It wasn't the way he squawked up and down the bridge or even the bits of drool moistening the edges of his mouth. It was the fact that when the colony was drifting on its own for however many years, he would be the only other person close to her age besides Khloe and Jerem. The two of them were already paired up, so it didn't take a big leap to figure out whom their parents hoped might one day contribute to the propagation of the colony.

No one had said as much to her or Willis yet, but Samra was old enough to know how these things worked on the patch. Parents always whispered things and made arrangements when new colonies began. Getting the Stormblowers and Mintzs to agree to come aboard would have involved many such conversations. Looking at the way Jerem and Khloe were swooning over each other, it was easy to see why their parents agreed, but did her father really think so little of her that he would subject her to a life with Willis?

She tried to shake off the thought. Years would pass till that was an immediate threat. There were plenty of catastrophes the globe might run into between now and then that might relieve her of that problem.

Far below, music drifted up from the surface. The Grounders had a band—playing strange instruments made of heavy keys and tight metal strings. She did like the drums. The rhythmic pounding echoed up to her like a heartbeat that skipped and danced. It reverberated off the cliffs and made the globe tendrils vibrate. She wondered if the Globe Mother felt it and dreamed of dancing herself.

The time finally came to descend for the welcome feast. Her family spiraled down the tendril bridges in a slow procession that made Samra's head ache. She could have plummeted to the surface a hundred times and floated back up after each one in shorter time than the Stormblowers took to walk down.

Mist clung to the edges of the valley despite the residual warmth of the late afternoon sun. As the sun set behind the high mountains, the valley was already mostly in shadow, even though the sky was still bright. The Grounders had lanterns and torches lit, party lights to dispel the very thought of nightbeasts.

There were protections in place, to be sure. Samra eyed the Grounder warriors with suspicion, tall men and a few women dressed in sheepskin coats and armed with pikes and spears. A few of them carried the unusual air-powered harpoon guns. She'd seen some in action at a previous festival when one of the men demonstrated how he could fire into the air and bring down lingering skyweed. The harpoon guns that the Grounders carried today didn't look like they were meant for plants.

Despite the threat of nightbeasts, the welcome feast was set outdoors. Samra had to admit the Grounders had done a fair job with the lights. Once the globe patch began to glow for the night, the combination of its light and the lanterns would keep all but the bravest of the creatures away.

A good contingent of guardians was on hand, too, but not all of them had been assigned to security. Harlan and Auralee were taking turns floating little Grounder children up in the air, eliciting shrieks of glee from their passengers. As Samra watched, Harlan lit himself up to a brilliant gold hue and hoisted a young girl of perhaps eight or nine into the air, drifting off the ground a few feet to a round of applause from the crowd.

Auralee, being much smaller in size than Harlan, was primarily hoisting toddlers. They both looked tired already. Samra knew that such an activity, while entertaining for the Grounders, took a lot of energy, and they wouldn't be able to keep it up long. It was said that Captain Bronks had once hoisted the town mayor into the air for the benefit of the crowd. Judging by the mayor's sizable proportions, Samra hoped for Bronks's sake that it had been in the Mayor's younger and leaner years. There were limits on what a Skylighter could carry and still get airborne, even for someone with the lift capacity of the guardian captain.

Enzo was there, too. He stood near *The Sunshine Express*, on display as part of the festival exhibition. She waved to him and was delighted when he immediately waved back, grinning his gapped smile and temporarily ignoring the line of curious patrons ogling his aircraft.

Enzo was a celebrity to the Skylighters, not only because of his flying machine, but also his ingenious inventions that brought pressurized air up from underground to be stored in little metal bottles. His family had delved deep into the mountainside and discovered caverns where the constantly falling water trapped the air in various pockets and kept it under pressure. His machine siphoned the compressed air up to the surface to be used for all manner of clever tools. Samra and Kipling had once gotten to see some of his machines, but that had been years ago, and only with a group of other school patchlings.

Samra admired Enzo because he wasn't like the other Grounders, or even like her dad. He never appeared to care about being famous. He seemed just as likely to climb into the *Express* and wander off into the sky as he was to stay. Samra would much rather have been spending the evening with him, but she plodded along behind her parents toward the feast nonetheless.

"Keep your back straight," her stepmother whispered, pressing a hand to her shoulder. "We want to make a good impression for your father."

Samra dutifully handed her food offering to the waiting Grounder attendant and followed her parents toward the raised platform that had been erected for the occasion. The platform faced the tables where the older Skylighters and Grounders were carefully arranged in places to socialize with one another. Kip was there, too, seated at the front table with his parents and the portly, smiling mayor of the village. Kip nodded to her. At least one friendly face in the crowd, although Kip didn't look especially happy to be there either.

Kaleb was on stage, along with a Grounder girl Samra suspected might be a relative of the mayor. She shared his same jovial, rounded proportions. Kaleb beamed out at the crowd and continued his speech about Skylighter and Grounder unity, and how he felt it was important for the younger generation to build relationships with one another to preserve tradition. In addition to the usual contingent of Khloe's friends that were hovering around the stage, a number of Grounder girls were also listening to Kaleb with rapt attention and seemed eager to discuss Skylighter-Grounder relations with him.

As Samra's group reached the side of the platform, they were met by a group of festival assistants including a cluster of Khloe's friends. The parents congregated near the steps while Samra was left alone with her peers.

"You look so good, Khloe," Dasha Cormunger said. "You and Jerem make the best-looking couple."

Khloe waved off the compliment but looked pleased.

"You do look amazing," Jerem added, staring Khloe in the eyes. "As radiant as a sun bloom."

Samra emitted a gagging noise from the back of her throat.

"Oh, they let the bloodstain come, too." Dasha stared down at Samra. "And here I thought we were trying to make the patch look good."

"Ha ha! Bloodstain!" Willis sputtered from next to his sister. "Cause she gets so red when she tries to glow." His finger stabbed toward Samra's face.

"Shut up, Willis," Samra hissed. She strained to keep from reacting, but could already feel her face starting to warm.

"You can't talk to Willis like that," Jerem said, resting a protective hand on Willis's shoulder. His other arm was firmly around Khloe — his hand lingering low on her hip. "Just because your father will be globe chief when we depart, don't think that means you'll be bossing Willis around. You'd better treat him with some respect."

"Yeah," Willis added, elated to have the approval of Jerem. He stuck his tongue out at her but retracted it immediately as Samra hissed at him again.

Jerem's father, Mr. Stormblower, appeared suddenly and shooed them toward the stage. "Time to line up."

Samra found her way behind her parents and was grateful that her family at least provided a narrow buffer between her and Khloe's crowd.

Her stepmother dabbed at her face. "Why is your paint already running?" Loara frowned, quickly reapplying some of Samra's markings with a stick of paint from her bag. She then stuffed it into Samra's tunic pocket. "You'd better keep that. I have a feeling we'll need it again tonight. I thought you were going to stay calm."

"I am calm," Samra muttered through gritted teeth. She pulled her eyes off Jerem and Khloe and found Kip in the crowd instead. Rufus had crept up from his table in the rear of the feast and was lingering next to Kip to watch her presentation. Rufus waved. Samra felt her skin begin to cool and gave a quick wave back. Rufus beamed.

" . . . and it's an honor to introduce our next globe colonists . . ." Kaleb continued. A few other members of the globe council joined him, and they stood ready to bestow the duty symbols on her father: a carved heartwood globe, a stone knife, and a goose-quill pen. "The Stormblowers will be tasked with the education of the young . . ." Jerem's parents stepped forward to receive their symbols.

Samra climbed to the second to last step and waited behind her parents. Khloe's friends were whispering and sniggering behind her, but she did her best to tune them out. Just a short walk. Stand next to her parents when they are called. Smile as her father receives his symbols of duty. Bow with the family and listen politely while her father gives his speech. Then she'd be free.

Councilman Thur addressed the crowd from next to Kaleb, his thin skin ghostly in the twilight. "And it's our great honor to now introduce the newest globe chief and his family. The first chief of Cirra Sola, Mr. Donlo Coley."

Samra's father stepped forward, beaming and waving, his wife at his side. Samra stepped up to follow them and was lifting a hand to wave as well, when her foot caught on something and she teetered. Panicked, she tried to wrench her foot free, but it was too late. The movement only propelled her farther forward. She inhaled instinctively to right herself, but the weight of the buoyancy belt had already thrown off her equilibrium. She crashed into the platform in a heap.

The crowd of onlookers gasped and groaned, and a smattering of muffled snickers emanated from behind her. When she looked up, all eyes were on her. The entire front row of council members and the mayor of the Grounders were right at her eye level. Kipling's mother looked concerned, but when Samra twisted to look up at her own parents, now at center stage, she only saw horror on their faces.

Her father was frozen mid-wave. Her stepmother's eyes were wide. She turned to look back at what tripped her and caught Dasha's eye the moment before she looked away. Heat flared beneath her skin. Before she could even think, she was on her feet again and diving for Dasha. A collective "Oooh!" went up from the crowd, but the only thing she could focus on was Dasha's hair wrapped around her fingers as she hauled the girl onto the platform. Dasha shrieked and flailed, but Samra only pulled harder, wrapping her legs around the girl's torso and pummeling her about the head.

"I hate you!" she shouted.

Her skin was on fire now, the heat inside her roiling through her body as she and Dasha rolled across the platform. Strong hands gripped under her shoulders and yanked her free from the terrified girl, but she came away with multiple strands of hair. Samra squirmed and flailed at her new attacker, kicking and biting the arms that tried to wrap around her neck.

"Get your hands off me, Kaleb Roose!" She kicked the boy hard in the stomach and scrambled backward till she was against the backdrop of the stage, staring at a ring of horrified festival hosts. Their eyes were wide and now they were keeping their distance. Samra was panting, and for the first time she realized her hands weren't empty. Her left hand held a clump of Dasha's hair, but her right held her cooking knife, blade pointed toward Kaleb. The older boy looked shocked and was cradling his forearm, one hand pressed tight against it. Stopping the blood?

Had she cut him?

The knife fell from her fingers and she began to shake, searching the faces around her for someone who might help. It was her father's that she found first. His eyes were hard, his nostrils flared. He kept his distance, too, but he would, wouldn't he? Stay as far away from her as possible — his failure of a daughter who had ruined everything.

She fled. She pushed her way through the banners at the back of the stage and fell to the ground behind it in a heap. She was up in an instant and running through the festival grounds, swerving past event tents and Grounder carriages, getting as far from the platform as she could and making for the wide open fields beyond. She raced around the corner of a striped tent and ran directly into the chest of a man on the far side. She ricocheted off him and almost fell again, but his hands clasped her shoulders and steadied her.

"Whoa, now!" It was Enzo, the old messenger pilot, his eyes wide with concern. "Samra, what happened? Are you okay?"

She looked up into his dark eyes and saw he was confused. Was he frightened of her? No. His hands were firm on her shoulders. "I didn't mean it," Samra whimpered. "I didn't mean to . . ." Her hands were still an embarrassing shade of blood red.

"It's okay, child. What happened to you?"

"It just does this, I don't—" She tried to stop her hands from shaking and dropped her eyes from the old man's face. She instead stared at the necklace that had fallen out of Enzo's shirt and was dangling beneath his scruffy gray beard. It was a triangular stone with lines etched into it. The lines glowed and pulsed faintly in the darkness. Viewed through watery eyes, it was mesmerizing.

"It's okay. You're okay," Enzo assured her. "Just breathe."

Samra choked on her own air, realizing that she had in fact stopped breathing. She gasped and then exhaled, trying to calm herself down.

Captain Bronks was the first to discover her. He dropped casually from the mist and landed next to them in the grass. "Evening, Mr. Mooreside. Nice to see you again." He seemed unconcerned with Samra's reddened state.

The tears on her cheeks had quickly evaporated from the heat of her skin and left cool trails down her face. Her hands had lightened again, fading back to a subtle orangish-yellow.

"Seems we have a bit of a situation on our hands," Bronks said to her. "You have a few people searching for you."

"Has our young Samra really done something worth all this fuss?" Enzo asked.

"So it would seem," Bronks replied. "Miss Coley does find herself in these predicaments from time to time."

"It wasn't my fault," Samra protested. "Dasha tripped me. Right in front of everybody. Nobody saw it, but it's true!"

"I did see," Bronks replied. "And I assure you that Dasha will face her own consequences. But it doesn't mean you get to attack her. Or the chief's son."

"I didn't mean to," Samra whimpered. "She made me. They always do."

Enzo laid a hand on her shoulder and stooped a little closer. "Hey. I ever tell you about how I came to be a pilot?"

Samra shook her head, not sure what this story could have to do with her problems.

"Had a bit of a hard time, too, when I was your age. Couldn't even get out of bed for a long time. All the other kids were running around, having fun without me. At school they used to play this game called 'frog pond.' Silly game really, but it was fun. And all I wanted in the world was to join them. Problem was, I couldn't even move out of my own way." He pulled up the fabric of his pants and revealed that his leg stopped just short of his knee. From the knee down, his leg was entirely mechanical—a combination of rods and joints with cables running up and down to actuate the boot on the foot.

Samra gawked at the contraption with wonder. She rubbed her nose with the back of her hand and wiped it off on her pants. She was in trouble, but she did have both her legs still.

The old pilot rambled on with his story. "Boy, I was determined. I was going to run and jump and play frog pond with the other kids, or die trying. So I built my first mechanical leg. Made it in my room. I wore that leg to school, proud as could be. I joined that game, and fell flat on my face in front of everyone. They laughed at me something fierce." He wagged a finger at Samra. "But I didn't let it stop me." He tugged his pant leg back down over his mechanical calf. "I went home and built another one. And then another. And you know what finally happened?"

"You learned to jump?"

"Nope." The old man shook his head. "Never jumped once. Fell on my face every dang time. Never ran either. Failed completely on both fronts."

Samra scrunched up her face in confusion. "Why would you tell me this story then?" She flung a hand in the air. "You mean I listened to that whole thing just so you could tell me to give up?"

Exasperated, she turned to Captain Bronks, but he was smirking at the old man.

Enzo smiled. "Just trying to be helpful. You see, I had to realize that I wasn't ever going to be like the other kids. I was going to be like me. I was never going to run or jump, but I learned other skills they never needed." He tapped his mechanical leg. "And then I learned to build that." He straightened up and gestured to the aircraft behind him.

Samra looked past the old man to the colorful wings of *The Sunshine Express*.

"Sometimes you have to skip jumping and go straight to flying."

She was about to speak when her stepmother appeared, flying out from between the tents, ceremonial beads clacking around her wrists.

"Oh, Captain Bronks, thank you for finding her." She crouched at Samra's side and grasped her arm in the same place Enzo's hands had been, but Loara's grip was pincers. "What were you thinking! A knife? And right in the middle . . . your father is furious. You're going straight back to the aerie and you'll stay there till we can come deal with you."

"Will dad still give his speech?" Samra stammered.

"How can he? How can he go out there now?" Loara said. "Don't you know what you've done? He's worked so hard for this."

"I'm sorry. I didn't mean—" Her eyes welled up as she spoke.

"Get back to the aerie. Don't even think about leaving your pocket till we are home." Her stepmother shifted her attention to Enzo. "I'm sorry if she bothered you, sir. I'll have her out of your hair momentarily. Captain Bronks, can you please take her home? I'd like you to get her back to our aerie right away and see that she stays. Don needs me right now and we have to sort this mess out somehow."

"It's not a problem," Bronks replied.

Loara gave Samra one last glare but didn't speak; instead she spun on her heel, gathered up the bottom of her tunic and sped back across the grass toward the lights and the stage.

Samra was back to shaking again. She looked to Enzo. The old man gave her a wan smile. "Bound to be a few crashes along the way."

Samra didn't know how that was possibly supposed to help.

"All right. Take off your buoyancy belt," Bronks said.

Samra fumbled at the bottom of her tunic but after the force of her stepmother pinching her arms, her fingers felt numb. She pulled the tunic up past the waist of her trousers but couldn't get the belt undone. Bronks flashed a hand to her waist and sent the belt flying into the grass with one swift motion. The next moment he was hoisting her onto his shoulder. "Breathe now, girl. Up we go." He took a deep breath and leapt into the air.

The figure of the old pilot receded below them.

"Samra!" Kipling was racing across the grass now, Rufus trailing behind. The pair sped across the grounds but grew rapidly smaller as she ascended.

"Now isn't the time, Kipling!" Bronks's voice boomed down to the field below. The two boys reached the old pilot and stood staring upward as if to bring her back with their eyes.

Samra watched the boys vanish into the mist and realized the fog from the hills had reached them. She let the darkness envelop her and closed her eyes tight. It was a mistake. All she found there was the image of her father's furious face and the feeling of Loara's fingers pressing into her arms. When next she opened them she was in her hammock and Bronks was closing the flaps of her tendril pocket behind him. He was blurry and watery in the darkness. He gave her one last glance, not unkindly, and closed the entrance.

Samra buried her face in her arms and cried.

9

THE ARRIVAL

"It's about spending time as a family," Amelia explained. "It's not like the festival won't be there tomorrow."

Atlas sat at the table and tried to understand her reasoning. "But I did all my chores already. That was the deal."

Cathy set the bread on the table and patted him on the shoulder. "This isn't so bad, right? Extra lumpy cheese noodles and fresh bread. It's your favorite."

The food did smell good. But it was the principle of the thing.

"You said I could go if I got all my work done."

"You can," Amelia said. "Tomorrow." She eased herself onto the bench on the other side of the table.

Atlas frowned at the food but stayed quiet.

The tension on the farm had simmered over the past few days. Atlas had done his best to not anger his aunt and had been attentive at school. As much as could be expected anyway. He hadn't seen Enzo at all, but he'd been counting on seeing him tonight at the festival. Now he wouldn't even have that. He stirred the cheese into his noodles and tried not to think about what he'd be missing.

The kids in town would all be at the festival feast tonight, sampling Skylighter food and swapping dishes from their homes. Was it the feast that worried Amelia? They had enough for themselves tonight. Plenty to have a good meal, but was there not enough to share in town? The cupboards did look bare. When was the last time Amelia had even been to town? She'd sent him on errands here and there, but never for food. Always other essentials. New saw blades. Horseshoes for Destro. He couldn't remember the last time Amelia had bought anything that wasn't a tool. Certainly nothing for herself. Meals lately had all been from the garden and the goats.

Atlas contemplated the bag of coins he had hiding in his sock drawer. He'd accumulated a few tips from townspeople while running messages. He'd been saving for a control wheel, but now that he had one, maybe he could take the coins to town tomorrow and get something nice for Amelia and Cathy. It would make them smile and relieve some of the strain. And then once they were happy, he could get them to come to Enzo's. They'd roll out the *Sun Dragon* and admire his work on it, and maybe even cheer for him as he took it up.

He could get his flight.

"What are you most excited to see tomorrow?" Cathy asked.

Atlas debated the question in his mind.

"Heather Lanford?" Cathy suggested.

"No way," Atlas retorted, but he could feel the color rising to his face.

"You don't think she'll be there waiting to see you?" Cathy said. "You going to ask her to dance?"

"No!"

"Why not? I plan to ask Amelia to dance. We'll be the stars of the ball. You and Heather will have tough competition."

"I'm not dancing with Heather . . ."

"Scared, huh?" Cathy grinned. "You should be. We'll put you to shame with our moves."

Atlas concentrated on his food. He appreciated that Cathy was trying to defuse the tension, but she was getting it wrong. "Heather Lanford won't want to dance with me."

"Why not? You're a handsome guy," Cathy said. "She should be so lucky."

"She's the prettiest girl in town. She's never going to want to dance with a stupid goat farmer," Atlas muttered.

When he looked up, he realized what he'd said. Amelia and Cathy were both staring at him. Cathy was clearly hurt. "I'm sorry. That's not what I meant."

"You think you'll only be worthy of her when you've got your fancy airship, like Enzo," Amelia said. "This life isn't good enough, huh?"

"I'm sorry," Atlas said. "I didn't mean that—"

"Why don't you go eat on the porch, Atlas," Amelia said. "Go get some fresh air."

"I'm okay here."

"I don't think you are." Amelia glared at him and rested a hand on Cathy's shoulder. Atlas got up and took his food. Halfway down the hallway he turned around to try to apologize, but Amelia had sat down next to Cathy on the bench and they were whispering to one another. He watched them for a few seconds, then continued to the porch.

Fog had rolled in from the mountains. The canyon was blanketed in it now and more was cascading down from above, slowly filling the valley.

There were still a few patches of sky visible, but they moved and shifted as the fog rolled in, the first few stars of the night blinking through the gaps. Down in the village they would be reveling in the light of the Skylighter patch, but even that would be hazy in this fog. He wouldn't see much of the festivities from here.

Atlas set his food on the porch bench and took up the lamp lighter from the corner. He lit the wick from the small oil lantern they always kept burning and used the flame to light the bigger lanterns on the corners of the porch. The light from the doorway spilled out onto the porch and that would possibly be enough to frighten off nightbeasts, but the rule was always 'the more lights the better.'

At the corner of the porch, Atlas gazed east to the high crags that made up the wall of the canyon. A footpath ran up the cliffside and wound its way high up the ridge to the Beacon Bell.

The watchtower light at the edge of the Rift was usually lit by now.

Danson Merkle, the usual night watchman, was a common sight at the warren, as he passed through their property almost daily on his climb to the Beacon. Sometimes Atlas would blink him messages from the porch and Danson would blink back using one of the smaller lamps from his post high on the crag. They said it had been ten years since the Beacon Bell itself had last rung in warning, and the big mirrored lantern of the Beacon merely marked time now, a symbol of security, letting the residents of the valley know that the Rift was clear, and no dangers of the outside world were encroaching on their peaceful valley.

Only tonight the lamp wasn't lit.

As the mist cascaded off the rocks, he only caught glimpses of the Rift in the gaps, but he could make out the windows of the Beacon, black and lifeless.

Atlas stood at the corner of the porch and flashed his lantern toward the watchtower—his usual greeting to Danson—but likely ineffective with the patchy fog. He wouldn't be able to blink a message, but perhaps just a hello? Danson could be having trouble getting the Beacon lit tonight. But he should have a lantern to blink back with.

Atlas flashed for a solid minute, but with no response. He was about to head back to his bench when he saw the shape. It was moving slowly out of the Rift, bulbous at the top with sharp fins at the rear. The two curved noses probed the darkness and began to descend. As the shape pitched downward, it revealed twin tails that oscillated in tandem. The side of the shape shimmered with silvery scales, but the way it moved in the starlight was not that of a living thing. It was mechanical. It was a ship.

Atlas doused his lantern immediately and frantically blew out the rest of the lamps on the porch. The nightbeasts might be a terror, but there were worse things in the skies. He raced down the main corridor of the warren, blowing out candles and lamps as he ran. He burst into the kitchen panting and out of breath. Cathy and Amelia were talking together over the sink full of soapsuds, but both turned to look at Atlas when he dashed to a stop in the center of the room.

"Sakes, Atlas, what is it?" Cathy asked.

Atlas gulped a breath and spurted out the word. "Raiders!"

Amelia was on the porch in a flash, scanning the sky. "Where?"

"Up there! Coming out of the Rift."

The ship that Atlas had first spotted had moved out of the cleft between the mountains and was gliding silently into the valley, but more shapes were emerging from the darkness behind it.

"We need to warn the village," Cathy said from behind him. "They'll be completely off guard."

"Danson . . ." Amelia muttered, looking up the rocky cliff face toward the watchtower. "He could be hurt."

"Someone needs to ring that bell," Cathy said.

"I can go," Atlas said. "I can make it up the path and—"

"No. You stay here," Amelia said. "I'll go." She raced back into the warren and emerged a moment later with a pair of hand harpoons in a leather quiver and her long knife. She slung the quiver over her shoulder and picked up one of the lanterns. "When I make the top, I'll ring the bell and light the beacon. Stay indoors and lock down the warren."

Cathy stepped off the porch and made a beeline for the woodpile. She plucked the ax from the chopping stump and returned to the porch. "Let's get going then."

"No," Amelia protested. "You should stay here with Atlas and guard the warren."

"Like hell I'm letting you climb into danger on your own," Cathy replied. "The raiders will have their sights on more than a goat ranch. But the nightbeasts will be happy to find you alone on the cliffs. I'm not letting you do this alone."

"I can go, too," Atlas offered.

"No!" both women responded at the same time.

Amelia pointed inside the warren. "You bolt the door and get into the caverns. I don't think they'll come here, but if they do you can lose them easily in the caves. You know all the hideaways. God knows you've used them enough to get out of chores. Get in there and stay out of sight. We'll be back as soon as we ring that bell."

"But I can help!"

"Inside. Now." Amelia shoved him toward the doorway. "We'll be back as soon as we can." Amelia let her hand linger on his shoulder for a brief moment, then gave it a squeeze before turning back to Cathy. "Okay, we need to hurry."

Atlas watched from the doorway as his aunt led the way up and over the berm of grass that covered the warren, headed toward the footpath up the cliffs.

He stood in the doorway even after they were gone, staring out at the canyon and the downward slope to the valley. He took a few steps forward to the edge of the porch and scanned the sky. The fog was even denser now, blotting out most of the view. He could no longer see the watchtower or what might be emerging from the Rift. The one bare patch of sky he could see held only darkness and distant pinpricks of stars. The raiders had perfect cover. No one would see them approaching. Womble was a pulsing glow in the mist on the valley floor. The lights of the festival would make everyone nearly blind in the darkness. Enzo would be busy showing off the *Express* with no idea what was coming.

Atlas looked back toward the Beacon. He'd made that climb enough times to visit the watchmen. Even at a run, as fast as he could go, the uphill climb still took nearly twenty minutes. His aunt might make it in fifteen at a dead sprint, but what if she couldn't? What if the nightbeasts came and they had to defend themselves? What if raiders had invaded the Beacon and they had to hide?

Atlas considered the dark hallway behind him and the safety of the caverns. How could he hide while everyone else was in danger? Enzo needed him.

He stepped inside and bolted the door, but once indoors he didn't head into the interior caverns. He made for the front passage instead, following it downhill toward the lower end of the warren. He unbolted the gates that led past the goat pens, but ignored their bleating as he leapt the underground stream. He ran up the path at the far side and through the passage to the next stable. Destro stomped a hoof in the darkness.

"We need to hurry," Atlas whispered to the horse. "Enzo's in danger." He snatched up a bridle and reins from the peg outside Destro's stall, but didn't bother with a saddle. Every moment counted. Destro balked once at the sight of the fog when Atlas led him outside through the livestock gate, but he soothed him with a few gentle strokes of his hand before leaping onto the horse's back. The horse charged forward into the night without further resistance, and Atlas urged him faster as they flew down the hill.

Shapes threatened and lunged from the fog, only to be revealed as tree limbs and boulders. Atlas would've known this path blindfolded and didn't flinch. He did listen, however, trying to hear past the thudding of the horse's hooves for any sign of impending danger—wings on the wind, or scratching of claws on the rocks. The horse's ears pivoted on occasion as well, but he kept up the pace, increasing steadily once the road began to level out into the valley.

He was making good time. The raider ships had been moving

slowly and being cautious. Destro flew along the main road now, hooves kicking sod and dirt into the air behind him.

Atlas only needed to make it to the mayor's fields. Thankfully it was this side of the village. He could already hear the band. Drumbeats pounded out a festive rhythm and the flutes and fiddles kept pace. Someone was singing. The glow through the fog grew brighter and he could make out the first shapes of globes overhead. The Skylighters and villagers were cheery with conversation. The steady hum of voices reached him over the music and the pounding of Destro's hooves.

The horse leapt the fence at the side of the mayor's pasture as soon as it appeared. Atlas groaned on the landing but righted himself and kept from slipping off. A frightened couple in the weeds relinquished their romantic embrace as Destro sped past. He was almost there. Lines of tables appeared in the haze, populated with feasters. Lanterns overhead bathed the festival in light. He was going to make it. He readied himself to shout.

An ear-splitting scream stopped the music.

Something dark plummeted from the night and crashed into one of the tables at the far end of the feast, overturning the head table and scattering the diners. Destro reared up and snorted, causing Atlas to clench the horse's mane to stay seated. Once the horse was back on four hooves, Atlas recognized the appendages protruding from the ruined table as human legs.

The black shape in the center of the wreckage twitched once, then went still.

A Skylighter swooped low over the head table and landed in the grass just before the stage. The winged warrior held a sort of hooked sword made of bone in one hand and a harpoon in the other. He spread his wings wide and shouted to the crowd. "We're under attack! Rally to the globes!"

Mayor Fillmore was white with fear. He rose from his chair and spun in place but could only stammer a few odd sounds.

"What's happening?" An elderly woman to Atlas's right shrieked up at him from her seat at her table.

"Raiders!" Atlas shouted. "Get out of here!"

The feast erupted in panic, with diners toppling chairs and knocking over glassware. Overhead, the fog echoed with shouting and the clash of weapons. Somewhere amid all this chaos, Atlas had to find Enzo. He scanned the fleeing crowd but saw no sign of his grandfather. Where was The *Sunshine Express*? Where would his grandfather hide? He spurred Destro and the horse leapt the table in front of him. Atlas urged him forward into the glowing fog and chaos.

Off in the distance, the Beacon Bell began to toll.

10

KIPLING

"Hey, gardener. How's it feel to be friends with a crazy girl?" Darian Wessel was smirking near the side of the stage when Kipling found his way back to the feast. His older brother's friend was accompanied by Tolmer Grange, the oldest and meanest boy in Kaleb's year. Tolmer stepped forward and confronted Kip and Rufus as they approached.

"Kaleb went easy on your little girlfriend. You better keep her away from the rest of us or she'd better have more than a kitchen knife next time."

"She didn't cut anyone," Kipling replied, straining to make himself heard over the noise of the band, which chose that moment to start back up again. "I saw what happened. She just bit him."

"Doesn't matter. She pulled a knife on your brother in front of everybody. She won't be seeing the light of day after this. They'll probably maroon her on her own kelp patch somewhere. Not like they'll let her aboard the new colony now."

"Would they do that?" Rufus looked to Kipling with wide eyes. "What will happen to her?"

"They won't maroon her," Kipling said, though he didn't have much conviction. What *would* happen to Samra? It was rare that anyone acted with violence aboard the patch. When it did happen, separation from the Globe Mother was usually the punishment. But they wouldn't do that to a patchling . . . would they?

Kipling pushed past the two older boys and rounded the front of the stage. The grown-ups were conferring near the head table. Samra's parents were there. Her father had taken off his ceremonial headdress and was wringing it in his hands. Kip's mother looked concerned and was listening to Mr. Coley apologize, while his father inspected Kaleb's wound. Kip could tell even from this distance that it wasn't serious, just an oval bite mark, but Samra had managed to break the skin. It would certainly leave a nasty bruise. He kept his distance, but his father spotted him and waved him over. He moved hesitantly toward the group under the condemning glare of his brother.

"Kip, I need your assistance," his father said. "I spoke to Mayor Fillmore and he's going to cancel the Grounder's lantern launch. Head up to the lower pods and tell them to keep the globe sons secured in the bundle. We were going to release them with the Grounder's lanterns, but we'll wait. No use trying to launch them in this fog anyway."

Kipling was relieved that the conversation had nothing to do with Samra, but couldn't help but ask anyway. "What's going to happen to Sam?"

His father shook his head. "We'll have to deal with her later. Right now we have an obligation to our hosts to repair the damage as much as possible. Luckily, none of the Grounders were hurt."

"She wouldn't hurt anyone, really. She was just scared."

His dad narrowed his eyes. "I think Dasha and her parents might disagree with you."

"Dasha is always mean to her and—"

"Dasha didn't pull a knife on anyone," Kaleb interjected. "And she didn't bite me either. It's your defective friend that's the problem."

"She's not defective! You haven't even heard Sam's side of the story. Maybe if you and your friends didn't always make fun of her, then this wouldn't—"

"Kipling." His father laid a hand on his shoulder. "Go to the pods and do what I've asked. There will be plenty of time to talk with Samra later."

He choked back the rest of his objections and nodded. Giving

Samra's parents a wide berth, he headed toward the center of the festival grounds, Rufus still on his heels.

"Do you think she's in big trouble? Will they let her out to see us anymore? Do you think she might stay living on the Globe Mother now?"

The last question stirred a small amount of hope in Kipling. Maybe she would get to stay on Corra Mara. That wouldn't be such a bad thing.

A scream sliced through the ambient noise and he swung around to see what had happened. The head table was broken in half, fractured by a body sprawled across the wreckage.

The band stopped.

Kipling looked up.

The air came alive with the whoosh of wings. Bronks descended into the crowd and alighted near Kipling's parents.

"We're under attack! Rally to the globes!" Bronks shouted. The guardian sprang into the air and ascended back into the fog. The feast erupted into screaming and chaos. Kipling scanned the crowd for signs of danger, but saw only fleeing Grounders and one Grounder boy astride a spotted horse. The horse reared once, then leapt a table and galloped off into the mist, taking the boy with it.

"What do we do?" Rufus exclaimed, grasping at Kipling's arm.

Kip turned and shoved his friend in the direction of the closest globe. "We need to get back aboard the patch!"

All around him Skylighters were dumping their buoyancy belts on the ground and leaping into the air. In every direction, glowing figures blazed into the fog before being swallowed up by obscurity.

Kipling kept a hand to his belt but didn't release it. He raced over the ground with Rufus panting behind, searching the luminous fog overhead for the right section of patch. He knew the emergency procedures. If he ended up aboard the wrong globe, he might not be able to connect with the Globe Mother. Everyone was meant to rally at his or her own globe, but the success of that procedure depended largely on not panicking, and that depended on what was attacking the patch.

Finally he reached the lowest tendrils of the Mother that had been tied to the ground to anchor the patch. Members of the landing crew were not bothering to untie the landing roots. They were simply hacking them loose with their long knives and hatchets. The roots groaned and then snapped loose, sending shudders up through the heart of the patch.

"Now! Jump now!" Kipling shouted.

Rufus struggled out of his buoyancy belt but forgot to leap. Instead he drifted free of the ground and began floating slowly upward. "Kip! Kip! Help!"

Kipling took a deep breath, released his belt, and leapt, flying into the mist and snatching hold of his friend on the way by. Rufus flailed behind him but they were aloft now, racing upward through the fog as their rapid breaths made them more and more buoyant.

He could hardly see anything. Vines and leaves whipped past but he merely kicked off the stalks he could reach, using them to propel himself higher and faster though the mist. He lit himself up slightly, but it didn't help. The fog was too thick. Even noises were muffled: shouts from Skylighters to meet at globes, screams for missing family members from frantic mothers, and above all that, the rumble and chuffing of mechanical engines and the blasting pops of pneumatic harpoon guns. This attack was no pack of nightbeasts. This was something different.

"Cut tethers and make for the Heights!" Someone shouted through the haze.

Figures illuminated themselves in the fog, glowing their warnings. Water gushed from above as someone released a ballast pod. The passing globe tendrils were slick in his hands.

Another whoosh overhead signaled a passing guardian. This was followed by a thud and an outcry of pain. But who were they fighting?

Another hundred feet and the fog began to clear. The globes were blazing brightly from the commotion and some were already detached from the Mother, rising swiftly into the night and dumping their water reserves. Protocol was being followed. When in danger, make for the sky, rise above the threat and back to the thin, cold air of the Heights where ground-based predators couldn't follow. Kipling finally arrested his ascent, grabbing hold of a stalk of the Mother and clinging tightly to its bark. Rufus scrambled for a handhold as well.

The sky was swarming with activity. In every direction globes were detaching from the Mother, which was rising rapidly herself. But amid the glow of the globes and the Skylighters aboard them, dark shapes were moving. Big shapes. Kipling stared into the vacant sky where the western arm of the patch used to be and found himself focusing on a moving form. Scales shimmered on the sides of the twin tails, but this was no animal. It was an airship, two cylindrical bodies with dorsal fins, linked together by a central hull. It was from this center of the craft that long, thin lines extended — harpoon lines — with sharp, shiny spines already buried in many of the globes.

The guardians were working at high speed, whipping around the globes to cut the lines and free them from the ship's grasp. But there were more ships. They hovered in multiple directions and the guardians weren't working fast enough to free every globe. One in particular was already lashed to the side of the twin-tailed ship and the Grounder crew was working hard to secure a second bundle into the recesses of one of the cylinders. Kipling recognized the cluster of globe sons that had been ripped from the central pods.

"What do we do?" Rufus stammered. He pointed a shaky finger toward the ship. "That's Cirra Sola."

"What?" Kipling had to look again to see what Rufus was talking about, but when he looked closer he did recognize the partially deflated globe attached to the side of the ship as the lately ripened globe daughter. "No! Samra!" He nearly came off the stalk to fly toward it but Rufus gripped his arm.

"Kip, they're Grounder pirates! We have to get away!"

The Globe Mother was rising fast now, though not quite as fast as the smaller globes around it, and the shape of the Grounder ship was diminishing into the fog below. Bronks would have rescued Samra from the globe before it was taken. He must have gotten to her. He knew where she was and wouldn't have let any harm come to her.

"Come on!" he shouted to Rufus. "We've gotta find Bronks!"

"What about our parents?" Rufus replied.

Kipling paused in his ascent of the vines. What had become of his parents? And Kaleb. Had they made it aboard the Mother yet?

Corra Mara was soaring upward, free of the weight of the water reserves and the bulk of globe sons at her base, and now unencumbered by many of her younger globes. In every direction more of the smaller globes were making their way out into the night sky. The citizens of the patch had wasted no time in cutting ties and making a break for the safety of the upper altitudes. Some were clear of the mountains already, but the sharp fangs of the ridge still loomed higher than the heart of the patch.

Kipling scanned the remnants of the patch. The Mother was burdened with the weight of the vine bridges that used to connect her various arms. In their haste to depart, most of the citizens of the smaller globes had merely chopped the vines at their end, letting the bridges fall and dangle from the Mother like so many umbilical cords. Without the smaller globes to share the burden, they were weighing her down and bearing her closer and closer to the rocky teeth of the ridges. Kipling spotted Jervil Plance, the patch routes ranger, working on one of the residual bridges with a knife. Kipling raced over to him and helped hold tension on the vine as Jervil sawed at it.

"Have you seen my dad?" Kipling shouted.

"No time to be looking," Jervil replied. "Quick and cut those other vines!" He tossed Kip a pruning knife and jabbed a finger toward the next vine bridge. "If we don't lose this weight, we won't clear the ridge!" Jervil let the vine he'd cut drop into the darkness and scrambled overhand toward the next tangle of dangling vines.

Kipling gripped the pruning knife between his teeth and leapt for the closest residual bridge in the other direction.

"What do I do?" Rufus asked, as he clambered behind.

Kip plucked the knife from his mouth and began sawing at the thick tendrils. "Go find Bronks! We need to know if he has Samra."

Rufus set his jaw and nodded, then scrambled upward on the globe, disappearing over top in search of the guardian captain.

Kipling couldn't help but watch the action below. Even as he sawed away the superfluous vines, he kept an eye on the dwindling shapes of the ships. There were half a dozen of them, most now loaded down with bits of the globe patch. He had no idea what they wanted them for. Never in his life had he heard of a patch being attacked by Grounders—certainly not flying ones. And now there was a whole group of ships endangering their patch.

Four of the craft were lumbering skyward, up and away from the chaos of the festival, but two were racing away, headed for the big cleft in the ridges. The craft in front was tiny compared to the rest and shaped more like a fish. The bigger ship was bearing down on it like a shark intent on a minnow. It was only after a few moments of watching the chase that he recognized the smaller airship. The red nose and yellow fins were a now familiar sight— *The Sunshine Express.*

"Get away, Enzo!" Kipling shouted from his perch on the Globe

Mother, though the two craft were far too low to hear him. Enzo's little *Express* banked and dodged its way through the foothills at the base of the ridges, making the chase a challenge for the bigger predator, but the larger ship was also faster, blasting up and over the rocky outcroppings with more thrust than the little ship could manage. "Come on, Enzo, you can make it," Kipling whispered, his hands temporarily forgetting their duty with the vines. *The Sunshine Express* was almost to the upper canyons where the deep clefts between rocks would give it the advantage in maneuverability. A little farther and the bigger craft would have to abandon the chase as the *Express* lost itself amid the rocks. But just when Kipling was about to cheer, the *Express* listed hard to one side and was wrenched laterally until it was sideways, presenting its broadside to its pursuer. The tail of the craft flailed back and forth and the nose tried to straighten back out, but the craft only skipped sideways now in lurches, closer and closer to the bigger ship. He couldn't see it from here, but Kipling recognized the cause of this strange maneuver. The bigger craft had hit the *Express* with a harpoon.

Far below, the little airship struggled to get free, but even as the pilot tried to cut away the harpoon, another spike flashed from the bow of the pursuer and struck its tail. A third hit the nose immediately after. The struggling stopped. The *Express* was dead in the air.

Kipling muttered curses at the ship below but his attention was quickly diverted by the first jagged ridge of mountaintop passing below the globe. He frantically returned to cutting the vines and as soon as the bridge was loose, raced to the next one.

"She's not going to make it!" someone below him yelled. The ridge they were headed for seemed impassible, but Kipling still sawed away at the vines with vigor.

"Come on. Climb!" he yelled at globe the below him. "Don't you dare give up!"

The Mother was glowing beneath his feet and the internal gases flared even brighter when the patch hit the ridge, but the impact didn't rupture the globe. She scraped her way up the rocky face of the uppermost tooth of the mountaintop and only caught her trailing roots on the ridge. Citizens down in the root system hacked and sawed rapidly to free the remains of the patch before the winds could dash it back against the rocks. In a few moments the entangled roots were cut away and the Mother soared upward again, out of reach of the rocky spires and into the safety of the Heights.

As the Globe Mother rose, Kipling looked back over the ridge into the valley at the dull glow of lights beneath the fog. Somewhere in that faint luminescence was the village of Womble, but whatever fate it had met was beyond their help now.

He slid and shinnied his way down the outside of the globe till he could delve into the thick tendrils below. After clawing his way through the damaged vines, he finally emerged into the central grove. The floor of the grove was littered with debris. Skylighters of all ages were wandering around the interior asking after family members and seeking assistance. One battered-looking guardian was at the end of the grove answering questions and directing people to help stations. Kipling pushed his way through the crowd till he could reach the guardian. He recognized her as Auralee, the patch deputy. Slipping through the adults, he waved a hand to attract her attention.

"Auralee! Have you seen Bronks?"

Deputy Auralee turned in his direction and waved him over. "Captain Bronks is in the Citadel, resting. He was injured in the attack."

"Do you know if he found Samra? Did he rescue her?"

"I don't know who he rescued. You need to report to the registrar down in the commons. We're taking all the names to see who made it aboard. If Samra is here, you'll find her name on the list."

Kipling swore under his breath and edged his way out of the crowd. He worked his way to the tendril ladder on the east side of the grove. The commons would be swarming with more frantic families seeking lost members, but the Citadel would only be in use by the guardians.

He reached the ladder and climbed upward into the thick of the colony roots. The ladder ended quickly and he was obliged to work his way along the wide stalks of durable heartwood that made up the roof of the central grove. Here, in the very center of the patch, just below the lower hemisphere of the Mother, the heartwood was the strongest and thickest. The rigid structure of the Globe Mother's internal frame was derived from this original husk. The globe bloomed upward and outward but always retained these first seed walls. The walls grew to become the strength and core of the patch, and therefore the home of its strongest warriors.

When Kipling reached the door to the Citadel, he found it open. An engraving in the wood over the Citadel door read '*We Rise Together. We Rise Forever.*'—the motto of the Guard. Inside, the rooms glowed constantly with the light of the Mother, since her bottom hemisphere made up the ceiling, but the glow was eerie, bluish and pulsating. He didn't know how the guardians could stand the constant flickers and turbulent flashes of light.

He found Bronks, not in his hammock, but propped up against the wall of the kitchen area, one hand on his bandaged chest, and one on the handle of his bone warhook. Bronks was still large, but here, indoors, and bereft of his mechanical wings, he was diminished. His eyes were shut but flickered open when Kipling approached.

"You shouldn't be here, Kip," the guardian captain whispered. "Your family needs you."

"I don't know where my family is," Kipling replied. He stood a few feet away from his hero, but didn't know how to help. "Are you hurt badly?"

Captain Bronks lifted his head and looked Kipling in the eye. "I didn't get there in time."

"Get where?"

"Cirra Sola."

"Samra," Kipling whispered.

"She got taken." The voice came from the side of the room and for the first time Kipling noticed Rufus ensconced in an alcove between two thick roots. He was stuck in the upper corner, his knees pulled to his chest. "The raiders took her."

"Raiders?"

"That's what they're calling them in the commons." Rufus sniffed once and rubbed a hand across his nose. "We'll never see her again."

"Don't say that," Kipling said. "We can go after her. Or she might get away."

"It's too dangerous," Rufus moaned. "You saw what they did. They fly against the wind and go where they please. We'd never find them."

"What do they want with Cirra Sola?" Kipling asked. "Why would they want to kidnap Skylighters?"

"We don't know what they're after," Captain Bronks replied. "But we need to be ready if they come for us again and be prepared for the next attack. We must defend the patch."

"What about Samra?" Kip sputtered. "How do we save her?"

Bronks shifted his weight and grimaced. "What happens now is out of our hands. I'm sorry to tell you the difficult truth, boys, but this patch isn't out of danger yet. And as much as it pains me to say it, Samra is on her own."

11

THE SUN DRAGON

The fog was too dense to see, but Atlas still had his ears. The spinning internal fans of the *Express* weren't especially loud, but they were a sound he knew like his own breathing, and he listened intently for it. The village was in disarray. Those festivalgoers who hadn't already gotten indoors were scurrying down cobblestone alleyways and into hiding places, intent on escaping the violence happening overhead. Only a few brave souls had taken up weapons and seemed inclined to fight.

Artemis Bartley, the town constable, had rallied a few stalwart men and women and the group was trooping down the main street with their eyes on the sky, waiting for the worst.

Atlas stuck to the festival grounds, circling Mayor Fillmore's property astride Destro till he found the tie-downs for the *Express*. A painted billboard showed the aircraft soaring through sunlit skies with a smiling Enzo waving from the cockpit. But the real *Sunshine Express* was nowhere to be seen.

"Quick on him, boys! That's one we want!" The shout came from somewhere overhead, and a silvery harpoon came plunging out of the mist and imbedded itself in the grass.

Destro reared and Atlas jolted in fright, thinking the harpoon was meant for him, but suddenly the air swirled into a whirlwind as the fans of the *Express* spun to life. The aircraft was just overhead, hovering out of sight in the fog, but now it had been discovered.

"Enzo!" Atlas shouted. He urged the horse after the aircraft. The *Express* was moving quickly, headed east through the fog and he doubted his grandfather could hear him from this distance.

Destro was tired from the run here, but he prodded the horse faster as the *Express* banked away over the rooftops of the village. Atlas was forced to dodge his way through the narrow village streets, Destro's hooves clattering on the cobblestones. By the time he reached the edge of the village, he could barely hear the fans of the *Express*, but there was something else overhead in the fog. Something bigger.

Atlas couldn't see much, but what he heard was the sound of at least a dozen men. Men shouting orders, men barking threats. Someone was laughing. Beyond that was the whoosh of rudder fins moving air and the steady chuffing of ducted fans. Engines rumbled with explosive power. But even those sounds passed him by.

"Enzo!" Atlas shouted vainly toward the retreating sounds. Then he was left alone.

He let Destro trot to a stop, the big horse's sides heaving. Sweat made the gelding's already spotted hide even more speckled. The sound of conflict was now far behind him, as were the lights of the village.

"We have to help him. He needs us." Atlas muttered the words to the horse but didn't see any way on. He'd never catch the aircraft on a horse. Even if they did catch up, there was no way he could get to Enzo in the air.

He didn't need a horse. He needed a *Dragon*.

"Come on, Destro! We can still do this." He turned the horse's head north and cantered forward, trying to get his bearings in the darkness. He was in another pasture—Minister Teague's maybe? Somewhere north he should hit the valley road and beyond that it was only a stream and patch of woods till he'd be on his grandfather's land. He could make it.

It took longer than he thought to hit the road, but he found it. Destro leapt the stream beyond without hesitation, but when they reached the woods the horse balked.

"Destro. Go!" Atlas dug his heels into the horse's sides, but the gelding merely shifted side-to-side, ears pivoting and eyes wide. The trees loomed like sentinels barring his path. Atlas had been through these woods plenty of times, but always in the daytime. In the darkness, the trees seemed ominous. "It's okay, Destro. We're almost there." He patted the horse's neck and urged him forward again. This time the horse took a few tentative steps. Atlas kept up the encouragement and the horse slowly threaded its way between the trees.

Inside the woods, the night became even blacker. Atlas regretted not bringing a lantern. They moved forward mostly by intuition, following the faint patches of light they could see and pressing themselves through the soft boughs of evergreens. Before long, Atlas's palms were sticky with tree sap and he wasn't sure which direction they were headed. He scanned the sky at every available opening, but the stars remained shrouded in mist and the moons were both out of sight beyond the mountains.

Each passing second weighed on his mind. Where was Enzo? Who were the men chasing him?

Enzo was smart. He'd head up into the canyons, lie low for a while till the danger passed. Nobody knew those canyons like his grandfather. He'd be okay. But he might have to hide awhile. He'd need supplies. Weapons maybe. He needed Atlas's help.

The claws came out of nowhere, swiping at his face.

Atlas rolled left, fingers clenching frantically at Destro's mane. The black shape hurtled past, crashing through the branches and shrieking. Atlas grunted and heaved himself upright on the horse's back, but it was all he could do to hold on now. Destro's ears were flat and he was galloping, plunging through the underbrush at full speed. Branches and vines whipped Atlas and the horse alike, scratching and tearing at his clothes and skin.

It was a terax, or some other forest raptor. They weren't big enough to lift a horse or livestock off the ground but they'd been known to tear animals to bits and carry off the pieces. He didn't want to know what they did to boys. The shriek from behind was echoed by one overhead. How many were there?

A branch struck Atlas across the face and he cried out. The sting made his eyes water. The whole world was dark and blurry, but up ahead the trees were clearing. Destro erupted into the meadow before Atlas could get his hands back on the reins. "No! Not the open!"

Atlas reached for the flapping leather straps and hauled back on them, but the horse only strained harder. Its mouth was frothy and its eyes wide. The fog was patchier here with little gaps of starlight peeking through, but the sky was turbulent, full of dark shapes circling overhead — a whirl of danger.

The foothills weren't far. Enzo's cottage. He could make it there, or maybe straight to the barn. The high grass whisked past his legs, almost up to the horse's shoulders. Just a little bit farther. Up over the landing strip. Down the gully. One short fence and they'd be there.

The impact of the creature unseated him immediately. Destro screamed.

Atlas's fists pulled tufts of hair and feathers as he flew through the air and crashed into the field.

His breath was gone. He gasped for air as Destro's foamy flanks disappeared into the long grass, the horse bucking and kicking at the dark shapes attempting to alight on its back.

Atlas rose to his feet and immediately fell, toppling forward to hands and knees in the damp grass. On his second attempt he stayed upright and staggered a few feet.

He wanted to yell for the horse, but choked back the urge. The cottage. He needed something to fight with.

He tilted forward and ran, keeping low in the grass but unable to stop himself from looking up and searching the sky. It was too black, too difficult to penetrate the darkness. He could only hope they were distracted enough to give him time. He concentrated on the distant shape of the cottage, partially buried in the hillside. He hurdled the fence at the end of the pasture and raced up the hill.

Wings beat the air overhead and he dropped, rolling out of reach of the talons. The terax hit the grass beyond him and immediately spread its wings again, lumbering upward and eager to make another pass. But Atlas was there. Leaping upright, he sprinted the last few yards. His feet pounded across the boards of the front porch and his body slammed into the door before he could arrest his momentum. Ricocheting off the door, he plunged his hands into his pockets, fishing frantically for the key. His fingers closed on the bit of iron and he stabbed it at the door in the darkness till he found the lock. Claws scratched the roof of the porch, knocking shingles loose as they worked their way toward the edge, but he was in now, slipping through the open door and slamming it behind him.

Leaned against the interior of the door, he jammed home the bolt and tilted his head up to catch his breath. His body begged for him to stop—slump right there against the door and rest—but there was still work to be done.

He rifled through the drawers of the kitchen till he found the flint and a knife. He struck it hard till he sparked the tinder in the fire bowl and used a strip of bark to transfer the flame to the lantern. He lit three just to be sure.

A sack in the pantry would be his carryall. He snatched it up but paused in the doorway, considering the shelves. Who knows how long he and Enzo might have to hide from the raiders? They'd need food. He scooped up things that were lightweight but filling. Strips of jerky, dried apples. A loaf of three-day-old bread. A wheel of cheese looked heavy but tempting. He grabbed it. He filled the water skins. There was no way to avoid that weight. He tossed a bag of grain cereal into the sack and decided it was enough. They might be able to forage or hunt for more. He dropped the sack on the kitchen table and headed for the back of the cottage to find the weapons. Enzo had a quiver of small harpoons, a pair of longer ones, and three reels of line. He'd seen him use the pivoting air tubes on the *Express* to launch them and bring down geese in flight. *The Sun Dragon* didn't have an air cannon, but he could make something work.

He took the quiver, two knives, and one of the long harpoons, and made his way back to the front of the cottage.

The sounds on the roof had stopped.

He strapped the biggest lantern to the end of his harpoon and slung the sack of supplies and the quiver over his back. He hooked the two small lanterns to his belt to illuminate himself from both sides. It wasn't as good as real bio-light, but thousands of years of evolution had taught the nightbeasts that glowing prey meant chemical reactions and burning guts when they tried to swallow. Some of the more dangerous bioluminescent creatures even came with acid sprays and glowing toxic spines, so it was their instinct to avoid all things that glowed. Atlas had none of the real bio-defenses, but he glowed now, too, lit to the best of his ability with flickering oil-fed flames. It would have to be enough.

He opened the door slowly, probing the night with the harpoon and lantern. He eased himself out cautiously after them, dispelling the shadows. He only spared a moment to lock the door, then wrenched his eyes back to his surroundings. The night was quiet. No sign of the terax.

He kept a sharp eye on the sky and his immediate surroundings, as not all nightbeasts struck from the air. He broke into a trot, moving as smoothly as he could so as not to jostle the lanterns too much. The heaviest was only half-filled. He should have taken time to fill them up, but it was too late now. He was nearly halfway to the barn. A hundred yards to go.

Shapes swirled in the night air, but didn't attack. A few dove low to investigate the commotion but he shook the harpoon at them and swung the lantern about. No creatures came close enough to make out their features. He was three-quarters of the way to the barn when he heard the snuffling. He paused his jog to listen. Somewhere in the dark close to the barn, another animal lurked. More than one? Perhaps just a wild hog. Atlas crept forward, shining his light ahead of him, wary for the first sign of movement. He was nearly at the barn when he saw the shape. Furry and dark, it was much too tall to be a hog. The bright eyes reflected the glow of his three lanterns and the creature emitted a long, low growl.

Canyon wolf. Not a nightbeast, but bad just the same. Atlas froze.

The Rift Valley wolf pack was a gathering of opportunists, no doubt drawn by the commotion of the terax. Atlas had heard of Altirian wolves that grew larger than horses. These weren't nearly that big, but the curved tusks protruding from their mouths were deadly just the same. They were here to scavenge a carcass, or add a new one.

Atlas raised his harpoon higher, making himself a bigger threat, and the wolf retreated. But there were more eyes in the darkness. Atlas fought the urge to run. Instead he took slow, deliberate steps toward the barn. Once he reached the doors, he again had to fish in his pocket for the key. This time it was all slow movements. He lowered the harpoon to horizontal, extending the light out as far as he could to reveal the threats. There were at least six of them. Likely more. They peered at him with large hungry eyes.

Something thudded into the top of the barn. A terax. The sudden impact scattered the wolves, just for a moment, but that was all he needed. He wrenched the lock loose from the latch and rolled the door open far enough to squeeze through. By the time he was inside, the snarling muzzle of the alpha wolf was back at his heels, its tusks scraping the wood as he slammed the door and held it tight. The pack snuffed and growled around the outside of the door for a few minutes before things grew quiet again.

Atlas latched the inside of the door and crept up to the hayloft to look outside. Prying open one shutter of the hayloft window, he scanned the barnyard. No less than eight wolves encircled the door, waiting for him to emerge. A few already had heads on forepaws, and a couple were sitting. One wolf, the alpha, was on his feet nearest the door. Perhaps hearing his breathing, the wolf pulled its gaze from the door and looked up at him. It stared into his eyes for a few long seconds, then tilted his head to the sky and howled. Somewhere in the distance came an answering howl. There would be more soon.

Atlas slumped to the floor of the hayloft and blew out two of his three lanterns. There was no way he could get the *Dragon* out now. He unslung his quiver of harpoons and the sack of supplies and propped them against the wall. He stared down at the aircraft below. Where was the *Express* right now? Had Enzo escaped the attack?

For all of his rushing around tonight, he'd failed to save him. He never even got off the ground. All he'd managed to do was lose the horse and get himself trapped.

He had to do better. Tomorrow he would succeed. Tomorrow he'd have the light and he'd have the *Dragon*.

"I'm coming, Grandpa. I'll come at first light. I promise."

He lifted the last lantern to his face and blew out the flame, then he leaned back against the wall and waited.

12

KALEB

"I'm in charge now. That's the way it is."

Kipling stared up at his brother and refused to accept the words. "You're not in charge of me. Mom and Dad are."

"And they aren't here," Kaleb retorted.

The interior of the council grove was still intact. No evidence of the raider assault could be seen here, except for the absence of his parents.

Witnesses had given conflicting reports. Some said the pair climbed aboard Mala Jutta—one of the last globes to detach. Others claimed Chief Roose and her husband were aboard the high-flying Tamra Ohna. Despite the varied stories, the common thread existed. While Kip's parents were alive and safe, they were nowhere near the Globe Mother, and weren't going to be back soon.

Kaleb seemed to think that meant he was the boss. Kipling wished he had someone to dispute the issue to, but the council had only made things worse.

After leaving the Citadel, Kipling had come to the Gate of Thorns to search for his parents in the council grove. He found only disagreements and discord inside. Councilman Thur had taken over in his mother's absence and was seated in the chief's chair, but the council was split about how to proceed. Three council members were missing, aboard other globes or otherwise unaccounted for. The four remaining members were divided on whether to continue sailing in the Heights or climb higher and make for the Bright, where only the Frost Kings could reach them.

Kipling listened to the debate after slipping through the throng of people crowding the gate. He'd pretended to be distraught and in need of his brother's comfort in order to get past the guardians. Luckily it was a couple of the newer guards and they didn't know that Kipling would just as soon kick his brother in the head as be comforted by him. Now Kaleb was just being stupid.

Common wisdom held that Grounders couldn't breathe in the Heights and the colony would be safe enough there. But that was before anyone had seen Grounders in airships big enough to haul off entire globes.

Tension was rife, and fear dominated the conversations at the gate. The colony's only contact with flying Grounders so far had been Enzo, the wizened messenger in his rickety old *Express*. No one suspected that the Grounders could be preparing attack ships with harpoon cannons. The council was in turmoil as a result, and maybe not thinking straight. Kipling could only assume that was the case, because they had already done the unthinkable. They'd elected Kaleb to the council as their fifth voter.

"I have greater responsibilities now," Kaleb said. "And with Mom and Dad gone, you have to listen to me. The patch needs everyone to pull together and work as a team." He shoved Kipling toward the council door, trying to keep him out of earshot of the rest of the councilors.

"Half the patch is gone!" Kipling shouted. He failed to see what Kaleb thought he was in charge of, when most of the biggest globes were now floating loose through the atmosphere. It could be weeks or even months till the globes were all accounted for, depending on the winds. If enough of the jettisoned globes were still visible in the morning, they might be able to signal a few of them and relay messages, but the winds beyond the mountains were already picking up and driving the glowing globes farther apart in the night sky.

"With Captain Bronks injured and the guard spread out across the globes, I agree it's best we rise to the Bright. Councilman Thur thinks that will give us the best chance to escape the Grounders and plan for how to defend ourselves."

"The Bright is frozen," Kip argued. "You can't take the patch that high in springtime. It'll freeze the new growth and kill off all the buds. How do you expect the Mother to recover from the damage if you freeze her to death?"

"This isn't the time to worry about the Mother. We have to look out for ourselves. The patch does us no good if we're all killed."

Kipling shoved his way around his brother and raced to the center of the horseshoe-shaped council table.

"You can't go to the Bright!" he blurted out. "It'll kill her."

"This is highly irregular," Councilman Thur intoned from the chief's chair. "You were not summoned to this council meeting. Remove yourself."

"Councilman Thur, I think it might be wise to listen to the boy." Councilwoman Somlee leaned in from her position at the right side of the table. "He is the master grower's son and apprentice. His professional observations might be helpful."

Kipling was a frequent guest in the Somlee aerie, as his mother and the councilwoman were close friends. Now Kipling was happy for the connection.

Councilman Thur frowned, his paper-thin cheeks crinkling in the process. "He's a patchling. I hardly expect he has a professional observation."

Councilwoman Somlee waved a writing quill toward Kipling. "Don't tell me your memory is so porous, Argus. You signed off this boy's Ascendare exam not two months ago. Kipling has earned the right to be heard."

Kipling faced the old man undaunted, the support from Councilwoman Somlee boosting his courage. "If you take the Mother to high altitude this time of year, she may never recover. She has too many fluids in her outer tendrils that would freeze. The new buds would die and the entire breeding season would be lost. And next year's, too."

"From what I understand, the breeding season is a loss now anyway," Councilman Podmire said. Podmire was the thickest Skylighter on the council, his proportions the most globular of all of his contemporaries. Kipling didn't know him well but his reputation was as a reasonable mind on patch matters and he tended to be even-keeled.

"The globe sons were taken," Kipling replied. "But there might be some still aloft from last year. The patch could still get pollinated and the Mother could recover from the damage, but not if you go to the Bright. The Bright will kill her."

"It may be the Mother's destiny to join the frost globes in the Bright," Councilman Thur said. "She would be a crystalline treasure there, and certainly worthy of admission by the Frost Kings."

Kipling had seen a Frost King only once at the height of winter. The Globe Mother had flown near one of the lowest flying frost globes from the upper altitudes. The frost globes were kept aloft by their internal gases, still catalyzed into buoyancy by the constant sunlight, but mere husks of their former selves. The frost globes were frozen and preserved—crystallized shells of exquisite beauty—but no longer living. Kipling thought the residents there to be frightening; thin, pale figures, stretching out their ends in a cold, dead world. Councilman Thur might feel comfortable there, but he certainly didn't.

"The Mother isn't showing any signs of aging," he said. "My father says she could be aloft and producing globes for my grandchildren's grandchildren."

"I've never heard father say anything of the sort," Kaleb countered.

"You would if you ever came out and pruned anything," Kipling spat. "All you do is sit in the shade and—" He cut himself off and fumbled for words, realizing he was about to criticize the entire council.

"I think Grower Roose makes some valid points," Councilwoman Somlee interjected.

"He's just an apprentice grower," Kaleb said.

"An apprentice currently without a master. Kipling is no longer a patchling, so I would say he's earned a promotion the same as you," Somlee replied, her eyes boring into Kaleb's and daring him to challenge her.

Kaleb looked away and kept his mouth shut. Kipling couldn't help but grin. He repressed it as best he could as Councilman Thur stretched and groaned. "Very well, let's put it to the vote. Those in favor of climbing to the security of the Bright, say aye. Those willing to risk the patch's safety to tarry here in the Heights, say nay."

"I vote aye," Kaleb blurted out, clearly enthusiastic about participating in his first vote.

"Aye from me as well," Councilman Thur growled.

"Nay," Councilwoman Somlee stated. She leaned back in her chair and rested her palms on the table as if settling the matter.

Councilman Podmire squished back and forth in his chair before gurgling out his response. "Nay from me. Too bugging cold up in the Bright. Just barely got thawed out from this past winter."

Kipling smiled.

All eyes now fell on the final council member left to vote. Magda Beezlebee was an old woman, but no one could say just how old. Some thought her older than Thur, but none of the patchlings had any idea. All Kipling knew was that Beezlebee had been on the council when his mother was young and his mother relied heavily on her wisdom. 'Old Mag' had been nominated for council chief multiple times over the decades but always declined. She claimed council leadership would dull her wits. Kipling's mother didn't seem to mind the implication. She said Beezlebee was always the first to arrive for council meetings and usually remained the longest, sometimes falling asleep in her chair after dull days of dealing with patch issues.

The old woman now looked between Kipling and Kaleb, as if the fate of the globe patch could be read on their faces. Her dark eyes blended into her wrinkled brown skin and Kipling couldn't read anything in her expression. The silence in the council chamber stretched till it was almost palpable, but then Beezlebee finally rasped out her response.

"Nay."

Councilman Thur stared at the old woman and frowned, but then turned to face the boys. "Very well. We'll hold our present altitude, but if we are attacked again I'll be less inclined to heed young Mr. Roose." He fixed his eyes on Kipling. "I trust you'll treat your father's duties with diligence in his absence. You'll be the youngest chief grower in patch history no doubt, and we don't have much in the way of persons to provide you assistance. I hope you won't expect much."

"No, sir," Kipling muttered. He hadn't expected to be gaining a position in the patch hierarchy today, certainly not his father's job. The promotion didn't give him the thrill that Kaleb so obviously felt.

The council members were leaned in toward one another now, moved on to new topics, and it was clear that his services were no longer required. Councilwoman Somlee gave him a nod and brief smile before turning back to a conversation with Podmire. Kaleb abandoned his side without a word and walked around the outside of the table to take the seat next to Thur—no doubt to suck up to him some more.

Kipling felt he should go, but he couldn't make his feet move. Not yet.

"What about Samra?"

The heads around the table slowly turned his direction.

"What are you saying now?" Councilman Thur inquired.

"Samra," Kipling repeated. "How are we going to save her?"

"Whom are we talking about?" Podmire asked, his second chin bulging out under his jaw as he tried to reconcile the name to his memory.

"The red girl with the knife," Beezlebee said, the only face at the table still listening intently to Kipling.

"The girl that's always plummeting past my aerie at ungodly hours? What happened to her?" Podmire asked.

"She was taken by the raiders," Kipling replied. "On one of their ships. We have to save her."

Podmire squished his face up again, and shook his jowls. "Blasted Grounder barbarians . . ."

"Kipling," Councilwoman Somlee said softly. "I'm sure we are all very concerned for Samra, as we are about all of our citizens. But mounting a rescue mission would be—"

"Preposterous," Thur interrupted. "Absolutely out of the question. Our mandate is the protection of those on this patch and the retrieval of persons we are capable of recovering from among the jettisoned globes. The patch is in chaos. We are in no position to chase after our attackers. Are we even sure she's with them? She could very well be on one of the other globes. We are nowhere near to having an updated residents list. Once the other globes have submitted their—"

"We can't wait that long!" Kipling said, losing patience with the conversation.

"I agree that it would be ill-advised to provoke more contact with these Grounders," Podmire replied, shifting in his seat again. "What makes you think they have her?"

"They took Cirra Sola. The whole globe. She was aboard it when they took it. I talked to Bronks and he said he didn't get there in time to save her."

"Has anyone checked with the Coleys?" Podmire asked. "We ought to find her parents. Perhaps they retrieved the girl themselves during the attack."

"The Coleys are not on the current list," Thur replied, holding up a roll of leaf paper and squinting at it. Perhaps once they've finished registration in the commons . . ."

"The other globes could be apart for months," Kipling said. "Samra doesn't have that long to wait for us. We have to go after her now! The other globes will be safe in the Heights. She's the one in real danger. We could send the guardians. Even one or two could do it. Bronks is hurt, but maybe if you sent Auralee or Harlan, they could—"

"Every guardian aboard is of urgent use to the patch," Thur replied. His eyebrows dipped into a deep V over his eyes. "If we had a dozen more we'd still be underserved. The Grounders could attack us again at any moment. Depriving the patch of defense in this hour of peril would be foolhardy and shamelessly irresponsible."

"You would think your priority would be to your family," Kaleb said. "Father and Mother are out there somewhere having just been attacked. You should show some concern for your own parents."

Kipling stared at his brother, dumbfounded. Of course he cared about his parents. But at least seven different people had assured him that his parents were safely aboard one of the other globes. True, the reports were a bit confused, but people saw them. No one had seen Samra. He tried to put words into a form that could get this across to his stupid brother, but nothing was coming out.

"Especially since this girl we're talking about already attacked me today," Kaleb added. "She acts like some kind of animal." He laid his bandaged arm conspicuously on the table.

The sound that came out of Kipling's mouth wasn't a word at all. It was closer to a snarl. Kipling wished he could show his brother what a real injury was.

"Unfortunate family history the girl has," Councilor Thur said. "We have to consider that perhaps she did escape her globe but was unable to float to safety. Her mother was a faller, too, wasn't she? Unable to ever pass her illumination tests."

"Tragic story," Podmire nodded. "Issues with her breathing, if I recall. Always passing out in excitable situations."

"A person with that sort of medical issue might not have survived the shock of the attack," Thur said, shaking his head. "Or if she did, she may have fallen to the surface in her efforts to escape."

"Sending guardians back would be a waste of effort in that case, wouldn't it?" Kaleb asked.

It took everything Kipling had to not leap over the table and pummel that smug look off Kaleb's ugly face.

"I know what the doctor said," Kipling replied. "She told me. He said she might light up any day now. He said there's at least a fifty percent chance —"

"It's too bad Doctor Kesh is no longer here to verify your claims," Thur interrupted. "As it is, we only know that she cannot currently illuminate. Her condition makes her less likely to survive a serious fall."

"Then that's more reason to go after her!"

"Kipling," Chairwoman Somlee's voice was smooth and controlled. He wrenched his eyes from Thur to look at her. "What Councilors Thur and Podmire are no doubt hoping to express . . ." she cast a withering glare their direction. " . . . is that we are all deeply concerned for Samra. She is an important part of our community and we will, of course, do all we can to ensure her safety. But we are dealing with a tremendous event right now and we need to think responsibly and act in the best interest of the whole patch. We must safeguard *every* citizen aboard."

Councilor Somlee stood up and moved to Kipling, resting a hand on his shoulder. "I think it's time for you to be going. The council will take your concern and deal with it as best we can. I promise you that as soon as we know more about Miss Coley's situation, you will be the first to know. For now, why don't you go home? Get some rest. We will all need your help in the days to come."

"Thank you," Kipling muttered, his years of manners training from his mother forcing the response from between his lips. He choked down the words he wanted to say to his brother and avoided looking at his miserable face as he turned to the door. He walked slowly and deliberately, not letting himself glow, though his anger was on the verge of lighting him up.

Outside, the crowd of citizens on the vine bridge had thinned somewhat, but still clogged the path too much for his patience. He took a running leap from the balcony of the Gate of Thorns and flew through the air toward the steady glow of the Mother. He landed in the tangleweed and scaled the perimeter of the globe, making another leap from the far side and catching hold of the vine bridge to Jana Luna.

The blossoms of the star lilies in the Starpark had not fared well in the ascent. The ones that hadn't been trampled underfoot by frightened citizens were bowed in the wind on the ride up. Kip scrambled down the path to the hideout and let himself imagine that he was wrong. Maybe Samra hadn't been taken. Maybe she was just hiding. Perhaps when he rounded the end of the globe he'd find her there, feet dangling over the edge of their fortress, safe and waiting for him.

The hideout was dark and tough to make out in the leaves, but even from here he knew the truth. It was empty.

Just to be sure, Kipling climbed into the doorway and scanned the interior. Just twisted roots. He ran his fingers over them, feeling more than seeing his way over the carvings. Symbols here told a story. The drawings and words etched into the roots were evidence of hours spent on adventures. The made-up runes and mystical spells that Samra had invented were meant to dispel the nightbeasts—or worse terrors from the depths of her imagination. Some were meant to summon the terrors.

Kipling stared out at the far-off mountains. The Ridge Valley was drifting farther away in their wake. Where was Samra now? He wished there was a rune carving on these walls that could summon her back, or some spell he could speak to take command of the high council. He'd send the guardians after the Grounder ships right now and let them smite the raiders from the sky. They'd return Samra by sunrise.

But there was no such thing as magic.

The council would sit idly by and make the guardians stay. As if the guardians were mere defenders meant for patch security. Guardians were meant for action. Bold action. How could Kaleb aspire to be a councilor when all the council ever did was fret and worry? Bronks was injured, but even one injured guardian was worth more than the entire room full of councilors. Guardians got things done. They rescued people. When danger struck they didn't wait for approval from a committee before acting. They just did what they were meant to do. What people needed.

And just like that, he knew what he had to do.

Samra was in danger. No one else was willing to do anything

about it. They made him a glorified gardener and told him to tend the patch, but they couldn't see what he was really meant for.

He was meant to be a guardian.

And he was going to save Samra.

13

RESTLESS FURY

The night was full of strange sounds—foreign, horrible noises—and Samra couldn't identify them.

Her world was muffled and constricted.

Pressed against the interior wall of her tendril pocket, the strands of her hammock were chafing her arms. She was vertical.

Vertical, upside-down, and stuck.

She'd squirmed for the first few minutes, shocked by the violent collapse of her most private space. She cried out when it happened, but quickly silenced herself as the world filled with strange mechanical clunks, breathy swooshing, ratcheting clicks, and rumbling bangs.

Some of the noises were voices—gruff, loud voices. A few shouting, some cursing, and none of them friendly.

Grounder voices.

Her legs were pinned. Something was tied across them. She should have run when she had the chance—not let Bronks or anyone lay a hand on her. Now they were coming for her—angry villagers, irate that she'd disrupted their festival. She found it odd that they would be up in the patch. What if it was the mayor? Was

Councilwoman Roose with him, here to formally exile her from the patch? Why had they compressed her tendril pocket around her? Maybe they didn't want to even give her the chance to apologize. Did they hate her that much?

The memory of her parents' disappointed glares on the festival stage pierced her again. Had they given up on her?

Samra strained to work her fingers through the vines and tendrils that made up the wall of her room. They were tightly compressed and hard to move. Her arms barely had room to work the vines but she dug at them, ripping and clawing with her fingertips till she could make a tiny hole. If this was going to be the end, she wanted to see it coming. Would they jettison her into the ocean? Maybe they'd set her pod afire in some sort of Grounder ritual sacrifice. Whatever her fate, she would face it bravely. No one was going to say Samra Rose Coley died a coward.

She tugged the last strands of fibers away and exposed the hole. Pressing her face against the vines, she strained to see what was going on.

This wasn't the patch.

Samra was staring at an upside-down world. Her feet pointed toward a sky bright with stars. She faced a rectangular deck of sorts. Worn wooden slats made up the top of the deck, and nets stretched up between two sturdy-looking metal supports. It was holding up . . . what? A silvery cylinder of some kind. Samra lacked the range of vision to see it completely. The netting beneath the strange silver shape permitted a view of shrouded mountain ridges beyond.

"Get that cargo stowed and secured, Hodges! No time to waste. All hands keep a wary eye out. Those flying devils might be back." The man speaking was a towering, fire-haired individual balancing himself at the middle of the rectangular deck next to a winch. Levers and other handles sprouted at various angles around him, and he had one hand resting on the handle of the winch. Other Grounders were scrambling about the rope netting, tying off lines or releasing them, and tethering green spheres into cargo holds.

The globe sons.

Samra recognized the smaller globes belonging to the Globe Mother's lower seedpods. What were they doing with them?

"Standby to diminish. Coming in tight." The muscular man at the center of the deck spun the crank and the surface Samra was attached to jolted. As he continued cranking, she progressed laterally toward a cylindrical shape opposite her.

She was aboard an airship.

Samra hadn't ever seen one this big, but she was sure of it now. The cylindrical shape growing closer to her was long and tapered toward the rear, and as she pressed her face forward and looked aft, two big silvery tails were pushing air back and forth—the source of the swooshing sound. Huge vertical rudders and sections of the tail kicked from side to side, shimmering in the starlight, and the whole craft swam through the air like two parallel sharks. She seemed to be affixed to the left-side shark in a bundle of netting and vines.

"Man those ballast tanks and get set to pump," the man ordered. "We're riding too high from this new lot and need to get back to equilibrium."

Samra could now make out more of the ship. The wooden deck hung between the two lifting bodies of the twin sharks. The deck was streamlined at the bow and glass windows revealed a front cockpit at the nose. The empty space between the various parts of the ship was rapidly shrinking as the man cranked.

"Do we need to take on more ballast?" a woman shouted from the opposite rigging.

"Shift it forward. We're almost there," the man with the crank replied. "You sorry lot nearly took on a balanced load for once in your lives."

Something was crawling in the vines and netting near Samra and suddenly a body was blocking her view. Thin, hairy-faced, and sparsely attired, the man was cinching something near her when he happened to look directly into the hole she was peering through.

"Agh!" The man flailed backward, caught his balance, and leapt into the netting below, rolling inward and sprawling on the deck. He scrambled to his feet and pointed to the vines. "Oi! That pod just looked at me!"

The man at the crank frowned and followed the skinny man's finger upward. "What are you on about?"

"It's got an eyeball! It's alive!"

The man at the crank appraised his comrade skeptically, but looked back to the cargo area where Samra was suspended. "What kind of eye?"

"I don't know. Big. Angry looking."

"Hold this." The muscled man grabbed his companion's arm

and pushed the winch handle into his chest. The skinny man wavered under the weight of it but held onto the handle carefully.

The big man leapt into the rigging with surprising agility, clambering up the ropes to the hole where Samra was now trapped. She squirmed harder in her leafy prison but could make no more progress than before.

The big man's face filled her view. His hair was wild, and a shade of red she'd never seen before. His face was heavily freckled and ruddy in the parts not covered by his thick beard. He stared into the hole she was peering out of and drew a long knife from his belt. He studied the area around her for just a moment, then plunged his knife into the vines.

Samra screamed.

She didn't stop screaming until a hand reached through the new opening in the vines and grasped the front of her shirt. The hand pulled her forward till she was nose to nose with the red-haired man.

"I'm not killing you, lass. I'm getting you out."

The vines around her snapped and cracked as she was pulled loose from their grip. Her arms were now sticky with tangleweed sap and bits of goo trailed down her neck. Her shark's tooth necklace was dangling in her eyes and she tried to bat it away unsuccessfully. Once the vines were cut back enough, the big man's arm scooped her out of the hole he'd made in the foliage. No sooner was she seeing the world from the right side up than he proceeded to hoist her over his shoulder.

"Let me go, Grounder!" She kicked at him and swung her fists at his back, but to no avail. She gasped as the man leapt into the air and dropped into the netting below. He didn't pause there, but swung onto an angled support of the airship's frame. He slid down it to the main body of the ship and landed on the top deck.

Samra was dropped unceremoniously on her rump in the center of the ship.

She bounced.

She was on her feet again in a flash but didn't get far. The big man caught her by the hair and held her down, calmly withstanding her flailing attempts to dislodge him and fly away. Unfortunately, his grip on the back of her head kept her from biting him. She tried unsuccessfully to remove his fingers from her hair but only managed to knock a few of her crow feathers loose.

"She's one of them sky devils, ain't she?" More curious onlookers had joined the skinny man from the rigging. Most were gruff, rugged individuals, and a few were armed with swords or knives. Samra snarled at them, hoping they'd see she was no one to tangle with. Her skin was turning red in patches. She tried to blind them with her glow—the Skylighter's natural defense—but once again the light failed to come. She hissed and shrieked but failed to evoke the fear she wanted from the red-haired man—though the others were keeping their distance.

"Hodges, inform Captain Savage that we have a stowaway."

The man named Hodges flinched and wrenched his eyes from her. "Me? The Captain doesn't like me to—"

"Now!"

"Yessir." Hodges spun around and lifted the hatch in the floor of the deck before scrambling down the steps below.

Samra stopped trying to get the man's hand out of her hair and looked around for another way to escape. Something. Anything she could use against them. As her eyes fell on the bundle of vines and leaves high overhead, she had a sinking realization. They hadn't just taken her tendril pocket. The entire globe of Cirra Sola was lashed to the side of one of the twin silver sharks. The globe was partly collapsed now, some of its internal gases deflated, but it still bulged from its tethers, many of its interior cells still intact. The skin of the globe flickered in spurts like she did. It was torn and hemorrhaging internally, ruptured cells flaring to life then fizzling out rapidly. It was dying.

She'd been silly.

These were no villagers. Womble villagers wouldn't have ripped a globe from The Mother. These people were something else. Something worse.

"What did you do to them?" She whirled on her captor and attempted to kick him. She leapt, swinging at his face with her fists. "Where's my family?"

The red-haired man grasped the front of her shirt and caught her in midair. "Little thing. Stop. Moving."

Samra froze. She was used to that tone from adults in the patch, and usually it meant bad news. She would have kept fighting anyway but there was something in the man's eyes. Something like concern. Perhaps he knew something she didn't about what was coming. Wind was blowing hard across the deck now, swirling down the cliffs from a gap between the high rocks. The ship was drawing steadily closer to a cleft in the mountains, despite the variable winds.

"You going to pitch her overboard? See if she can fly?" One of the other airship sailors had edged closer, her features shadowy in the darkness.

"Heard these sky folk glow. She might light our way through the Rift." A second sailor pulled a knife from a sheath on his hip. "Maybe we should let a little light out and show us the way."

A crack resonated across the deck as the knife went soaring out of the man's hand. He hissed and recoiled, shaking his fingers. Samra craned her neck toward the rear of the ship and the person standing at the edge of the open hatch. The end of a striped whip glided back across the deck toward her feet, like a snake after a strike.

"No one gave you permission to threaten captives, Wallace. Don't forget whose ship you're on."

The woman with the whip stared down her crew from the shadow of dark, windblown hair. The long strands were being kept in check by a loose scarf wrapped around her neck that trailed down the front of her fatigued leather jacket. Nothing else was in danger of being displaced by the wind. Her tight jacket blended into dark trousers and high-laced boots that permitted no argument from the unruly air.

"Found this one in the cargo nets. Must have been hiding in the vines when we took the goods aboard." The man holding Samra elevated her farther so the captain could have a better look.

"Bring her here."

Samra didn't struggle this time, but watched warily as she was set on her feet in front of the captain. The red-haired man kept his hands resting on her shoulders, weighing her down. She was fascinated by this woman with the whip who was so readily obeyed. She wasn't old—surely no more than twenty—but these men and women in the crew seemed to respect her.

The captain lifted a pricklefish spine away from Samra's face, then examined the shark tooth necklace with her fingertips. "What's your name?"

Samra glared at the woman with as much ferocity as she could muster. "What did you do with my family? Where's Kip?"

The captain let the necklace fall from her fingers and

straightened up. "Your people attacked us, then fled into the sky. If that's who you're talking about, they're long gone now."

"My family didn't attack you. You're lying."

The captain slung her whip around her shoulders. "Someone from your clan did. My back-up pilot was impaled by a harpoon and sent overboard because of your kind. Some of my crew are injured. Crews on the other ships as well. Your people have a lot to be accountable for."

Samra looked past the captain, and for the first time noticed that there were other shapes in the darkness behind them. Other airships.

"Let me go!" She struggled again but the big man's hands encircled her biceps and kept her from floating.

"I'm afraid I can't do that just now," the captain replied. "Your people may attack us again and if they do, things are likely to go badly. I'll need you here to explain that we didn't steal you. It was you who stowed away with us."

"I didn't stow away. You took my globe. You took Cirra Sola!" She attempted to jab a finger toward the partially deflated globe daughter. Clearly this woman needed to get her facts straight.

"That globe?" The captain pointed. "That is a plant we found in the sky. It's not yours. It's ours now."

"That's my home!" As Samra stared up at the ruins of her family's globe, she couldn't believe that her family's future and that of the other members of her new colony could be so tidily disposed of and bundled away. What would they do now? What was going to happen to her parents?

The captain's eyes were fixed ahead of the ship now. "We're nearing the Rift. Tie up that vine rubbish and get the girl below. Leave nothing above deck that might attract the wildlife." She spun on her heel and moved toward the hatch.

"But you have to let me go!" Samra shrieked. "I have to get back to the Mother!" The captain paid no attention, and merely descended the steps.

The big redheaded man scooped her up again and followed the captain.

"I have to get back . . .to . . . the Mother." Samra repeated as she thrashed in his arms.

"Looks like you have a new mother now." He reached for the hatch and closed it over top of them as they descended into the depths of the ship. "And her name is *Restless Fury*."

14

NIGHT THIEF

Kipling didn't own much that would be useful on a rescue mission. The closest thing he had to a weapon was his pruning knife he used for work. The obsidian blade was now secured into the waist of his pants, but he needed more. He needed the armory.

Kaleb had come home late, still obscenely giddy at having been elected to the council. You could see it on his face plain as day beneath the mask of false sincerity. Circumstances being what they were, he could have at least shown some real regret at Mom and Dad being displaced. All he did was bark orders about getting to bed and not making him look bad as a new councilor.

Kipling went to his hammock but didn't sleep. He merely waited for Kaleb to finish waltzing around like he owned the place and get to bed. A couple of grown-ups stopped by to check on them, delaying the process. Kipling listened through the wall as they praised his brother for his courage and wished him well in coping with the tragedy. Kaleb assured them he could handle it and agreed that he had a responsibility as an older brother now to manage the family. Kipling wanted to march out to the front door and inform all of them that he was not in need of any management, but held himself in check. He had a responsibility, too, and after tonight his brother wouldn't be a problem.

The glow of the Mother had shifted to a soothing light green by the time Kipling snuck out of his hammock. The aerie was quiet and Kaleb was asleep, no doubt dreaming smug, self-important dreams. The grove was likewise silent. Kipling moved quickly to the tendril ladder and climbed silently to the Citadel.

There was usually a guard posted near the entrance to assist citizens in time of need, but tonight they were out on patrol. With their depleted numbers, every guardian who could fly would no doubt be watching the skies, alert for more Grounder attacks. It was a lapse he could take advantage of. Even so, he moved softly, floating down the tunnels and touching as few things as possible.

Kip paused at the door of the Citadel's main entrance. He searched his pockets till he found the key. It wasn't his. He'd never even touched it before tonight, but he'd always known where it was. His mother wasn't an official member of the guard, but she was chief of the patch, and this key was a symbol of her power. She had access to anywhere aboard the Mother other than private aeries. There were drawings in the histories of previous chiefs wearing their keys around their necks constantly, but his mother had never followed that trend. The key hung unused on a hook. But Kipling remembered.

Kipling opened the circular key, twisting it until its five arms extended like the points of a star. He then inserted it into the star-shaped receptacle in the door. As the lock turned, he felt a pang of unease. It's not really breaking in when you have a key, is it? It's not like he wasn't allowed to be here. He had visited earlier tonight — though for a decidedly different purpose. He crept through the main living area and scanned the tunnels to the barracks. All was quiet. He slipped through the doorway to the armory.

It was a tight space, as nearly any pocket of the Globe Mother was, but this seemed even more restricted, resembling a closet more than a treasure trove of weapons. Fortunately, many of the guardians had their equipment in use and the space occupied by their mechanical bone wings was now free.

Kipling scanned the racks of what was left. It seemed most of the guardians had been wearing their wings during the festival, and still had them out, so pickings were slim, but a few must have had duties that didn't require them because five sets of wings still hung

in the racks. Three were too large for Kipling to dream of using—
one belonging to Captain Bronks, and two others that were nearly
as large.

Kipling found himself wishing that Auralee had been off duty
on another patch. She was nearly his size. Her wings would have
been a great fit. As it was, he had to make do with a pair usually
worn by Corky Altos. Corky was taller than Kipling by several
inches but at least he was skinny. Kip bundled the silken wings into
a blanket he'd brought from home, careful to not bend any of the
bone ribs, and moved on to the weapons.

He'd have to be careful here. There was no way he could sneak
out with a long harpoon. Even some of the clubs were far too heavy
for him to dream of wielding. He searched the options till he found
a medium length warhook with a heartwood handle. It was about
the same weight as the pruning ax he used with his father and the
handle fit comfortably in his palm. The hook was shaped from the
tusk of a shadow raptor and inscribed with runes. The end was
sharp at the point and then again at the end of the curved hook.
The hilt was notched in a few places from previous battles, but the
shaft still had all of the blackened shark's teeth fitted into the saw
tooth back edge.

One of the shark's teeth still had a bit of something stuck to it.
Fur? Feathers? He wondered what beast had unwisely threatened
the patch and met its end.

Kipling untied the tether and let it dangle from the handle, then
slung the weapon over his shoulder.

"I carried that warhook the day I killed my first dreadwing.
You could certainly do worse."

Kipling spun to find Bronks leaning against the doorway. His
face was pale—a dusty brown many shades lighter than normal.
His chest was bare with the exception of the stained bandages.
Kipling didn't know whether to be concerned that he was caught
or worried that Captain Bronks looked so weak. The big man's face
was beaded with sweat.

"Off to battle the world, are you? Going to defeat our enemies
single-handed?" His eyes lingered on the warhook. "I remember
those days. The flame of youth flares brightest against the darkness."

"I have to rescue Samra. Someone has to save her."

"A rescue is a task for the guard," Bronks said, his voice raspy
in the darkness.

"The council won't send you. They won't go after her. That's . . . that's why I have to go."

"Kipling, you are very brave, but you're too—" his words were suddenly cut short by a coughing fit—moist, bloody coughs that racked the big man's frame. Kipling took a step forward, not knowing how to help.

"What are you doing out here?" The voice was frantic. Ellea Conlay, the guardian healer, emerged from the hallway and raced to Bronks' side. Kipling stuffed the warhook into his bundle to hide it. "You are in no state to be out of bed! What are you thinking?" She lifted Bronks' arm and threw it over her shoulder. Holding a towel up to his face, she wiped his brow and then gave it to him to aid in his coughing. She glared at Kipling. "What are you doing here? You shouldn't be encouraging him. Get home. It's too late for visiting." She immediately began guiding Bronks back down the hall. Bronks struggled to get his coughing under control and speak, but all he could manage was a few words.

"Bright, Kip. Glow bright."

Kipling backed away down the hall and placed a hand on the front door handle.

"Get!" Ellea shooed him away before guiding Bronks back into his room.

Kipling fled down the ladder and back into the central grove.

He had his prize. He was halfway to the vine bridge when he realized the gear in his arms didn't weigh nearly enough. The warhook was solid, but the wings were hollowed and light. The silk between the bone ribs was strong but nearly weightless. Without the harpoon and the armor that guardians wore, he wouldn't be able to sink very quickly. He could exhale his breath in spurts and he'd probably get to the ground eventually, but from this altitude, he might drift for hours or days before settling to the bottom of the sky.

He needed a faster drop. He'd need a buoyancy belt.

His own was now lying on the ground in Womble and he didn't have a spare—but he knew someone who did.

Rufus and his family lived aboard Brumla Sing, one of the lowest-flying globes in the patch. It was a water reserve globe, so, despite its size and strong ties to the Globe Mother, it constantly trailed aft and below the main bulk of the patch. Kipling crept down the bulky water roots that led to the underside of the globe and threaded his way into the grove hidden below.

Rufus's end of the patch was significantly worse for wear after the attack. Brumla Sing's grove had been connected to three other globes in a long arm that typically made up the tail of the patch. The other globes had cut loose and were now making their own way through the skies, and their departure had ripped a hole in the tendril wall that made up one side of the grove. Water droplets from severed xylem veins still dotted the perimeter of the tear and raw heartwood was visible in places where the green protective skin of the structure had been torn off. Family aeries around the grove were now exposed to the outside winds.

Rufus had a window in his tendril pocket that overlooked the grove but it was currently shut. Securing his bundle on his back, Kipling climbed to the window and whispered through the thin gaps between closed tendrils. "Rufe. Wake up, Rufe. Rufe!" The last call came out a bit too loud but it resulted in some stirring inside.

"Kip? Is that you?"

"Yeah. Let me in."

"Did they find Samra?" The tendril vines parted and exposed the rotund boy's sleepy face.

Kipling climbed through the opening and hopped to the floor of Rufus's room. He then illuminated himself to a dull glow and looked around. Rufus's tendril pocket was even bigger than his, and far bigger than Samra's. The walls were cluttered with oddments from school and souvenirs from their adventures around the patch. Kipling recognized a thick root that Samra had carved into the shape of a monster and decorated with pillberry seeds. He'd thought the creation long lost, as Samra had decreed that the monster be banished from the patch in one of her more elaborate imaginary rituals. But here it was, preserved among other similar treasures.

"Where do you keep your spare buoyancy belt? Can I borrow it?"

Rufus blinked a few times to clear his vision. "What for? Are you too full? I barely even had a chance to eat at the festival with all the —"

"I need to get back to the ground." Kipling began searching

corners of the room.

"The ground?" Rufus looked out the window, checking the view of the night sky. "But we just got back to the Heights. I thought we were staying up here."

"The patch is, but I'm not." Kipling found a buoyancy belt under a pile of clothes near Rufus's hammock and began checking the belt's various weight pockets. "I need the heaviest rocks you've got."

Rufus rubbed his hands across his face and finally came around to the situation. "Who else is going down?"

"No one. Just me. I'm going after Samra."

Rufus spotted the handle of the warhook tucked in the folds of Kipling's blanket. "Oh wow! Where did you get this?" He grasped the weapon and drew it from the bundle.

Kip straightened up and looked at the saw-toothed shaft. "That used to be Captain Bronks' hook. He said he used it to kill a dreadwing once."

"Flaming mother . . ." Rufus swore softly. He held the warhook up with both hands and waved it around. "And Captain Bronks gave it to you?"

Kipling looked away and continued searching the floor for rocks. "I'm just borrowing it. I'm going to bring it back once I've rescued Samra."

Rufus's face grew serious. "You think she's in bad danger? Where do you think she is right now?"

"I don't know, but the stupid council isn't sending anyone after her. No guardians. They only plan to gather the globes. But we saw Cirra Sola get taken. We saw the ships take her."

"So . . . wait. Why did the council agree to send you?"

Kipling stuffed the handful of rocks he'd found into the pockets of the belt and began fastening it around his waist. "I decided to go. It's my choice."

Rufus stared at him blankly for a moment, but then dropped his eyes to the belt. His brow furrowed. "You'll need more. You should use the lead ones." He moved to the wall and parted a section of tendrils revealing a secret compartment. Inside was a trio of shelves loaded with more weights. A few were rocks but most were smooth, dark metal. He scooped a few up and handed them to Kipling.

Kipling gasped at the weight of them. "Whoa. Where did you get these?"

"Dad traded with some Grounders for them," Rufus said. "He said if I wore smaller belts, I wouldn't look like as much of a patchling. These weigh a lot more than the rocks. I've been using them for years." Rufus's skin was glowing faintly having admitted this. "My dad actually still uses them, too."

Kipling had often wondered how Rufus's father, who shared his son's hefty proportions, never drifted off the patch. Feeling the density of the metal in his hands, he now understood. Weights this heavy should have been registered with the council and the balance officers in charge of keeping the patch properly weighted, but he'd never heard anything about them. The consistent surplus of weight on this end of the patch had been throwing off his father's water ballast calculations for years. They'd attributed the discrepancy to undiscovered water pockets in the tendrils, but the math was now adding up. It was a violation of patch rules to own things this heavy, but right now, the contraband would certainly come in handy.

"I should go with you." Rufus blurted the statement out as if unable to contain it. "For Samra. I don't have a warhook, but I could come, and I could —"

"I think you should stay," Kipling said.

"Why? She's my friend, too. She needs rescuing and she'd do it for me. I know she would."

Kipling didn't doubt that was true. Samra certainly would have leapt into danger to save one of them, but the truth was, he needed to move fast if there was any hope of catching up to the raiders. He had no idea how long it would take or how far he'd need to go, but he knew he'd get there a lot faster if he weren't waiting for Rufus. The boy was determined, and Kipling didn't doubt that he'd go anywhere to find Samra, but endurance and stamina were not words typically used to describe him.

"You can't come. I need you to stay here and see if you can convince my brother that I'm still on the patch. If I get past the guardians tonight without them noticing, they won't be able to drag me back right away. But Kaleb will still be looking for me in the morning. If you cover for me, you can buy me time. You can tell him I'm working on the repairs of the patch. Doing grower stuff. Tell people you've seen me and I'm just moving around. It'll throw them off the trail. If you don't do it, they'll know I'm gone and they might catch me. Once the patch is far enough downwind, I'll be safe, but not unless you help." Kip rested a hand on his friend's shoulder. "You know how good the guardians are about nabbing overboard movement. One person might sneak off the patch but I don't think they'd miss seeing two."

Rufus stared out the window again. "Is Auralee on guard?"

"Everybody is. Everybody except Bronks."

"Then you won't make it either. They'll be looking down to spot Grounders. They'll see you jump for sure."

Kipling frowned at the thought of being dragged back aboard the patch after never even making it to the surface.

"Unless..." Rufus continued, "...someone created a diversion."

Kipling smiled. "If only I knew someone good at those . . ."

He was in position. The wings were tucked in tight against his back, covered by the blanket he'd thrown over himself. The straps were as tight as he could get them and he'd rigged the controls to his wrists. It was harder than he'd expected. He'd never actually used guardian wings before but he'd certainly watched it done enough times. That would be enough, wouldn't it?

He'd snuck down the central helix of the Globe Mother's internal root structure, past the empty globe son pods, all the way to the cloud net. Below this point, the thin, water-absorbent strands were too delicate to descend. He was heavy now, too. Heavier than he'd ever been in his life. It took extra care and more time than he expected to not tumble the entire way down the core of the Mother and ricochet out into the night. He'd be plummeting soon, but not yet.

He'd had to sneak past two guardians perched on the outer tendrils, but luckily both were watching the sky. Now he waited for the signal.

He didn't have to wait long.

Rufus's shout carried from the trailing end of the patch, floating on the wind as he shrieked. Rufus was lighting up, too, flashing as much as he could to draw eyes to his position. The guardians stationed above Kipling muttered and moved upward, one ascending the roots and the other spreading his wings and soaring out toward the source of the noise.

That was his cue.

Kipling kept the blanket wrapped tightly around him, shielding any involuntary flashes of light he might be emitting from stress. He crept out of his hiding place among the roots and eyed the long drop to the darkened terrain below. The mountains seemed to seethe and roll in the darkness, though he knew that was just a trick of the light. It was over fifteen thousand feet to fall. A long way in the dark. But this was his chance. He was really leaving.

He'd never feared a fall before, but with the weight of all his gear, his knees began to quake.

"Help! Help! Look over here!" Rufus shouted into the night. The lights of the guardians were almost on him. So fast. They were reaching him too fast.

Kipling tore his eyes away from the rescue going on above and forced himself to concentrate.

Just let it out.

He exhaled forcefully and took a step. The overloaded buoyancy belt did the rest.

He ripped through the soft trailing membranes of the cloud net and plunged into the darkness below. The blanket whipped and flapped around his shoulders, straining to rip itself from his grip. Why hadn't he tied it to himself? He could have used tether rope or creeper. For now only his straining fingertips clenched the fabric to himself, with the wind whipping past his face and pulling at his hair.

He was falling face-first, the buoyancy belt pressing into his abdomen like an anchor. He lost his grip on the blanket with one hand, then the other. The fabric soared away from him as he fell, thrashing upward into the ripping wind and then fluttering slowly after him. It disappeared into the darkness as he continued to fall.

His eyes scanned the night above and the slowly shrinking patch around the Mother. So far none of the guardians were pursuing him. Their attention was still at the tail of the patch, or what was left of it. The patch looked so much smaller now. He'd only ever known the globe patch of the Mother to be this enormous network of life. A city in the sky. Now it looked fragile—torn and vulnerable.

Something brushed his face with a cawing swoosh. The faint, sudden caress of feathers or fur—it touched his skin and then was gone. But it happened. Contact.

He wasn't the only creature in the sky tonight.

His wings were still tucked in and he was only drawing tiny

sustaining breaths, then expelling hard. He couldn't tell how fast he was falling. He also couldn't see the ground. Everything below was blackness. Fog? Trees? How would he know when to open his wings? The wind was so loud around his ears. He couldn't even hear himself think.

Look for reflections. Starlight on water or moonlight on leaves. Something to use as a reference.

There. Water. A glint in the darkness. Reassuring but close. Too close!

He spread his arms and deployed the wings. The cords on his wrists yanked upwards, but his momentum barely slowed. He kicked back to move the tail fin attached to the back of the wings, hoping to level out his dive. Nothing happened.

What was wrong? Had he not rigged the controls right?

One wing caught the air and spun him, a momentary lift on his left side, but then it was too much. He toppled to the other side, whirling and banking out of control in a terrifying spiral. His other wing ripped back and the control line came loose from his wrist. The weight of the belt around his waist was still pulling hard toward the surface, but his wings were only making him spin. The world was a dizzying cyclone of starlight and darkness, the faint glow of the Mother above, the reflection of moonlight on the water growing rapidly closer below.

Kipling gasped. He sucked as much air into himself as he could to arrest his fall. He slowed, ever so slightly, then a little more. He struggled to orient his vision and prepared to light himself up. The ground was there, wasn't it? Somewhere between that inky sky and murky glow.

Something hit him.

A creature's talons sank into the wing attached to his left arm and wrenched it loose.

He yelled and fell faster. The other wing was now just a hazard, flailing about his head and thrashing in the wind as the belt pulled him down. He gulped air as fast as he could but there was too much weight. He wasn't slowing fast enough. The creature struck him again from the side. This time one of the talons dug into his shoulder and he screamed. The flailing wing caught the creature in the underbelly and dislodged it. The black mass of feathers and claws dropped off to his left, then flapped away.

The nightbeast wheeled and turned, keening into the darkness before tucking its wings and diving hard for Kipling again. He watched in terror as the talons advanced, boring straight toward him. He channeled his fear and lit himself up, flashing to life and burning as bright as he'd ever glowed. The light poured out of him and beamed into the night. Inches away, the creature pulled up.

He hit the water.

Cold blackness swallowed him. Bubbles churned and frothed, racing around his face, glittering jewels desperate to reach the surface—a surface that was slowly retreating. The water was murky, encroaching on his glow. It dimmed him and robbed his heat.

He wanted to breathe. He wanted to rise, but this was not his element. He needed the air and he needed to be free of this crushing weight. His fingers found the straps of the wings first, shedding the now useless contraption into the darkness. Next his fingers dug into the belt, prying loose weights from their pockets. Not all of them—he still needed them—but just enough.

He began to rise.

Faster and faster he raced to the surface, overtaking the bubbles and erupting into the air.

He gulped and swallowed the night sky—only stopping when he felt in danger of drifting loose from the water's surface.

He was victorious, no longer in danger of sinking. He only needed to make the shore.

Kipling had never swum before. He'd never had the need. Only with this weight belt dragging at his waist had he ever been heavy enough to sink below the surface. He'd seen it done before though, so that was enough, right?

This time his plan didn't fail him. He paddled and stretched for the shoreline, hitting the reeds on the bank in a matter of minutes. He clawed his way through the grasses and weeds till his fingers sank into thick mud.

Kipling's skin was dim when he reached firm soil and finally felt the first satisfying crunch of pebbles and shell. He walked, feet making sucking noises in the muck, till he reached the rocky terrain beyond. He collapsed to his knees and sat on his heels. Slinging the tether of his warhook around till he could reach the handle, he hoisted the weapon and waved it at the sky.

"I made it! You didn't stop me!"

Overhead, shadows still whirled in the darkness, but nothing plunged to attack him. High, high overhead, he could just make out the glow of the patch, the Globe Mother in the center, drifting off beyond the wispy clouds. The sight of his home so unreachably far away quieted his jubilation at having reached the ground. As his body came down from the high of his success, his shoulder began to throb. He used the warhook again, not to threaten his airborne enemies this time, but to prop himself up. He climbed to his feet.

He studied the dark line of the horizon and began to walk, unsteadily at first, but then with greater conviction. He'd made the ground. He'd taken the first step. From here on out, he'd either rescue Samra or die trying.

Overhead, the nightbeasts shrieked and circled in the sky.

He'd know soon one way or the other.

15

DAYLIGHT

The sky was only a fraction less than black when Atlas woke. By the time it faded into gray-blue on the horizon, he had the *Sun Dragon* completely uncovered and it floated close to the door.

The wolves were gone. During the night, as many as twelve had sniffed around the barn, but they didn't last. The pack was hungry, and their patience was not up for the long wait till dawn.

Atlas made the most of the delay.

He reminded himself that a good pilot is never in a hurry. Enzo had repeated the phrase so often he could hear it in his head almost as though his grandfather was standing right next to him.

He'd been foolish last night. He'd rushed. Once his mind had settled, he realized he hadn't even packed the maps. How did he expect to find Enzo in the canyons without any references?

It was an oversight he remedied before the dawn light had even reached the tops of the canyon walls. It took two runs to the house to gather the rest of the supplies he needed, but he made the trips with efficiency and none of the clumsy rush of last night. He was an aviator now. He had to think like one.

He opened the doors to the barn and pulled out the *Sun Dragon* with careful but efficient movements. The air tanks were full.

Safeties and gust locks removed. The craft hovered above ground, tugging gently at its tether. His cargo was all carefully stowed. He'd done the math. Once he was aboard she would be perfectly balanced. Ready to soar.

He climbed into the cockpit and took his seat. His hand rested on the tether line. This was really it.

"Atlas!"

The canyons echoed with the yell.

Amelia raced down the trail. Her braid was undone and her hair flew about her shoulders in a messy wave. Her shirt was torn at one sleeve.

"What are you doing out here? Don't you know how worried we've been?" Amelia's face was red from exertion as she forged through the high grass toward the *Sun Dragon*.

"I'm going after Grandpa," Atlas shouted. "They're chasing him. He needs help."

Amelia reached the side of the airship and grabbed hold of the lateral fin. The *Dragon* sank under her grip and the tail fin bumped the grass.

"They were raiders, Atlas. And they're dangerous. You're not going up there."

"I have to!" Atlas threw off the tether line and tried to float free of the ground. Amelia clenched the fin harder and held the airship down. She only weighed perhaps 130 pounds, but it was enough to keep the craft from climbing. Atlas kicked the rudder fins to turn and dislodge her, but she held tight.

"Atlas, they raided the village! They got into the town hall and stole the village relic. Dale Merritt is dead."

Atlas stopped kicking the pedals. "Mr. Merritt?"

School wasn't exactly Atlas's favorite thing, but his teacher was about as close a friend as he had in town when it came to grownups. The idea of him being dead . . .

"Put this thing on the ground, Atlas!" Amelia was struggling to keep her grip on the stowed lateral fin as the breeze coming down the canyon attempted to lift the *Dragon*'s tail.

"Grandpa needs me." Atlas refocused his attention on the task at hand. "If they're after him, then I have to hurry!" He kicked the rudder hard and the tail skidded around till it was perpendicular to the barn and facing into the wind. Amelia hung on.

"You're just a kid, Atlas! You're lucky to be alive as it is. You can't do this."

"I have to!"

Amelia struggled to hold the *Dragon* but her feet were skidding in the grass now. "You're not your mother! Okay? I know you want to be like her—to be like Enzo—but you have to stop this. You're not a pilot! Your parents wouldn't have wanted you to do this either. They wanted you safe."

Atlas fumed. She didn't understand. She couldn't. How could she when she'd spent her entire life on the ground and hiding from the sky? This was his moment, his chance, and Enzo needed him. His fingers found the air valves to the lateral fin deployment system.

Amelia was grunting now and she spoke through gritted teeth as she dug her heels into the dirt and wrenched the *Sun Dragon* downward. "You're my responsibility, Atlas, and—"

"Not anymore," Atlas said. He pulled the deployment lever and the air charge burst into the lateral fin actuator. The fin sprang from the side of the fuselage into its open position, lifting his aunt off her feet and flinging her into the grass. She landed in a heap on her back as the *Sun Dragon* sailed backward and upward. The deployed fins caught the wind and Atlas shoved the control wheel forward to climb.

"I'm sorry!" Atlas shouted. "But I have to do this."

Amelia stared up at him from the ground with eyes wide. "No!" She scrambled to her feet and ran after him, but he was already much too high to catch. Atlas kicked the rudder and turned the *Dragon* downwind, reversing his movement on the control wheel to now climb forward. He flung open the lever for the upper fins and they sprang into position as well. They caught the wind and carried him up and away from the barnyard.

He leaned over the edge of the cockpit and watched the steadily shrinking figure of his aunt running through the field below him.

"I'll be home soon!" Atlas shouted. "And I'll bring back Grandpa!"

Amelia shouted something else in return but he couldn't make it out. She was falling too far behind and the breeze down the canyon was propelling him faster and faster. Atlas turned forward and immediately wrenched the control wheel back to avoid the tops of the pines stabbing up from the woods to spear him.

"Whoa!"

The *Dragon* responded and rose higher, clearing the treetops and soaring up and into the open valley. Atlas realized he was already headed too far south and banked left, dipping the left fins and kicking the rudder around at the same time. He trimmed the lateral fins and opened the fan valves. A rush of wind surged down the channels near his feet as the forward fans spun to life and blasted air through the tail. The air motors chunked and ticked as the pistons pumped their way up and down, driving the counterbalanced shaft that spun the fans.

Atlas tapped the mariner's compass affixed to his dash and slipped his goggles over his eyes. Ahead, out the abbreviated windscreen, the deep cleft in the mountainside marked his destination.

Last he saw, the raiders were headed for the Rift. So that's where he'd go too.

He twisted in his seat and looked back once more, but Enzo's farm was now just a grassy patch at the foothills of the canyon. Amelia, if she was still watching, would be just a speck beyond the forest.

"It's okay," he whispered. "I'll be back." He wasn't sure if the assurance was for him or for her, but it made him feel a little better.

It wasn't the maiden journey he wanted. It wasn't the way Amelia should have seen him fly for the first time. The image of her frantically running behind the airship made his stomach twist thinking about it. He wanted her to see what he could do and be proud. Why couldn't she see that he was ready for this?

Atlas shook the thought away and concentrated on his heading. Finding Enzo would fix it. If he brought his grandfather home, how could anyone argue that he wasn't a pilot? He was a pilot right now!

The trailing edges of the lateral fins fluttered ever so slightly in the wind and he made a few corrections to his heading to find the most efficient path through the valley. The *Dragon* was soaring along beautifully, even better than he'd imagined. He'd ridden in the *Express* enough times to know what the rigging should feel like and this was even smoother than that. The sun was up now and lighting his aircraft in all its glory.

Atlas spotted the schoolhouse, and for a moment he was tempted to bank that direction and buzz the schoolyard — see if any early arrivals were there to witness his flight. Then he remembered Mr. Merritt.

Killed by raiders.

Amelia said they stole the town relic. What on earth for? As far as Atlas could tell, the relic only taught them about farming techniques and grazing animals. It did have some useful medical information—safe health and medicine practices—but the rest was just boring technical stuff: math, physics, reading, and writing. He'd learned all that in school. Why would raiders steal that? Could it have some information Mr. Merritt never told them about?

Atlas had seen the relic a few times when the class was allowed to visit it in the town hall. Mr. Merritt was proud to be its chief custodian. He called it a treasure and a priceless artifact of the Old World. Not much to look at though. Just a sturdy cube with smooth sides. One side lit up like a window, but you couldn't see inside. It showed other things, other places. Occasionally Mr. Merritt had to drag it outside and set it in the sunlight. He said the relic would request that sometimes. He talked to it a lot in his free time, sometimes for hours. Used to anyway. Atlas pulled his eyes from the village.

The Rift was getting closer.

He banked left and swept low over the slope of scattered boulders that had fallen loose from the mountains. The boulders were as big as houses and the gaps between them weren't a bad place to hide if you needed one.

"Grandpa!" Atlas shouted over the rail of the cockpit and scanned the terrain for any sign of *The Sunshine Express*, but there was no yellow aircraft in sight. He dipped into the ravines and checked the crevices between the biggest promontories. No Enzo.

After circling for a few laps around the boulder piles, he finally righted his craft and turned it to face the next challenge.

For as long as he could remember, Atlas's world had existed within the confines of the Ridge Valley. Womble and all of its neighboring villages fit comfortably within the great bowl between the mountains. The walls of the bowl collapsed on only one side, and that side faced the sea. To leave the valley in any other direction was impossible, with one exception: the Rift.

Atlas used to imagine that an enormous giant had made the cleft in the mountains with a tremendous axe. Some days he dreamed that *he* was the giant and was able to knock down the mountains that hemmed in his valley.

Some travelers had made the rocky climb through the cleft on foot, but it was a slow passage over difficult and sometimes deadly terrain. And all was done beneath the watchful eye of the Beacon. For years the high peaks and narrow passage had protected the valley from the outside world. Till last night when their defenses had failed them.

For Enzo, the Rift may have been the only escape route left to evade the raiders.

Atlas applied power to the fans and worked the rudder pedals back and forth, propelling the *Sun Dragon* forward like a fish. He angled the lateral fins for a climb and slowly gained altitude heading into the Rift.

High overhead, the fires of the Beacon were still lit. Amelia and Cathy had made it to the top, but too late to save the village. The warning bell hung mute as he passed beneath it. What warning would it toll for him now if it could?

It didn't help that the Rift was always in shadow. Even if he entered it with the sun directly overhead, the sunlight wouldn't last long enough to traverse the entire cleft. The deep gash in the mountainside was miles long and twisted in places, not a clean cut, but a jagged tear — sharp and unforgiving. The towering walls on either side stabbed into the sky to an altitude well above what was safe for breathing. The *Dragon* might survive a flight that high, but he wouldn't.

Atlas spun the crank at his knee and ratcheted the airship's lateral fins in tighter, narrowing the *Dragon*'s width and streamlining the fuselage. He took a deep breath, shut down the forward fans to save air power, then went back to kicking the rudder fin.

He would move slowly.

He would be careful.

He would make it through.

16

THE RIFT

"Needle webs!"

The shout went up from the forward deck and heavy footsteps thudded across the ceiling of Samra's place in the hold. The noise drew her back to consciousness. She hadn't remembered falling asleep.

"Stave off those spikes. Get below and man the oars. Full stop here!"

More yelling echoed above. Men and women scurried about the ship, taking positions. Samra rubbed her eyes and shoved off the blanket that someone had wrapped around her.

"Oh Lord — she's a mother. Look at them eggs!"

More footsteps pounded overhead, but Samra could only imagine what terror might be lurking outside. She stretched out a hand and concentrated. She needed light to better determine her surroundings. Her fingertips flickered, but went dark again. She muttered at it and tried again. "Come on. Work."

Something scratched the table and a match sputtered to life a few feet from her face.

"Ahhh!" She shouted involuntarily as the glow revealed the wild face of her red-haired captor. He was seated on a bench across a table from her. His fiery beard and billowy hair made him look elemental—a force of nature more than a man. Her memory came back to her. He'd brought her down here last night and held her still while she raged and fought him. It had done no good. He'd simply wrapped her up in a blanket and stuffed her in the corner, his big hands keeping her from going anywhere. Sometime after, she must have fallen asleep.

"Welcome back, Little Weed." The man's eyes were not unkind. His freckles formed dark constellations across the bridge of his nose.

"I'm not a weed."

The man lit an oil lamp dangling from the ceiling. "You look like one. But if you say you're not, then you must have another name."

Samra folded her arms across her chest and looked away. She was stuck in the corner of a narrow galley. She discovered there was a chain around her waist. It was clasped with a lock, but she wasn't shackled to anything. Apparently the man had just wanted to weigh her down and keep her off the ceiling. A buoyancy belt of sorts. It was working.

The table and benches took up one quarter of the room and cupboards and supplies occupied the rest. Two doors opened off the galley but the one she wanted, the one leading back above deck, was directly behind this red-haired giant. She didn't see a way around him.

"If you don't have a name," the big man continued, "someone will pick something to call you, and all of a sudden, that will be how you're known. That's how it works. Stop calling something by its right name and one day you forget you ever knew it. That's what happened to me aboard this ship. Might happen to you, too."

Samra's eyes wandered back to the man with the fiery beard. "They changed your name?" Despite her best efforts to hate him for capturing her, he was fascinating to look at. And now she had to admit she was curious about the name.

"Didn't just change it. They forgot my old name so completely, it's like it never even existed."

Khloe and her friends had certainly called her enough terrible things, but no one had ever lost track of what her name really was. "What did they call you?"

The man studied her. Crinkles lined the corners of his eyes. "They call me Sunburn." He folded his arms across his chest and mirrored Samra's defensive posture.

"Because you hurt them?" Samra asked.

The big man laughed. "No. They called me that the first time I took my shirt off to go for a swim. They said my skin was so pale I would blind them and give them sunburn."

Samra studied the big man's arms. They were freckled like his face but the insides of his wrists were indeed very pale. "Does your skin light up?" She had never heard of a Grounder glowing like a Skylighter, but wondered what this already fiery man might look like lit up.

The man called Sunburn grinned at her. "No. I don't glow. Just in the crew's imagination. But that is how they saw me that day, and that is why no one aboard even remembers my real name."

Samra considered the situation. She didn't plan to be stuck here long, but even after she made her inevitable, daring escape, she didn't want anyone calling her 'Weed.' She would much rather be something fearsome, or at least a name they would remember not to tangle with in the future. It had never occurred to her that her name was something she could lose. The thought made her suddenly possessive of it.

"My name is Samra," she blurted out. "Samra Rose Coley."

Sunburn nodded gravely. "I see. That's a strong name. I thought you might have a strong name." He leaned forward and rested his elbows on the table. "I'm glad you told me. I think it will help you stay strong now. The captain wants to speak to you, and I didn't think she wanted to talk to a little weed. A 'Samra Rose Coley,' however . . ." He laid his hand on the table. " . . . that's a different story." When he lifted his hand, it revealed a key that appeared to match the lock around her waist. He stood up and moved to the second door, swinging it open for her. "The captain will be up at the cockpit. I'll show you the way."

Samra stared at the open door and the big man waiting for her to enter it, then snatched up the key.

He'd left the other door exposed now. She could make a break for it, maybe get back above decks and jump overboard before he caught her. But why was he giving her the chance to escape? Did he know something she didn't?

He knew her name now.

He said it was strong.

She *was* strong. Whatever this raider captain wanted, she would have to listen to her, too. She'd tell her a thing or two, and make them return her to her patch. If this was how they'd remember her, they needed to know that she was the fiercest Skylighter on the patch and they'd abducted the wrong person today. They'd better return her or suffer the consequences.

Samra slid off the bench and out of the corner of the galley. She unlocked the chain around her waist and let it fall to the floor. Controlling her breathing to keep from floating, she straightened her shark tooth necklace and marched through the doorway Sunburn was holding open. She staggered a little with the subtle swishing motion of the ship, but kept her balance and continued, flinging open a second door at the end of the short corridor. She marched into the next room, prepared to give the captain a piece of her mind, but stopped short at the sight of what was happening in front of her.

The cockpit of the ship was roughly triangular. The top featured a ceiling of tapered windowpanes. The panes narrowed at the front of the ship, offering a view forward, a wider view above, and a narrow view below the prow. The room reminded Samra of the head of a snake. At its center—the brain of the snake—there was a chair on a raised step. It was empty because its owner was standing, arms clasped behind herself and peering up through the glass windows.

Outside the windows, two men were standing on the bow deck, stabbing harpoons at an immense, hairy spider. The spider was dangling from its web with its hind legs and slashing at the bow of the ship with its front limbs. Great chomping jaws scissored the air above the heads of the men, and eight shining eyes gleamed in the pale dawn light. Its belly contorted and the spider attempted to skewer the men with a sharp appendage protruding from its rump.

"Sunburn, I want you to tell Hodges that if he dislodges any more of those egg sacks onto my ship, I'm assigning him to galley work for a month. Last thing we need is a brood of spider babies crawling all over the rigging."

"Aye, Captain," Sunburn responded. He'd stepped through the doorway behind Samra, but waited calmly behind her. She noticed he was also blocking the exit. On the other side of the glass, the men were having little luck with the spider. One of them threw a harpoon, but the weapon sailed wide of its target and flew into the spiny webbing beyond the beast, piercing a sack of eggs. The hole immediately widened and a swarm of spiders the size of melons clambered out and rained onto the windows above them. Sunburn groaned. "No one aboard appreciates Hodges' cooking. I'll see that he mends his aim." Sunburn rested a hand on Samra's shoulder. "The young stowaway is here, Captain. Her name is Samra Rose Coley."

The captain turned and appraised Samra with a disinterested stare. "You can leave her here. I'll deal with her."

Sunburn turned to the door and ducked back through it, but before he closed it, he gave Samra a wink. "See you soon, Little Weed." The door clunked as he closed the latch on the other side.

Samra had intended to give this captain an earful immediately, but there was something about the way she stood staring out the window that didn't invite interruption. She was a steel rod unmoved by the events unfolding outside. Captain Savage had shed the tight-fitting leather jacket she had been wearing above decks and was now wearing a loose-sleeved white shirt. The striped whip was still coiled at her belt.

Two people occupied chairs near the window: a pilot, and beside her—seated at a table of maps—a man serving as navigator. Both crewmembers had their eyes fixed on the action taking place on the bow.

Samra screwed up her courage and took a step forward. "I need to get back to my patch. You have to take me home."

Captain Savage turned slowly. Her deep green eyes looked Samra up and down, then turned back to the spider-fight going on outside. "I don't *have* to do anything."

Samra struggled to come up with a response. "They'll be missing me. They'll send the guardians and make you give me back. You don't want to anger the guardians."

"If you're talking about those flying assassins who impaled my back-up pilot and sent him to his death, then I would agree with you. And it's more reason to *not* get near your people again." Captain Savage stepped down from the raised platform and strode over to Samra's position. She wasn't terribly tall, not compared to Sunburn, but she still loomed over her. Her piercing eyes had none of his warmth. "But, since you are here, you can tell me more about this patch of yours. Are there others like it? More giant globes like the ones that escaped? The big one must have been four hundred feet tall. Biggest thing I've ever seen in the sky. Where did it come from?"

Samra didn't know the dimensions of the Globe Mother. She'd never bothered to think about it. The Mother was simply a fact of life, constant and eternal. It was home. "There aren't any other ones like her. She's the Mother."

"Mother?" Captain Savage asked. "And these littler ones?" She gestured through the ceiling windows toward the back of the ship where the ruin of Cirra Sola was strapped in the cargo nets. "Where do they come from?"

"That's mine," Samra replied. "That was my aerie." She found herself growing angry at the sight of it. "You ruined it."

The captain glanced through the rear-facing panes at the back of the cockpit. "You're right. My crew did a poor job of harvesting that one. Most of the lift cells ruptured and we'll probably have to cut it loose. It's going to cause too much drag up there." She crossed her arms. "My men had never seen anything like it. We didn't know the big ones ever came down this low."

This conversation wasn't going at all how Samra wanted. She needed to get home, not educate this Grounder pirate about patch life.

"Where else do they come down? Does this 'Mother' land in other places besides the valley?"

"We only come to the one valley," Samra replied. "In springtime."

"We saw the rest of the globes cut loose, after your people attacked us. Where do they go next?" The captain advanced toward her and Samra backed up, bumping into the windows on the side of the bow.

"We didn't attack you," Samra retorted. "We were having a festival."

"Believe that if you want, but we were just doing a bit of harvesting on an abandoned patch of skyweed. Next thing we know your people came flying out of the fog throwing harpoons. You can hardly blame us for fighting back."

"That's not true," Samra stammered. Though she hadn't seen anything from her tendril pocket. Was it possible she was wrong? Had the guardians been the first to attack?

"Captain, looks like Wallace is injured." The woman at the helm gestured to one of the men who had been battling the spider.

"Bitten?" the captain asked.

"By one of the small ones," the pilot replied.

The man called Wallace was retreating from the bow, cradling his arm.

Something thudded into the window next to Samra and made her jump.

She shrieked.

The spider was the size of her head and gnashing its fangs at her against the glass.

Then it happened.

Samra lit up to a brilliant white and gushed light in the direction of the spider before she even had time to think. The spider cowered away from the light and leapt off the window, tumbling into the darkness below the ship. Samra looked down and found she was hovering a foot off the cockpit floor. She made the mistake of touching her own reflection in the glass and the movement spun her around.

She rotated to find the captain and the other two crewmembers shielding their faces from her light.

"Bleeding guts that's bright," the navigator swore, his hand covering both eyes.

Her light flickered, then blinked out as suddenly as it had come on, dropping her ingloriously back to the floor.

The woman in the pilot position stood with mouth agape. Her face glinted with jewelry, a nose piercing and silver studs through her ears. She was close to the captain's age but her expression had none of the captain's intensity.

The captain's expression changed from indifference to something more calculating, her mouth pressing into a thin line.

She'd done it! She'd glowed. Samra studied her hands with amazement. She never imagined it would be like this, but it had finally happened.

The captain looked past Samra to where the little spider had been, then glanced out the front windows of the ship. The mother spider had retreated from the light as well, back up onto her web, leaving the lone crewman on the bow blinking in confusion. Even he was now looking inside, curious about the sudden brilliance.

"Can you do that again?" Captain Savage asked. "Could you do it to that one?" Her finger stabbed forward toward the giant spider outside.

Samra was suddenly apprehensive. She hadn't even thought about lighting up. Not that she hadn't tried plenty of times before.

It just never worked. Only now, it had. It finally happened.

"Look." Captain Savage took a step closer. "The longer we wait here in this oversized gully waiting for the critters to get out of the way, the farther away your patch gets. We saw them fly over the ridge, so that means they're already on the far side of this range, moving east. You won't catch them on your own. You're welcome to try, but the fact is, you need a lift."

She pointed at Samra's chest. "I'm willing to consider going after them, but there's no such thing as a free ride in these skies. The berths on the *Restless Fury* are for crew only. You want to fly with us, you'll have to earn your keep."

The captain jerked her thumb toward the bow. "Move that hairy behemoth out of our way and I'll let you stay aboard."

Samra clenched her sharks tooth necklace in her hand, the edges of the teeth pressing into her palm, grounding her and giving her nervousness a distraction. There was too much to process. Did she want to stay aboard this ship? She had only thought as far as escaping, but the captain was right. How could she catch the patch on her own? What chance did one Skylighter patchling have alone in the Southfang mountain range, or even adrift in the wind? The patch was miles up by now. Suddenly, the security of the ship was an asset she couldn't afford to lose.

"I just have to get it to move?" She glanced out the window to the dark mass in the web and then back to the captain.

Captain Savage crossed her arms. "You get rid of the spider, my crew can hack through the webs. Then we'll be on our way."

"You'll get me back to my patch? You promise?"

"Sure, kid. You tell us where it'll be and we'll get you there. But first things first." The captain moved to the wall and opened a hatch leading to the bow deck.

Samra steeled herself and climbed through it.

She could do this. All she had to do was light up again. Easy.

Her stomach turned over as she climbed to the bow.

The captain and the cockpit crew stayed inside but watched from the safety of the interior. Hodges, who had been left alone on the bow, glanced at the captain, then retreated, looking relieved that someone else was facing the hairy threat.

The spider was monstrous. Samra had seen needle spiders before. Every once in a while the guardians would find one clinging to air kelp or drifting in the breeze on ribbons of webbing, but she had never seen one this large. This spider was as fat as a globe son and its eyes as big as oranges. It studied her, watching her movements across the bow.

"Get her closer!" the captain yelled.

At the sides of the ship, fabric wings extended and flapped, like fins on a fish, creating a bit of upward thrust in the otherwise dead air. The airship rose, ever so slowly.

The spider was only a dozen feet away now. The front legs of the beast were spread wide and spanned the width of the hull. Samra was in range of the clawed feet. The spider gnashed its jaws twice and twitched. It repositioned its back legs on the web.

"What are you waiting for?" the captain called from inside.

Samra clenched her fists and concentrated, but her pale, yellow-green skin stayed dim. The fangs of the spider clacked above her head.

"You can do it." The voice came from the deck behind her. Samra glanced back and found half a dozen raiders watching from rigging. Sunburn was standing in the middle of the deck. He held an axe in his hands. "We'll help." He began walking toward her.

Samra turned back to the spider, but before she had time to concentrate again, the spider leapt. The great hairy body launched itself toward her, the needle on its underbelly aimed straight for her. Samra screamed and ducked, rolling sideways to avoid being skewered. The needle of the spider scraped across the bow, then retracted again. The spider turned to find its target once more, climbing across the front of the ship and pivoting to face her. Now Samra had only the ravine behind her, the webbing above, and the spider clawing its way toward her. It dove at her, the jaws closing in around her.

Samra leapt.

The fangs snapped beneath her and she tumbled upward, turning a flip and suddenly finding herself sitting astride the spider's head, facing the wrong direction. The skin of the creature was clammy but abrasive, covered in spiny hairs that scraped the insides of her legs.

She shivered in disgust, but held on.

The arachnid retreated from the bow rail, spun, and spread its fangs toward the raiders on the deck. Samra craned her neck to see what it was doing. Sunburn took a step forward and raised his axe. Samra, not knowing what else to try, grabbed big handfuls of the spiny hair at the back of the spider's head, and pulled.

The spider twitched and jolted, pivoting around again, then leapt for its webbing.

Samra shrieked, but held tight, her fingers digging into the creature's rippled skin. The spider didn't stop. It scurried up the web, all the way to the side of the ravine and raced vertically up the rock wall. Seated the wrong direction, Samra never saw the hole in the wall coming. The spider crammed its fat body into a cavern and Samra collided with the rocks.

She twisted in the air and grasped for a handhold as the spider's hind legs contorted themselves into the hole beneath her. Her fingers scraped the stones but found nothing to grab and she fell to the open mouth of the hole, landing on all fours. The spider continued burrowing itself into the mountain, thudding into the walls of the tunnel and vanishing into the darkness. After a few seconds, even the sound of it disappeared.

The ravine was quiet.

Samra took a breath.

She'd done it.

She stood and stared at the abyssal lair her enemy had retreated into.

That's right. It'd better run.

Despite her victory, Samra didn't feel inclined to linger. She looked down the ravine to judge her descent and found herself fifty feet above the *Restless Fury*. The twin shark nacelles of the airship gleamed in the bits of dawn light finding their way down the cleft. There were more airships in the ravine — the ones she had spotted before. They were much larger now. Behind the *Restless Fury*, a few hundred yards farther back in the Rift, a cylindrical, single-envelope airship took up nearly the entire space between the ravine walls. The fabric of the ship's lift envelope was solid black with a red sunburst on the nose. Beyond that, she could just make out the lower gondola of a third, slightly smaller ship. How many of these raiders were there?

Samra eyed the gap between the two shark-shaped nacelles below her and leapt. She expelled her breath and plummeted, splitting the gap between the two envelopes, then flipping upright again as she reached the deck of the ship between them. She thudded into the boards next to Sunburn, and straightened up.

The captain and the navigator had exited the cockpit to see

what happened and were now standing on the bow deck. When Samra turned to face the front of the ship, Captain Savage's lips split into a grin.

"Can't say as I like a show-off, but I guess you did the job." She gave Samra a nod. "Sunburn will get you a berth. Eckers is dead. I suspect you can have his." She turned her eyes on the rest of the crew. "As for the rest of you, clear those webs. I want to be out of this ravine by noon. Get to work." She stepped past the navigator and climbed back down into the cockpit.

Once the captain was below decks, the remaining crew gathered around Samra. Besides Sunburn, there were three men and two women. One of the women's skin was so brown and leathery, she looked like a dried apple. Her wispy chestnut hair was streaked with gray. She grinned at Samra with a crooked smile. The other woman was young, with hair so light it bordered on white. A corset held in her curves, but beneath the tails of her shirt was all business—trousers and high boots. She wore a long knife at her waist and a smaller blade on the opposite hip. The handles were carved into the shape of wolves. "Looks like I'm not the greenie anymore," she said. "About time we had a new fish."

A man with a scraggly beard ran his fingers through it as he sized Samra up. "'Cept she ain't a fish, is she? She's a spider rider." He gave her a nod. "I'm Cogburn. They call me Cogs."

"She showed that thing a new trick, didn't she?" the man next to him chimed in. He was still cradling a hurt arm. Samra recognized him as the man who had suggested stabbing her the night before. His expression was slightly more congenial now. "Guess we've got a spot for you on the bow from now on. See how you do against the rest of the night baddies out here."

"She's done enough. She's earned her place," Sunburn replied.

Cogs spoke up again. "So what do we call you, spider rider?"

She lifted her chin and puffed her chest.

"My name's Samra. And nobody better forget it."

17

THE LEAK

The crags of the Rift stabbed from every direction. Atlas was two miles in now, but with every bend, turning back became more tempting. Three stones the size of his head had plummeted past already, knocked loose by unseen creatures scurrying along the cliffs above.

Atlas held tight to the controls and forced the *Sun Dragon* forward. Enzo needed him. There was no quitting now.

Daylight had at least brought some reassurance. Birdsong echoed through canyons and at one point Atlas spotted a wild goat. It watched his slow progress with curiosity, then went back to plucking weeds from the near vertical cliff walls.

As he continued on, he was swallowed by shadows again, the towering walls of the ravine blocking out all but a sliver of sky above.

Progress was slow and the twists of the ravine were confusing. His maps had guided him this far, but he was worried he may have taken a wrong turn up a dead end. He was about to turn around when he saw the ruined web. Massive strands of webbing hung in tattered ribbons down the cliff walls. The ends were tangled in clumps, but some of the cuts were clean and deliberate.

Someone had been here.

The web had been destroyed by something big. Something that had wanted to get through this particular passage.

The airships.

Atlas grinned at his luck. He was getting closer. Maybe he was even catching up. Whoever was chasing Enzo wasn't that far ahead. He would have to be careful, but he had the element of surprise. If the *Dragon* was fast enough, he would sneak past them when they weren't paying attention. Somehow he'd find Enzo and —

Something thudded into the side of his airship. The *Dragon* rocked and he corrected the controls to stay level.

What was that?

He craned his neck to check the tail, but didn't see anything. Another rock?

He wiggled the tail controls and everything still worked. He kicked the rudder fin a few times and scooted the aircraft forward, getting out of the way in case something else fell.

The thud jerked his head forward. This time he saw the black mass bounce off the nose and cling to the air intake. It wasn't a rock. It was a spider. A spider the size of a watermelon.

The third thud came from the right. The oversized arachnid landed aboard the lateral fin and caused the airship to list.

Atlas fought the controls and kicked harder on the rudder fins. Looking up, he spotted three more spiders on the rocks, eyeing his craft.

"No!" the word burst from his lips as he frantically spun the air valves to start the pneumatic motor. "Get away!" The *Dragon* lurched forward, the forward fans spinning to life and sending a blast of air down the channels below the cockpit. The jet of air propelled him forward and gave his rudder more authority. He shot away from the wall as one of the spiders leapt.

This one missed and plummeted into the ravine below.

His problems weren't over. The spider on the nose was now sitting astride the front of the airship and inching its way closer. A thin barb protruded from its underbelly and it flexed the weapon as it advanced. The spider on the lateral fin was stationary, but watching him as well. Atlas wrenched on the fin controls, wiggling the fins back and forth, but the creature held on.

He'd seen plenty of spiders in his life, but none like this. The claws on the closest one were digging into the fabric of his airship.

"Get off!" Atlas yelled, and waved a fist. The spider didn't move. He rummaged in the hold next to his seat till he found the small harpoons. Setting the locks on the controls, he cautiously stood up and brandished the weapon. The spider canted its head and watched him.

"Off!" Atlas swung the harpoon and connected with the spider's hairy abdomen. It flew off to the left of the ship and disappeared into the ravine. No sooner had Atlas turned around than another spider landed in its place. He looked up and discovered that the entire rock wall he was passing under was covered with the creatures.

"You've got to be kidding me."

He slid back into the pilot seat and unlocked the controls. Jamming the wheel forward, he forced the nose lower and pushed the thrust lever. The fans spun to full speed and he cranked hard on the pump handle, shifting water ballast forward as fast as he could.

Thud.

Thud.

Thud-thud-thud.

The creatures rained down onto his aircraft.

He yelled as he engaged the rudder with the air motor. The rudder fin now whipped back and forth on its own, faster than he could kick it, but the spiders were still jumping aboard quicker than he could descend. They were on the wings and the tail controls now. The nose was crawling with them. One was creeping closer to the fan intake.

"No! Stay away from that!" Atlas shrieked at the creature but it had no effect. Last thing he needed was a spider sucked into the fans. It could jam up the entire system. He pulled back the thrust lever and let the fans spin to a stop. The rudder was still oscillating, but even that was having trouble. It was bumping into creatures on both sides now.

The airship was sinking.

Atlas realized with horror that the spiders were too heavy. They were bringing the ship down. He spun the lateral fins all the way in with the hand crank, then slung them open again with the air actuators. The maneuver dislodged a dozen spiders into the ravine, but it wasn't enough. They were almost in the cockpit now. He snatched up his harpoon and batted another spider off the nose. When he turned around, another was looming over him from behind, its barbed needle aimed to strike. Atlas wrenched his harpoon around to block the blow, but he never got the chance. The spider was suddenly dislodged and sent overboard by something brown and furry that careened into the fray and landed on the tail. The creature's fangs snapped and chomped, tearing limbs from the spiders around it and crunching them furiously.

Atlas's heart jolted in his chest until he recognized the pointed ears and webbed black wings of the creature that had come to his rescue.

"Fledge?" Atlas stared incredulously at the cliff fox.

Fledge shook out its wings and bit through the remainder of the spider in its mouth. His big orb eyes were bright with excitement. He leapt off the tail and snatched another spider off the lateral fin as he dove. The cliff fox spread its wings, banked into the turn and flapped overhead again, turning and diving for the nose of the *Dragon*. Two more spiders fell victim to his attack. The rest grew suddenly apprehensive and watched with intensity as their companions were plucked from the ship. The exodus started on his next pass, spiders leaping from the rigging, aiming for the cliffs, but many of them falling short and plummeting to the distant rocks below.

The *Sun Dragon* began to rise.

"Yeah, Fledge! Get 'em!" Atlas cheered on the cliff fox as it plucked another spider off the tail and flung it into the ravine. He slid back into the pilot seat and made his adjustments. He reengaged the thrust fans and climbed, making for a beam of sunshine breaching the shadows ahead. As he soared upward into the sunlight, Fledge came flapping out of the shadows behind him, a thick spider leg still dangling from his jaws.

"Good boy, Fledge!" Atlas grinned as the cliff fox alighted on the rim of the passenger cockpit. The animal was extra weight and would throw off his balance calculations, but it was a fix he could make easily enough. The sight of Enzo's pet boosted his spirits so much, he felt like he could float the ship himself.

Then he heard the hissing.

It was faint, but definitely there.

"Oh no!"

Atlas straightened up and peered over the nose. The fabric on the front of the airship all looked taut. He spun around and checked the tail. Something was definitely wrong. He couldn't see it, but the hissing was louder in that direction. He scanned the tail surfaces till he spotted the puncture. It was halfway back on the right side. A hole with a bit of canvas flapping in the breeze. One of the gasbags was breached.

Atlas leaned over the rail of the cockpit. It was all jagged precipices and sharp rocks below. To make matters worse, thick, thorny vines scaled the walls of the ravine here, adding danger to an already unfriendly landscape. There was nowhere to land. He'd have to repair the leak in the air.

He rummaged through the storage locker for the patch kit, then opened the tail access hatch. It was a tight fit, even for him. The main lift bag was directly behind his pilot position and looked to be intact. The leak was farther aft and he'd have to squeeze back there to find it. He frowned at the tiny patch kit in his hand, but then got to work.

He spun the ballast pump and passed more water ballast forward to make up for his movement. The nose tipped and the aircraft began to sink. He opened the dump valve and shed some of the rear water ballast. The craft rose a little but he didn't dare jettison too much. He might need it later. Every direction he looked held threats. It was only a matter of time till he hit a ravine wall or struck the patches of thorns. The wind in the ravine was too variable to try to predict where it might blow the ship. He'd just have to work fast. He stuck the patch kit between his teeth and began to crawl, squeezing his way aft.

The hissing was louder back here.

While bollite gas wasn't exactly toxic, it wasn't breathable either. It tended to force other denser gases out of its space, and with the exception of the lumium gas in the plants it lifted, it left little room for breathable elements. The tail already had the smell of it, an oily scent, smelling vaguely of butter.

He held his breath and squeezed through.

The rip was two gasbags away and up at the top. He wasn't sure if it was a barb from the spiders that did the damage or Fledge's claws, but something had gotten through the external skin and punctured the bag. He worked the kit open in the near darkness of the tail. The only light coming in was the faint beam through the puncture of the outer skin. Luckily that shone right where he needed it. He opened the tar bottle and smeared it over a patch of fabric, then stuck the patch over the puncture. He dolloped more of the tar over top and spread it around the edges. It was a sloppy repair job, but it was the best he could do under the circumstances. The bag was loose now but still had a good amount of gas left in it. He waited thirty seconds, and when the hissing didn't return, he crawled back out of the tail, leaving fingerprints of tar the entire way.

Fledge chirped a raspy screech in his direction as he reemerged into the cockpit. The wall of the ravine was mere yards away and approaching fast.

"No you don't," he whispered at the *Dragon*, plopping back down in the seat and spinning the air valve handles. He reversed thrust with the forward fans and pressed hard on the control wheel, climbing back and away from the rocky wall. Once clear of danger, he stopped the fans and spun them back the other direction, pushing the aircraft forward and banking for the passage between the walls.

"See, Fledge? We can do this."

The cliff fox flapped its wings and hopped into the front seat of the aircraft. When Atlas leaned forward and peeked over the dash into the passenger area, Fledge was already circling the cushion, tucking his head under one wing and settling in for a morning sleep. Atlas leaned back in his seat and set his eyes on the passage ahead.

The *Dragon*'s damaged gasbag would need a better repair, and some fresh lift gas to refill it, but he could find that once he was out of the Rift. For now they were still flying. He'd survived his first crisis, and even more importantly, he was getting close. If Fledge was here, that meant Enzo wasn't far. Having the cliff fox aboard was proof he was on the right track.

As the Rift began to straighten out, he caught his first glimpse of the highlands beyond. Rolling, grassy hills opened up beneath a sea of blue. Puffy clouds dotted the horizon. This was farther than he'd ever been in his life. Farther than almost everyone he knew, except Enzo.

Atlas lowered his goggles over his eyes and pushed forward on the thrust lever.

The grin spread across his face.

"Open sky, here I come!"

18

THE BARGAIN

It was past midday when Kipling realized his mistake. His quest had barely started but he was already failing. Not only had he lost his wings, he was on the wrong side of the wind.

He stood in the grassy heather of the highlands staring up at the sky. He'd struggled his way free of the lake, survived a long night on the surface, and wended his way back toward the mountains. Against all odds, he'd done what he'd hoped. He'd found the airships. But now he couldn't reach them.

"Samra!" He cupped his hands and shouted at the sky.

High above him, the raider airships were moving away, departing the Rift and making slow but steady progress eastward. Against the wind.

Kipling ran and took another flying leap. He'd shed as much of the weight in his buoyancy belt as he dared, but left enough to counterbalance his own higher buoyancy at this low altitude. He shot into the air, soaring upward, hoping to get free of the airflow along the ground, but the wind immediately repelled him, flinging him back and sending him tumbling away from his target. He somersaulted through the air, flailing his arms till the relentless current forced him to ground again. He dug his fingers into the roots of the heather and arrested his flight, sliding to a stop even farther away from the ships than when he started.

"Come back!" He screamed at the diminishing shapes of the ships, but he may as well have been yelling underwater. They were upwind and flying away, powered by engines he didn't understand and couldn't hope to compete with. He could jump at them all he wanted, but he would never reach them.

Muttering at the sky, he dug around in the grass till he found more stones. He piled them into his buoyancy belt until his feet had more traction. He cinched the strap of his warhook tighter across his chest, and set his eyes on the ships. If he couldn't fly after them, he would run.

He leapt through the heather and bounced along the hills, timing his breathing with his leaps. He sprang over streams and cleared gullies in single bounds. His arms pumped and he worked his legs as fast as they could go. His skin beaded with moisture as he raced through the grass, the sun soaking into his skin and reacting with the chemicals beneath. Despite the daylight, his body took on a pale glow as he ran.

The landscape was deceptive. The fields of waving grasses hid sinkholes and deep crevices. Kipling leapt the gaps when he came to them, undeterred by the sight of the long drops into the ground, but didn't envy the non-buoyant travelers who might stumble upon one of these chasms unaware.

It felt like hours had passed when he finally let himself stop to rest, but the sun hadn't moved much. The airships were now just specks on the eastern horizon. If he blinked or took his eyes off them for too long, he'd lose them and have to frantically search again. It was getting more difficult every time. What would happen if they changed course beyond the horizon? How would he know where to pursue them? The fear moved him and he broke into a run again.

Another mile was all it took.

The airships were gone.

No matter how hard he searched the sky, he couldn't find them. He panted and fell to his knees.

He was tired.

He was thirsty.

He had failed.

No. Not yet. He wasn't going to give up.

Kipling staggered back to his feet and looked around.

He'd give anything for a drink. If he had some water he might be able to think straight. He could make a new plan. He'd leapt multiple streams along the way, but now there were none in sight.

In all directions, there was nothing but puffy tufts of grass, some of it blossoming with tiny lavender flowers. It spread from the base of the mountains all the way to the eastern horizon. He knew from experience that the Northern Sky Forest lay in that direction. It always seemed so close to the mountains when they'd spot it from the patch. From here there was no sign of it. This ocean of grassy hills had expanded to swallow him.

He considered going back to the last stream he'd passed, but that was at least a couple of miles ago. He couldn't go back. Samra needed him. He had to go forward.

He kept going.

Kipling didn't run anymore. He walked now, his legs already complaining from the strain of the morning. He hadn't slept at all last night. He'd been foolish. He should have planned better. He could have waited and dropped down farther from the mountains. He could have dropped into the Sky Forest. He wouldn't have as far to go then.

But no. What if the ships had turned south when they left the Rift? How would he have known how to pursue them?

There was no right answer. It was too late now to change things. He just had to go on.

Three miles. Five miles. Ten? He was beginning to lose hope of ever finding another stream. Where was the water here? How did anything grow? He plucked stems of grass and tried to chew them. They were woody and tasteless. He found a few fresh shoots of grass and plucked those but it wasn't enough. It was only making him hungry.

Why hadn't he packed food? He should have thought about this. The sky floor was nothing like the Heights. Up there food was plentiful. The patch never lacked for growing things to eat. They encountered food in the air as well. Even from here he could spot the floating kelp columns drifting along the wind currents. Tube grass. Lemon bulb fronds. Even a bright clump of cloud lettuce. It was all up there, ready for the taking.

He was tempted to take off his buoyancy belt and leap. But then how would he get back down? He'd be adrift in the sky and end up who-knows-where. Certainly nowhere close to Samra. The winds were too unpredictable. He needed to stay the course.

He tore his eyes from the sky full of food and kept walking.

The sun was definitely lower now. Despite his afternoon of progress, he still hadn't reached the forest. He could see it now though. When he climbed to the top of the grassy hill he was on, he could make out the wall of darkness on the horizon. Trees in the Sky Forest grew to enormous heights. Trees sprouted from other trees. Plants climbed plants and produced floating balls of lift gases to raise themselves even higher. Airplants and vines competed in columns for the sunlight, climbing thousands of feet into the air.

As he studied the horizon, something closer caught his attention. It was a big pile of bright green in the otherwise dry grass. Skyweed!

He raced down the hill and up the next. A kelp patch had come down. Could be rotten. Best not to get his hopes up, but there had to be something edible on it. It was still bright, and his stomach was empty enough that even slightly fermented kelp might do. He could deal with the repercussions later.

As he crested the final hill he could nearly taste the greens already. But then he saw the ship.

His heart jolted in his chest and he dropped, flattening himself to the grass as quickly as he could. Had they seen him?

He poked his head up just enough so that he could peer over the grass and get a better look.

This airship was small. Much smaller than the ones he'd been chasing. It was almost completely hidden from view behind the fallen column of skyweed. The ship resembled a fish. The big tail could clearly be used for propulsion. Four fins protruded from the sides but were currently tucked in close to the body of the aircraft. The big nose section of the ship had an opening in front like a mouth and there was an exit under the tail. The lift bags that kept it afloat had to be internal because this airship didn't dangle from a bigger balloon of gas the way the other ones did. It looked like it only had room for one or two people. So where were they?

His ears located the pilot before his eyes did. A great crunching noise from the far side of the clump of skyweed preceded the figure that walked into view. He was a kid!

The Grounder boy was dragging a section of the kelp patch behind him and he dropped it next to the airship. He next extracted a knife and set to work sawing at the stalks surrounding one of the lifting pods. He had to be after the gas.

Kipling considered his options.

He could wait him out. The Grounder would have to move on eventually. But who knows how long that might take? It could be hours. He was too hungry to wait that long. The kelp patch looked old and slimy but it couldn't be all bad. Even just a sip of its juices would quench his thirst.

This was just a kid Grounder, not any bigger than he was. Maybe he could scare him off. Kipling reached over his shoulder and found the handle of his warhook. He had a guardian weapon. Certainly much more fearsome than the knife the Grounder kid had. A person would have to be crazy to want to fight against a guardian sword. He tugged on the handle and slowly began to ease the tether over his head. That's when the second creature emerged from the cockpit of the aircraft and climbed into view. Brown and furry with pointed ears, it stretched its pleated wings and yawned.

Fledge!

Kipling sat up at the sight of the cliff fox perched on the rim of the cockpit. If he was here, did that mean Enzo was too? Had he gotten away from the raiders? He scanned the area around the skyweed pile but saw no evidence of the old aviator.

Now that he looked at it, this aircraft did bear a resemblance to The *Sunshine Express*. It was close to the same size and the lettering on the tail looked similar.

He kept the warhook on his back and stood. The boy, intent on his project with the skyweed bulbs, didn't look up. But Fledge noticed and the cliff fox let out a friendly squeak.

The Grounder boy glanced at the animal, then followed its gaze to the hillside and Kipling.

They just stared at each other for a moment, then the Grounder boy stood as well.

"Who are you?" he challenged. Kipling noticed that he hadn't released his grip on the knife. The bollite pods of the plant were tangled around the boy's feet. They were leaky and wet. He'd been right. This patch was nearly rotten.

"They'll last longer if you leave the root nodes on," Kipling offered. "When you cut the stems that close to the pod, they die and lose all their lift."

The boy glanced down at the sticky pile of pods he'd been sawing loose, then back to Kipling.

"I could show you how to cut them if you want," Kipling added.

The Grounder boy seemed to be considering the offer. "Where did you come from?"

"The Globe Mother."

The boy's shoulders relaxed. "Were you at the festival?"

The memory suddenly came back to Kipling. "Hey, I saw you there! You were on a horse." Kipling took a few steps forward. "I was there with my parents. My mom is chief councilor. Chief Roose. I'm Kip."

The Grounder boy met his gaze. "I'm Atlas." He looked pensive. "Look, I'm going after the raiders who attacked the village. I'm not going to stay here long and I don't have time for talking." He bent back down and started hacking away at the gooey kelp stalks again.

"Why do you need those? Are you trying to eat them? The greens actually taste better and they—"

"I need them for the *Dragon*. If I'm going to catch the raiders, I need more lift. There's only so much water I can lose if I want to get back down."

"You have water?" Kipling jolted at the words. He scanned the area around the boy. Where was it? In the airship?

Atlas kept sawing at the stalks till his knife nicked the pod he was trying to liberate and it promptly deflated. He muttered at the plant and kicked it aside, snatching up another one.

"Look," Kipling said. "I'm going after the raiders, too. They took my friend and I need to rescue her. If you let me have some of your water, and let me come along in your airship, I could help you. We could hunt the raiders together."

"I don't need help," Atlas replied. He sawed even more vigorously at the next pod. "And I can't take on any more weight. The *Dragon* is too heavy as it is."

Kipling strode over to one of the pods next to Atlas, snatched it up and spun it in his hands. He twisted the root tendrils, tied them in a knot and repeated the process with the flowering leaves, then tucked them in on themselves. He gave the pod a quick tug and it popped loose from its main stalk, coming off in his hand in a neatly compact ball. He held the pod out to Atlas. "I can help you find lift pods twice that size that will last way longer. This patch has been cooking in the sun so it looks more buoyant than it really is. All of this is dying and it's going to wilt at altitude." He tossed the pod into Atlas's lap. "And I don't weigh anything unless I want to. When I breathe deep and light up, I can even fly. So I could lift your ship more than a dozen of these little pods."

Atlas studied the leafy ball in his hands with curiosity, then lifted his eyes to Kipling. "You're sure you can fly?"

Kipling took a deep breath and lit himself up. With the weight of the warhook on his back he had to glow a little brighter than usual to get off the ground, but he drifted a few feet above the tips of the grasses before exhaling and dropping back down. "Okay, more like a hover, I guess." He glanced up at a fresh batch of kelp drifting past. "But if we go fast, we could catch dinner, too."

Atlas glanced up at the sky and then back to him. "Kip, huh?"

"Kipling Roose," Kipling added. He extended a hand.

Atlas shook it and grinned. "Well, this is the *Sun Dragon*, and fast is what she's made for. Get in, and I'll show you how to *really* fly."

19

THE FLEET

"That's one hell of a problem," Captain Savage declared. She stood on the foredeck studying the wall of plant life looming off the bow. "What's the altitude there?" She pointed a finger at a section of the forest off the starboard side.

Samra stood on the middeck next to Sunburn, watching the action.

A man holding a brass contraption with a lot of dials peered through a viewfinder before turning a knob and scribbling on a scrap of paper. "Looks like fifteen thousand, Captain." He double-checked his readings and bobbed his head. "It's fifteen if it's one."

"Can we clear that with our current load?"

"It'll be difficult," the man with the brass instrument replied. "If we dropped most of the water ballast and shed a bit of surplus here and there, we might make it."

"What if we shed all of the ballast?" the captain asked.

"Well, sure, that would get us up and over. There'd of course be the matter of getting back down again."

The captain ignored Samra and turned to Sunburn. "Tell Warehime to signal the other ships. They'll want a meeting."

They'd left the Rift around noon, and for the last few hours had been overflying miles of grassy highlands. Sunburn had permitted Samra to follow him around the ship during the day, learning some of the duties of crewmembers.

She hadn't been impressed by much below decks. She'd already visited the galley, sleeping berths, cargo deck, and ballast pumps. What fascinated her, however, were the twin shark-shaped nacelles overhead and the powerful air engines inside. The channels that ran beneath the lifting cells were big enough for her to climb into, but with the engines running there was too much air blasting through from the forward fans. She'd stuck her hand into the channel and felt the rush of wind tickling her fingers. It'd made her want to stick her face into it, but she didn't feel like getting ejected into the slipstream behind the ship, so she stayed out.

Despite unfavorable winds, the airship had made good progress across the highlands, even slowing on occasion to let the other ships catch up.

Throughout the afternoon, she'd watched the crew pack more of the lifting gas cells from Cirra Sola into cargo compartments on the two sides of the airship. It had taken all of her self-control to not scream at them. The little globe was nearly stripped clean and was almost unrecognizable. What buoyancy it had left was now going to use holding the *Restless Fury* aloft.

"I want my things back," Samra said, finally grabbing Sunburn's arm and pointing to the ruins of her aerie. "That's mine."

Sunburn looked aft to where one of the crew was sawing away tendrils around the remains of her home. The man had discovered her silkbug rope hammock, and after admiring the iridescent colors of the strands, he was attempting to stow it into his shirt.

"Wallace! Leave that be. It belongs to Samra."

Wallace glanced down at them and frowned, then grudgingly withdrew the hammock from his collar.

"Best get up there and grab what's yours," Sunburn said. "We'll be cutting that lot loose once the lift pods are out."

Samra crawled up the netting to the side of the engine nacelle. Wallace handed her the hammock with an exaggerated bow. "Here ya go, Your Brightness. Won't have it be said I was stealing nothing from the captain's pet."

Samra narrowed her eyes and snatched up the hammock. "Good." Wallace climbed higher in the rigging and began cutting away a different section of Cirra Sola. "And I'm not a pet!" Samra called after him.

Samra studied the gash in the tendrils that used to be her home. It didn't look like much now. Whole sections of the globe were missing. There was a corner of the Holcomb's aerie protruding from the netting, but most of the living areas had been jettisoned. The section of the tendrils that Khloe's family occupied was missing completely.

Samra couldn't help but wonder what they were doing now. Khloe was probably having fits about the loss of her clothes and her rock crystal jewelry collection. Jerem Stormblower would probably adjust okay. Last Samra had seen, his personal belongings mostly consisted of bad portrait drawings he did to impress girls, and dirty sketches he did to impress his guy friends. The patch archives wouldn't exactly suffer from the loss of his art.

Samra's eyes settled on the section of the aerie that used to belong to her parents and her thoughts flashed to the last time she'd seen them—her father's disappointed glare, her step-mother's crushing grip on her arm. Had they forgiven her in her absence, or were they now relieved to no longer have her chaos in their lives?

If the ship successfully carried her home to the patch, would she even be welcome?

The thought chilled her and she did her best to cast it away. Kip would at least welcome her. If her parents wouldn't have her, perhaps they could run off together, the way they'd imagined before things went so terribly wrong.

The old woman named Warehime waved a pair of colored flags from the rear of the ship, signaling the aircraft behind them. As Samra plucked whatever clothing and personal belongings she could salvage from the ruins of her tendril pocket, the other ships advanced on their position.

There were four of them.

The closest was the black, single-envelope airship with the red sunburst on the nose. It was significantly larger than the *Restless Fury*, and by the time Samra had climbed down from the cargo nets with her armful of belongings, it was looming overhead blocking out the sun. There was something strapped near the stern that looked like a smaller ship, or parts of one. It looked familiar, but with the sun behind it, she had a hard time making out its details.

A flagman on the bigger ship was signaling back to Warehime.

"They ask for permission to board, Captain!" Warehime called from the tail.

Captain Savage stalked across the deck to the stern rail and looked up at the hulking airship. "Permission granted."

A few moments later, ropes were hurled from the nose of the bigger ship and secured to the deck of the *Restless Fury*. Two men climbed off the nose of the higher ship and glided down the ropes in a feat of acrobatic athleticism that was impressive even by Samra's standards.

When the men reached the deck, they immediately linked their lines together and began to operate a device that made the rope ratchet through it. Up above, a sort of swing, dangling between the lines, began to descend. Standing on the swing was a young man that Samra couldn't take her eyes off of.

It wasn't that he was handsome. He was, but it was his smile that commanded her attention. It was as though he was in the middle of telling a joke and had yet to deliver the punch line. As he descended to the *Restless Fury*, his amusement only seemed to grow. The expression on the captain's face was suffering the opposite effect. She was scowling at the man by the time he set foot on the deck. Her fingers tapped impatiently at her hips.

"Hello, my darling sister," the young man said, as he spread his arms. "So good of you to consider the opinions of the rest of the fleet for a change before dragging us off course again." He grinned his bright smile at the rest of the assembled crew. "And everyone looks surprisingly well, considering the cramped conditions aboard your—" His eyes landed on Samra and her armful of belongings. "Oh my! What's this you've found?"

Captain Savage crossed her arms. "If you and the rest of the fleet could keep up for once, I wouldn't have to do all the navigating."

The man strode over to Samra and leaned over to be at her level. "Well, look at you. A regular little plant person, aren't you? Green and everything."

"I'm not green," Samra retorted. "Babies are green. I'm twelve."

"Oh, well, pardon me," the man replied. "You talk, too!" He stretched out a gloved hand and attempted to poke Samra in the shoulder. She backed away.

"We need to make a decision, Eric," Captain Savage said. "There are more of those giant pods in that group. If we want to catch them we need to get over the forest."

"Well, your little dinghy might wriggle through, but there's no way the *Savage Stranger* is fitting through those trees. The rest of the fleet either. We don't all share your diminutive proportions."

"I wasn't talking about going through. I'm talking about going over."

"Over?" The man turned and scoffed at his sister. "It's nearly frozen up there this time of year. Cold enough here as it is. Not to mention the air being too thin. The crews will pass out in five minutes at that altitude. I had a hard enough time getting them through the mountains. Eight thousand feet and it was like they were all smoking mush leaf."

"We've been to that altitude before," the captain retorted.

"And the men never let me forget it," Eric replied. He looked up to where the forest reached its apex. "I think my first mate lost a finger on one of your high altitude routes."

Samra checked the hands of the men standing on the bow, but neither of them appeared to be the one missing a finger. She was vaguely disappointed.

Eric straightened the lapel on his jacket. "Go after the sky people if you like, but I'm taking the *Stranger* south. We'll go around this forest and see what we can find worth scavenging on the way."

"Father wants lift pods," Captain Savage said. "Those are the biggest we've ever seen. Just a couple could equal months of harvesting kelp patches and tree nodes. Plus, they'd be worth a fortune. I'm not going to just let them go."

Samra scowled at the captain's back.

"My hold is nearly full," Eric said. "Father will be happy with what we've got now. Besides, he doesn't know I'll be bringing him home a missing piece for his collection. While you were antagonizing plant people and salvaging gasbags, I was finding what father is *really* after."

Captain Savage let her arms drop from her hips. "You found another relic?"

Eric grinned. "Seems these mountain people used it to unlock lighter-than-air flight the way we have, but it looks like they're using some kind of pneumatic motors to fly them. Who knows what else they've unlocked? Trust me, this find will more than make up for the lack of pods."

"Stored relic knowledge is only dispersed to the individual learners who've earned it. Without the relic key of the person who unlocked the information, having the relic won't do father any good."

"Then it's a good thing I have the guy who opened it."

Captain Savage glanced up at the airship hovering overhead. "You abducted one of the villagers?"

"I'm finding the people father can use. You're apparently just kidnapping natives." He gestured vaguely to Samra. "If you'd spend more time at home with father, you'd know what his real goals are and the sort of people he finds useful. Who knows, if you were a little more attentive, perhaps he would have given you command of *Savage Stranger*, and you wouldn't have to settle for this rattletrap floating dustbin."

"I command this ship because it's mine," Captain Savage snapped. "You can fly his ship all you want, but it's still his. That means I own one more airship than you do, little brother."

"Borgram told me you've still got this tub leveraged to his bank for all it's worth to cover your expenses. Can't claim you own it without the note." Eric Savage smirked and turned his back on her. "Chase the plant people if you want, Erin, but without the rest of the fleet, you'll have no way to get those pods home. I plan to explore the forest edge with the *Stranger*, but then I'm turning for port. Father will be eager to have his prize."

Eric stepped back aboard his platform and his crewmen began hoisting him up. As he swung out into the open air overhead, he gave Samra another glance and smiled. He took one hand from the ropes and saluted. "Enjoy the flight, ladies. I'll see you in port." He then turned his back on them and kept his eyes aloft the rest of the way to his ship.

Captain Savage muttered a few curses under her breath before turning back to the crew.

"Sunburn, how much room do we have left for lift pods?"

"None, Captain. Unless we plan to stow them in our bunks."

"Blasted trees. Two weeks we work ourselves ragged salvaging low-altitude junk pods and only when we're full do we find the ones that could cover our entire costs. If we could anchor down even a few of those high-flyers . . ."

"They're not yours," Samra said, her arms still full of her clothing and oddments. "You can't just take people's homes without asking."

Captain Savage blinked and looked at her as if she had forgotten she existed.

"They're just plants, kid. And your people have plenty to spare. I must have seen fifty pods in that patch when we came into the valley. Any one of them is ten times bigger than what we could glean from a forest vine. You can't possibly need them all."

"They're called globes. Not pods. And they have names."

"Names?" the captain asked. "What, you talk to them or something?"

Samra stayed silent. She *had* talked to the Mother. Lots of times. Oftentimes she'd lie in her hammock and wish for things—wish for the Mother to fly them somewhere new. Somewhere better. But she wasn't going to tell these Grounders that. Not like they would understand.

"We're turning south," Captain Savage declared to the crew. "Cut that refuse loose and trim for speed. My brother may be changing our course but I'm not giving him the satisfaction of getting there first. I want to be docked and offloaded by the time he pulls into the harbor."

"Wait! You said you would take me home!" Samra said. "We had a deal."

"And we still do," the captain replied. "Believe me, the first thing we'll be doing once we've offloaded our cargo is hunt down the rest of those pods of yours. You're going to help me find them."

"You can't steal our globes," Samra said. "The guardians will stop you."

"I'm not going to *steal* anything," Captain Savage replied. She fixed her arms to her hips again and stared at the horizon. "I'll trade for them. What is it your people want? Food? Weapons?" She reached down and plucked an item from Samra's arms. It was the little leaf-paper book that Rufus had made from her stories. The captain thumbed through a couple of pages and tossed it back to her. "Maybe they need some decent writing supplies. Whatever it is, we can get it for them and they can part with a few of those mothers of yours."

"They don't want anything from Grounders," Samra said. "Not from you. You attacked them."

"We've had this discussion, kid. Your people attacked us. As a matter of fact, they owe us for killing my pilot. They'd better be ready to trade now, or they'll have a different kind of negotiation on their hands."

Samra glared at the captain but kept her mouth shut. She didn't like the implication of what might be traded if they couldn't find anything else of interest. She didn't have any intention of becoming a bargaining item.

She could jump off the ship right now and leave this bunch of pirates to their delusions. But what would she do then? The Sky Forest loomed like a wall to the east, and to the west lay mile upon mile of grassy highlands. She'd seen nothing out there in the way of settlements or civilization. What hope could she possibly find out there?

No. She was committed now. If these raiders were going to reach her patch again, she'd need to be there.

The patch didn't know the danger they were in.

Samra would have to warn them.

20

THE SKY FOREST

The winds were changing.

Atlas watched the attached bits of string dancing on the nose and put a hand on the fin extension lever. He powered off the air motors and the telltales began to straighten, forming taut lines. He popped the lateral fins open and pivoted them to catch the wind. The aircraft surged forward.

He smiled.

The *Dragon* was soaring.

Atlas stood up and spread his arms, letting the air push him as well. He felt as one with his aircraft as a pilot could be. He was riding the wind.

The sky boy in the front seat didn't seem impressed.

"We can soar without power now," Atlas explained, leaning over the partition between the two seats. "Give the air motors a break and save pressure in the tanks."

Kipling was busy petting Fledge in the front seat. The cliff fox had found a place in the boy's lap and was now fast asleep. Only his whiskers twitched sporadically.

"My ship is faster than the *Express*." Atlas continued. "If Enzo is still flying ahead of us, we should be able to catch up."

Kipling looked up. "He isn't. It got harpooned."

Atlas's mouth fell open. "What?"

"*The Sunshine Express*. It got harpooned," Kipling said. "I thought you knew."

"When?"

Kipling stared up at Atlas for a moment longer, then went back to petting Fledge. "I saw from the Mother before we went over the ridge. A big black airship was chasing it. It caught him with harpoons and pulled the ship in."

"Is he okay? What happened to Enzo?"

Kipling shook his head. "I don't know. I didn't see anything else. We flew over the ridge. When I saw you in the field I thought it might be him and he got away somehow, but it was you."

Atlas glared at the horizon and clenched the dashboard. He'd suspected that Enzo might have been caught by now but hadn't wanted to admit to the worry. This made the situation even more serious. He'd hoped that he could simply catch up to Enzo, get him aboard the *Dragon* and outrun the raiders on a race for home. If he was a prisoner, that meant this was definitely going to be a fight.

"They have your friend, too?" he asked.

"Samra," Kipling said.

"Why did they take her? What do they want with them?"

"Doesn't matter," Kipling replied. "I'm getting her back."

Atlas could respect that. This kid might have come from the sky but at least he had his priorities straight.

Ahead, the wall of trees loomed closer. That was going to be another problem.

"Do you know anything about the Sky Forest?"

Kipling slid the sleeping cliff fox off his lap and onto the seat, then stood up to study the trees. "We've only ever flown over it."

"You think they made it through?" Atlas pulled a chart from his bag and unfolded it till he found the section with the Sky Forest illustrated on it. "Are there paths that make it across?"

Kipling stared at the barrier of plant life. "We were always so high up, it was hard to tell. There's a river. A big one. We could always see that from the patch. But I can't remember where it started."

Atlas pored over the map and traced his finger along the line of blue running through the forest. "It comes out of the mountains. But that's too far north to start. We'd have to cut through the trees to meet it."

He scanned the horizon from north to south, hoping for any glimpse of their quarry. Kipling was doing the same.

"Why can't we just go over?" Kipling asked. "Wouldn't the raiders just do that?"

Atlas frowned. It's true there was no sign of the other airships. If they had continued east, the way the patch had drifted, they had to have either gone over the forest, or found a path through. If they went over, it was with equipment the *Sun Dragon* didn't possess. "I can't fly that high."

"Too cold?"

"No," Atlas declared. He slumped back into his seat. "Too hard to breathe." He jolted upright. "But wait, I think I saw . . ." He fumbled through the cargo locker until he found one of Enzo's breathing masks. He traced the rubber hose to a little tank. Elated, he yanked it from the locker. He checked the gauge and his heart sank. The little dial on the pressure gauge was on empty. Enzo had outfitted the airship with a breathing air tank, but Atlas hadn't thought to fill it.

"Is that the special air Enzo breathes?" Kipling asked.

"No." Atlas passed the spherical tank and mask to Kipling. "It's empty."

He sighed and unlocked the controls, then sat back down and aimed the airship for the tree line. "Okay. We'll find a way through down here."

Kipling studied the wall of green ahead, appraising its mystery-laden shadows, then searched both other directions. He frowned but apparently had no argument. After a moment he put the tank in the front cargo locker and sat back down. Before he got settled, he propped his bone sword up next to him where it would be easy to grab. Atlas watched the maneuver but didn't say anything. He did free up one of the harpoons in his gear to keep it handy.

The wall of plants rose gradually from the heather, giving the false impression that the terrain was leveling out, when in fact the hillside continued to slope away below it like a sandy shore disappearing beneath the sea. Farther across this new floor of green, the trees rose.

Atlas had seen airborne trees before. Even in the Rift Valley there were plants that survived off moisture in the atmosphere and didn't require roots. But these specimens were far larger than anything past the Rift. Great towering spires twisted into the sky spreading broad leaves, or waved in the breeze with thin ribbons that resembled lace. Balls of lifting gases bulged from knotted trunks. There were huge fans of fronds that spread toward the sun, and determined spikes of twisting branches aimed skyward. Smaller plants climbed along with them: kelp, ivy, and plenty of tangleweed, connecting the trees and allowing other platforms for yet more growth. The ensuing wall of life was a slow-moving battleground, each plant clawing its way upward over the bodies of its competitors.

As the wind blew the *Sun Dragon* over the first ranks of trees, Atlas searched for the best way through. He cranked the bottom fins in tighter against the hull and readied himself to drop the upper fins as well when things got tight.

It didn't take long.

He first dodged the dry spires of rugged trunks that stubbornly maintained the edge of the forest. Some were twisted carcasses, casualties in the war for moisture and sunlight. Others were the new recruits.

Fresh seedlings, nestled in the crooks and ruins of their fallen comrades, bloomed with fierce color and broadcasted their lofty intentions toward the highlands. They boldly challenged the hills with all the exuberance of their youth.

The march of the forest was being propelled from behind. The farther they flew, the denser the push became. The forest was a wave—a swell of green that surged and broke across itself in slow motion. It stretched outward and skyward until it crested and curled beneath its own weight. The efforts left tubes and hollows, long tunnels of dappled sunlight and deep caverns of shadows. Time moved too slowly to display its violence, but this ocean of green was raging against its shores nonetheless.

Atlas steered through the peaks and valleys as best he could, climbing the thermals over the treetops whenever the wind allowed, and using the air motor when he needed to push the *Dragon* over a particularly high crest. He donned a blanket for the chill and pressed on, but he finally hit a wall of green he could not hope to float over. The air was already too thin up here. His head felt light and his skin tingled. The altimeter read 12,750 feet.

"We have to dive through. There's nothing else for it."

Kipling was unperturbed. He merely nodded and kept his eyes

ahead.

Atlas envied his constitution. The Skylighter wasn't bothered by the cold or the thinning atmosphere. If anything, he looked more comfortable. The skin of his forearms had a faint glow in the fading daylight and Atlas wondered if the chemical reactions inside kept him warm as well.

The sun was painting the distant cirrus clouds in pinks and purples in a farewell salute on the horizon. Atlas checked that the lanterns were within reach near his sides, then steeled himself and pushed the control wheel forward. He found himself holding his breath as he dove into the shadows of the upper boughs.

The forest eagerly swallowed them up.

"We need to watch for whisper wings," Kipling said. "They get you when you aren't looking. Too quiet to hear." He tapped his fingers nervously on the cockpit walls. "And horned tree bears. I've heard they have those here."

Atlas shivered. He'd learned the local catalog of nightbeasts in school. Every child in the Rift Valley knew the dangers of the dark, but the valley only held a limited number of species. The Sky Forest would bring new threats. Birds were calling one another in the boughs, but there were other noises, too, screeches and caws. Off in the distance, the eerie lilting song of a grim wailer searching for a mate filtered through the branches.

Insects were already glowing in the canopy. Some of the plants were also shifting into night mode. It was rumored that the height of the Sky Forest rose and fell with the sun. The solar rays fueled lift reactions in the pods and inspired surges of plant life that were not worthwhile in the darkness. As a result, the canopy of the forest could sometimes shift and sink, compressing the already dense spaces below it even tighter. As Atlas guided the *Sun Dragon* beneath the ceiling of plants overhead, he kept his eyes open for signs of collapse.

He tapped the vertical compass on the dash. The ball inside bobbed in its liquid prison. They were still headed east.

"How wide is the river?" Atlas asked. He squinted at his map, but could barely make out the blue line in the dim light. He fumbled in his cargo hold for a box of matches.

"It's big," Kipling replied. "We can see it easily from the Heights. Plenty wide enough to fly down."

Atlas got a lantern lit and hung it on the edge of the instrument panel. It gave a warm glow to the cockpit, but it made the darkness around them even deeper. The line of the river on the map wended its way through the patch of green but forked in two near the heart of the forest. The upper fork continued eastward, while the second bent south. The southern fork was slightly wider, though for some reason, the ink turned from blue to brown partway along its length.

Atlas brushed a finger over the point where the color changed. An error? Perhaps the artist had simply run out of colored ink? He flipped the map over to check the notes in the legend, but nothing mentioned the color change. Whatever the reason, he wouldn't be finding out. They would need to take the eastern fork to cross the forest.

A shrill screech penetrated the wall of plants to his right and brought his attention back to their surroundings. The canopy shuddered and a flock of birds exploded from the foliage. The tiny black birds surged in a cloud and broke around the aircraft, darting away and vanishing behind them in a cacophony of chirps and flapping wings.

Atlas centered the controls and cast a wary eye toward the place the birds had vacated. One of the boughs shook. Kipling stood up and peered into the leaves. The back of his neck was glowing.

The thing in the trees didn't reveal itself.

After twenty seconds of tense waiting, Atlas eased his power lever forward and steered away. The *Sun Dragon* glided onward through the trees.

Kipling pivoted in the front seat, his eyes lingering on the vegetation behind them.

"What do you think that was?" Atlas asked.

"I don't know," Kipling replied. "But I think it's following us."

The leaves on the trees behind them shivered in spurts. Bits of bark tumbled into the darkness below and something leapt from trunk to trunk above them.

Fledge crawled out of the front seat and perched atop Atlas's windscreen. His ears pivoted from side to side and he sniffed the wind.

"There's more than one," Kipling said. He lifted his bone sword and braced himself against the side of the cockpit.

"You can light up and scare them off, can't you?" Atlas said.

Kipling's head swung upward and he kept his eyes trained on the canopy. "I think you should fly faster."

Atlas pushed the control wheel forward and dove for a gap ahead. The *Sun Dragon* banked and yawed at his commands, dodging boughs and glowing lift pods. He cranked the fins in tight and strained to navigate the foliage, picking out pinpricks of light from distant lantern flowers and the eerie luminescence of ghost beetles. He blew out the lantern in the cockpit so he could see the faint outside lights better, but it was still difficult to navigate. The airship scraped past tree trunks that seemed to spring from the darkness.

In the front seat, Kipling was glowing steadily brighter. His eyes still lingered on the trees above. "I don't think it's nightbeasts," he whispered.

Atlas looked up as a figure leapt between two trees overhead. It was tall. A lanky, hairy shape with long arms. The figure swung from branch to branch and disappeared again.

Two more leapt into view on a wide bough ahead. Their hairy coats barely concealed lean frames and they flashed wide, flat teeth, gnashing them in the direction of the airship. The faces on the creatures were hairy too, with heavy brows and deep-set eyes. They were carrying spears.

Tree people.

"Go! Go faster!" Kipling shouted.

Atlas kicked hard on the rudder pedals, swishing the tail fin back and forth and trying to assist the fans. The motors whirred at high speed but he had to pull back power every time he collided with some new plant in the darkness. He couldn't afford to suck a bunch of moss or creepers into the blades. He was sure he'd already ingested some by now. Much more and the fans were liable to seize up.

Fledge took to the air as the *Sun Dragon* collided with a wall of vegetation. Atlas muttered curses at the net of green blocking their path. They'd run into a dead end. Kipling leapt onto the top of the aircraft and blazed to life, a brilliant white that streamed from his bare arms and face. He gripped his bone sword with both hands, ready to fend off the imminent attack.

Atlas could now see how outnumbered they really were.

The canopy overhead was filled with tall, hairy creatures. They began to whoop and chatter, raising their spears and shaking their fists.

But they didn't attack.

They were all waiting for something. The eyes of each would-be attacker turned repeatedly in one direction. Atlas followed their gaze to a gap in the leaves high overhead. A figure was hunched over and studying her palm. She was big. Streaks of gray lined her beard and scars shone through the hair on her shoulders. She stretched a hand toward them, fingers opened wide. Atlas caught the hint of a smile on her lips as she clenched her fist shut.

A heavy net fell overtop the *Sun Dragon*. Atlas tried to push it off and Kipling slashed at it immediately with his sword, but the cords were too thick, and before he could cut his way through, the swarm of hairy creatures was upon them. Tips of fire-hardened wood spears menaced them from every direction.

There would be no fighting their way out of this.

They were prisoners of the tree people.

21

THE TREE PEOPLE

Kipling had to be smart. That was the key now.

Anyone could wield a weapon. Not everyone could survive without one.

As he and Atlas were escorted through the canopy along twisted pathways of linked boughs, Kipling tried to recall anything he could about their captors. His culture lessons in school had seemed dull and useless at the time, but as a chief's son, he'd been expected to learn the basic customs of the various sentient species from other altitudes in case his family had to interact with them.

The forest folk, known as the Horokim in the patch, weren't killers. Not arbitrarily anyway. But they had a reputation for being territorial and superstitious. To them the world was a frightening place full of creatures bolder and cleverer and more capable than they were. Evolution had left them wallowing somewhere in the depths of the intelligence spectrum. They weren't smart enough to compete with other sentient species on the planet, but they were smart enough to notice the disparity. It was a circumstance that made them dangerous.

"Where are they taking us?" Atlas asked from ahead of him. Despite having his hands bound, he was doing a good job of keeping his balance on precarious footing. Their route was taking them steadily downward, sloping from tree to tree via lashed together branches.

Kipling couldn't see far enough ahead to spot a destination but he did have a few ideas. "They might want to display us." He kept his head bowed, doing his best to look defeated. "We might be prizes."

"They aren't going to eat us, are they?"

"No." Kipling reassured himself with the fact that Horokim were plant eaters—one of the cultural similarities they shared with Skylighters. The presence of all the spears did make them look like a hunting tribe, but in the Sky Forest, defense was nearly as essential as food. Weapons were not always an indicator of diet.

Their captors had rifled through the items in the aircraft they could reach, but had been uninterested in most of it. They found Atlas's supply of dried fruit and ate it immediately, but hadn't seemed particularly concerned with having captured an airship. Kipling wondered whether they realized how valuable it was. They had certainly understood the warhook, but that had more practical uses. The weapon was now slung around the body of one of the leaders of the group. Kipling kept an eye on it. He'd be needing that back. They hadn't found the pruning knife lodged in the waistband of his trousers. He was grateful for that as well.

Despite Kipling having waved a warhook at them, the bulk of the group now seemed intent on guarding Atlas. They chattered back and forth around him and prodded him roughly with their spears.

Trailing the group, Kipling was certainly a prisoner, too, but he felt like a mere afterthought. One of the smaller troop members had been assigned to guard him and even she didn't seem all that concerned he might escape. Kipling appreciated the lack of abuse, but a part of him would like to at least be considered a threat.

The group proceeded into a clearing arranged in the tangled boughs, not unlike a grove aboard the patch. It appeared to be a group habitation, individual nests collected in a circle and tucked into nooks of trees. Similarities with his home ended there. This grove was filthy. The nests of stripped tree bark and marrow leaves were heavily bedecked with fur. Clumps of matted hair clung to any available surface. It had done so for a long time, judging by the smell. The pungent scent of rotting fruit mingled with an odor of stale urine that wafted up from somewhere beneath his feet. The Horokim themselves seemed fairly clean, but now he understood the grooming it must take to remain so in this environment.

Kipling and Atlas were guided to the bottom of a central tree and pushed to a sitting position to wait while one of their group climbed into the canopy. Kipling could only assume it was to notify the rest of the troop of their arrival. His suspicions were confirmed when a few minutes later the grove began to fill with tree folk of all ages and sizes.

In his mandatory diplomacy lessons in school, Kipling had done his best to keep his teachers happy. His tutor, Master Freebold, had a favorite quote: 'Communication is the backbone of peaceful coexistence, so never enter a conflict without your spine.' For more evolved species, communication sometimes meant being able to tell the difference between sarcasm and sincerity, and in other species, the fine line between a snarl and a growl. Kipling expected that communication with the Horokim would involve more of the latter, especially from the look of the gray-bearded female that lumbered toward them. He recognized her as the same scarred tree-woman he'd spotted before.

She snarled at Atlas before sniffing the air around him. She was definitely a force to be reckoned with — muscular, intimidating, and a powerful leader. That was why Kipling was surprised when she stepped aside and a young female behind her worked her way into the light and began to sign to him in High Altirian.

The girl was covered in light-brown fur but she hadn't yet grown a beard. In terms of tree folk years, she was likely only Kipling's age, but the big, gray-bearded matriarch was very clearly deferring to her now. The girl scowled at Atlas with unveiled hostility but seemed less offended by Kipling's presence. Her hands formed the question: "Are you his prisoner?"

Kipling shook his head.

"Slave?"

Kipling lifted his bound hands and attempted to sign a response but he lacked the range in his wrists. The girl chattered something at his captors and one of them untied him. He looked up at the hulking male who had freed him and nodded. The tree-man nodded back. Atlas was watching the action with curiosity, but no one made a move to free him. Kipling caught his eye and tried to read the boy's expression. It wasn't fear yet. That was good.

"We are travelers," Kipling said the words aloud as he signed them, so Atlas would at least be able to follow part of the conversation.

The tree girl concentrated on his hands, then signed her next question. "Why here?"

Kipling tried to recall the sign for rescue but couldn't remember it. He signed out an alternative. "We're searching for friends."

"The Horokim do not have them."

Kipling nodded. "We know. They were taken by . . ." He didn't know a sign for raiders. He couldn't sign pirates either. "Sky ships," he concluded. "Big sky ships."

The girl pointed a finger at Atlas and signed something Kipling didn't understand. He signed for her to repeat it. Her fingers flashed again but he still didn't understand.

"What is she saying about me?" Atlas asked.

Kipling frowned. "I think it might mean dirt-man?"

The girl signed the word once more.

"Oh. Maybe it's her word for Grounder," Kipling said. "But it's got the sign for sand in it."

Sand man? Desert maybe.

Kipling signed an explanation. "Not desert. He's from the mountains." He pointed west. "Fanged Mountains."

The girl eyed Atlas skeptically, but her glare softened slightly. She grunted something to one of the others and the group chattered back and forth in a guttural debate. Finally the girl signed again. "We'll take you to the Knower. He'll decide."

The troop whooped and hollered and one of the big males promptly hoisted Atlas over his shoulder. Atlas blurted protestations but they were lost amid the shouting. The group broke into a run and leapt off the edge of the clearing. Kipling was prodded forcefully with a stick, and before he could think, he was plummeting over the edge with the rest.

Kipling was used to falling. The buoyancy belt hampered his usual agility, but he did his best to follow the troop. Even with the added weight, he had to minimize his breathing to try to keep up. The tree folk were fast. They dropped from bough to bough and took huge leaps into the open, only to catch themselves on trailing vines or ricochet off a tree trunk before dropping downward again.

For creatures without the ability to float, Kipling couldn't help but be impressed by their courage. It took all of his speed to stay with them.

Atlas was not faring nearly as well. The big tree-man who held him was not being especially gentle in the descent, and with his hands bound, Atlas had little chance to fend off the leaves and creepers that lashed him in the face. By the time the troop reached its destination, the boy's head was festooned with shreds of greenery, cobwebs, and sticky wads of tree sap. His face bore multiple scratches, though none of them looked deep.

Kipling straightened up on the final landing and allowed himself a deeper breath. The air was thick. They were low now. Ground level? The piles of detritus and rotting wood scattered around made it hard to tell. It could very well be just another tier of the ever-climbing forest. Kipling was the only light here, though he wasn't glowing especially brightly. The tree people seemed not to mind the darkness and gathered outside the ring of light.

Atlas was deposited on the floor of this new grove. He glared at him. "Why am I still tied up? What did you tell them?"

Kipling moved closer and crouched next to him. He kept his voice low. "They've taken us to someone. She called him the Knower. I don't know why."

Atlas squeezed his nose and cleared his ears from the rapid descent. "What's a knower?"

Kipling didn't have time to wager a guess. More shapes emerged from the darkness. A pair of towering tree-men were followed into the clearing by a shorter person in a gray, weatherworn overcoat. He had a wooden crutch lodged under one arm. The face was hard to make out in the darkness, but despite being bearded, he was clearly not of the Horokim. He was a Grounder.

As the tree-men stepped out of his way, the man in the overcoat was preceded by a raspy, wheezing sound. He was laughing. He stepped into the glow of Kipling's light, limping with the aid of the crutch, and loomed over the two boys.

"And they told me they'd captured sky bandits. Naught but a pair of pups, you are." The man leaned hard into his crutch and lifted his right foot off the ground. "They told me they captured a skyship, too. You don't look like aeronauts to me."

"Bet I can fly better than you," Atlas declared.

Kipling frowned. 'Never begin a conversation with an argument' was one of Master Freebold's first tenants of peacemaking. Atlas had clearly not learned that lesson.

"Is that so." The man reached beneath his coat and extracted a knife. Atlas's defiant stare didn't flinch. The man made a flicking motion with the blade. "Raise those hands."

Atlas complied and the man began severing the strands. Once Atlas was freed, he turned to Kipling. "And you must be one of the sky nomads. What do they call you? Cloud Burners?"

"Skylighters," Kipling replied. "My name is Kipling Roose. I belong to the clan of Corra Mara. My mother is chief of the globe council."

"I'm sure that means something where you come from," the man replied. "But down here your mother won't be helping you none. Don't care if she's the almighty queen of the moons."

Kipling kept his mouth shut. Rule number two from Master Freebold had been: 'When opposition is met, allow opportunities for your adversary to reveal their own weaknesses. Do not burden the conversation with information you already know.'

Atlas piped up next to him to fill the silence. He was eyeing the canopy of leaves overhead. "We need to get to my ship. How do we get back up there?"

"You'll have a rough go of that this time of night," the man replied. He stood up to his full height and sheathed his knife. "It's a far climb, and dangerous."

Atlas didn't seem discouraged.

"Plus, you'll have to take it up with the locals. They're the only ones who know where you left it." The man brushed his hands off and looked like he was done with the whole incident.

"Who are you?" Kipling asked, anxious to gather some kind of useful information from this encounter. "Why do they call you the Knower?"

The man's eyes turned to him. They reflected Kipling's green glow. "Used to be I did know a few things worth knowing. Enough to teach these folk anyway. Little ones still learn the best." He gestured toward the girl who had signed to them. "Shoa there is the brightest of this bunch. Couldn't get the hang of speech, but she picked up the signing all right. Others are coming along, but she's the shining star. Makes life more passable here. They didn't have too much to offer in return that's worth boasting about, but I'm still alive at least. They fend off the nightbeasts and keep me fed. Could certainly do worse in this forest."

"You're a knowledge trader?" Atlas asked. "What's your specialty?"

"Seen a few traders in your day, have you?"

"No. Not many. But my granddad told me about you. Said he's traded with some before."

"Your people live on the trade route?"

"I'm from Womble."

"Ah. Mountain people. I can see why you don't get many traders. I was actually headed your way before I ended up here. Don't think I'll make it now." He stomped his crutch up and down.

"How did you hurt your leg?" Kipling asked.

The man sniffed. "Same as most ground folk. I fell. Bleedin' sinkhole opened up right underneath me. A wonder I didn't break my neck. The low roads are getting harder and harder to travel these days."

The tree folk were still watching respectfully, keeping their distance but maintaining a circle around them.

"Why'd you teach them to attack airships?" Atlas asked. He didn't seem at all interested in avoiding confrontation.

"The tree people didn't start this fight," the man replied. "Can hardly blame them for defending their territory. Didn't need no prodding from me."

"What fight?" Kipling asked.

The man with the crutch shifted his weight and surveyed the two of them. "Now that would be the kind of knowledge some might call useful. Especially a couple of travelers headed through the forest into what is clearly the unknown for them. Seeing as I'm in the business of trading knowledge and not just giving it away for free, maybe we might come to some sort of reasonable agreement."

"But we don't know anything," Kipling said. "What would we be able to tell you?"

The man smiled and rested his free hand on his hip. "Well, I reckon you could tell me plenty about this sky people of yours. Where they go. What their fightin' numbers are. You fill in a few of my blank areas, and maybe I'll fill in some of yours, like where your airship is, and what kind of trouble you can expect on the other end of this forest."

Kipling frowned. He didn't normally mind talking about patch life with Grounders in Womble, but he'd never considered that it was information that would be useful to anyone. The knowledge seemed suddenly more precious. "Why do you want to hear about Skylighters? We aren't part of any fights."

The man with the crutch straightened up and turned away from them. "Trading the knowledge is up to you." He hobbled slowly out of the circle of light, back the way he came. "You might not have noticed, but the sky's gettin' to be a crowded place. Way I see it, it won't just be a fight. I'm getting ready for a war."

22

ERIN

Samra sat on the bow of the *Restless Fury*, and waited for her doom. When she died, they wouldn't be able to say she shirked her duty. They wouldn't say she lacked courage, but they might mention that she wasn't even glowing when she went, and that would certainly raise a few eyebrows.

It's hard to fend off a nightbeast in the dark.

She balled her fists and gritted her teeth, but to no avail. The more Samra attempted to light herself up, the dimmer she got. The most she had managed so far was an eerie flicker from her shins for a few seconds. Hardly an intimidating display.

Perhaps when people told the story of her demise, they'd wonder why she chose to stay dark. Maybe they would think she was protesting something noble. She was fond of a good protest, but only her parents or Kip would be able to remember that. If she was going to die for a cause, she should have mentioned it to someone on the ship before now.

She observed the silent and otherwise empty deck. These airmen weren't likely to mourn her mysteriously noble death without a good morality tale behind it. Samra knew a thing or two about how to tell a story, and nobody ever wanted to listen to a tragic death where the heroine got eaten for no reason.

What was wrong? Her glow had worked once. Why not now?

The *Restless Fury* was sailing on a southeasterly breeze along the outer edge of the Sky Forest. In the dark, the expanse of vegetation resembled a storm cloud. Lights flashed from the interior spaces and lit up the foliage, outlining various trees and casting others into deeper shadow.

The sky overhead flickered as well. Drifting kelp towers blinked past one another in the dark or vanished beyond columns of real cloud, otherwise invisible in the sky. There were hardly any stars tonight. The Heights were masked by a flat, formless overcast.

Danger weather.

Samra had finally gotten her wish. For as long as she could remember, she'd wanted excitement. She'd wanted thrilling action and feats of courage. She wanted some magic to take her away from the tedium of life in the patch. Now that her wish had come true, it felt different.

She was scared.

She fished in her pocket and found a hunk of obsidian she'd recovered from her tendril pocket before Cirra Sola was jettisoned. The glassy black stone had been a gift from Kipling. Registered, weighed, and legally obtained—as all of Kipling's gifts came—the rock was a useless trinket to most, but in their imagined adventures it had taken on myriad roles. It was the eye of a seven-tentacled sea monster. It was the frozen heart of a cursed king. It was a talisman of untouchable virtue, or sometimes the secret source of all evil. In their imaginations it was priceless. Jewel. Artifact. Memory.

Samra looked up at the eastern sky and wondered what Kip was doing now. Were he and Rufus in the hideout searching the sky for her return? She supposed she'd never know.

A school of iridescent kettle rays swam beneath the clouds overhead, drifting lazily through the kelp towers. It was safer up there.

Somewhere near the forest edge, claws scraped at bark and a long, piercing howl shattered the night. Shadow raptor. Or maybe a dreadwing.

Despite the low altitude, Samra shivered. Death would come soon.

"I think you've proved your point."

Samra turned and found Captain Savage at the door to the

cockpit. She was holding it open and leaving room to pass.

"You won't actually be a whole lot of use to us dead. Come on inside."

"But I'm supposed to guard the ship from nightbeasts," Samra replied. "The crew said so."

"And it's a wonder we've lasted so many nights really, without you here to save us," Captain Savage said. "I suppose we'll have to suffer through one more."

Samra got up and moved toward the captain. In the soft glow from the cockpit lights, she looked younger. Not so much older than Samra really. Seven or eight years? It made Samra wonder what it must be like to be captain of a skyship. To fly wherever you felt like and have people do whatever you commanded. Could there be a better freedom?

The captain let Samra inside and slid the door closed behind her.

"Take a seat."

Samra eyed the few options for seating in the cockpit. There was a pilot's seat, a navigator's position, and the raised captain's chair. The captain was still watching her so she pulled her eyes from the chair and settled into the navigator's position. The seat was cushioned and soft and had a little desk attached to one side that wrapped around the front. The desk had pockets built into it with various instruments of measurement sticking out. There were pencils, too, and a small compass to match the big one that rode at the front of the cockpit. Samra noted the bundles of charts racked alongside the seat. She turned her attention back to the captain.

"I bet you've never been aboard a skyship before, have you?" the captain asked. She stood next to the pilot's position and toyed with the gust locks on the controls. Samra eyed the wheel.

"I got to sit in the *Express* once. Enzo let me."

"Enzo, huh? He's someone friendly with your people?" She leaned on the back of the pilot's seat. "What's he do?"

The captain didn't have the scowl on her face she'd maintained on deck with her brother. Here, without the rest of the crew around, she looked at ease. She no longer carried the whip and her eyes were actually friendly.

"He brought us messages," Samra replied. "And candy."

"Sounds like a nice guy. Why did your people choose him to carry their messages?"

"I don't know. He always has. Every time we come to the valley."

"Awfully nice of him. I suppose your people have some sort of deal worked out. Maybe they give him something in return?"

"I don't know."

"He doesn't get something from your people? Maybe some of those big pods to help him lift his ship?"

Samra was noticing a trend in the captain's line of questioning. She crossed her arms and turned toward the front window, but watched the captain out of the corner of her eye. The captain studied her quietly for a moment, then reached down and flipped one of the latches on the controls. "I'll bet he never let you fly his ship, did he?"

Samra couldn't help but look.

"Go ahead." The captain gestured toward the pilot seat. "Give it a try."

Samra eyed her cautiously, but then slid across to the pilot seat. She settled into the cushioned chair and her fingers found their places on the sides of the control wheel.

"These are the power levers," the captain explained, pointing to a pair of handles to her right. "Push those forward and it will give the engines a kick. Go ahead, you won't hurt anything."

Samra rested a hand on the twin levers and gave them a gentle push. Overhead, the big shark engines growled. The nose of the ship tipped forward slightly as the engines ducted more air through the nacelles and thrust it out the tails.

"Uh-huh, now pull back on the wheel a little to compensate for the dive," the captain said. She reached over Samra and rested a hand on hers, giving a slight pressure backward. Samra moved the wheel and the airship leveled out.

Samra smiled.

"There you go." The captain released her hand. "See? You're a natural."

Samra turned the wheel to the right and the nose yawed that direction.

"She's a bit of a dog in the slow turns," the captain said. "But if you give her a little more power, the tail fins get more effective."

Samra pushed the power levers and the ship surged forward.

"Here's a fun trick for you," the captain said. She leaned over and split the power lever inputs, pulling back on the right side while pushing the left farther forward. The ship kicked hard right and Samra was forced sideways in her chair. The captain reversed the inputs and the ship swung back the other way. Samra laughed.

"That'll wake the crew up," the captain said.

A moment later a rap came on the cockpit door and then it popped open. Sunburn stuck his head in and surveyed the situation. "Everything all right up here, captain?"

Captain Savage leaned back in her chair. "Everything's under control, Sunburn. No need to worry. Just giving our new airman a flying lesson."

"Aye, Captain. Understood."

"Everything all right back there?"

"Oh, aye, Captain. Cogs came a bit unstowed from his hammock, but we're all fine."

"Good."

"Also Wallace did mention that the state of his dinner is a bit precarious at the moment. Seems that might come unstowed, too, if you take my meaning."

"Tell Wallace to buck up," the captain replied. "Can't have him wasting good rations."

"Aye, Captain. I'll pass that along." Sunburn gave Samra a wink and closed the door.

Captain Savage looked out the front window, then turned and smiled at Samra. "Want to do it again?"

Samra grinned back.

The captain showed her how to repeat the maneuver, and as the ship oscillated back and forth, it drew a cacophony of fresh swearing from beyond the bulkhead.

Samra and the captain laughed.

Once the ship settled, Captain Savage trimmed the controls for straight and level again. "I suspect that's enough for the moment. Don't want the whole ship smelling like Wallace tomorrow."

The captain slumped in the navigator's chair and let Samra manage the controls. Samra peered out the window and hoped there wasn't anything ahead to run into.

"I like it best up here at night," the captain commented. "Peaceful."

Samra glanced back at the captain's chair, then over at the lounging form of the young woman next to her. She seemed very different than when she'd first encountered her on deck. "Isn't that other woman usually the pilot? The one I saw earlier?"

"Landy? Yeah. When I want her to be. My ship, my rules." The captain stretched a leg over the navigator's desk. "But with Eckers dead, I need another back-up pilot. Who knows, maybe I'll switch it up and make the back-up into chief pilot one of these days. Those are the perks of being in charge."

Samra grinned and took a tighter grip on the controls, imagining herself in the role. Samra Rose Coley: skyship pilot. She liked the sound of that.

"'Course everybody has to pay their dues and earn their promotions," Captain Savage added. "Nothing comes free in this life. Especially for us." She gestured back and forth between them.

"What do you mean?"

"You're kidding, right?" the captain asked. "Us. Women. Maybe it's different where you come from, but down here a woman has to work twice as hard to get the recognition she deserves. At least on most ships."

"What about on yours?"

"Well, like I said—my ship, my rules."

"What about on your brother's ship?"

The captain frowned. "Eric. Yeah. Let's just say he's the reason I need my own ship. And exactly my point. My father has a fleet of ships. I'm the oldest, but who did he pick to command his flagship? Eric, my baby brother." The captain stared out the window. "I guess he connects better to my father's brand of crazy."

The captain lapsed into silence as Samra steered them through the dark.

Samra glanced over twice before finally opening her mouth. "My dad wanted to move us away from the Mother so he could be a chief of his own globe. I think he wanted it more than anything."

"Chief? Would that make you some sort of princess?"

"No. It just means I'd be stuck playing with Willis Mintz like a little kid. He's my neighbor Khloe's little brother." She frowned. "And it means someday they'd probably want me to marry him."

"Ah. I see." The captain pointed toward the moonlit horizon. "Little more to the left. We want to follow that tree line south."

Samra concentrated on making the correction.

Captain Savage picked up one of the charts next to her. It was only partially illustrated. The navigator had been sketching in new details, but most of the sheet was still blank. "I guess it's a good thing you ended up with us then. Out here in the wilds, we don't have to care what our parents say. As an airship pilot you could spend time with whomever you please. Do a good job, you'd even get paid. Maybe buy your own ship someday like I am."

"It's not yours yet?"

"Nearly," the captain replied. "We get back to port, I'll sell this load to the pod dealers and have enough to provision the ship for one more run. Should be enough to pay the crew, too. One more good load and I'll be able to pay off the loan."

Samra brushed her fingertips across the power levers. She tried to imagine what Kip and Rufus would say if they found out she'd gotten to be an airship pilot. Maybe when she got back to the patch, she could get them positions too, and they'd go off and have grand adventures together.

But that was impossible.

The raiders had attacked the patch. Joining them would be traitorous, wouldn't it?

She studied the captain. "You said my people attacked you first, but I don't believe you."

Captain Savage nodded. "Yeah. I didn't think you did." She leaned over and looked Samra in the eye. "Listen, I'm not going to try to con you, okay? We usually go after anything that floats up here and sometimes that involves taking things from other people. We weren't out to take your house specifically, or attack your people. We didn't know anyone was onboard that pod of yours when we took it, but even if we did, it wouldn't have mattered much. We needed the pods. I know that might make us seem like your enemy," the captain continued. "But it wasn't personal. It's just life."

Samra swallowed once and looked back out the window.

"If it makes any difference, that was before I knew what your people were really like," Captain Savage said. "Where I come from, people consider sky folk to be another variety of wild animals. I didn't know we'd be attacking someone like you. That's the truth."

"And now that you know?" Samra asked.

"Well, now I know you are something different. And we were wrong," Captain Savage said. "And if there's a way to work something out with your people—some way we could trade for those globes without stealing them, then I think that would be better for everybody. Nobody should need to get hurt."

"Why do your people want them? Don't you already have

enough to fly with?" Samra asked.

"Sure. We can keep the fleet afloat easy enough with the little pods we find floating around, especially up here in the north, but down in the Thunderlands, pickings are getting slim. They've harvested most of the decent pods already, and people always need more."

"Why?"

"To keep their homes from falling down some ghastly hole, mostly. You sky people have it easy. You float around all day and never have to worry about setting your foot on the wrong patch of ground or disappearing into a crevice. Sinkholes are so bad in some places, you can fall for a thousand feet before you finally go splat. Down south we've got underground rivers and shifting sand lakes. They swallow up whole villages while people are asleep in their beds. Not a fun way to wake up."

Samra had seen sinkholes from the patch. In the east, there were some that were miles wide with glittering lakes at the bottom. From the Heights, she'd always thought they were pretty. She'd seen the shifting sand lakes, too, but hadn't thought much about what it would be like to live near one.

"Why don't you just move?" Samra asked. "Go somewhere where they don't have sinkholes. People in Womble live on the ground and their town hasn't been swallowed up."

"Trust me, I've thought about it. Plenty of folks down south wouldn't mind finding a stable mountain for a change. But my father won't leave the desert," Captain Savage replied. "So his people won't either. He's looking for something out there, and he's not going to leave till he finds it." She swung her leg back down from the desk and rested both feet on the floor. "So that means we still need lift pods. And the bigger the better."

She leaned over and rested her elbows on her knees, leveling her stare at Samra. "If you can help me get in good with this patch of yours, I could make it worth your while. You could be the key to a whole new era of trade. Those big globes of yours are worth a lot of money where I come from. You play your cards right, work with me a little on this, you might even end up rich."

Samra searched the captain's face. "I don't want to do anything to hurt the patch. I have friends there. My parents live there." The thought of her father's angry glare came back to her, as he stood embarrassed on the stage. Then she remembered Kaleb and the knife she had threatened him with. Maybe the high council wouldn't even let her back on the patch at all. Maybe they'd get one look at her aboard the raider ship and banish her forever. Would she even be allowed back?

"You want to see your friends and family. But you want your freedom, too. I can read it on your face." Captain Savage leaned closer. "It's one thing to be loyal, but you don't want to be just a pawn in someone else's chess game."

"What's a pawn?"

"It's someone always getting sacrificed for the greater good, and never getting any choice in the matter. It's an old game with old rules. The piece you want to be is the queen. The queen does what she wants and controls the game."

"Are you a queen?" Samra asked.

The captain brushed a strand of hair away from her face and let her gaze drift out the front window. "Not yet."

At that moment a dark mass swooped down from above and alighted on the prow. The creature had wide, flapping bat wings but its body was much closer to that of a bird. Its beaked head swung from side to side as it stretched its wings and searched the bow. Its taloned feet scraped the deck and it waddled its way toward the glass of the cockpit.

Captain Savage stood and calmly fastened the locks back onto the controls. "Go to bed, Samra Coley. We'll talk again later. You're relieved of duty for the night." Samra glanced out the window at the creature pacing the bow.

"I don't have to . . ."

"This one I can handle," the captain replied.

Samra moved to the door, and by the time she got there, the captain had picked up her whip and opened the hatch to the bow walk. Samra stood in the interior doorway and watched the captain work her way around the front of the ship.

The nightbeast turned and faced the new threat, cawing hungrily in her direction. The beast took two steps forward and was partway to the third when the whip moved. It was almost too fast for Samra to see. The striped lash ripped away fur from the creature's body and it shuddered. The beast recoiled a step, studied its adversary, and extended one wing. The whip flashed again and this time the creature made up its mind, extending its other wing and spinning around before launching itself into the black.

Samra waited for the captain to turn around, but she didn't. She took a few more steps instead and took up the position the beast had vacated. The same position Samra herself had previously occupied, staring at the horizon.

Samra finally conceded her need for sleep and trudged back through the ship to her hammock in the hold. The room was stuffy with hot breath and snoring. It took her a while to get comfortable in her hammock, strung up in the position last belonging to the dead man whose spot she'd taken. As she drifted off to sleep, she wondered if the captain was still outside, one woman against the elements. She assumed that she'd come back in by now, but part of her could see her in her imagination, still straddling the bow and facing off against the night.

Samra thought that whatever lay ahead, the night would lose.

23

CHANE THE KNOWER

Atlas couldn't sleep. He knew he ought to, but his mind wouldn't let him. He blamed it on the smell.

The grove of the tree people was musty and dank. The canopy was a blanket, smothering the air and pressing it down on them. He'd spotted several worms the size of his finger in the floor of dead moss and desiccated leaves. To make matters worse, there was a hole. It was only five inches in diameter and at least three feet away from where he was lying, but he'd made the mistake of noticing it. He'd made a further mistake by looking down it.

They were not on the ground. They weren't even close. There were things glowing in the night down that deep dark hole that were either very small or very far away. He knew which one.

This wasn't how it was supposed to be.

Atlas didn't mind heights. At least he didn't mind them when he was flying above them. But he ought to be happily ensconced in the *Sun Dragon*, sleeping in the pilot seat, secure in the comfort of the airship's lift bags. He ought to be safe in the cockpit with Fledge for company, his harpoons for protection, and the glow of his lanterns for cheer.

He didn't know where the cliff fox was now. He didn't even know where the *Sun Dragon* was. This was all wrong.

The sky boy was sleeping. Kip.

Atlas studied the huddled figure of the Skylighter curled against the base of one of the trees. His skin glowed, ever so faintly, as he breathed. Something inside the boy was reacting to the dense air here, even as he slept. It left beads of moisture on his forehead. He was hot.

Atlas pulled his jacket a little tighter around himself and wondered how that could be possible. If anything, the damp and dank of this grove seemed to be robbing him of all his warmth. The few tree people he could make out in the dim light didn't seem concerned with the damp either. Perhaps their hairy coats kept them warm and insulated enough in the night. Atlas couldn't imagine what it would be like to live this way. Especially to choose it.

He let his eyes wander to the area where he had last seen the knower. The old man had limped his way back to a grotto at the far side of the grove. It was treacherous footing, but the man had managed it. At least he hadn't fallen through the floor.

Beyond the distant branches, light flickered against a backdrop of vines. A fire? Perhaps the old man was cooking something.

Tree people apparently didn't believe in dinnertime. While the creatures had variously disappeared into the canopy and come back munching fruits or other edibles they'd found, no one had offered anything to Atlas. Every man or woman for themselves, it seemed.

Atlas was no longer bound, but he still felt like a prisoner. Every time he shifted in place or rolled over, it was with eyes on his back. Still, the lure of the fire was strong, and he felt it was worth investigating.

He carefully got to his feet. Somewhere in the darkness to his left, a creature grunted. He waited, but when nothing else came of it, he took a few cautious steps. He crossed the grove slowly, casually. He wasn't running anywhere. Not trying to escape.

He scanned the canopy, but a few more grunts were his only opposition. The creatures in the trees let him continue.

Atlas glanced back to where Kipling was sleeping. The Skylighter hadn't taken the invitation to trade with the knower yet. Despite Atlas's encouragement, he seemed reluctant to share any information about his patch. It was an obvious choice as far as Atlas was concerned. Trade some general knowledge on Skylighter life for some actually useful and needed information about his ship and their route? The deal couldn't get any better than that. Finding the *Sun Dragon* was paramount. Every moment they wasted here, Enzo and his captors were getting farther away. When the sun came up, they'd need to be in pursuit.

If that meant letting this knower learn what he needed about Skylighter life, then Atlas could help with that. He knew plenty from what Enzo had told him. He'd simply have to take matters into his own hands.

Atlas crept up to the tree that the knower had turned into a sort of lean-to shack. The front face of the abode was a latticework of branches woven together and covered with wide, slick leaves. The top arched inward and connected to the trunk of the air tree. From this makeshift roof a rolled-up bit of metal protruded at an angle and acted as a chimney. Smoke and the occasional spark drifted out the top and wafted lazily into the air, only to settle back down around the tree in a hazy cloud. The entire situation seemed to Atlas like a disaster waiting to happen, but the smell issuing from the chimney along with the smoke made him think that perhaps the risk was worth it.

"Come on in. I've got plenty to spare."

The voice came from the gap at the side of the lean-to. Atlas had thought himself stealthy as he approached, but apparently his presence was obvious enough. He ducked his head and peered into the side of the knower's space. The man was seated cross-legged on a cushion, facing a wide, shallow metal bowl. Inside the bowl a little fire was burning, and above the fire a plucked bird was roasting on a spit.

"Tree grouse," the man said. "With a bit of herb seasoning and sea salt. It'd be better with a coat of pepper sauce, but I'm all out. But it beats chewing roots and berries like the tree folk. I'll bet you're hungry."

Atlas had been hungry before, but in the close proximity of this new delicacy, he felt famished.

"Sit down before you fall down," the man said, and tossed Atlas a cushion from the little pile of belongings on the far side of the lean-to. In the corner, the man had organized the remainder of his goods. There was a tall travel pack, some saddlebags, and a pile of miscellaneous sacks and boxes. The boxes were small, wooden units, tied in bundles and neatly stacked together.

One of the boxes lay open at the man's feet, empty with the exception of a few remaining bits of straw. The straw from the box appeared to have ended up as kindling for the fire, and the primary content of the box was now in the man's hand—a fat, stumpy glass bottle, half-full of brown liquid. The man corked the bottle and tucked it away behind him as Atlas settled onto the floor. "Thought you might drop by."

Atlas watched the man for a moment, then let his eyes drift back to the bird on the spit.

"I failed to get your name, son. Afraid our introduction lacked a bit when it came to pleasantries. What do they call you?"

"My name's Atlas."

"Ah. Holder of the sky, are you?"

Atlas shrugged.

The man ran a hand through his beard and scratched at his chin. "Well, maybe they don't teach the Old World tales where you come from. Back there, Atlas was one of the Titans. A god condemned to hold up the heavens and keep them from touching the ground. Do they still teach you about the place we came from? The world before this one?"

"My grandfather told me no one really remembers the Old World. He says we can learn about it in school, but no one has ever been there. He says it's long gone now."

"Gone? Hmm. I think it's still out there. Far away maybe. Hard to get to. But there's folk who think it can be done. Hard to say." The knower leaned forward and prodded the roasting bird with a knife. "Just about ready now. Here, grab yourself a piece." The man pulled at the bird's leg and gingerly pried it free with the help of the knife. "Use one o' them leaves there."

Atlas fumbled through a pile of the wide, glossy leaves stacked near the wall and folded one into a dish to hold the grouse leg. The man dropped the hot leg onto the leaf, then stuck his fingers into his mouth to cool them off. He sucked on them a moment, then shook them. "Nothing fancy around here, but it gets the job done."

Atlas's mouth was watering, but he waited for the man to pry his own piece of bird loose.

"What's your name?" he asked. "Do you have an Old World name, too?"

"Can't rightly say," the man replied. "My name's Chane. Don't know how I came by it. Suspect I had a daddy who knew at some point, but he was long gone by the time I could ask him." He blew on the piece of meat at the end of his knife and took a tentative bite. He spoke again as he chewed. "And I can't say it doesn't pain me a bit, the not knowing. Seeing as I'm in the profession of knowing things and all. But I suppose there are some mysteries we're just meant to carry around with us."

Atlas knew he was at risk of burning his tongue but he couldn't hold back any longer. He held the bird leg up to his mouth and took a bite. It was juicy on the inside and browned around the edges, just how his aunt Amelia cooked fowl back home.

As he chewed, he could sense the knower sizing him up.

"So you're the pilot, huh? You flying around all on your own? How'd you manage that?"

Atlas angled more of the grouse into his mouth. "It's not hard," he mumbled. "My grandpa taught me. He's the best pilot there ever was."

Chane leaned back. "Is that so? Well, I'm surprised I haven't heard of him. Or maybe I have. What's his name?"

"Enzo Mooreside." Atlas licked his fingers. "He builds the best airships, too. Fast ones."

"And he does this all the way up in the mountains?" Chane asked. "Where does he get the fuel, being so far north? The way I hear it, all the fuel is either out in the desert or down in the Thunderlands."

"We don't need fuel. We have his air motors."

"Air motors?" The man leaned forward. "What's an air motor?"

Atlas paused in his consumption of the grouse leg. "You said you'd tell us where my ship is."

"Said I'd trade that for information on the sky peoples."

"You've been asking lots of questions, and I've been giving answers. Isn't that worth something?"

"Seems you were just chatting with me freely. Can't fault me for taking what was offered. Besides, you're getting a bit of reward right now." He gestured toward the remains of the grouse leg in Atlas's hands. "I'd say a bit of supper's worth something."

"Can't fault me for taking what was offered," Atlas replied.

Chane grinned. "Quick study. I like that. You have a bit of the trading arts in you, son. Maybe you've found yourself a future profession."

"I already have one," Atlas replied.

Chane nodded. "Right. I guess you did mention a certain aircraft. Suspect you're powerful keen on getting back to it." He tossed the bone from the grouse out the opening of the lean-to, and it disappeared into the darkness. He began carving off another piece. "So how about you and I make a trade then. You tell me what you know about this flying machine of yours. And a bit of what your granddad uses it for. Maybe tell me how he gets in so good with the sky folk. And then I promise to have these tree folk take you back to your ship at first light. I'll even tell you the best way to get to where you're going."

"You don't even know where we're going," Atlas said.

"I bet I can figure it out," Chane replied. "Or you can tell me. Besides, there's really only one way on through this forest. At least if you plan to take that ship with you." He extended a hand. "Do we have ourselves a trade?"

Atlas hesitated only a moment, then reached out and clasped the man's hand. "But you have tell me the way out first."

Chane let out a laugh. "You want to know which path to take before you even have your ship back? I appreciate your enthusiasm. Since you have to wait till morning for my assistance to be of much help, I suppose it's only fair for me to go first." He reached into his pile of belongings and came up with a small towel that he used to wipe his hands. Once they were clean he extended a hand, pointed his index finger, then aimed at the floor. "Your way out is down."

"Down?"

"Something most folk don't know. The Sky Forest is so thick at the edges that it touches the ground. Gets plenty of sun out there. But here in the wild bits, trees get so dense you'd never find a way through. Not up top. But not much sun makes it through either. Means all the old low trees can't compete. They died off years ago. You sink down past the forest floor, you'll find it's hollowed out. What's growing in the middle of this forest is growing high. Ground might be treacherous down there, but in an airship? Well, I'd say you could scoot right through underneath."

"But if it's rimmed at all the edges, how am I supposed to get back out?" Atlas asked.

"Smart question." Chane tapped his nose. "But there's where things get interesting for you. You can follow the river. Trees grew up and over it in some parts, but down low you should be able to find it. Follow it south."

"We aren't going south. We're headed east."

"Not meaning to tell you your business, but whatever it is you're after, you won't be finding it in the east. Nothing gets through that way. Whoever you're after, they either tried to smash their way through like you did and failed, or they wised up from the get-go and turned. If they didn't go back the way you came, then they went south."

"What's down that way?"

"For an airship? Everything. Civilization. Fuel. Work. Whatever's worth doing these days is down in Smoketown and Port Savage. Your people will head that way. Foolish not to. Smart move would have been to follow the edge of the forest south to the coast, then follow that around till you reached the bottom of the forest, but since you're this far in anyway, you should go under. River will lead you straight to it."

Atlas ruminated on the idea, rearranging his thoughts around it. "South. You're sure?"

"Sure as the sun rises." The man rubbed his knuckles and shifted a little closer to the fire. "Now a deal is a deal. Seems your granddaddy had quite a business going up in those mountains. Time to tell me all you can about his dealings with the sky people."

24

THE RIVER

Kipling woke damp with sweat.

His dreams had been strange—a menagerie of terrors stalking him in his sleep. Some he wasn't convinced were dreams at all. There had been shrieks in the night, and shouts and grunts from the Horokim. No nightbeasts had penetrated the confines of the grove, but evidence of action during the night was now littering the floor of the domed enclosure. Black and gray tufts of feathers clung to bits of moss or waved apathetically in the feeble morning breeze. There was a broken spear near one of the tree trunks. The shaft was speckled with dark stains.

Kipling's mouth was dry. His stomach was rumbling as well, but it was his thirst he was most intent on resolving. It was only after a few minutes of searching the vine pods near his sleeping place for any type of drinkable fluids that he realized what was different this morning.

Atlas was gone.

Kipling scanned the dingy grove but only saw a few of the older tree folk up in the branches and a handful of furry children scampering about the grove floor. How long had he been asleep?

The lack of direct sunlight was addling his sense of time. In the patch, he nearly always rose with the sun. Here the sun was a distant and vague presence. Was it later than he thought?

The idea suddenly occurred to him that Atlas could have left him here. Had he escaped during the night? Perhaps he'd cut his losses and gone off to try to find the airship on his own. Kipling dashed into the center of the grove and spun around. "Atlas!" He cupped his hands and tried again. "Atlas!"

All he got was mute stares from the children.

Before he could do anything else, a whooping shout went up from the canopy. A quartet of Horokim leapt through the boughs overhead, moving north. Kipling hesitated only a moment, then followed, keeping his eyes on the troop.

He pried his way through some boughs at the far side of the grove, then leapt into the trees beyond, doing his best to keep up with the raucous group overhead. They led him to a diagonal shaft of light that was piercing the gloom, and as he stepped into the warm morning glow, he looked up to find another cheery sight above him. The *Sun Dragon* was descending the beam of sunlight, fins spread wide and gleaming with a halo of morning dew.

The airship sank to the level of the tree folk and they whooped some more. This time no one brandished weapons. Kipling spotted the knower in the front seat while Atlas steered from the cockpit. He leaned his head over the cockpit rail and waved. Kipling lifted a hand and returned the gesture.

"There's our man," the knower declared. He let his eyes rest on Kipling and smiled.

Kipling moved back as the *Sun Dragon* settled into the boughs. Atlas threw out a line. "Tie that off!"

Kipling secured the line to the trunk of an air tree and waited as Atlas and the knower climbed out of their seats. The old man was clutching his overcoat close as he stepped over the rail, then accepted a hand from Atlas as he stepped onto the bough. One of the tree people was waiting nearby with his crutch and sprang forward to deliver it when the knower glanced her way. The woman bore a strong resemblance to the little girl who had spoken to them in the grove.

"There you have it. Safe and sound," the knower said. "I'm true to my word, you can be sure of that."

Atlas shook the man's hand and grinned, then turned to Kipling.

"Chane says the airships went south and he told us how to get there. We're going under the forest."

"Under?" Kipling said.

Chane stepped past him and found surer footing on the twisted boughs of the air tree. "You stick to the river, you'll find your way. The people you're looking for will be south. Mark my words."

"Are you going south, too?" Kipling asked.

"Me? No. Not no more. I was headed north, up into the mountains. Heard rumor there might be more knowledge traders up there. The old relics have been scattered but I hoped there were still a few in the north." He turned toward Atlas. "Suspect you lot must have had a knower up in your range that taught you what's what. Someone certainly unlocked some knowledge to get you this bit of machinery. Who was your relic keeper?"

Atlas frowned. "My teacher, Mr. Merritt, was in charge of our relic, but my aunt says the raiders took it when they came. Mr. Merritt's dead now."

"Raiders?" Chane asked. "Not surprised. Someone should have gotten word up into the mountains before now. I might have gotten there in time myself if it hadn't been for this leg. Raiders been on the move all year. Lord Savage and his Air Corps have been snatching up relics and keys anywhere they find them and killing the knowers, too. The Old World relics aren't safe in the open anymore. Knowers with any sense are going into hiding."

"Why do the raiders want these relics?" Kipling asked. "Don't they have any of their own?"

"That's the problem," Chane replied. "They got most of them in the south already and they'd like to have the rest. Rumor is that Lord Savage keeps all the citizens of Smoketown under his thumb by hording all the relic keys to himself. Anybody wants to know anything useful, they have to pay him for it. The time of free trading knowledge is coming to an end. If the Port Savage raiders have their way, the relics will all get claimed and the free knowers will get snatched up or killed. Only knowledge to be had will be in the south and only for folk willing to be governed by their rules. Not safe for the likes of me down there anymore. I know too much."

"Why do you need these relics?" Kipling asked. "Can't you just learn in school?"

"Hard to find out what to learn, if you don't know what you don't know," Chane replied. "Life experience is a good teacher in its own way, but a relic is a shortcut. More knowledge inside one of those than any teacher that ever lived."

"Do you have a relic?" Atlas asked. "Like Mr. Merritt did?"

"Used to be I did," Chane replied. "And I got pretty far with it, too. Learned from it for years. But in the end the ground got its way. Village I was teaching in got swallowed up one day and took the relic with it. Been wandering on my own ever since. Thought I might find more of the free relics up north, maybe get in good with someone who'd opened one. I'd go back to being an apprentice even. Get some new knowledge that way. Getting scarce now though. Who was the learner in your village?"

"Everybody learned in my village," Atlas said.

"Sure, but somebody must have been the apprentice to your knower," Chane replied. "That's how these relics do it. They teach you by having you teach someone else. That way someone can always open the relic and carry on where the first knower left off."

He pulled a cord around his neck and removed an object from under his shirt. It was a metallic triangle with rounded corners and hole through the center. The edges had ridges carved into them. They reminded Kipling of the runes carved into his warhook.

Chane dangled the pendant in front of Atlas. "You ever see this symbol before? Or something like it? Your teacher must have had one. Somebody else in your village have one? Maybe someone younger who might have been training to be a knower?"

Atlas was staring hard at the symbol. "Nobody younger, but my grandpa has one of those. He wears it under his shirt. Isn't metal though. It's stone. Says it's his lucky rock."

"How old is your grandfather?" Chane asked.

"I don't know. Old as you maybe?"

Chane frowned. "And this Mr. Merritt, was he your grandpa's age or older?"

"Mr. Merritt was young. Well, younger anyway. I think he was in school with my aunt."

"Ah." Chane replied. "So your grandfather had already passed the relic on. Not many do that. Most keep it till they die, but I've heard of exceptions."

Kipling was losing interest in the conversation. For one, he didn't know much about relics. Secondly, his mouth was so dry he was having trouble thinking about anything else except getting a drink. Something about the density of the air down here was making it hard to concentrate on the words Atlas and Chane were speaking. Was Samra having this trouble, too? What must she be feeling like right now?

"If the raiders have your grandfather, then I bet they won't be looking to let him go," the knower continued. "And if he didn't pass his relic key on yet, then there won't be any more knowledge trading going on in your parts. Your folk will have to get on best they can without Old World help. I may as well stay on here a while in that case."

"You're going to live with these tree people?" Atlas asked.

"It's not so bad," Chane replied. "They're so starved for knowledge they treat me like a king. All they want to do is compete with the rest of the world. Lots of change going on outside the forest and it's passing them by. But I don't know how much hope they have.

"The older folk don't have much capacity for language, but these young ones do all right." He flashed the sign for 'good morning' toward the trees and Kipling spotted the little girl from the night before now standing near her mother. The girl signed back and smiled.

"You said the south is dangerous," Kipling said. "Is it dangerous for Skylighters, too?"

"Dangerous for anyone not flying a raider flag."

"Then how do we get there?" Kipling asked.

"If you're asking how to stay safe, then I don't know what to tell you. Nothing about what you're doing is safe and I'd be a liar to say it was. Just seems to me that you wanted to know the way to find your people. If that's what you really want, then you head south. You want to stay safe, then I suspect you ought to turn around now while you still can."

Kipling looked to Atlas and found the boy staring back. He had his jacket on and was wearing his leather pilot's gloves. He already had one foot on the lower fin of the *Sun Dragon*. "I need my weapon back," Kipling said. "It's important."

The knower signed to the little girl and she shook her head. He signed something else that looked like 'Find him' and she nodded, then disappeared into the trees. It was only a matter of a minute before the girl returned. She stepped aside for the tree man who followed carrying Kipling's warhook. The tether was tangled and the haft was dirty, but otherwise the weapon looked all right.

"Fancy bit of handiwork there. Looks like it has some history." Chane crossed his arms. "How'd a half-pint like yourself come by a weapon like that?"

Kipling ignored the question and stepped over to the tree man holding the warhook. He held out his hand. Chane nodded and the tree man let out a grunt. He then set the weapon back in Kipling's palm.

Chane leveled a stare at Kipling. "Now, he only did that because I told him to, and lately what I say goes around here. So you might consider this a favor . . ."

"Thank you," Kipling replied, looping the tether of the handle and hanging the warhook across his back.

" . . . a favor you might return some time in future, should the need arise," Chane added.

Kipling eyed the man skeptically. "What kind of favor would you want?"

"Hard to say," Chane replied. "The future's a surprising place. Even I don't know what will happen. I just know it's useful to have allies. And it's more useful when those allies owe you a favor."

"Where I come from, we just have friends," Kipling said.

Chane extended his crutch and shifted his weight. "I'll stick with allies. Too many friends will get you killed." He shuffled toward the heavier foliage. "You flyboys have a good adventure down south, now. If we're all very lucky, maybe we'll meet again." He gave a salute with his free hand, and with that he disappeared back into the forest.

Kipling turned back to Atlas. "I guess you must owe him a favor now, too."

"I don't think I do," Atlas replied. "He only wanted to hear about the village and the festival from me. And about the *Sun Dragon* of course. Oh, and he wanted to know what I knew about Skylighters."

"And you told him?"

"Why not? I got us the ship back, didn't I? You'd rather try walking to find your friend?"

Kipling frowned, but stayed silent. He climbed back aboard the *Sun Dragon*. Atlas untied the tether line, then leapt aboard and slid into the cockpit as the ship drifted away from the tree.

Kipling blinked as the *Sun Dragon* passed into the beam of sunlight streaming down through the canopy. Instead of cheering him, the heat only worsened the sense of unease in his stomach.

"Do you have any water?" He shifted in his seat and lifted the lid on one of the cargo compartments.

"In the other one," Atlas replied. "There's a canteen under the breathing cylinder."

Kipling lifted the lid on the second compartment and found the canteen — relieved to find it full. He uncorked the canteen and took a satisfying gulp. His body welcomed the water eagerly, and before he knew it, he had consumed nearly half the container. He forced himself to stop so that he could savor the rest.

The *Sun Dragon* continued to sink. They were in the middle of a spiraling turn to avoid the wall of foliage ahead of them, when a familiar furry creature came flapping down from above.

"Fledge!" Atlas put a hand out and the cliff fox nipped at it as he glided by. The animal squeaked once as it turned above them, then dipped below the level of the *Sun Dragon* to lead the way into the undergrowth. "I knew he'd come back," Atlas said. "He knows we're going the right way."

The airship slipped out of the beam of sunlight and sank lower, continuing its spiral down into the waiting mouth of the forest. As the light faded, Kipling tried to share his companion's optimism.

Atlas leveled the ship temporarily when they heard the sound of the river, but they had to sink still lower to find the way onward. In these deepest depths of the forest, the air trees had long ago given up on finding the light. The boughs were twisted and leafless, thin fingers stretching vainly upward from the black. Even the air seemed lifeless.

Only the sound of the water drew them on. Kipling lit up the bow of the ship as best he could in the dim hollow, and Atlas let the *Sun Dragon* sink till they were nearly touching the flowing current, carefully navigating the tunnel of ancient roots formed by the striving war of plant-life above them.

Kipling watched the needle of the mariner's compass bob and waver on the instrument panel then finally settle in one place. South. Beyond the cockpit, hardly anything could be made out in the murk. He realized that he'd never in all his life been this long without a true horizon. He tried not to let himself worry about that problem. According to the compass, they were headed the right direction. That would have to be enough.

Kipling unslung the warhook from behind his back and rested

it on his lap. The swishing of the tail fin and the working of the air motor kept him alert. If ever there was a place for danger, this looked like it. He had to be ready. He gripped the handle of the weapon tightly.

Atlas lit one of the lanterns and hung it from the side of the cockpit.

The path through the undergrowth ahead was a speckled labyrinth of deteriorating roots and petrified limbs.

The view was bleak, but this was no time to turn back.

Somewhere ahead, Samra was a captive. And somewhere ahead, Kipling would find her.

25

PORT SAVAGE

Sunburn was reading her book.

Samra had only rolled over in her hammock to try to get more comfortable, but as she did, she'd opened her eyes and found the fire-haired first mate perched in a hammock on the opposite side of the cabin, thumbing through the leaf-paper journal.

Samra must have held her breath for too long because when she exhaled, it came out loudly. Sunburn looked up and caught her watching him.

He kept his thumb between the pages as he spoke. "I didn't know you told stories, Little Weed."

There was nothing in his tone that was apologetic for being caught looking through her things. His intrusion might not even have been recent, as it appeared he had already flipped through most of the book.

"That was a gift," Samra said. "It's personal."

"We don't get books on board anymore," Sunburn commented, almost as if he hadn't heard her. "But I like them. When the inspectors come aboard in port, you should hide this."

"Why would I need to hide it?"

"Because of the law. No writing allowed in Port Savage

anymore. Except for conducting public business or if you belong to one of the high families."

Samra tried to process this. Reading books had never been a favorite hobby. She much preferred making up her own stories, but even so, she couldn't imagine the patch making a law to ban writing.

"Sounds like a stupid rule if you ask me."

The big man nodded thoughtfully. "I think so, too." He closed the journal gently and put it back with her other belongings. "Ready for breakfast?"

Samra cocked her head. "Breakfast?"

Sunburn led the way into the galley and held the door open for her. "Most of the crew was up early and ate what they could before shift, but nobody knew what it is that you sky people eat. We took our best guess and grabbed what we could." He gestured to the galley table that was now loaded with a variety of skyfruits and vegetables. Samra spotted cloud grass and bell clover and a good amount of chopped skyweed fronds. It all appeared to be unwashed and there were a fair number of plants included in the pile that she was pretty sure were poisonous, but having not eaten in a full day, she wasn't about to complain.

"Thanks. Looks delicious." Samra proceeded to the table and picked up a handful of tangleberries.

Sunburn beamed and bowed his way out of the doorway. "Glad we did okay. I'll see you up top."

The *Restless Fury* was clearing the coastline at the western edge of the Sky Forest when Samra climbed above the deck. The ship had caught a strong tailwind out of the northwest and was sailing over the rocky cliffs that barricaded the landscape from the brunt of the sea's assault.

High overhead, the forest edge strained for altitude but couldn't withstand the eastward thrust of the sea winds.

The sight of the sea raging against the rocks thrilled Samra, but as morning stretched on and there was still no sign of the forest ending, she began to worry about the patch. The farther south the ship traveled, the farther away the patch became. It would be beyond the forest to the east by now, perhaps traversing the Oralay Ridge. Were her parents somewhere up there searching the sky for her? Had they even been looking? Had they sent someone out searching for her? A guardian perhaps?

"Not a bad view, eh?" Samra turned to find Sunburn leaning against an engine strut behind her. His tempestuous red hair was mostly pulled back behind his head, but much of it was still flailing in the breeze, giving the impression of an inferno as much as a man. "I've seen these cliffs on a dozen trips, but it always feels like the first time."

"You've crossed the forest before?"

"In different parts. This is the northernmost end of the airway. If you look, you can see the guides." He pointed ahead to a spot on the cliffs where a rocky outcropping had been made even taller with piles of stone. A ragged red flag protruded from the top. "From there, we can follow the signals all the way to Port Savage."

Samra studied the signal tower, then turned back to Sunburn. "Are you happy to be going home?"

Sunburn smiled. "I'm already home." He spread his arms to the breeze. "Out here is where I live." He looked down at Samra. "A port is safer. But it hems you in. You can't fly in a port. And no one there is as free as we are."

Samra ran a hand along one of the stabilizing ropes, letting the rough bristles tickle her palm. "I don't think flying is what makes you free. We fly all the time in the patch, but people still tell you what to do."

"The captain tells me what to do here, too," Sunburn replied. "But rigging this ship is what I want to do anyway, so I'm still free."

The sliding door on the front cockpit opened and Landy, the pilot, stuck her head up above the deck. "Hey, Plant Girl! Captain says you're supposed to be my relief today. You want to learn this, or what?" She waved Samra over.

Samra let herself smile.

"You see?" Sunburn said. "Still free."

Samra climbed down into the cockpit and found the captain seated in the central chair. She was in all black today. Her jacket was slung over the back of her chair but the whip was once again curled at her waist. Despite the severe outfit, her greeting was pleasant. "Samra. Time for more training. Landy here is going to go over the rest of the controls. You'll be flying us down the airway."

"Me?" Samra balked at the sight of the cliffs looming closer out the window.

Landy guided her toward the pilot's seat. "Someone has to teach you how to fly this thing without tumbling the whole crew out of their hammocks at night."

"Oops," Samra said.

Behind Landy's back, the captain smirked.

"Remind me again why this is a good idea?" the navigator asked. He eyed Samra skeptically, then pulled a chart of the airway out of his basket and unrolled it on his desk. The navigator was a thin man with graying temples, though his lean, youthful face offset the gray and left him looking somewhat ageless. If he said he was anywhere from thirty to sixty, Samra would believe him.

"Samra is going to be the key to us making nice with the sky peoples," Captain Savage said. "And when we do that, you'll all be getting raises." Samra could feel the captain's eyes on her as she got situated. "And I think she's going to like it a whole lot better coming home to her people as a prestigious skyship pilot than as an accidental stowaway."

Samra let the image run through her head—her piloting the *Restless Fury* up to the globe patch. She could almost see the look of shock on Khloe Mintz's face. She definitely liked it.

"So we're prestigious now?" Landy joked. The pilot was in the loose-fitting shirt and rugged pants Samra had seen her in before, but today she had her hair tied up in a bandana, revealing even more piercings through her ears. The shining silver jewelry was adorned with turquoise stones that matched the stud in her nose. It looked painful, but Samra thought the beauty of it might make it worth it.

"Your life is certainly a lot more glamorous than when we were working on my father's ships," Captain Savage said. "Not that Eric wouldn't enjoy seeing us all back under my father's command." She rubbed a hand slowly over the armrest of her chair. "One more good load of those big pods. Then we'll all be free and clear."

Samra carefully pulled on the control wheel the way the captain had shown her the night before and felt a surge of delight as the ship rose. The way the airship climbed made it feel like her stomach was dropping. She liked it.

"Follow that channel," Landy said, pointing a finger along the cut that carved through the cliffs. "If this tailwind stays steady, we'll make good time."

Samra made the turn toward the cut and let the wind push her through. Before long the ship was rushing over the cliffs and into the gorges on the far side.

Landy hovered nearby initially, making suggestions and showing Samra tricks to keep the ship properly trimmed, but after a while, she gave Samra longer and longer sessions alone at the controls and even left the cockpit entirely. Samra fretted about being at the helm of the powerful ship, but she felt her trepidation fade as each passing moment failed to bring any catastrophe. After each successful maneuver, her hope rose that perhaps she really could be a skyship pilot.

The captain also seemed at ease with Samra in the pilot's seat. Other than a few clarifications of commands, Samra had been able to follow her orders and get the ship through the pass without trouble. Before long they had outdistanced the other ships and were making great time. It helped that the *Restless Fury* was vastly more nimble and able to corner efficiently in the turns. They climbed the mountainside along a route Eric and the rest of the fleet would be hard-pressed to follow.

Samra was just at the point of feeling confident enough to relax, when she rounded the corner of a high promontory and found herself facing a sheer wall of rock. She wrenched the power levers back to idle and balked as the wind shoved the ship onward anyway.

"Um, Captain?" Samra turned toward the central chair. Captain Savage was smirking.

Landy chose that moment to breeze back into the cockpit. "All right, move over Greenie, time to let the real pilot back in the seat."

Samra hopped out of the chair and retreated behind it. Landy slid into her spot and began working the controls. She shifted the power levers over to the side a fraction of an inch, then pulled them back farther. Overhead, the engines roared to life again but now thrusted air forward out the fans.

Landy reversed the tail control inputs and the ship rose. She pulled the dump lever and dropped water ballast from the nose and the ship pitched upward sharply. Samra finally saw what she was aiming for.

Another hundred feet up, the rock wall revealed a circular cavern opening. Rimmed with stalactites and stalagmites, it had the appearance of a gaping mouthful of fangs and wasn't at all welcoming. But Landy wasted no time. She elevated the ship to the proper altitude, centering it with the opening, and plunged ahead. The engine noise echoed off the cavern walls and reverberated through the cockpit.

Samra glanced back through the narrow windows that looked up to the deck and saw that the rest of the crew was dangling in the rigging, watching the ship's progress. The obstacles in the cavern were not only stalagmites and rocks. It had Grounder architecture, too. Carefully constructed stone walls and an elaborate latticework of wood beams held up sections of the cavern that seemed especially fragile. Samra spotted a few dirty-looking Grounders shoring up a particularly hazardous section of wall with protective wire netting.

"You look like you've never seen a cave before," the navigator said. Samra turned to find him watching her.

"I haven't. Not from the inside. I've never been underground before."

Despite the apparent dangers of the route, Landy calmly steered the ship into a hard right turn and emerged into a secondary set of caverns. At the far end, a wide beam of sunlight lit the floor. Samra found herself creeping closer to the windows to get a better view. As Landy steered the ship into the light, Samra got her first glimpse of what was on the other side of the tunnel.

It was a floating city. Or nearly. The high rock walls of the valley created a protective cove, and at its center, hovering in mid air, was a cluster of airships and kelp globes. If it wasn't for the riot of colors and fluttering flags aboard the airships, she'd have said the cluster resembled the globe patch. There was no mother here. No single unifying ship even, but the overall effect was the same. The air was alive and heavily populated.

As the *Restless Fury* exited the caverns and entered the mountain valley, Samra pressed her face to the glass to take it all in.

Stone stairways and walkways were carved in zigzagging patterns up the rocky walls. The rugged pathways intersected dangling rope bridges that swung out over the canyons to meet the ships that were moored in the air around narrow spires of rock.

These rocky mooring towers varied in height, creating tiered layers of ships. Some of the ships looked like they hadn't moved for decades and were bedecked with vines and ivy that had crept along the rope bridges to find them. Other ships were clean and bright, efficient machines of commerce glistening in the afternoon sun. There were hulking behemoths with dozens of decks, and also tiny single-envelope skiffs flitting about the port, moving from berth to berth.

"I never knew there were so many of you," Samra said.

"The teeming masses of humanity," the navigator muttered. "Ready to drain us dry."

"Buck up, Wade," the captain said, rising from her chair. "We won't be in port long. Nobody will have time to rob you at cards this trip." She raised an arm toward the far side of the valley. "Borgram's transport ship is next to the hopper today. Should make offloading and getting paid that much quicker. If we provision overnight, we could be back on our way in the morning."

Landy steered the *Restless Fury* toward the ship the captain had indicated. They passed near another cavern opening, this one facing south. The mouth of the cavern was worn to a V at the bottom and an inconsistent flow of sand was cascading out and falling hundreds of feet into a seemingly bottomless chasm. Samra tried to make out how far down it went, but the sandfall had bored its way deep into the crust. An airship was perched above the chasm dangling a brightly colored line. Sections of the line had small matching spheres attached to them. A squadron of smaller ships was clustered around the central ship, their decks teeming with observers.

As Samra tried to divine the purpose of the rope, three figures leapt from the ship and tumbled downward, freefalling into the chasm and disappearing into the darkness. "Whoa," Samra exclaimed.

"What?" Captain Savage asked.

"Those people. They just jumped. Were they Skylighters? How can they do that?"

"Jumpers? Oh, you mean the rope fall. It's a sport. They do it for money."

"Someone pays them to die?" Samra asked. "Why would they want that?"

"They don't die," Landy explained. "At least not usually. They have arresting hooks to grab the rope once they get far enough down. And they have drag chutes. The one who falls the farthest before grabbing on wins."

Samra looked for any sign of the jumpers as they passed over the chasm. If they had successfully hooked the rope, it was a long way down. The ship moved on and the scene passed behind them. There were other fascinating things to look at too. There were Grounders eating at hovering restaurants. People idled away the time on swings, and some were riding up and down the valley in elevators. Attached to one rock wall, there was a long tube where children were lining up to go sliding down. They erupted from the bottom of the slide into a pool of water. The children were all laughing and splashing one another. Samra found herself wishing she could try it.

Landy was lining them up with a set of floating docks instead.

"Wade, tell the crew we're headed straight for the hopper," Captain Savage said. "If they've got any contraband, they'd better hide it quick."

The navigator rose from his desk and shuffled aft. "Aye, cap'n."

Samra watched him go. "Um, what about me?"

"What about you?" Captain Savage replied.

"What if I have contraband?"

"Just having you on board is probably contraband, now that I think about it," the captain replied. "But yes. If you've got something the inspectors shouldn't see, you'd better get it out of sight. I'll think of a way to explain the rest of you."

Samra nodded and followed the navigator through the hatch.

In the cabin, the rest of the crew were stowing their belongings. Samra found her paper journal and looked for somewhere to hide it. She watched Cogs take a packet of green crystals from his trunk and fit them inside one of the speaking tubes that extended from the cockpit. Warehime was bundling her handful of recipe cards into a secret compartment in the bottom of the overhead lamp. It seemed the *Restless Fury* had plenty of nooks and crannies built into her construction, but Samra didn't know where to find one.

She tugged at Wade's shirtsleeve. "Um, do you know where I could hide this?" She held up the journal.

"A book?" The man squinted at it and frowned. "What are you trying to do, get us sent to the mines?"

"Give her a break," Warehime said. "She's new." The old woman held out a hand for the journal. "Give it here, honey. I'll let you use one of my spots." Samra handed over the book and Warehime pressed the end of a board in the wall next to her hammock. The board popped loose and revealed a stash of other knickknacks squirreled away behind it. Warehime squeezed the journal inside, fit the board back into place and gave Samra a wink.

Landy walked into the cabin, elbowing past the others, and quickly began rooting through her belongings. When she turned around she had a knit cap in her hands that she proceeded to fit atop Samra's head. She frowned at it. "You'll need a lot more," she muttered. She gestured to the blonde woman wearing the corset and knives. "Ylva, you see what you can do with her, will you? Captain says she wants her to not look like a greenie. Wants to pass her off as a cabin boy or something. Maybe you use some of your face kit on her?"

"What's a cabin boy?" Samra asked, confused by the sudden attention.

Ylva stepped over with a bag of brushes and powders. Her own face was made up with rouge and lipstick, and her eyelids were a sky blue. "Don't worry, kid. I'll at least make you a good-looking cabin boy. You've got cheek-bones to die for."

When the ship lined up with the docks, Samra and the rest of the non-essential crew were on the main deck waiting in a row. Sunburn was busy tossing lines to the dockhands so Samra felt frightfully exposed to the eyes of the inspectors on the dock. She would have liked to hide behind him.

She was dressed in cast-off men's clothing that was much too loose for her, but at least it covered her up. Only the tips of her fingertips protruded from the oversized shirtsleeves. Her hair was tucked into the cap and she was told that her face had been shaded some manner of dirty brown. She had also been instructed to wear the chain and lock around her waist to weigh her down and make her walk more like a Grounder. She didn't especially love the sensation of heaviness the chain created and didn't like that it was locked on, but the key she'd tied around her wrist made her feel a bit better about the situation.

She had only caught a brief reflection of herself in some of the brass on the way upstairs, since Ylva had already packed up her mirror, but she doubted she would have recognized herself anyway. Ylva had used what seemed like a bucketful of face powder on her and she had no idea what color she was anymore.

Once the ship was tied off, the gangplank was extended and the line of inspectors filed aboard. They each wore long coats down to their knees and brimmed hats to shade them from sun or possibly rain. It was neither raining nor sunny here in the shadow of the mountain, but their uniformity was unmarred by common sense.

An eager young man led the charge onto the deck and swept past Sunburn without a second glance. He immediately began pointing to holds. "Get these open. You have the manifests? He wasn't speaking to anyone in particular, but as Samra did her best to seem invisible, Sunburn unfolded a sheet of numbers from his pocket and handed it over. The man scanned the sheet, then turned his nose up. "This is not to our standards. We'll have to do our own count. Expect to be charged for the delay."

"What delay?" Captain Savage had emerged from the cockpit and was making her way aft across the deck. The young man balked at the sight of her and let his eyes flit to one of the other inspectors stepping aboard. This man was twice his age with severe eyebrows that seemed intent on swallowing his eyes. His mustache was encroaching on his face from the other direction, making his small eyes and angular nose seem lost in the forest of gray.

"Captain Savage," the man said. "Your arrival is most timely. You have quite a few people looking to speak to you at the moment."

"They'll have to wait," Captain Savage replied. "We're doing a quick turn. Offloading now, provisioning tonight, and gone again in the morning. We found an opportunity for a major haul and we don't want to lose it."

The man's mouth contorted into what might conceivably be considered a smile, but his words were icy. "You haven't heard then. I'm afraid you may have to reconsider your plans. The pod market is closing."

"What? Why?"

"Your father has uncovered the wreck. He's given the order to move every bit of pod stock we have out to the dig site tomorrow. We're taking every ship that flies and every lift pod that's not in structural use. Including these. You'll get paid for what you brought in today, but rates are down to half. If your father indeed raises the wreck, I suspect they'll be all but worthless afterward."

Samra struggled to follow the conversation. How could globes ever be worthless?

"You're devaluing the pods? We spent weeks harvesting this batch," Captain Savage said.

"Then count yourself lucky that you came back today while they still have some value. Come next week, you might be selling them yourself to the ore miners to prop up their shanties. I'd take what you can get now and be happy with it. Especially in the financial condition you're in."

"What's that supposed to mean?" Captain Savage spat.

"Ah. That's the other bit of news you won't have heard. Virgil Borgram is calling in all his loans. His men have been repossessing skyships and homes all week. If you haven't paid him off yet, I'd make that your first stop. Otherwise his crew might be flying your ship out to the desert tomorrow instead of you." The inspector waved the rest of his cohort over. "All right, search the ship. It's going to be a busy night for Miss Savage. We'd best get her on her way." He moved away and began directing his people down the hatches.

Captain Savage stood in the middle of the deck and fumed.

Samra waited as long as she could but her curiosity couldn't be contained. "What did all that mean?"

The rest of the crew huddled a little closer to listen. Captain Savage finally brought her attention back to the people in front of her. "It means that if I don't find a way to pay off this ship tonight, I'm going to lose it. You're all about to be out of work." She turned toward Samra. "And you won't be going home."

26

BORGRAM

"It's blatant thievery and you're not going to do this to me!"
Captain Savage stood outside the banker's cage and shouted. The
attendant was a skinny little man with a greasy ponytail trailing
over his collar. He was keeping his distance from the metal bars,
perhaps worried the captain might reach through and throttle him.
Samra felt that was probably a valid threat.

Samra and a few members of the crew had followed the captain
across a shaky rope bridge to the reinforced façade built directly
into the cliff wall. Each of them now had a stake in the fate of the
Restless Fury.

The cavern opening had only one metal door and it was clear
the attendant wasn't about to open it. "We issued the notice weeks
ago," he murmured. "As per your contract. You had adequate
warning about the loan terms."

"I've been out harvesting. You know I haven't been here to read
any bank notices!"

"Be that as it may, Miss Savage, Borgram's bank is still within
its right to request the funds. We've adjusted your interest costs
to account for the early termination but you still have quite an

outstanding sum. Ten thousand marks."

"I want to talk to Borgram. Where is he?"

"Mr. Borgram isn't here at the moment. If you would like to leave a message —"

Captain Savage had her arms through the bars so quickly that Samra barely had time to see the whip. It lashed out and wrapped around the banker's neck and she used it to haul him closer. When he stumbled forward, she grasped his shirt with her other hand and yanked him the rest of the way to the bars.

"I'll ask you one more time," she hissed. "Borgram. Where is he?"

The banker coughed and tugged the whip away from his throat. "He's—he's on the jump ship. He's betting the rope fall."

Captain Savage ripped the whip back through the bars and left the banker sputtering in her wake. She turned back to the group and muttered curses under her breath. She looked up to get her bearings, then pointed the coiled whip toward the far side of the valley. "We'll have to hike the bridges or find a skiff to give us a ride out there. The *Fury* isn't an option."

Ylva had her hands on her hips. "I've still got a few friends in this town. I can find us a lift."

Captain Savage nodded. "Good. As long as they know we can't pay them. We need every mark we've got left."

While Ylva walked off to find them a ride, the rest of the crew lingered in the shadow of a dingy inn. Its various rooms were hollowed into the rock face but appeared to be mostly empty. It seemed the majority of the residents preferred the safety of the open air to the crumbling mountainside. Samra didn't blame them.

"We might be able to pool our money, pitch in for the loan ourselves," Landy said. The crew was down to her, Sunburn and Cogs. Warehime had shuffled off to visit her grandchildren, while Wallace, Hodges, and Wade had made straight for the taverns.

"It won't be enough," Captain Savage said. "Even if I sold each of you shares in the *Fury*, I doubt we could pool that much. I know how much I pay you, and I've seen how you all spend it in port."

"Warehime might have a stash somewhere," Cogs mused. "She never goes in for the gambling and drink when she's aground."

"She gives it to her daughter to raise her kid," Landy said. "You know that."

"Hmm. That's true." Cogs tapped his foot, apparently out of

ideas.

"We know anyone else in town who likes us enough to give us a loan?" Sunburn asked.

"No one who isn't indebted to Borgram themselves and probably just as badly off," Captain Savage replied.

"Do you think you could ask your father for—" Landy cut herself off after the glare from Captain Savage. "Sorry, just thinking out loud."

Captain Savage crossed her arms. "Believe me, if I thought there was any chance of him donating so much as a mark, I'd try. But that bridge was burned a long time ago."

The group lapsed into silence until a single envelope skiff bobbed up from somewhere below containing Ylva and a smitten-looking young man with shaggy hair and an optimistic but sparce goatee.

"Micah here said he'd be happy to give us a ride to the rope drop."

"For free, right?" the captain asked.

"Just enjoying the pleasurable company, ma'am," Micah responded. He grinned and pulled the skiff up to the dock so the group could step aboard. A few moments later, they were whizzing away toward the far side of the valley.

Samra couldn't help but be amazed at the complexity and efficiency of the Grounder machines. Aboard the patch, there had never been anything so heavy as a propeller motor. The Grounders seemed to have made up for the extra weight through ingenious use of wings on their craft and dispersing the buoyancy pods carefully throughout the lightweight, rigid frames.

The metal was a miracle all its own. Samra had seen metal down in Womble, but it was relatively rare. Here the finely worked material was everywhere, and the population was putting it to good use.

She looked up as they passed an especially elaborate cluster of lift pods. High up top was a structure with wide landings and broad glass windows. It wasn't a ship. It was much too bulky and would present nothing but flat planes and hard angles to the wind, but it was beautiful.

"What's that?" Samra pointed out the structure to Landy.

"That's the Library of Knowledge. It's where the high families keep the relics."

"Like a school?"

"Sort of," Landy replied.

"Is that where you learned to fly?"

"Me? Psshh. I couldn't afford to learn there. None of us can. I got my training from Captain Savage. Paid for it out of my wages."

"Why did you have to pay for it? Doesn't she need a pilot?"

"Yeah, but that's the law. If you can't show you paid for what you know, you'll get charged with knowledge theft. They'll send you to the mines."

"What about me?" Samra asked. "I didn't pay anything to learn to fly the *Fury*. Am I a knowledge thief?"

"If the captain teaches you something, you can bet she's keeping track of the cost. You always pay the price, kid. Sooner or later."

The skiff bobbed its way around the floating pod city and approached the south end of the valley. Samra had a better view of the sandfalls leaking out of the rock face. The cliff itself was enormous, even taller than the other sides of the valley. It went on and on into the sky to where she had to squint to see the top. The jump ship was still hovering over the chasm beneath the falls. The various streams of sand leaking out of the mountainside had carved grooves into the rock over the centuries and then cascaded downward, hollowing out sections of crust below till it was pockmarked and porous like a honeycomb. The rope from the ship was dangling down the largest and blackest hole and she couldn't see where it ended.

Samra stood next to Sunburn and leaned over the railing of the skiff. "Why doesn't the sand fill up the hole?"

"There's a river down there. Deep underground. It carries it away," Sunburn replied.

Samra studied the spurts of sand being pushed over the edges of the falls. Higher up, there was another large opening in the cliff similar to the one they had flown the *Restless Fury* through, and airships were coming and going through the opening, but down at this level there were just a dozen or so smaller holes leaking sand. Many of the holes were augmented with Grounder architecture. Braces and beams kept the tunnels from collapsing and let the sand pass unimpeded. "Where's it all coming from?"

"On the far side of this mountain range is the High Somorian Desert," Sunburn said. "The sand storms push the dunes up against it and over time it leaks in. The mountain is full of pits and caverns.

The desert winds blow hardest during the day and push it through. Most of the crevices inside the mountain are already brimming with sand, but we make sure to keep the main tunnel open. We use it to navigate out to the desert. We call this the Storm Gate."

Samra tried to count all the holes. "Seems like a dangerous way to get through a mountain. What if it falls on top of you? Why would anyone risk that?"

Sunburn smiled. "I suppose it depends on what you find on the other side."

Micah pulled the skiff up to a dock suspended from one of the pod clusters near the rope fall ship. Multiple airships had moored themselves together here and slung bridges between decks to traverse them. Airmen and townspeople were mingling on the decks and watching the spectacle. The crowds were thickest near the rails overlooking the pit.

"Borgram is here somewhere," Captain Savage said. "Probably with whoever's winning the most money."

"I see Admiral Orloff's ship," Sunburn said, and pointed to a gleaming vessel decked out in burgundy canvas. "He's the biggest gambler in town."

They made their way through the crowds, crossing bridges and narrow gangplanks between ships. Samra noticed that not all of the locals walked with the confidence of the *Fury's* crew. Many people sported belts, fashionable or otherwise, that included leashes that they could use to tether themselves to safety. Samra had noticed that the crew of the *Fury* frequently tethered their tools and weapons to themselves in an effort not to lose them but she hadn't noticed them needing additional help getting around. With the weight of the chain around her waist making walking a heavier experience, she had a newfound respect for their balance and confidence, especially considering the long drop below them.

"I see him," Landy said. "He's aboard the Wind Devil." She gestured toward a cluster of people near a huge winch on the main ship.

The ship dangling the rope had a wide deck with multiple levels. The lowest was teeming with the public, but other, higher tiers offered more private views of the entertainment. Across the chasm, more ships were outfitted with balconies and terraces to provide prime viewing.

As Samra and the crew of the *Fury* forced their way through the crowd, she spotted the next group of jumpers lingering near a ladder on an upper deck. A few of them were waiting calmly in specially designed jumpsuits or testing out various accessories like extendable fabric wings under their arms. Others didn't look nearly so optimistic. A pair of desperate-looking men stood clutching rough poles with hooks on the end and squeezing them so tightly their knuckles were white. One man was nervously knotting and unknotting the tether cord to his hook, muttering to himself all the while.

The crowd around them gave a shout, and Samra just had time to glimpse the individuals leaping off a jump deck high overhead. The quintet of jumpers fell from their place in the rigging and plummeted straight through the bottom of the ship. The energy of the crowd made Samra's skin tingle. Their enthusiasm was kinetic.

When Samra finally got through the throng to Sunburn and the rest of the crew, she found them fanned out behind the captain, who was facing a ponderous man in a bulging waistcoat seated near the opening for the rope hoist. A hole had been designed into the bottom of the ship so that the giant winch in the rigging could spool the colored rope directly through the center. A pair of sooty-looking men were standing at the winch motor, but weren't currently operating it. The crowd was instead waiting breathlessly while watching the rope. The section of rope exposed in the hole was white, and as the crowd watched, it gave a quiver.

The audience whooped. A few people laughed and referenced an elaborate clock secured to the ship's central spar.

"Borgram," Captain Savage shouted across the opening of the hole. "We need to talk."

The big man in the waistcoat glanced up from his seat and looked for the speaker, but when he saw the captain he merely frowned. His eyes went back to the rope. After what seemed to Samra like an impossibly long time, it gave another quiver and the crowd cheered. A third and fourth quiver went through the rope immediately after and the onlookers cheered again.

A hush immediately followed as their eyes lingered on the rope. There was a scoreboard on the wall with five names scrawled on it in chalk. As time elapsed, more and more eyes turned to the clock. Samra had never used one before but she was able to recognize that the moving hands were not telling a time of day but were counting down to something.

The captain was edging her way around the hole to get closer to Borgram. As the clock wound down to its ultimate position, the crowd groaned. The rope failed to quiver a fifth time.

"Well, four out of five isn't bad." A man with a black mustache and top hat near the clock signaled to the men at the winch. "Reel them up, lads." The men heaved on a lever and the winch motor coughed to life in a cloud of black smoke. As the rope rose into the ship, a crew of individuals unhooked the colored spheres from the line and threw them into a basket. Samra noticed they were numbered.

Captain Savage shouted over the din. "Borgram, you can't hide from me."

Borgram looked up from his conversation with a fancily dressed man next to him and scowled. "Who's hiding, girl? You think I have something to hide?"

"Just the scandalous way you run your business. You knew I was out on a trip. How dare you try to foreclose on my loan."

Borgram turned toward the man next to him. "Admiral, I believe you'll remember Erin. She's Lord Savage's eldest and least promising child."

The admiral was a square-jawed man with a broad forehead. He fixed a golden monocle to his eye and squinted at Captain Savage. "Ah, yes, I recall the poor girl had aspirations to be a flyer one day. Pity she didn't have what it took to make my crew." His eye raked over the captain with a look that made Samra instantly dislike him. His view through the monocle lingered longest on the tightest places of the captain's clothing.

Captain Savage scowled. "I've been flying since I was a child, no thanks to you and your useless Air Corps. Sorry I didn't want to join a bunch of elitist thugs in extorting decent people for protection."

The admiral recoiled from the words as if from a bad odor. "And still disrespectful of your betters. No wonder your father disowned you."

Samra watched the captain, half expecting her to unleash her whip and send the man tumbling out the hole in the ship. But the captain's voice was cold and measured. "I'm not here to clue your friends in to their obnoxiousness, Borgram. If you want to spend your time with arrogant asses like this, I can't stop you. But I've got work to do. I was in the middle of a big run. I've found pods that could lift the whole city. I just need to get back out there."

"The pod market is closing," Borgram replied. "It's a fool's investment now. Once your father raises his wreck, all the pods he's been using in the project will flood the market again. We'll have enough pods to haul the city to the moons if we want to. Your harvesting days are done."

Enough pods to raise a city? Samra wondered just how much of the sky they'd already cleared. On the way through the valley she was fairly certain she'd spotted some of the patch's missing globe sons in catch nets, but he seemed to be talking about a lot more than just those.

"The *Fury* is my ship," Captain Savage spat. "Mine."

"It certainly could be your ship," Borgram smiled. "But I still hold the note. Seems there's a matter of ten thousand marks to account for. If you don't have it, then I'm afraid the ship will be claimed by the bank."

The crowd outside gave a shout as the first jumper was reeled from the hole. The rope running through the spool was now yellow, and at the bottom of that section, just before it turned to orange, a man had his legs wrapped around a sphere and was clinging tightly to the rope above with his arresting hook. Samra noted that the huge fabric streamer dangling from his back and twisting in the wind beneath him was yellow as well. The crowd began to laugh as he was raised into the afternoon light.

"Matches the color of his courage," someone commented.

"Or what's leaking from between his legs," another said.

The man with the top hat affixed a yellow disk and the number ten to a peg beneath the man's name.

"I could give you two thousand," Captain Savage offered, ignoring the spectacle. "If I delay the pay to my crew for a month and take on half rations, I can get you two now. I can pay the rest off in a few months like we originally discussed."

"How do you expect to earn the money with the pod market closed?" Borgram scoffed. "Every pod barge in the valley will be turning into air taxis and security patrols after tomorrow. Seeing as I now own most of them, I can assure you that the competition for employment will be considerable. If I was you, I'd be a little nicer to Admiral Orloff. You might be begging him for a job in the Corps come next week."

Captain Savage now really looked like she wanted to murder

someone. Samra decided that if she were the banker, she wouldn't be sitting nearly so close to the hole in the ship. But the situation didn't seem to concern him.

"I'll make you an offer, Erin. I'll buy the *Restless Fury* from you right now. I'll give you twenty-five thousand marks for it. You can take the money and go buy yourself a little skiff and fly off into the sunset. If the flying is what you care about. It's a wonderful offer, considering the circumstances."

"A wonderful offer?" Captain Savage said. "With the modifications I've made it's worth seventy, easy. I've already paid you forty on the loan. You want to give me twenty-five and I'm supposed to just walk away from my investment? You're out of your mind."

Borgram merely grinned at her. "Very well, where's your payment then? Ten thousand tonight or my men repossess it tomorrow. What'll it be?" He leaned forward. "What's that? Oh, you don't have it. I see. Then I guess I can just sit here, enjoy the show, and wait to collect my ship. I'm sure the Admiral might buy it off me tomorrow." He turned to his companion. "You said you needed a few more old crates for target practice, didn't you? Maybe you could test out those new harpoon launchers you were discussing. The ones with the flaming tips."

The admiral was back to ogling the captain. "I'm sure there are other skills she might employ for a bit of credit, or she could always join the rest of your foreclosures." He gestured to the deck with the gaggle of nervous jumpers. "Try to win her last payment in the jump. Popular option today."

"Now there's an idea, Orloff. Young Erin says she wants to keep her beloved tub. Let's see if she has the courage to jump for it. I hear the prize for a black ten is up to twenty thousand marks. For ten thousand, you'd only have to fall to a what? A black five?"

"Eight," the games master with the top hat declared. He'd clearly been listening in to the conversation. "Black eight is worth ten thousand."

The crowd cheered again as more of the jumpers were lifted clear of the hole. One of the men was at the bottom of the orange section of rope and the next two had landed in the red section. A man with a spyglass was peering down the hole and shouting out the numbers. "Orange eight. Red four and . . . Looks like a red ten!"

"A thousand marks to the winner!" the man with the top hat

declared. The crowd erupted into hoots, whistles, and applause.

Samra absorbed the fervor of the cheering. They were this happy just about someone falling part way? She checked the results board. She'd never had a use for money aboard the patch, but a thousand marks definitely sounded like a lot. Certainly worth a lot of respect here. Even the captain seemed to respect it . . .

Borgram frowned as the red circle and number ten were hung on the peg beneath the winner's name. "Well, it looks like Mr. Gibran gets to keep his house after all."

"Told you he had more gumption than you gave him credit for," the Admiral said. He held out a hand and Borgram passed him a few bills. "Goes to show what a sense of desperation can do for you."

"Downright inspiring," Borgram grumbled. He turned back to Captain Savage and his mood lightened. "So what do you say, young lady? Is your ratty little ship worth a bit of risk?"

"I'll do it!" The words were out of Samra's mouth before she'd had time to think them through. All eyes turned to her. Borgram squinted to try to make her out in the now smoky half-light.

"Who's that you've got there?"

The crew all wore surprised expressions on their faces. Captain Savage stammered out a response. "That's my . . . cabin boy, Sam . . . son."

The admiral leaned forward and reattached his monocle.

The captain elbowed her way to Samra and leaned down to whisper in her ear. "What do you think you're doing?"

"I can do it," Samra whispered back. "It would be easy."

The captain grabbed her arm and tugged her into the crowd, away from the watchful eyes of Borgram. "This isn't your responsibility."

"I want to do it," Samra said. "But if I win the money, you make me an airship pilot and take me home. And nobody steals anything, and I'm not a knowledge thief."

"What makes you think you're a thief?"

"Because you taught me to fly the *Fury* and Landy says you always keep track of your debts. I don't want a debt to anybody. Not even you."

"You'd do that? Do a rope fall just to save my ship?" Captain Savage was studying Samra's face with what looked like awe. Samra liked it.

"I told you. It's easy," Samra said. "I fall all the time. If I go too far, I can just float back up."

"Not with a chain around your waist you won't." Sunburn had squeezed through the crowd to listen to the conversation and pinched Samra's oversized shirt where the chain was looped above her hips.

"But I have this," Samra said, pulling her sleeve back and revealing the key strapped to her wrist. She carefully covered it again as the crowd around them started to take an interest.

"No one's ever made a black eight," Sunburn objected. "Hardly anyone lands in the black at all. It's too dark down there. They say the black rope just vanishes. May as well be invisible."

"Yeah, but she lights up," Landy whispered from the other side of the captain. "And flies. We saw her do it on the ship. It's brilliant. This would be a piece of cake for her."

Sunburn looked unsure but didn't raise another argument.

Samra had to admit the darkness might be an issue, judging on her spotty lighting abilities, but she'd have a long way down to get ready.

"You're sure?" Captain Savage asked, keeping her eyes fixed on Samra.

Samra nodded. "I plummet all the time at home. I can do this."

"Okay then." Captain Savage forced her way back through the crowd. Borgram and Admiral Orloff were in murmured conversation.

"We accept your challenge," Captain Savage said.

"It's typically up to the winner what to do with the funds of course," Borgram said. "But we don't let minors place any wagers. There is also the matter of the fees. If your cabin boy can't pay the entrance fee and you're indebted as it is, might I suggest a little side wager between us? I always think it's best if everyone has a bit of skin in the game."

Captain Savage squinted at him skeptically. "What's the wager?"

"You bet on your cabin boy. I'll bet on my own man. If you win, Admiral Orloff here will cover your entrance fee, I'll forgive the loan on your ship, and the boy can keep the prize to do with as he sees fit. If my man wins, I get the *Restless Fury*, and you sign a contract to work off the entrance fee and the remainder of your debt to me in Admiral Orloff's Air Corps."

Admiral Orloff smirked his leering smile at her.

Borgram leaned forward and rubbed his hands. "How's that for an exciting proposition?"

Captain Savage turned to look at Samra. They stared into each other's eyes for a long moment. Samra couldn't tell what the captain was searching for, but when she turned away and faced Borgram, her voice was steady. "I'm in."

Borgram laughed and held his arms out to the crowd. "Ladies and gentlemen, we have ourselves a wager."

27

SCARABS

Kipling was empty. Leaning against the cockpit rail, he felt as though his inside had been hollowed out and purged of any potential source of energy. Probably because it had. Atlas had offered him the hunk of goat cheese that was now somewhere below the *Sun Dragon* in the foaming swirl. Kipling had optimistically attempted to eat it but his body had rejected it immediately, along with most of the water he'd drunk to quell his stomach's rumblings.

Now he was truly out of options.

The tunnel of ancient tree limbs had given way to more and more rock as the river carved its way through the terrain. The noise of the rushing water had risen as they progressed and now it had swelled to a throbbing roar as it tumbled over the edge of the falls.

Atlas was leaning over the cockpit rail as well, though for reasons other than his stomach. He was studying the gaping hole in the ground that the river was disappearing into. His eyes kept flitting from the view below them to the map in his hand.

"I just don't know," he muttered.

They'd been hovering overtop the falls for fifteen minutes, pondering their predicament.

They'd reached a dead end. The tunnel of dead trees had brought them this far, but the path had been closed off. The river vanishing below ground left a wall of rock and twisted roots ahead, with no conceivable way through.

"Didn't he say to just follow the river?" Kipling asked. "Was there another branch?"

"This is it," Atlas replied. He pointed to the map. "It's the only one anywhere near us." He dragged a finger across the line of blue to the point where it changed to brown as it met the mountainside. "It goes underground from here. I just didn't know that's what this map meant."

"So what are we supposed to do?" Kipling asked.

Atlas took one more look at the tangled canopy of boughs overhead, then returned his gaze to the falls. "I guess we follow it. We go underground, too."

Kipling frowned.

It was dark enough here as it was. By his calculations it was midday and, even so, he doubted there was enough light to see a quarter mile in the murky haze. If the trees would ever allow it. He leaned over the rail and looked at the chasm the river was plunging into. "What if it doesn't make it all the way through the mountain? What if we get trapped under there?"

"We can always turn around if we have to," Atlas said. "We can backtrack."

Kipling felt he barely had the energy to move forward as it was. He hadn't had anything to eat that would stay down since the day before yesterday. He needed to get to the Heights to find food, not delve even further into this foreign world of rock and water. But there was no choice. If Samra was on the other side of this mountain, then he needed to be too. Even if he did turn back, where would he go? The patch had moved on. There was only forward. Success or utter failure. And only one way to find out which. "Okay," he said. "Well, let's do it so we can get it over with."

Atlas nodded and sank back into his seat. He pushed the controls forward and powered up the fans. The nose dipped in response. Kipling watched him maneuver the dials and levers. Atlas had taken hold of a handle and was pumping it up and down. "What does that do?"

"Moving ballast to the front. It'll help trim the nose down for the descent." Atlas tilted his head skyward and shouted. "Fledge! Come on!"

Kipling turned and spotted the cliff fox leaping from the

roots of a banyan palm. Fledge banked and glided down to them, alighting on the front windscreen. He squeaked once and hopped into Kipling's seat.

The falls raged past, coating the ship in mist and spray in intervals. Kipling wiped his face and let the water rejuvenate him. He stayed standing with his hands firmly gripping the rail so as not to waver.

As the *Sun Dragon* reached the bottom of the falls, Kipling could barely hear his own thoughts over the noise. He stared up at the yawning mouth of the cavern and steeled his nerves. He glanced back at Atlas one more time, but didn't attempt to speak. Questioning Atlas again wouldn't be possible. And they'd made their decision. Atlas gave him a nod and pressed the control levers forward.

Within moments the darkness swallowed them. Kipling glanced back a few times toward the mouth of the cave as they advanced and thought that as dim as it had been outside, that faint light seemed like a beacon now—a glowing half moon fading slowly back into the cosmos.

Atlas lit the lanterns.

The river calmed itself and the noise of the falls receded with the memory of the light. Underground, stillness reigned. Over the gurgles of the river, Kipling began to make out new noises. Waiting noises. The noise of patient moss and determined fungi dripping condensation from the cavern ceiling. The noise of mysterious beasts hunched in alcoves, sleeping the patient sleep of the timeless. This place seemed the realm of dragons and trolls, goblins and wraiths.

But no. That was only Samra's stories. He had spent too many nights in the darkness of their hideout, listening to her describe imaginary threats in the starry skies. Real dangers didn't need magic, or sleep.

Real threats were already awake and prowling.

"Keep an eye out," Atlas said, his eyes sweeping from one side of the ship to the other. He steered the ship with a steady hand, well away from the dripping cavern walls. Kipling wasn't sure if he meant to look for nightbeasts or the route forward, but either way he had no choice. He kept a firm grip on his warhook and kept his eyes fixed ahead.

They came quietly.

Scarab crabs. They perched on ledges and peered out into the tunnel with bright iridescent eyes. The eyes flickered in the lantern light. The smallest were perhaps two feet across, the largest more than six. They stayed motionless as the *Sun Dragon* passed, black, shiny statues arranged to decorate the passage. They didn't blink, didn't flinch, just observed and catalogued the ship's movement through those flickering orbs. And then, once the darkness shrouded them again, they followed. At first only a few, and then a growing wave. Their noise gave chase.

Scratch. Scratch. Scratch.

Scuff, scurry, splash.

Scurry scurry scurry!

Leap.

The scarab whipped past in the darkness. A flash of shiny armored shell, then it was gone. A brave soldier making a grab for the dark end of the tail.

"Keep the lights on them!" Atlas shouted. He hung one of the lanterns on a harpoon and propped it up to illuminate the tail.

Kipling looked down at his hands and found them glowing. Not as bright as they usually did, but enough. He hoped it was enough.

He brandished the warhook and waited for the scarabs to come closer.

They didn't. But the snakes did.

The lightning snake flashed from the darkness, generating its own light as it moved. The perfect adaptation. Venomous to its prey, poisonous to its predators. It landed on the right lateral fin of the ship and lashed out toward the cockpit. In one instinctual movement, Kipling caught the snake mid strike with the warhook, separating its head from its body and sending both parts tumbling into the river below. The snake was still glowing as it hit the water, but flickered and dimmed as it sank.

"Careful of the fins. We're going to need those," Atlas said.

Kipling looked and saw that his swing had nicked the fabric on the trailing seam of the fin. A thin slice exposed the glossy wood beneath.

"Sorry," he said.

"Look out!" Atlas shouted. His pupils were wide pools in the lantern light.

Two snakes tumbled from the rocks overhead. Kipling knocked the first overboard in mid-air, but the second landed on the windscreen, lashing out and nicking his arm before he could hurl it away. Kipling hissed in pain and studied the scratch from the creature's fangs. It hadn't been a proper bite, but it had punctured his skin nonetheless.

"You okay?" Atlas said.

"Yeah," Kipling responded. "I think so." He wiped his arm on his pants and tried to shake off the numbness in his skin.

Atlas steered down the center of the cavern for what must have been another mile before they faced their next obstacle. The river forked.

The air was thick here. Thick enough that Kipling ought to be floating out of the ship with every breath. But the pressure was too great. His head ached with it. Each breath he took left him smothered. All air and no lift. His hands had dimmed to a faint luminescence. He could brighten when he concentrated, but not nearly enough to light the way ahead. When he tried it, it only made his vision blur and set his head swimming.

The scratch on his arm was beginning to burn.

"I think we go right," Atlas said. The boy was studying his map again but not seeming to find answers. "It's wider there. At least I think it is."

Kipling couldn't tell. Both passages were a blur to him. Something bumped his leg and he shouted. He scrambled to the side of the cockpit, raising his warhook. But when he looked down, it was only the cliff fox, staring up at him with its brown orb-shaped eyes.

"Fledge," Kipling gasped.

"Hey, are you okay?" Atlas asked.

He grunted in response and turned his eyes back to the blackness ahead. The monsters were all out there. Waiting. He shivered involuntarily and his skin prickled.

The ship moved on. The rudder fin flapped and the air motors churned. How far? Miles? Somewhere in the darkness behind them, the scarabs fought their way over the rocks. Scratch, scratch, splash.

Kipling found himself muttering the old rhyme. The one Samra would chant to scare Rufus and send him scrambling for the safety of home. It always made her laugh.

"Beware the clatter of claws at night,
What clicks and screeches outside the light."

"What did you say?" Atlas peered at him over the panel of his instruments.

The rhyme continued to slip from his lips.

"Pincers that clench, mouths that bite,
Don't stir, don't whisper, or set them to flight."

Kipling found himself leaning over the edge of the cockpit. The darkness was porous down there. So many holes. So many eyes.

Where was the river taking them? Where had the river gone? The sound of the water was far away now—lost, down some hole or pitfall. Had it been swallowed up again?

Ahead it was just blackness. They weren't going the right way. He should tell someone. He should tell that boy. What's-his-name. The one he knew from outside. Kipling turned to find him. He had to tell him to turn around. His skin burned.

"Pincers that clench, mouths that bite," he whispered.

The boy was there. He was speaking but his face was blurry. The lanterns were turning him orange. Their flames seemed smaller now. Dimmer. Almost extinguished, like he was.

"Don't stir . . ."

The air motors were spinning faster. Louder. The boy had his hands clenched on the controls.

"Don't whisper," Kipling whispered. "Don't . . ." He couldn't remember the end. How did the rhyme end? There was another verse yet, wasn't there? Samra would know.

He turned to the blurry boy in the back seat. *"Don't set them to . . ."* It was too late. The tunnel behind them was full of noise. Not scratching. Not splashing. Wings beating and legs kicking. Eyes watching and claws pinching. A swarm of them. A wave. " . . . *to flight,"* he said.

The boy in the back seat wrenched the control wheel toward himself and climbed. Up through the ceiling. He steered the ship through tunnels and spiraled up through caverns. The wings of the horde beat around them. The cockpit shuddered. A big shiny face with pincers was staring at Kipling from the front windscreen. The claws were poised to strike. Kipling swung the warhook at the scarab's eyes and cut one of them off. He screamed at it and glowed.

The light poured out of him and flooded the cavern. Winged things took to flight again. Scarabs and snakes and a cliff fox, darting in all directions. The boy with the airship raced on. On through the caverns. Straight through the mountain. Kipling brandished his warhook again and caught another of the scarabs in midair, sending it tumbling into the darkness without its legs.

And then there was a crash. The sickening crunch of wings against stone. The feverish whirl of the motors now spun down into oblivion. An arm was holding him up, dragging him across water, across rocks. The warhook trailed behind him on the ground, tethered to his wrist but no longer in his hands. He'd chipped out one of the shark's teeth along the spine of the blade. Would Bronks be upset?

He flickered. The tunnel was tiny now. Too tiny to fly through. That must be why the boy was walking. The blurry boy with the lanterns. He was down to two.

"I saw some light up ahead," the boy was saying. "But it's high up. I need to climb to see where it's coming from and I can't carry you."

"Rustleberry leaves," Kipling whispered. The blurry boy's face leaned closer, so he spoke again. "Good for poison."

Then the boy was piling rocks around the entrance to the cavern. "I'll be right back. Back before your lantern burns out."

It was good the boy was leaving. He wouldn't like it here. It was dark and cold, and the air was heavy.

"I'll be back. I'll find help and I'll be back." The boy had some rope coiled around him and was holding a harpoon. He looked a bit like a guardian. One day when Kipling was a guardian, maybe he would invite this boy to be one too.

But then he was gone.

Kipling blinked at the lantern. It was propped up in the hole. The hole that the boy had left in the wall for him. Big enough for a lantern. Not big enough for a monster. Well, maybe a little one.

It went black for a while.

He opened his eyes again when the hairy bat thing tried to shove the dead lizard into his mouth. The ponderous brown eyes were waiting, expectant. The bat fox was kind. Thoughtful fox. But Kipling didn't like lizards.

It went dark again. When he opened his eyes the second time, the flame on the lantern had turned blue. It was tiny now. A blue pixie dancing in a glass jar. Samra would have liked to see it dance. He watched through watery eyes till the pixie was done. It curled up into a pinprick and vanished. Then all that was left was the darkness, and the faintest scent of smoke.

28

THE ROPE FALL

"This is Ranginui," Borgram said, grinning. "He'll be my champion."

Ranginui was a huge man, broad chested and decorated all over with elaborate tattoos. The most intimidating symbols adorned both sides of his face. Ranginui stared at Samra down the length of his broad nose, then opened his mouth and let his tongue hang out. He grunted at her and she took a step backward.

A hand braced her back.

"Don't go falling off just yet, young man." The games master with the top hat eased her away from the edge of the deck. "You won't want to go without this." An assistant passed the games master a pair of goggles and a wooden hook and he in turn handed them to Samra. "And here is your streamer bag. Don't lose it." She accepted the armful of items clumsily. He smiled at her and patted her shoulder, then moved on to the next jumper.

Ranginui scowled at her another moment, then snorted and moved away with Borgram, who seemed intent on giving him extra advice. The men glanced back at her once as they spoke, then moved out of earshot.

Samra perched the goggles atop her head, then grasped the hook and studied the design of it. It was primarily a pole with a curved rigid hoop at one end. One side of the hoop opened with light pressure from the outside, a feature used to hook the rope, but it was kept closed by means of a spring. The handle of the hook had a stack of shock-reducing springs that divided the hook end from the handgrip. A cord ran through these springs and out the bottom. The apparatus ended in a tether loop big enough to wrap around her body.

Samra opened the canvas bag next and peeked inside. A wad of colorful fabric was bundled into a dense ball.

"So you don't rip your arms from their sockets when you latch on," a man on the platform near her said. "Throw out the ribbon as you fall. Creates drag and absorbs a lot of your momentum. You'll regret it if you don't." He was watching her from a few feet away, holding his own hook. He had his hook's tether tied to a harness that was affixed to various parts of his body and he was testing the springs. The young man was lean and sinewy with dark skin and shaggy hair. His clothes were extra baggy and he had them tied with cords around his wrists and ankles.

"Has that happened to you?" Samra asked.

"Me? No. But I knew a man once who got his hook caught on a rock on the way down before he'd deployed his streamer. Only had the hook tied to his wrist, so it pulled his arm clean off."

Samra screwed up her face in disgust, then looked away. "Well, I'll be okay," she said. She fingered the key under her sleeve and loosened the cords to make sure she could palm it easily. The sinewy man nodded and moved toward the ladder.

The game master hadn't wasted any time getting them in line. There was one team ahead of them and another already lining up behind. It seemed there was no shortage of desperate competitors today.

The crew of the *Restless Fury* was a deck below her, huddled at a table near the bar. Sunburn and Landy had their heads leaned close to one another, whispering and casting occasional glances her way. Cogs was making quick progress on a flagon of beer, while the captain had opted for something smaller but presumably more potent. She fidgeted with the glass in her hand and was looking outside with a far-off stare. Samra wondered if she could see the *Fury* from her seat. Was she regretting this decision already?

The signal bell for the jump team ahead of her sounded and the group leapt off the upper deck and plunged past. Samra leaned over the rail and watched them plummet through the open sky, each angling for positions near the rope before vanishing into the hole at the bottom of the sandfall. Two jumpers deployed their streamers prior to entering the hole and floated in gently, while the other two vanished beneath the surface at full speed.

The sinewy man with the baggy clothing was next to her again, also peering downward.

"How deep does it go?" Samra asked.

The man scratched at the stubble on his chin. "Well, we're nearly at the top of the mountain. The river is all the way down near the bottom of the mountain, so I guess you could say we have an entire mountain worth of fall."

Samra nodded. She'd plummeted off the Globe Mother for as long as she could remember, but jumping from the top of the patch to the bottom was still only a few hundred feet. This fall was many times that. Thousands upon thousands of feet. It was going to be a long drop.

"I'll give you some free advice," the man said. "That rope?" He pointed to the giant spool hanging above them. "Doesn't always reach the bottom of the pit. It stretches pretty low, especially when you've got a few guys hanging onto it, but it usually comes up a bit short. If you plan on grabbing on and not pancaking into the river, I'd grab hold earlier than you think you need to. Otherwise you might miss your chance altogether."

Samra nodded again, trying to absorb the information.

The crowd cheered as the rope began to stretch and twitch.

"And another bit of advice. Stay away from that one." The man pointed to Ranginui. "Cutthroat as they come. Wherever he is on the fall down, you want to be someplace else."

"What's your name?" Samra asked.

"Robinson." The man stuck out a hand. "Jake Robinson."

"I'm Samra. Er, Sam," she replied. The games master was gesturing for them to move toward the ladder. Jake directed her ahead of him. She watched Ranginui scale the rungs, then turned back to Jake. "Have you done this a lot?"

"Enough to know it's a bad idea. But not enough that I don't still need the money."

"What do you need it for?"

Jake glanced down to the crowd. Samra caught sight of a young woman in the corner watching the crowd nervously. Her hand was resting on her slightly swollen belly.

"I'm trying to make a few things right," Jake said.

"You have to jump to do that?"

"There were probably better chances I missed along the way. This is just the latest in a long line of bad decisions. But if I do this, maybe I'll have an opportunity to make some good ones."

The woman's eyes had found his. She raised two fingers to her lips, then held them out toward him.

Jake smiled and held his fingers to his lips in return.

Samra turned her attention to the ladder.

Carrying all the jump gear was cumbersome. Samra seemed to have one fewer hands than she needed to manage it all and had to stop at the base of the ladder to shift the streamer bag to her back. The other jumpers all wore theirs by the straps and hung them somewhere near their hips for easy access. Samra followed their example and swung the bag over her head before hoisting the hook in her free hand and climbing the ladder with the other.

Never in her whole life had she felt so heavy. The chain around her waist had been manageable. It provided a constant but not unbearable downward pressure on her that made it unlikely she'd float away, and gave the impression of Grounder walking. Now she was positively suffering under this additional burden. The fabric of the streamer seemed to be made of a lightweight silk, but there was a lot of it, and wrapped into a ball it weighed plenty. Considering her usual buoyancy, she now felt as nimble as a stone. How would she plummet with all of this? She found herself looking forward to being out of sight below ground. She'd shed the chain, shed the bulky gear, and just do like she always did—drop as far as she wanted, and float back up.

The crowd hollered as the winch began to turn. Somewhere in her climb up the ladder, Samra must have missed the countdown. The long length of colored rope was reeled back in. White, yellow, green, blue, orange, red, and finally, black. Samra spotted the top few spheres in the black section. No one had bothered to remove them since the rope was headed back down again and that section didn't need to be wound into the winch. The winner of the jump had once again been chosen from the red section, and the closest competitors had never made it past blue.

Samra searched for the black #8 sphere she would have to reach to win the money for the *Fury*. It was so far down she could barely make it out. To make matters worse, the last sections of rope had progressively smaller spheres to get a hook around and use to arrest the fall. She hadn't counted on that. She glanced down at the lower deck and found Captain Savage looking back. Once again, her expression was unreadable.

Samra averted her eyes first this time and concentrated on the rope. She would do it. She had to. She'd save the *Fury*, become a pilot, and then she could go home with proof. Proof that she was good for more than just being a lousy colonist. Proof she wasn't just another faller. She'd be coming home victorious from a dangerous adventure. That would show them. Nobody had to save her. Not even the guardians. She'd see if Bronks would dare try to kick her off the prohibited globes then . . .

"Places, gentlemen, and lady."

Samra started, and turned to look at the games master. But he wasn't talking about her. The fourth competitor in their jump challenge had climbed to the platform. She was middle-aged and even skinnier than Jake. Her threadbare clothes and undernourished frame gave her away as yet another of Borgram's desperate foreclosed-upon customers. Her expression was grim.

Samra lined up at the edge of the platform next to Ranginui, but when Jake shook his head, she stepped aside and let the other woman take that spot. Ranginui tied his long black hair behind his head and flexed his thick neck. Samra noted that his streamer bag was much larger than the others, no doubt to make up for his oversized proportions.

The crew of the jump ship completed the rope extension and the men with the winch motor shut it down. The games master reset the clock and the crowd grew silent in anticipation. Samra noticed Borgram and Admiral Orloff were both staring intently at her. Borgram was smirking.

Her heart was racing now. She hadn't expected to be this nervous. This wasn't like jumping off the Mother at all. There were never eyes on her like this. On the patch she could plummet right past the entire globe council and no one would even bat an eyelash. No one ever cared what she did, unless she was screwing up. But here, everything was suddenly riding on her. And everyone was watching.

The captain's expression was stoic. Landy and Cogs stood with lips pressed tight and worry in their eyes. It was only when her gaze found Sunburn's that the pressure lessened. He was smiling at her. Not a broad smile, but a subtle one. He lifted a fist her direction with one thumb raised. She didn't know what the gesture meant, but it was encouraging. It was enough.

She lowered her goggles over her eyes and took a deep breath.

"Jumpers ready!" the games master yelled. He lifted a hand to the signal bell, then struck it.

Samra exhaled hard.

The woman to her right leapt feet-first, even as the bell was still resonating, but Ranginui was out immediately after—head down and diving after her. Samra and Jake left the platform simultaneously. The fall through the bottom of the ship was over in a flash, a blur of faces, a riotous shout from the crowd, and then they were in the open sky, angling for the rope and the distant hole in the rocky surface.

The woman who jumped first was flailing. She'd fallen in a tumble and was now flipping end over end in the wind. Samra watched with amazement as Ranginui fell straight for her, almost like she wasn't there or he intended to pass clean through her. A moment later he had hold of her streamer bag. There was an instant of relief and maybe even gratitude showing on the woman's face as her tumbling body was righted, but Ranginui had his hand inside her bag. He then used his brute strength to hurl her aside. The woman screamed as she went flailing once more, this time aimed for the sandfalls gushing out of the rocks. The streamer came unfurled from the woman's bag as she angled away and it was twisting behind her as she flew, but Samra never saw what happened after that, she was below her now and plummeting through the hole in the surface of the mountain.

Ranginui spread his arms, using the fabric wings stitched into his jumpsuit to angle himself back to the rope. The drag on his winged suit was slowing his fall and Samra realized too late that she was about to catch up to him.

Ranginui was not surprised. He rolled over onto his back as he fell and snatched at her.

"No!" Samra spread her arms and inhaled deeply, pulling air

into her body and generating just enough lift to slow her fall. She spun and dodged Ranginui's attack. A rocky promontory flashed by and she rolled to narrowly avoid it. Ranginui dodged as well but turned again to snatch at her. Samra exhaled hard and tucked her arms in tight, plummeting past Ranginui and angling away.

She was too far from the rope.

Samra held the arresting hook streamlined against her body with her left arm and spread her legs and other arm to turn. The baggy clothing was helpful, especially as it kept filling with air from her fall, but it wasn't nearly as effective as Ranginui's wing suit. As she angled toward the rope again, Ranginui was nearly on top of her.

The rope was green, but getting harder to see in the darkness.

Which color came next? Samra tried to recall but couldn't. She needed to be ready. The numbered spheres were whizzing past at alarming speed. She aimed closer but was suddenly wrenched around toward the snarling face of her competitor. He had ahold of her right wrist and was pulling her toward him. He reared back with a meaty fist and aimed it for her face.

"Let him go!" Jake slammed into Ranginui's back and the three of them went tumbling in a mass of arms and legs. Ranginui snarled and threw an elbow toward Jake's face. Jake dodged and pushed himself clear, throwing out his streamer so that the drag pulled him up and away. But he wasn't done. As Samra and Ranginui fell away from him, she saw he'd had his hands full pulling the streamer out of the big man's bag, using his own trick against him. The huge wad of fabric unfurled in a cloud of billowing silk, wrenching the two of them upward. Somehow Samra's bag had gotten tangled in Ranginui's and when his streamer unfurled, it yanked her closer to him and partially deployed her own streamer as well.

The wind resistance was making them spin. Rock formations flashed past dangerously close. Even worse, Ranginui had ahold of her streamer, keeping it from fully deploying, and he was using it to reel her back to him. He pulled furiously on the streamer to hoist her toward him, then stretched out a hand the size of her face, no doubt ready to crush her skull.

It was time to go. Samra squirmed out of the streamer bag's straps and dropped, narrowly avoiding his swiping hand. He caught the top of her hat, yanking the cap free as she fell.

Jake yelled as she tumbled backward into the blackness of

the pit. She just caught a glimpse of him, hanging from one of the orange spheres by his hook. His yell was distraught. Then he was too far away to see.

Her own hook was flailing around at her feet by its tether, but she didn't care. She gasped a deep breath to try to slow herself down, and fumbled under her shirt for the lock on the chain. Her hand found it immediately and pulled it to the center of her waist. She felt for the key with her other hand. It wasn't flapping around inside her shirtsleeve any more. She pushed the sleeve up with her other hand and tried to make out her wrist in the darkness. She couldn't see the cord. She searched frantically up and down her forearm with her other hand.

No!

Where was it?

She inhaled as deeply as she could and tried to light herself up. If she could glow, she could float better, or at least see. But her wrist still throbbed from where Ranginui had been yanking on it, and now she knew the key was gone.

Her vision was darkening from the intense pressure and her head ached. Where was the rope now? She pulled frantically at her hook tether, got the handle in her hands, and swung for the last place she recalled seeing the rope. It was so dark now. What color was it? Red? Had it turned to black already? A heavy grunt sounded above her. Ranginui had grabbed hold somewhere. His groan from catching himself echoed down the cavern. There was another sound, too. A rushing sound rising up to meet her.

The river.

Where was the rope?

Samra gasped and gasped again, trying to arrest her fall. The pressure was horrible. It pressed on her ears made her feel like she was smothered under a rock. Under a mountain.

She wasn't plummeting as quickly as she was before but she was still falling too fast. The chain felt like it had gained ten pounds and was dragging her toward the sound of the river at alarming speed. Would she survive the impact? Would it drown her anyway if she did?

The blood was pounding in her ears and her skin felt like it was burning—but it still wasn't glowing.

Glow.

Find the rope.

Glow.

And then there was light.

But it wasn't from her.

She tumbled into the opening of the last cavern and had only an instant to register the scene. The massive sand dune from the falls. The river. A figure near the edge of the water holding a lantern.

The rope.

She swung the hook with all her might toward the rope and caught the last sphere just as it flew past. She gasped again, this time from the jolt, as the springs of the hook stretched and the tether around her body grew taut. Her shoulders strained to bear the deceleration as her fingers slipped down the handle to its very end. The hook handle snapped, but the tether held it together. She swung back and forth at the bottom of the tether and at the very bottom of the rope. She twirled around once, then was flung into a wild arc, up and around. Her view kept changing.

Forward, back.

Sandfall. Boy with lantern.

He was a definitely a boy. Young and covered in dirt. He had a coil of rope slung over his shoulder and a bunch of contraptions hanging off his jacket. She'd seen a jacket like that before. He reminded her of Enzo, the old messenger pilot. But this boy was young. Her age. He was crouched at the edge of the sand, right where it met the swift-flowing river. His boots were muddy with mountain grit and he was holding something by a dangling cord. Something he'd just picked up from the sand.

The key.

"Hey!" she yelled. She swung away again and the rope twirled her around the cavern in its wide, slow arc. As she swung back his direction she twisted to face him again. "That's mine!" She was nearly over the top of him now. He strained his neck to watch her.

He was lit in a strange way from the lantern below him. His face was mostly in shadow but it looked kind. It looked tired.

"Where did you come from?" the boy yelled. "What's up there?"

Samra swung away again, but this time her arc was much smaller—gentler. When she faced him again it was more direct. "It's a sky city."

The boy was standing fully upright now and shifted the rope on his shoulder. "Are there airships?" he yelled.

"Lots of them!"

Samra was spinning again. It was making her dizzy. The boy and his lantern were a yellowish blur. She swung back around to face him, but felt the rope above her lurch. The winch was engaging, pulling her up.

"How do I get up there?" the boy yelled. "Is it far?"

So far. Just the thought of being hoisted back up was making her irrationally nervous. Her heart still hadn't stopped racing from the fall, from Ranginui and the way she came so close to hitting the river face first in the blackness. She would have, if not for this boy and his lantern.

"You have to fly!" she shouted. She didn't know why she said that. It wasn't as though he could. He was just standing there with those muddy boots and his dimming lantern. But there was something about him that somehow suggested he could. Maybe just that jacket.

She rose steadily through the air now. The winch was reeling in the rope. She cupped a hand around her mouth and shouted down to the rapidly diminishing figure of the boy. "What's your name!"

"Atlas!" The shout came back as an echo, bouncing off the walls of the cavern. He was just a speck now in his tiny orb of light.

"What's yours?" The yell was faint and distant, but barely discernible.

"Sam!" she shouted.

Her voice ricocheted back at her from the rocks. She listened for any kind of response, but got nothing. She was in a new cavern now and she could no longer see him. The rope was picking up speed. She whipped through the darkness toward the growing disc of twilight, high, high above. By the time she reached the upper caverns, she could make out a distant planet in the darkening sky.

The whole fall had only lasted minutes. It wasn't more than five or six minutes in total now since she left the ship. It felt like a lot longer. Had she somehow plummeted through the mountain during the day, but come out at night?

But it was just an illusion. As she rose, the caverns grew lighter. Sections of the pit she thought dark on the way down now seemed cheery in comparison to the blackness she'd just suffered in the bowels of the mountain.

The pressure on her ears was lessening. Her vision was clearing, too. The valley was coming into view, and the port town around it. The little planet far up in the sky grew dimmer again. At least it seemed so as she was dragged back into the light.

She rose out of the pit in the mountain and breathed an involuntary sigh. It was only then that she took a look at the number on the sphere she was dangling from.

Black ten.

She'd done it!

She was the champion. Far up the rope, Ranginui was dangling from a sphere near the top of the black section. Number one or two perhaps. Way, way up in the distance, just about to climb aboard the ship, was Jake Robinson. She watched him step aboard, but he immediately turned around to scan the rope. He was waiting for her. As she cleared the last edge of the pit, she gave him a wave.

She was worried that without her hat, people would easily tell that she wasn't a Grounder. Her hair still had a decidedly greenish tint and she'd not seen any Grounders sporting anything so colorful. But as she neared the jump ship, hardly anyone was paying attention. The observation decks and rope bridges were nearly vacant. Even the jump ship had cleared out. As the rope was wound up into the giant spool overhead, all the spheres were being put away, not just because she was at the bottom, but because the waiting jump teams had all disappeared.

She looked around to see what could have caused the drastic change, and her eyes finally settled on the airship hovering just inside the Storm Gate, high above the sandfall. The ship was rigged with black canvas and sported the same red sunburst she'd noted on Eric Savage's ship. The airship certainly hadn't been there when she left. This craft was longer and leaner than Eric's. It was bristling with harpoon weapons and smaller, nimbler skiffs strapped to the side. Some of these skiffs were deploying crew and moving off to different parts of the port.

Samra was hauled up through the gaping floor of the jump ship and found the interior decks nearly empty. The games master was still there and he only paused briefly at the sight of her hair before helping her aboard and shaking her hand.

"Congratulations, Sam. You did it after all. Had us worried there for a bit. Thought that rope was never going to move a third time."

"Third?" Samra asked.

"Yes. Ms. Turngrass didn't fare quite so well as you in the standings, but not to worry. Search team said they found her alive in one of the sand pits. Bit worse for wear. Maybe a fracture or two but she's still among the living. Lots to be said for that." He reached into his pocket. "Usually there'd be a lot more fancy to-do about your victory, but I'm afraid the show's been cut a bit short. Here are your winnings, however, as promised." He tucked the note into her palm and donned his hat. "Must be off now. Congratulations again, young man." He spun on his heel and rushed out through one of the doors to the side deck.

Only Jake Robinson and the crew of the *Restless Fury* remained in the bar. He strode over to Samra the moment the games master departed and grasped her by the shoulders. "Thought you were a goner for sure," he said smiling. "A black ten. In all the years I've seen this sport done, I've never seen it done like that."

Samra smiled. "Thanks to you."

"Me? No. I was the one who almost got you killed. I was convinced I had when you went tumbling down that hole with no streamer pack on. Boy, when you came up out of that hole hanging onto the very last sphere . . . man, I thought I'd seen it all." His eyes flitted to the doorway. Samra spotted the young woman from before, lingering just outside the door. Her eyes were smiling but she still looked nervous. "Look, Sam. I gotta run, but if you ever need anything in Port Savage, you come look me up, all right?"

Samra smiled and nodded. "Okay, thanks."

"See you around, kid." Jake clapped her on the shoulder and ducked through the doorway.

Samra moved toward the bar and the rest of the waiting crew. Landy and Sunburn were grinning. Cogs looked more or less drunk, and the captain still had the same serious stare, but Samra noticed she was now holding a rolled-up piece of paper in her hands and she was treating it gently.

Ranginui chose that moment to emerge from the swinging door behind the bar. Samra froze while still a dozen feet away and waited for him to start hurling the crew of the *Fury* about the place or smashing the bar to pieces, but the big man didn't give any of them so much as a second glance. He merely hoisted one of the brown liquor bottles from the bar, gathered a second in his other hand, and disappeared back through the swinging door again.

The tension in the room ebbed, and Samra finally reached the crew.

"You did it," Captain Savage said. Her words gave no indication of what emotion she might be feeling. "You saved the ship. Borgram left a guarantee that we can retrieve the note from the bank in the morning."

Samra let herself smile. "So does that mean we can head back to my patch now?"

The captain hadn't been smiling, but her eyes lost whatever humor they had. "We've got one more job to do first. And it's one we don't get to refuse." Her eyes flitted out the windows to the skiffs being deployed by the newly arrived behemoth of an airship.

"I thought we were free now," Samra said.

"Not yet."

Samra followed the captain's gaze up to the red sunburst. "A job we can't refuse? Who's up there?"

Captain Savage frowned. "That's my father. And he's waiting to see us."

29

THE KEY

He'd climbed over too many boulders to count. He moved slowly and stopped often because there were periodic screeches in the dark. The scarabs were down there, clacking their claws and waiting.

Atlas hated leaving Kipling alone in that tiny crevice, but he was running out of time and he'd need to move quickly. The oil in the lamp was running low and the last thing he wanted was to be stuck inside a mountain with no way out. Even if the *Sun Dragon* hadn't struck ground so hard, he wasn't sure he could find his way back the way they came, even with the lights.

No. He'd have to keep going, find help or at least some medicine for the Skylighter boy and come back for him. Rustleberry leaves. He didn't have any idea what they looked like or where he would find them, but he had to try.

The light was coming from somewhere ahead. He shielded his lantern periodically and watched for it. He could also hear the river. Somewhere in their desperate flight from the scarabs, he'd lost it. It burbled and gurgled in the distance but he was getting closer. If he could find the river again, he was sure he could find the way out. There was another sound, too. Somewhere nearby. It wasn't the smooth flow of water. It was scratchy. An underworld sound. A whisper from the earth. It said, "Shhhh."

He climbed down a long slope of boulders that had tumbled out of the mountain's innards. He worked his way out the end of the cavern and into a new one—a cavern with a distant light, high overhead.

The dim glow shimmered faintly on the rippling water. The walls of the mountain itself were disturbing it. A steady flow of sand pouring down one side of the cave was pooling into a giant dune. The sand ran over itself in rivulets till it skittered off the end of the dune and into the water. From there it washed downstream and disappeared again into the darkness.

Atlas saw a way out.

Up in the circle of dim light, near the cavern ceiling, there was a rope. He couldn't imagine its purpose, as it was so high up he saw no way to reach it, but someone must have put it there. People must use it somehow.

The rope was almost as black as the cavern. It swayed gently, due in part to a shiny sphere bobbing at its end. Once again, Atlas could divine no purpose to the item, but he wished he could reach it nonetheless. Could he use it to get out somehow? Was it an escape route? He stood near the water's edge and tried to see up the hole.

Something whizzed past his head, followed by a tiny thump.

He looked down and saw a metallic object with a bit of leather cord sticking out of the sand. Whatever it was had just barely missed him. He crouched down to investigate and tugged on the cord.

A key.

As he crouched there, trying to decipher the purpose of the key and its mysterious appearance, something else incredible happened. A girl came tumbling out of the sky.

She was some kind of daredevil acrobat, catching hold of the very last bit of the rope and swinging around by a mechanical contraption tied to her body. She swung about the cavern, spinning and twirling till finally she seemed to notice him.

"Hey! That's mine!"

Atlas didn't care that the key was hers. He was far more interested in where she had just fallen from.

"Where did you come from?" he yelled. "What's up there?"

"It's a sky city!"

Sky city. What kind of sky city? A friendly one where he could get help, and medicine for Kipling, or a city full of raiders?

"Are there airships?" he asked.

"Lots of them!"

He scanned the walls for any kind of stairs or a path up.

"How do I get there? Is it far?" Wherever this place was, it sounded like his best option.

The girl continued to twirl. Her hair flew around her face in little wisps. He had a hard time making out exactly what she looked like. She was dressed like a boy, but was still as pretty as any girl he knew.

"You have to fly!" the girl shouted.

Did she mean there were airships that went up and down this hole? Perhaps that meant he could get the *Sun Dragon* up this way.

The girl was getting farther away. The rope was being pulled up and out the top of the cavern, and her with it. He wasn't ready for her to leave. He still had so many questions. But she was the one who asked first.

"What's your name?" she yelled.

He could barely make her out in the distance now. "Atlas!"

He cupped his hands and shouted again. "What's yours?" The girl was out of sight now, up past the rocks, and he couldn't get nearer because of the river. A sound echoed down the cavern walls but he couldn't make out the words over the burble of the river and the subtle shushing of the sand cascading down the rocks.

He stood there for a while, holding the key and waiting to see if perhaps the rope would come back down, but it never did.

After a few minutes, he followed the edge of the river till he could nearly see straight up the hole in the ceiling, but he still couldn't make out the top.

It had to be up there somewhere. If the girl had come down, how far could it be? He'd find a way up it somehow.

He considered his options.

If the rope did come back down, maybe he could ask the girl for help. Ask her to lift Kipling out. If he couldn't find a way to bring the *Sun Dragon* to this cavern, he might at least benefit from the knowledge of someone who knew the caverns better than he did. He could map it, and get the airship out later. He'd have to work quickly, however. The Skylighter boy was fading fast and their lights weren't going to last much longer. This cavern was his best chance.

He picked his way over the sand and up the rocks, then back through the hole he had emerged from. He moved slowly again, not only because he didn't want to stumble into a den of nightbeasts unannounced, but also so he wouldn't end up down a wrong passage. There was no time for getting lost.

Atlas finally reached the tunnel where he had left Kipling, but there was no light coming from it.

"Oh no," Atlas muttered and raced along the passage. He skidded to a stop at the section of wall he had constructed to barricade Kipling in. It was a mess. The stones he'd piled up at the entrance of the alcove were scattered and the lantern was lying cracked and unlit on the floor.

Kipling was gone.

Atlas searched the alcove with grim determination, but found no sign of the boy. His fear that Kipling had been taken and eaten by the scarab crabs seemed unlikely. There was no blood. No evidence of a struggle, other than the broken-down wall.

A tuft of brown fur was fluttering against his boot. From Fledge?

What in the world had happened?

Kipling had been unconscious. Weak. Certainly in no condition to be tearing down walls and vanishing. Where had he gone?

Atlas headed around the corner into the larger cavern where he had anchored the *Sun Dragon*, hoping Kipling and the cliff fox had simply made their way back there.

When he rounded the corner and lifted the lantern, his heart sank. A scarab crab was facing the other direction and picking at a bit of detritus caught between the rocks, but there was no airship.

The *Dragon*.

Atlas swung the lantern side to side to see if perhaps it had simply come untethered and drifted off to another part of the cave. The lateral fin had been bent, but the ship was still floating when he left it.

The scarab crab turned in the light and appraised Atlas with its glossy black eyes. Atlas shivered and backed up a step. What now?

The flame on the lantern was growing dim and the scarab was taking more interest in him.

This was bad.

The *Dragon* had been his only hope of getting to Enzo. Now

he'd be lucky to get out of this cavern alive.

The flame of the lantern flickered and began to smoke. Atlas set the lantern down, whipped off his leather jacket and tore at his shirtsleeve. It took a bit of help from his teeth, but he was able to quickly rip the fabric off his arm, tearing it away from the seam at his shoulder. He formed the fabric into a ball and skewered it onto the end of his harpoon. From there it was a matter of lifting the glass housing of the lantern carefully enough to not extinguish the already perilous flame.

The cave had sunk into darkness, and somewhere ahead of him, claws clacked on stones.

The fabric caught fire and sputtered to life. He raised his makeshift torch just in time to press back the advance of the scarab crab. The creature dodged to the side, then retreated a few steps. Atlas backed up, too. He gathered up his jacket and worked his way blindly backward till he got a hand against the cavern wall. From there he felt along it, still keeping his eyes on the scarab and his torch aimed directly at it.

He found the entrance to the passage and sprinted inside. The scarab followed.

It was only when Atlas was partway down the passage that he realized it wasn't the one he had come from. This passage sloped steadily upward, making progress difficult. He alternated the torch from front to rear as he fled, keeping danger behind him at bay, while simultaneously trying to navigate the tunnel.

The *Sun Dragon* was gone. How was that possible? There was no way Kipling could have taken it, unless . . . what if Kipling hadn't really been unconscious when he left? Was it all some kind of act? What if the feverishness and fainting was all an elaborate ruse, so he could steal the airship?

But why? They were already traveling together. And how could he have flown away in the dark, and with a busted lateral fin?

The situation baffled him. Atlas shrugged back into his jacket. As he climbed steadily through the passage, he tried desperately to identify the sounds in the tunnel behind him. Was the scarab in pursuit? Were there more? Or perhaps some other creature had joined the chase. His torch was nearly out. He'd soon be finding out the answer in the dark. The thought goaded him into running faster. So much so that he rounded a corner at full speed and almost ran off the edge of a cliff.

Atlas teetered on the precipice and watched the pebbles he'd dislodged go skittering downhill.

Ahead of him was a vast pit, hundreds of feet across, lit by fading daylight. For the first time in hours, he could see the sky. The pit was part of a vast gorge that somewhat resembled the Rift back home, but the walls of this gorge were perforated with dozens of holes, many of them lit with lanterns and bustling with activity. Heavy ropes dangled down the cliff walls and supported scaffolding and rickety, winch-driven elevators.

Atlas gaped at the complexity of the scene.

Pathways along the cliff walls linked the various openings, some of them as narrow as goat trails, but it didn't impede the progress of the people using them. They were miners. Lots of miners, swarming in and out of passages like ants. It was difficult to make out the details of the work in the fading light, but it was evident that they were dragging ore from the mine and hauling it away toward a blackened end of the gorge where great fires were burning and coating the cliff walls with soot. A cloud of smoke wafted up from the distant smelters and drifted north into the twilight.

Atlas had emerged from a disused section of tunnels midway up the cliff face. The action was all taking place on the canyon floor as gaunt miners loaded ore into metal carts and pushed them along the road to the smelters.

The last bit of shirtsleeve on his harpoon fizzled and went out as it fell from the tip of the weapon. Atlas took another look down the passage, but could see nothing. Somewhere inside, claws scratched on rocks and echoed down the passage, but no creatures dared the light of the mine. At least not yet.

Atlas moved cautiously away from the passage, uninterested in being dragged back into the darkness by some especially courageous scarab. Whatever his next direction of travel, it wouldn't be back through that tunnel.

A horn sounded overhead and drew his attention to the skyships hovering over the mine. They were small craft, capable of carrying no more than five or ten people but they were illuminating the gorge with periodic light. The aircraft had fires aboard, and seemed to be using the heat to keep themselves aloft. They also deflected the glow from the onboard fires via curved mirrors to highlight different sections of the mine in sequence. The lights swept over the holes with the most activity.

"All out, now!" someone shouted. "Final call! Close up those tool carts!"

The shouting was coming from a craft, hovering near the center of the gorge. The men aboard were all dressed alike, in coats with shiny buttons and sabers at their sides. They looked significantly better fed than the miners and their clothes bore none of the soot and grime.

Other men in uniform stalked the walls. They clustered in groups toting long lances and a few held shields. Some of them carried whips. A promontory jutting over the mine was outfitted with a mechanical contraption bristling with harpoons. A man seated in the machine swiveled it about, aiming the business end of the device at various tunnels in turn. At first Atlas thought it was a weapon for use against nightbeasts, but then he realized it was being aimed at the miners themselves.

His attention didn't linger long on the machine, because something new was entering the gorge. Multiple somethings. Overhead, rounding a bend in the gorge from the west, was a massive black airship. It had a red sunburst on its nose and was followed by a couple of other smaller craft. It motored through the gorge sending rumbling vibrations along the cliffs. Atlas could only glimpse a few of the crew in the rigging, but what caught his attention was a smaller ship, partially disassembled and lashed to the rear of the hull. Even without the distinctive coloring and hand painted name emblazoned on the tail fin, he would have recognized the ship anywhere. The *Sunshine Express*.

Enzo!

Atlas's heart sped up, along with his thoughts. He had to get up there. He could find his grandfather. This was his opportunity.

He'd lost the *Sun Dragon* and Kipling. He'd lost nearly every asset and tool he'd come with, but he still had a chance. He just needed to seize it.

The ship was making for a passage in the rocks at the south end of the mine. No matter its destination, it would have to make a turn to avoid the fiery smoke over the smelters. It would turn and disappear through the wall on the far side of the gorge. From there it would be lost to him. But there was one other possibility.

In order to make the sharp turn to the right, the ship would have to hug the left wall of the gorge just prior to the turn. It would pass beneath the rocky promontory with the harpoon turret. If it came close enough, he could make it. He had to. And that was his only hope.

Atlas frantically scanned his options. The cliff was too steep to climb. He'd never make it to the top in time. He scrambled along the goat-sized trail, careful with his footing so he wouldn't slip and tumble into the mine. He needed a way up.

Ahead, he spotted his salvation.

The elevator. Miners were forming a line and stepping into a cage at the bottom of the canyon. The cage was nearly full. High overhead, a motor was coughing to life. The gate to the elevator swung shut and elevator ropes quivered. Atlas ran.

The elevator was moving, but in a matter of moments it would pass by the end of the path he was on. It was a hundred feet down if he missed, but if he timed it right . . .

No time for hesitation.

He raced down the path and kept his eyes on the point where it ended and the quivering ropes beyond. He lost sight of the elevator briefly as he had to cut into a hairpin turn of the cliff, but as he rounded the bend, it rose into view ahead of him. He tossed his harpoon aside and sprinted, leaping the few feet of distance between the path and the elevator car, watched by the load of startled miners. He collided with the side of the cage, caught one hand on the bars, then lost his footing on the narrow ledge between them, slipping off the edge with one foot and teetering precariously on his other. A hand reached through the bars and grasped his shirt to steady him.

He looked through the bars to find a dozen dirty faces looking back. The man grabbing his shirt had a massive beard coated in dust and flecks of rock. He only had one arm, but it held Atlas tightly. His eyes were questioning as Atlas righted himself and got a better grip on the bars. "Thanks," he murmured.

The man holding his shirt looked up to the elevator's destination, a wooden platform high overhead, loaded with more of the uniformed mine supervisors. "Don't know who you are, kid, but the Air Corps won't like you being here," the man said. "If you have business you got to do, you best get to it in a hurry."

Atlas nodded to him. "I will." He shifted his feet to the space between the next set of bars and began working his way around the cage. The one-armed man released his grip on Atlas's shirt, but as he moved, more hands reached through the bars to find his shoulders, his back, or his waist. Some of the hands were missing fingers, many were skeletal and gaunt, but they held on—not detaining him, but clasping and releasing as he moved, a wave of security, keeping him steady and safe from the long fall to the mine floor. Atlas reached the other side of the cage just before the elevator approached the landing platform. He nodded to the miners in the cage, then leapt onto the last footpath that ran beneath the cliff top. He caught himself on the rocks and gripped the side of the gorge wall as the elevator continued up through the bottom of the wooden platform above. One of the youngest miners gave him a wave.

The fire-propelled balloons were scanning the floor of the mine and the various tunnel openings with their mirror-assisted lights. A beam of light passed along the path beneath his but didn't reveal his position.

He watched for an opening in the surveillance from the Air Corps on the landing platform, then ran along the path, searching for a less conspicuous way up.

The airships in the gorge were nearing the promontory. One of the smaller airships had passed the big one and was making the turn up the canyon first. The uniformed man in the harpoon turret leaned over the edge of his machine to watch.

Atlas was a mere eight feet below the top of the cliff now, perhaps a dozen feet from the turret, flattened against the rocky wall. He eased himself up slowly, trying to scale the last bit, but footholds in the rocks were unstable and each one he tried was loose. The last thing he needed was to knock a rock free and send it tumbling down the mountainside. Or send himself with it.

The rocks above him were slick and hard to hold on to. He pressed himself close to the cliff and searched with his fingers for handholds, but despite his best efforts, he couldn't make it up the last few feet without slipping. He was tempted to leap for the top, but if he missed, or there was nothing up top to grab, it would be a long fall down to the bottom of the mine.

The airship with the sunburst on the nose was nearing the promontory. The man in the harpoon turret yelled something down to the deck of the ship. Atlas cringed. It was only a matter of time till someone spotted him. He had to act fast. The airship was approaching its closest point. If he had a running start, Atlas could almost leap the distance. It was so close.

He couldn't miss this chance.

He crouched and pulled the coil of rope off his shoulder. He didn't have any kind of hook to use but he knew what he had to do. His fingers worked fast, yanking one of the stones loose from the cliff wall. He pinched a length of the rope beneath the stone and wrapped furiously. It didn't have to be pretty, but it had to hold.

He knotted his makeshift grappling hook and stood up, balancing the weight of it in his hand. The ship was pulling beneath the turret. It was now or never.

Atlas spun the rock around in an overhand arc, faster and faster as he lengthened the rope. He gave it one final spin and heaved, sailing it up and over the turret's harpoon launcher at a slight angle. The rope hit the barrel of the launcher and kinked hard. Atlas held tension and let the rock end complete its arc around, once, twice, and a final tight spin, overlapping itself at an angle. The rock clanged into the metal launcher.

The turret gunner popped up and looked around. He spotted the rope around the harpoon gun and gave a shout, but Atlas was already on the move. He pulled once on the rope to check the tension, hauled back, and leapt. He swung out away from the cliff wall and over the top of the airship. He was about to let go, when the rope came loose from the gun turret anyway — the rock spinning free from his hastily tied knot.

Oops.

He dropped.

Atlas let go of the rope and flailed for the canvas of the airship's envelope. He hit the ship in a belly flop, just shy of the apex of the frame, and bounced slightly, but he dug his fingertips into the fabric as hard as he could to grab hold.

Stop stop stop.

He managed to pinch the fabric just enough to make a wrinkle and arrested his slide with all the strength he had in his fingertips.

The turret gunner pivoted the weapon to face him, surprised by the sudden movement, but whether it was because he was aiming at a kid, or because he was also aiming at the airship, he did nothing else. He merely stared in shock as the aircraft finished rounding the turn and motored up the canyon.

Atlas shimmied his way up the envelope, staying flat and using his clammy palms to spider his way up. Moving slowly, he was able to not slide downward at all, and finally gained the rigid walkway that ran atop the airship's longitudinal axis. He gripped the narrow rail with satisfaction.

He'd made it.

Atlas folded himself over the low-profile rail and collapsed onto the walkway beyond with one hand still firmly gripping the bar. He looked back to the harpoon turret but the man inside had disappeared. That was probably trouble, but he'd bought himself some time.

He let himself smile, just briefly, but then remembered his mission. He was almost there.

As the ship lofted steadily upward in a turn through the rocky canyons, Atlas worked his way farther astern. The ship passed villages built into the sides of the mountain walls. Recently returned miners and their families were sitting on stoops overhanging deep vertical drop-offs.

The homes themselves were carved directly into the rocks or adapted to fit into previously bored-out tunnels. A few people spotted him atop the airship as it cruised by, but no one opened their mouth to say anything. Everyone viewing the passing ships was doing so with hostility. Not a single one of the children was gazing with the sort of incredulous adulation these aircraft would have received in Womble.

In Womble, the kids would have come racing from their homes, hollering the whole way through the fields and begging for a ride. These children—the few he could spot—stared out from behind mothers and fathers with sullen eyes and snotty noses, not the least bit thrilled to be witnessing this particular aerial wonder.

The ships climbed on, circling the mountain, and eventually reached a passage that bored straight through the mountainside. The passage was lit with lanterns and guarded by more of the stern-faced Air Corps. Atlas slunk aft behind the vertical fin and hid himself on a maintenance deck near the rudder. Careful to not be spotted by the lower-flying airship trailing some distance behind, he climbed down the access ladder and cautiously scanned the aft deck of the ship. There was some type of captain's quarters built into the stern, and a rear observation deck, but no one was on it.

As he continued down the ladder, he spotted the bulk of the crew. The few that were above decks were huddled along the starboard side of the ship, watching a spectacle coming into view on the other end of the tunnel. It was only then that Atlas saw where they were.

They'd entered the flying city the girl had talked about. He'd made it. For all the climbing and turning over the outside of the mountain, he'd come back to where he started, just a whole lot higher up.

Hundreds of airships hovered in the valley between the cliffs. Big ones, small ones. Atlas hadn't ever dreamed there were so many in the entire world. In any other circumstance, he would have simply hung there on the ladder and gawked as they drifted by. But now was not the time. His grandfather was aboard this ship, and he was going to find him.

He jimmied the lock on one of the captain's quarters windows and slipped inside. The cabin was compact, as would be expected aboard an airship, but it did have a few accessories he doubted most other ships boasted. One was a full-sized two-person bed instead of a hammock. The other was a framed oil painting of a man with a bristling black beard and a double-breasted coat seated next to a sickly woman in a flowery dress. There was no plaque or description of the painting, but the position on the main wall of the cabin suggested persons of importance. Atlas didn't have time to notice anything else because voices sounded just outside the door.

Atlas scrambled for a place to hide, but the only option in the cramped cabin was under the bed. He fell to the floor and rolled underneath, just as the cabin door opened and two men entered.

He couldn't see much. Two pairs of boots, one shiny and black, one battered and brown, standing near the doorway.

"I don't care about the crew's families. They can wait," Shiny Boots was saying. "My father has reached the wreck. We'll simply keep the cargo aboard and ferry it out there tomorrow."

"And the shore leave?" Brown Boots asked.

"They can have leave tonight, but the rest is cancelled. I expect them all back aboard by morning. They can loaf about the saloons when the work is done." He walked to the mirror. "This is my father's finest hour and he's likely to be in a festive mood. Getting what he wants makes him almost bearable to be around. If I'm going to ask for full command of the fleet, this will be the time."

"Certainly well due, sir," Brown Boots mumbled.

"My father is giving his speech tonight. Admiral Orloff will no doubt be there. I'll present him with his gift then. Can't wait to see the look of jealousy on Orloff's face. It will be the perfect time for my father to see how irreplaceable my talents are, and note the admiral's need for a permanent retirement."

Brown Boots walked to the windows. "It seems your sister beat us to port by a matter of some hours. I heard she paid off the *Restless Fury.*"

"I couldn't care less what Erin does with that rattletrap bucket," Shiny Boots said. "She's Father's problem, not mine."

"So no more deals with Borgram?"

"Undercutting my sister's harvesting earnings is small potatoes now, Aspen. You need to show some imagination. You're never going to get anywhere in life if you don't learn to improve upon your ambitions."

"What would you like done with the captive, sir?"

"Is he still chained up?"

"Aye."

"Given you any trouble?"

"None to speak of, unless you count his snoring. Makes a din with that. But he's an old wreck. Suppose we all can expect that at his age."

Shiny Boots walked to the writing desk and scribbled something. "Leave the old man aboard. Does he still have the relic key?"

"Hangs on to it for dear life anytime the men get near him. We could get it away from him, but we'd have to break a few fingers."

"Let the old man hold on to it for a few more hours. We'll bring him to my father once I've had time to present him with the relic. No use spoiling the surprise. Take this message to my father's attendants as soon as we dock. Inform them I'll be along presently."

"I was planning to dress for the party, sir."

"Don't be ridiculous, Aspen. No one will be looking at you anyway. Now get out. We're nearly there."

Brown Boots left and the door was shut roughly behind him. Shiny Boots walked to a cupboard and poured something into a glass. The first contribution disappeared quickly, but when the bottle clinked against the glass a second time, he stood there for some minutes sipping it. It was another fifteen minutes by the time he'd finished standing in front of the mirror and primping. Finally, when Atlas was despairing of ever escaping from under the bed, the man dropped his coat over the footboard, retrieved another from the closet, and exited the room.

Atlas waited five more minutes before climbing out from under the bed. He crept to the door and listened, but the passage was quiet. He snuck out into the mid-decks, found the stairs heading upward, but only poked his head up far enough to spot the sentry, leaned lazily against the stern rail and spitting something over the side. The ship was docked.

Atlas crept back down the ladder and peered into the other cabins. All were empty, but there was another set of steps at the forward right of the ship, just aft of the cockpit. Atlas descended quietly and emerged in the cargo hold.

The space was crammed with supplies and ballast tanks. What little room there was left had been stuffed with miscellaneous lift pods. None were especially well cared for and a few were oozing goo from punctures due to rough handling.

Atlas crept along the narrow keel corridor until he reached the center of the ship. He found a wooden pen with bits of straw protruding under the door. The pen looked to have been used to haul livestock of some kind, but when Atlas reached it and peered over the top, there were no animals inside. Instead, he found Enzo, curled up in a ball in the hay, and chained to a wall.

"Grandpa!" Atlas flung the latch open and swung the door wide. He sprang through the doorway and fell to his knees, skidding across the straw to the side of his grandfather.

Enzo stirred in the hay and rolled over to face him. When he saw who it was, he broke into a smile. He raised a weathered hand to clasp his grandson's. "Atlas, my boy. I knew you'd come."

30

MARLOW

Samra felt lighter than air. She wasn't at the moment—not technically speaking, as she still had the persistent weight of the locked chain around her waist—but the thrill of her victory in Borgram's wager made her euphoric nonetheless. She'd saved the *Fury*, ensured the jobs of the crew, and now she was rich!

She read the bank note she'd been given by the games master. Twenty thousand marks. She didn't know what she'd buy with it, but it surely meant she was important now. She was a rope fall champion. The title brought a grin to her face.

She followed the crew over the gangplank of the jump ship and across the valley via the web of bridges and floating platforms toward the main cluster of ships that made up the city.

People were bustling about, dizzy with apprehension about the arrival of Lord Savage's skyship. Some she passed were thrilled at the prospect. Ladies in fancy jewelry and men in fine clothing scurried to primp and fine-tune their looks for the evening. Ship captains and crewmen frowned and complained over notices being handed out by the Air Corps and the crew from the newly-arrived ship.

The skiffs had deployed to different parts of the city, making announcements and giving notices. Sunburn grabbed one of the slips of paper from a passing messenger and scoured the writing, spelling out the words and attempting to read it aloud. He wasn't making much progress.

"My father is giving a speech," Captain Savage said. "He's issuing orders to move the city." She'd only taken a quick glance at the paper. "And of course throwing a party. Heaven forbid we ever get anything done in this town that doesn't require an excuse to show off. At least my brother will be happy."

A party? Samra wondered if she'd be invited. Would they celebrate her rope fall victory there?

Samra stopped smiling when she saw another skiff pull up from the direction of the sandfall. Four men were aboard carrying a stretcher. They hoisted it over the bulwark of the ship and handed it off to men in white uniforms on the dock. The men leaned over the woman in the stretcher, probing her arms and legs, then lifted the stretcher and carried it in Samra's direction. The crew of the *Fury* stepped aside as the medics passed. Samra had a long look at the person in the stretcher. It was Ms. Turngrass, the woman Ranginui had forced into the falls.

Samra's good mood disappeared as the woman was borne past. Both of her legs were in splints as well as her left arm. Her right arm was the only one still working and she had her hand over her mouth, sobbing softly into it. Her watery eyes found Samra's for an instant as she went by.

Samra recalled Jake's warning about Ranginui and how she had stepped aside to let the woman take her place next to their tattooed competitor. No one had warned this woman, already desperate, and now even worse off for her bravery.

The crew of the *Fury* moved on, up to the next ship deck they needed to traverse, but Samra was frozen on the floating dock, watching the medics prepare to cross the next rope bridge. Captain Savage turned and waved her on. "Come on. We've got to go."

But Samra couldn't leave. She spun around and shouted to the medics. "Wait!" They paused near the bridge and Samra sprinted back to them. She positioned herself at Ms. Turngrass's side and grasped her good hand. The woman recoiled in surprise at first, but Samra held onto her hand and pressed the note with her winnings into the woman's palm. "I'm sorry I didn't warn you."

The woman lifted the note and tried to read it.

"It's twenty-thousand marks," Samra said, "I hope it helps."

The woman's eyes widened, then welled with tears again. She clutched the note to her chest and sobbed. Samra stepped back and the medics hoisted the stretcher again, carrying the woman away across the rope bridge.

When Samra reached the deck of the next ship, the crew of the *Fury* was still waiting. They were all studying her.

"You know those winnings would have provisioned the *Fury* for a year," Captain Savage said.

"Or you could have bought your own skiff," Landy added.

"I know," Samra said. It was a lie. She had no idea what an airship cost. But she didn't want them to second-guess her decision.

"Could have bought a lifetime of ale," Cogs muttered from behind Landy.

"Not the way you go through it," Landy replied.

"I think you did a noble thing," Sunburn said. "I don't know that I could have been so generous."

Captain Savage turned on her heel and led the way on again. "Let's move. If we don't answer my father's summons, he'll be considerably less than generous with us."

The black skyship had moved to the center of the city, high above the other ships. It was docking at the glass-paned Library of Knowledge. Observation decks and balconies overlooked the rest of the city from the library, and they provided a view of every part of the valley. Samra noticed that a main portion of the building was held up by a netted cluster of globe sons.

The crew crowded onto an elevator operated by one of the Air Corps guards and were propelled upward toward the pinnacle of the city via a system of weights and pulleys. As they climbed, there were more of the sunburst flags flying on the ships. Some ships had hoisted other colors as well, but the sunburst flag always rode on top.

"Why does your father need to see you?" Samra asked. "Does he miss you?"

The captain laughed. "A daughter should be so lucky. My father is not much for sentiment. He only has one interest these days, and it's not me."

"He likes Eric better?"

"Probably," Captain Savage sighed. "But Eric won't win my father's attention either. You can't compete with mad obsession, and that's what my father's goals have become to him."

Samra studied one of the flags as they passed it. A motto under the starburst read, "Family First." She considered the captain's statements about her father, and wondered if in the Grounder culture the words meant something different than at home.

The elevator stopped at a row of landing docks near the peak of the city. They were met by a quartet of armed Air Corps guards. Two held crossbow-powered harpoon launchers, and the others carried sabers.

"Your crew will have to wait outside, Miss Savage," the head guard said. "Your father wishes to speak to you alone."

"It's *Captain* Savage," she corrected.

The guard nodded. "Yes, ma'am. If you'd please follow me?" He led the way through a gate wrought from ornate hollow tubes, then he and the captain promptly disappeared inside the library. The other Air Corps guards resumed positions blocking the entrance. Samra and the rest of the crew were abandoned unceremoniously on the docks and left to their own devices.

"Could have at least invited us inside for something to drink," Cogs said. "Waiting around goes a bit easier with something cold and wet in hand."

Landy turned to Sunburn. "You still have that notice?" Sunburn pulled the crumpled paper from his pocket. "Can I have it?" Landy asked.

Sunburn handed over the piece of paper and Landy studied it. Samra noticed she was having an easier time reading it. Landy straightened up and looked around. "Look. I've got to see about something. Will you tell the captain I had to go? I'll be back by morning. I'll meet you at the docks."

"Sounds like we'll be leaving early," Sunburn said. "It's a fair piece of flying out to the dig site, and treacherous terrain."

"Don't worry. I'll be sober, if that's what you're implying," Landy replied. "Just let her know. I'll be back in the morning." She pocketed the notice and moved to the elevator. The attendant frowned but dutifully climbed back inside with her and actuated the lever. The ropes creaked and the pulleys shimmied as the elevator disappeared again below the landing.

"Where's she going?" Samra asked.

"Well, she's got a man in town, don't she?" Cogs said. "Running off to see him no doubt. Night of frivolity while the rest of us mind the captain. Should have lit out by now myself. Bet ol' Wallace and

Hodges are having a good time in the pubs. Could've gone with them, not bandied about with you lot all night."

"You haven't got any credit at the pubs anymore," Sunburn said. "We all know they won't serve you."

"Details," Cogs replied. "Always a decent man or woman about who don't mind spotting a hard-working sailor a bit of ale. Just got to find yourself a generous one. Like young Samson here." He looked to Samra.

"It's Samra," she replied. "And I'm out of money now."

"Ah. So you are," Cogs replied. "Would have liked if you could have saved a mark or two for your own crew mates."

Sunburn smiled and shook his head.

Samra put her hands in her pockets and Cogs wandered over to slump against the wall. She liked that he'd referred to her as part of the crew. He might not have much else in the way of charm, but he'd at least welcomed her into the group.

It was nearly an hour till the captain reappeared. The night had grown dark and, in the meantime, more and more guests had arrived at the library. Some brought skiffs or their entire ships. Others came up the way Samra and the crew had arrived. They exited the elevator, careful to not spend much time looking at the ruffians on the landing, and proceeded inside.

The guests were mostly elegant couples, though more than a few single men and women arrived as well. Most were wearing well-tailored clothing. Brightly colored dresses were standard for the women, with scarves and elbow-length gloves. The men arrived in vests and jackets with shiny buttons and fancy ties around their collars. Few wore hats, but many women used their scarves to cover their hair until they could get inside and out of the wind.

When the captain returned, she was quiet, her mind elsewhere. She gestured to Sunburn and Cogs, not seeming to notice Landy's absence. "One of you has to be my date for the evening, it seems. Otherwise I'm going to be swamped by a bunch of my father's miserable friends trying to court me and get in his good graces. Either of you know how to dance?"

Cogs brightened. "I know the grab-a-bottom two-step. Do they do that one up here?"

The captain simply turned to Sunburn.

"I can manage a simple waltz or two," Sunburn said.

"That'll do. I only need an excuse to turn down other offers."

She addressed Cogs. "Head back to the *Fury*. Make sure no one tampers with our cargo. We need it fit to fly at first light."

Cogs's face fell a bit. "So no dancin'?"

The captain pulled a coin from her pocket and tossed it to him. "You can buy yourself a bottle of ale on the way back and drink it aboard the ship while you stand watch, but no lingering around the taverns on the way." She held up a finger. "Just one bottle. I want you alert when I get back."

Cogs waved the coin and bobbed his head. "Aye, Captain." His spirits were clearly lifted. He inspected the coin on his way toward the elevator. "One big bottle . . ."

"What about me?" Samra asked.

"You're coming with me," the captain replied. "You can be my bodyguard."

Samra grinned.

When the captain led them through the gate, they were met by a servant in a long-tailed jacket. "Miles, I need you to find Mr. McGuire a jacket to wear. See if you can commandeer something from one of the guest suites." The servant nodded to Sunburn and led him away down a hallway.

"Mr. McGuire?" Samra asked. "That's his real name?"

"Connor McGuire," the captain replied.

"So someone remembers his real name after all."

"Of course I do. I'm the captain."

Samra followed Captain Savage to a wing of the floating library featuring a number of rooms for guests. It boasted intricate metalwork of a thin, lightweight variety Samra had never seen before. She wanted to ask the captain how it was made but they reached their destination too quickly. The captain shuttled her into a rectangular room full of mirrors. Dresses and wraps hung on rails in a row and two servants were chitchatting in the corner. They sprang to attention when Captain Savage walked in.

"Why, Miss Erin, we didn't expect to see you here tonight. The party's already started."

"Then you'll have no excuse to dawdle," the captain said. "Father will be furious if I miss his speech. We need to get ready for this event quickly."

"We?" the older of the two servants asked. She looked at Samra over half-moon spectacles. "Are we also meant to dress this creature?"

Captain Savage straightened up. "This is Samra. She's part of my crew. You'll treat her with the same respect you give me." The two women shared a glance with one another. "In fact I'd suggest you treat her better than you treat me, since I already know how I rank in your estimation."

"Why, that's a terrible thing to say," the younger woman replied, and lifted her skirts to walk closer. "You know we hold you in the highest regard, Miss Savage."

"You can save your breath, Alora. Just make us look presentable as quickly as you can and you can get back to your gossiping."

Alora's mouth tightened into a line, but she didn't say anything else. Instead she picked up a kit of supplies and turned to face Samra. "Well, let's see if we can't turn you into something a little *less* savage," she muttered.

When Samra emerged from the room, she couldn't even say all that had happened to her. She wasn't dressed as a boy anymore, that was certain. She'd been outfitted in a light blue dress meant to complement her yellow-green skin tone and her hair was formed and twisted into a complex ball atop her head. What few strands escaped this fate had been curled and tugged at and arranged to perfection at the sides of her face.

Her face itself had also been remade, removing the previous layer of color and contour Ylva had provided, and replacing it with newer and lighter colors that she was informed would bring out her natural radiance. She was then told not to touch anything.

She didn't feel radiant. She felt heavy.

The women had tried in vain to free her from the chain around her waist, insisting that it would ruin everything about her outfit. Despite calling in help, however, they were informed that no tools for removing locks or cutting chains were to be found anywhere on the library grounds, especially not at this late stage with a party already beginning. So after attempting an abundance of soap, lotions and painful, old-fashioned squeezing, the duo admitted defeat and simply decided to cover up the bulge at her waist with an even bulgier dress.

The outfit featured a sash and bow at the waist, a wrap for her shoulders, and long gloves for her arms, and, by the end, the two women looked at each other and admitted that she was in fact quite lovely, despite being a Skylighter.

The captain had kept her mouth shut during this whole ordeal, so Samra followed her example. The captain had selected her own outfit, a simple black dress with shoes that latched around her ankle. To this she had added a thin gold necklace and a matching bracelet. She had cleaned up and permitted the ladies to arrange her hair, but she applied her own make-up, declined gloves, and was ready by the time Samra's transformation was complete.

The captain strode out of the room with the same expression she had on going in, and Samra tried to exude the same confidence, despite feeling entirely unlike herself.

They made their way into the center of the floating tower and crossed a bridge to the main building. When they walked into the heart of the library, Samra had to take a breath.

It was beautiful.

Colored panes of glass formed intricate geometric patterns across the ceiling. Even without sunlight to illuminate them, the windows were exquisite.

The walls of the library held hundreds of miniature alcoves, most of them full of shiny cubes.

A dance floor was suspended a foot or two above the rest of the room, but no one was using it. People milled around the perimeter instead, drinking from thin glasses and tasting bits of food passed around on trays. Nearby conversations muted themselves as Samra and Captain Savage walked in, and various sets of eyes turned their direction.

Samra quickly scanned the room for Sunburn, but the big man wasn't in sight. She could use the assurance of his smile at the moment. Captain Savage was also searching the room, but was forced to greet a contingent of young men that approached her from the dance floor.

Samra listened to the captain deflect small talk for a few minutes before losing interest. None of the men even commented about her presence, and while the women in the vicinity gave her plenty of sideways glances, none approached to speak with her.

Finally, a bell rang and the musicians in the corner of the room ceased playing. A man stepped up to the dance floor. He was wearing a white tie and gloves. He addressed the crowd in a commanding voice. "Ladies and gentlemen, if I could have your attention, please. I'd like to present to you the man of the hour, our gracious host, Lord Marlow Savage."

Samra stretched to peer over the shoulders of the people ahead of her as the crowd applauded. Murmurs rippled through the room as a man stepped up to the wooden dance floor from the far side of the room.

He was different than Samra expected. She somehow thought Lord Savage would be an older, possibly angrier version of Eric Savage, but that was not the case. Eric was boyish and handsome with an impish grin and laughing eyes. He dressed smartly and seemed to relish his appearance. This man, while finely dressed, didn't seem like he fit the clothes at all. They were tailored to his dimensions, but Samra thought he was the sort of man you'd find building a house with his bare hands or hauling great hay bales across a field the way Grounders sometimes did in Womble during the festivals. He had a bushy beard that fell all the way past his collar and rested on his broad chest, and thick unruly eyebrows. His hands looked like they were better used for swinging an axe or digging with a shovel than holding a delicate drink. Samra had a hard time imagining Eric with hands like that.

The most unusual feature of the man was his jewelry. Around his neck, Lord Savage was wearing not one or two, but dozens of necklaces. Each one was a cord or chain with a triangular pendant on the end. The pendants appeared to be made mostly of stone. A few were metal. Samra couldn't help but wonder how heavy they all were piled together around the man's neck. She couldn't imagine hauling around such an oppressive weight all day.

Marlow Savage shuffled to the center of the dance floor and looked around with eyes that seemed ready to judge every figure in the room.

"Well, I've done it," he declared. "I said I would. I've found the wreck of our ancestors' ship." He pulled a paper scroll from his coat pocket and held it up. It was a map with a lot of scribbles on it and a broad red X near one side. Samra noticed glistening metal rings on the man's thick fingers. He seemed to be organizing his thoughts. When he spoke again it was more slowly. "My . . . *our* search is over. After generations adrift on this infernal, deadly world, we'll finally have the answers we seek, and will be rewarded with the truth." He chewed at a bit of his beard that kept getting in his mouth.

His eyes were wild. Samra thought he looked out of place here. The thick coat he wore made him look like a bear. Not a creature she expected to find at a party.

"A long time ago, our people journeyed to this place from

another world. The Old World. Presumably to give us a better life. Couldn't have known what this place was really like. Or maybe they did. But tomorrow we'll unearth their true gift to us."

He spun in a slow circle, searching the faces in the crowd. His eyes found Captain Savage, then rested briefly on Samra. She felt like he was looking straight through her. His gaze flicked back to Captain Savage, however, then drifted around the room. "The proud family of Savage, and the other families present tonight, rose to our ancestors' challenge. We've carved out a new life on this brutal world." He held up a clenched fist. "We've reshaped its dangers and bent them to our bidding.

"We've faced rockslides and tremors—and still built mines. We've battled the winged terrors of the night intent on devouring us, but learned their weaknesses and built ourselves a city of light. We've survived. Not only have we survived, but we've thrived! We took the knowledge given to us by our ancestors, preserved in these relics they left behind, and constructed the greatest city on the face of Altiria.

He held out his arms. "We are the owners of this world."

The crowd applauded again, and he paced back and forth on the floor. Samra couldn't help but think he looked unhappy. Even in the midst of his victory speech, his expression seemed to waver on the brink of rage. He thundered across the floor, feet stomping, but seemed to have no destination.

"Tomorrow morning, we're going to bring our city home. We'll harness the power of flight we've gained and use it to resurrect the vessel of our ancestors' mission. I believe that once we do, we'll learn the final secrets of our history that have eluded us. Its sciences. Its weapons. Its mysteries. We can learn how they traveled across the stars. We'll know how to escape this—"

"We'll be as powerful as the old gods!" A shout emanated from the back of the room. "And what a glorious new future we will build together."

Marlow Savage looked up, seemingly irritated at the interruption, but his expression softened when he saw the speaker. Eric Savage was striding through the crowd. He smiled at the guests around him and shook a few hands as he passed, then leapt up onto the dance floor with his father.

Eric bowed to Marlow and then spun and gave another theatrical bow to the guests. A smattering of applause went up from the crowd.

"I apologize for being late, Father. When I inform you of the reason, I trust you will forgive me."

"He's late because his ship is too slow," Captain Savage whispered to Samra. "If his pilot knew how to fly half as well as you, he'd have been here sooner."

Samra smiled.

Eric gestured to someone in the crowd. "I hope you will pardon the interruption, Father. I've brought you a gift to celebrate your victory."

A man in a stiff coat and battered brown boots stepped up to the platform and offered something covered in paper to Eric. He in turn passed the object to Marlow. Marlow ripped the paper off the gift unceremoniously and revealed a shiny cube made of a material matching those along the walls. It shimmered in the light when Marlow moved it.

"For your esteemed collection," Eric said.

Marlow nodded in appreciation and held up the cube. "Another jewel in our crown!"

The crowd applauded again.

"What is that?" Samra asked the captain.

"Another addition to his Library of Knowledge," Captain Savage replied. "It's one of the lost relics. Part of my father's obsession."

Marlow Savage was turning the relic over in his hands. He brushed his fingers over a corner and one surface lit up. "Do you know which secrets this contains?" he asked his son.

"I hope more than we shall ever need," Eric replied. "But honestly, I do not know. However, I have someone who does. I plan to present him to you soon." Eric turned to the man who had brought him the relic and whispered something, then turned and smiled to the crowd. "Now, Father, should we let these people dance and be entertained?"

Marlow seemed slightly annoyed to be cutting his speech short, but after a moment's hesitation he gestured to the musicians. "Very well," he said. "Enough talk. We are men of action."

The crowd applauded again and the musicians started back up. Eric Savage consulted privately with his father for a few moments while people slowly climbed up onto the dance floor. Marlow's eyes once again found Samra in the crowd, and this time he frowned. A whispered conversation ensued, then Marlow Savage nodded to his son, and moved the other direction to hand the relic to one of his attendants.

Eric noted Captain Savage in the crowd and walked over, hopping down from the dance floor and smiling at them. "Why, Sister, I almost didn't recognize you. Without the whip, you're nearly presentable, aren't you." He looked down at Samra. "And I see you brought your plant friend. Aren't you a bit old to be playing with dress-up dolls, Sis?"

The captain narrowed her eyes.

"I'm not a doll," Samra protested.

"Keep telling yourself that, kid," Eric replied. "Did you think you were actually invited to this party? Erin here is just using you as a way to rebel against our father." He turned to Captain Savage. "Father specifically asked you not to bring her, didn't he?"

Captain Savage didn't respond.

"See?" Eric said to Samra. "What did I say? Looks like she just wanted to play dress-up with someone besides herself, and act out like the child she is."

"Hard to take your insults seriously while you're in that jester suit," Captain Savage replied, flipping the end of Eric's frilly tie. "How many hours did you spend getting into that?"

"Just enough to show I actually care about our father's events. Did you even talk to any of the suitors he picked out for you tonight? Can't turn them away forever. This life in the sun isn't making you look any younger, you know."

"Everything all right?" The voice came from behind Samra and she spun to find Sunburn standing behind her. He was wearing a jacket but had left the collar of his shirt open. He'd trimmed his beard and washed his hair, and his wild mane was now pulled back behind his head. He looked far more civilized than Samra had ever seen him. Handsome even.

"About time you showed up," Captain Savage said. "Where have you been?"

"Waiting for the ideal moment," Sunburn replied.

"Perfect timing indeed," Eric said. "We were just discussing the continuing erosion of Erin's future." Sunburn stood almost a head taller than Eric and dwarfed the man by comparison. Eric tilted his head to look up at him and frowned. "So nice you brought your crew to the party. First the plant girl, now the redheaded giant.

What's next, you going to introduce us to your ancient mess cook?" He looked at Samra. "I know you enjoy disappointing Father, but I'm sure one freak in the room is quite enough to do the job."

Samra felt her face heating up. "I'm not a freak."

Eric cocked his head and smiled at her. "And I'm not the heir to the Savage Empire." He grinned. "Thanks to my sister being such a screw up."

Samra wanted to kick him in the shins, but she held herself back. She wasn't going to make a scene. Not again.

"Enjoy the party, Eric," Captain Savage said. She turned her back on her brother and grabbed Samra's arm. "Come on. We've got better places to be."

Eric smirked and watched them go. "So glad you could be here, Sis. Have fun with your toys."

Samra fled from his laughing stare and followed the captain and Sunburn. They were navigating the crowd of partygoers and making their way toward the exit. Samra caught the captain slipping her hand into Sunburn's and giving it a squeeze, before releasing it as she forged ahead through the crowd.

There was something about the gesture that spoke of another world between them. A world Samra was not a part of.

They burst onto the landing platform and into the cool night air.

The wind pulled at Samra's dress and tugged at her carefully coifed hair. When they reached the elevator, it wasn't there. They were forced to wait.

The captain patted Sunburn on the arm and turned to look at Samra.

Samra's view of the captain was blurry through her watering eyes. She ran a hand under her nose and sniffed. Her hand came away smeared with make-up powder.

"Don't let him get to you," Captain Savage said. "Eric is a terrible person. They pretty much all are, but mostly just the ones I'm related to."

"Why did you bring me tonight?" Samra asked, brushing a tear away from her eye with her fingertip and trying not to let her lip quiver.

"Because I needed a reminder," Captain Savage said. "That underneath all this, we're still creatures of the air. We both are. And no matter how they dress us up, we'll never belong here. We'll never be like them. Not ever."

"You don't think I'd ever fit in here?"

"Lord, I hope not," the captain replied. "But having you with me tonight was a way to show them. You were my talisman of the wild. Evidence to these people of what's really out there. Our true life in the sky."

"But I don't want to be anyone's talisman," Samra replied. "I want to be me."

"So do I, kid. So do I." The elevator arrived and the captain moved to the door. "Come on. We'll get back to the *Fury* where we belong." She gestured for Sunburn to follow but he wasn't moving. He was simply waiting in the middle of the landing, silhouetted by the party lights behind him.

"I can't leave," he said. "I haven't completed my assignment." The captain cocked her head in confusion, but Sunburn simply extended a hand toward her. "It was my captain's order."

The music from the party was drifting through the windows. Couples now whirled around the dance floor.

Samra watched with curiosity as the captain's resolve slowly melted and a smile turned up the corners of her mouth. She took a step toward Sunburn and finally took his hand. He grinned and spun her to him. The captain laughed. Samra couldn't help but smile, too. She felt she was witnessing an entirely different person who had replaced the captain. This woman looked happy.

Sunburn and Captain Savage stepped in time to the music and turned circles around the dock. After a few minutes, they separated and Sunburn turned to Samra, bowing low and extending a hand. "May I have the honor, young lady?"

Samra smiled but shook her head. "I don't know how to dance."

Sunburn took a step forward and simply scooped an arm around her waist, hoisting her in the air and spinning her around the dock. She laughed as they spun, the lights of the party blending with the starlight and streaking across her vision in a blur.

The blur suddenly stopped when Sunburn froze. The world was still spinning a little as he set her down, and she turned to face what he was looking at.

Marlow and Eric Savage had emerged from the party accompanied by their attendants. Eric was chatting with his father gaily and grinning his self-assured grin, but as they approached the boarding ramp of the *Savage Stranger*, they paused and watched what was coming down. Two men were struggling out of the hold of the ship and they were carrying something heavy. Another person?

Samra rested a hand on Sunburn's arm and gripped it tight. The something was dragged onto the dock and brought into the light.

It was a dead body, and Samra knew him.

31

ABDUCTED

Lights flickered in Kipling's brain. They flashed by like his thoughts, and the voices came with them.

"There's something else up here. Looks like an old lantern." It sounded like a young girl speaking.

"Oi! Watch out!" someone else shouted.

Something hissed and flapped around Kipling's head.

"Grab it! What is that thing?"

The hisses and squeaks filled the alcove.

"Oh lord. Should we kill it?"

"No. Grab one of the sacks. Might be worth something."

Some rocks shifted around. "Hey, looks like that creature might have been guarding something . . . there's a kid back here."

The voices and lights faded away, and when they returned, Kipling found himself moving. He was being carried on some sort of stretcher, borne beneath the flickering lights of torches and the dangling stalactites of the caverns. A man walking beside the stretcher was carrying a heavy hammer with his torch.

"You think the ship still flies?" the young girl's voice asked.

"It will once we get it back."

"Never had such a lucky day."

"Hey! Shut up back there and keep an eye out. Still more critters in these holes."

Kipling drifted away again.

When he opened his eyes the next time, he was being given water. It was sweet and tasted like rustleberries. He gulped at it.

"Hey, now. Not too fast." The person speaking was glowing faintly and squatting next to him. He was the pleasant brown of an aged Skylighter. A young girl was there, too, staring down at him. A pair of round-lensed goggles held her hair back.

"Samra?" Kipling muttered, his eyes only partly open. But it wasn't Samra. This girl was a Grounder.

As the girl leaned closer, he got a better look at her. She had freckles across the bridge of her nose in the places that weren't sooty, and her hair was a mousy brown under the lantern glow. "You think he'll live?" Her voice was the same as the one from the cave.

"Oh, certainly," the glowing man said. "Poison was minimal. Just got to get some decent food in him now." He tipped the container of juicy water again and Kipling sputtered a bit, but drank.

He was next offered a slightly battered-looking clump of air kelp bulbs. Not his favorite food usually, but right now it seemed like the best meal he'd ever seen.

"You'll start to get your strength back soon," the man said, as Kipling devoured the bulbs.

A poultice of soggy leaves was wrapped around the wound on his arm.

Kipling propped himself up a little straighter to get a better look at the man. He was a Skylighter, though nobody he recognized. Based on his skin color, Kipling guessed he was around his mother's age.

They were inside a room hollowed out of the rocks. One side had a doorway leading to some other interior spaces and another door looked like it led outside. A single window broke up the wall near the door but beyond it was darkness and Kipling could get no sense of the outside world. His warhook was lying on the floor nearby, along with a burlap sack tied at the neck. The sack moved a little and issued a squeak.

"Oh no!" Kipling said, and crawled toward it.

The Skylighter tried to hold him back. "Whoa, where are you

going?"

"That's Fledge," Kipling blurted out, his fingers stretching for the bag and finding the cords.

"Hey, don't let that thing loose in — " the Skylighter was saying, but Kipling already had the knot free. Fledge did the rest. He burst from the sack, flapping and screeching, bouncing from the floor to the ceiling and off the walls. The Skylighter dodged an attack on his head and flung open the door, ducking as the cliff fox soared over him into the passageway outside. The old Skylighter slammed the door shut.

"No!" Kipling yelled.

But the flapping and squawking subsided, and when the Skylighter cracked the door again, the cliff fox was gone.

"He'll make it out," the man said. "There are openings."

Kipling stared forlornly at the door, then collapsed on the floor again. It was only when the Skylighter came to prop him back up that he tried to assess his situation again. He needed to get out of here. Find Atlas. Find Samra.

"Which colony are you from?" the man asked.

"I'm from the Globe Mother," Kipling replied, wiping dirt from his face with the back of his hand. He righted himself and slid back to the wall, picking up the strand of kelp greens again. It was already making him feel a little better and he was going to need his strength. He noticed the girl with the freckles studying him. She was crouched on a woven rug near his feet and watching him take another bite of a bulb.

"You're from Corra Mara?" The man raised his eyebrows. "What in the world were you doing under the mountain?"

"I'm looking for my friend," Kipling replied. "Why are you here?"

The man frowned. Instead of replying, he leaned back on his haunches and lifted the leg of his pants slightly, exposing the remnants of a metal shackle around his right ankle. "Didn't have a choice. Got brought here to work the mines after they found us."

Kipling stared at the shackle in disbelief. "They stole you from your patch, too?"

The Skylighter shook his head. "Patch came down on its own. We went three years with no globe sons to pollinate the daughters. It never bloomed and the families on the patch started getting sick from lack of new growth. We ran into a big column of kelp near the end, thought it was going to keep us fed for a while, but it was infested with drift rats. They got aboard the patch and started eating everything they could get their teeth into. Didn't have enough folk left to salvage the globes and keep the patch afloat. Went down in the desert. That's when the raiders found us. Never even had time to get word to the council."

"What was the name of your colony?"

"Loma Dura."

Kipling studied the face of the man with new appreciation for the lines and creases in his skin. Loma Dura had disappeared years ago. Samra had been wrong about the flying sharks. It was the lack of globe sons that had spelled its doom. Had this man been living underground all that time?

"We haven't seen any of the globe sons reaching the Mother, either," Kipling said. "The council has been receiving messages from colonies all over the skylands. None of them have been getting pollinated."

"And none of them will," the Skylighter said. "The globe sons are here."

"In this cave?" Kipling asked.

"No. Up top. In Port Savage."

Kipling recalled the last bundle of the Mother's globe son pods getting stowed aboard the ship that had stolen Samra. As much time as he had spent thinking about getting her back, he hadn't fully considered the repercussions of their loss. This weathered Skylighter in front of him gave him an entirely new appreciation for the patch's potential future.

"I'm Laslo Marku. I studied aboard the Globe Mother when I was young," the Skylighter said. "I apprenticed under Grower Master Roose for a time."

"That's my father!" Kipling exclaimed.

"You're Kole Roose's son? How is he? Has he made a plan to save the colonies?"

"We got a message from the patch messenger just before I left," Kipling said. "Near the Rift Valley. A Grounder pilot had brought word from the other patches. I think they were trying to get him to communicate back with the other colonies for us."

"Oh, good," Laslo said. "Your dad will know to preserve the pod stores he has left aboard the Mother and get them out to the other growers."

"But the pilot got abducted in a raid," Kipling added. "Our pod stores got taken, same time they took my friend. And Father got separated from the patch. We're all split up now."

Laslo frowned. "That's terrible news. Who did the council appoint as your father's successor? An apprentice grower perhaps? Who is giving them guidance on how to save the patch now?"

Kipling fidgeted with the kelp stalk in his hands. "They did appoint a new grower, but it was me."

The Skylighter wrinkled up his forehead in confusion. "The council appointed you to care for the patch? Then how is it you're here?"

"I . . . I left," Kipling said. "I needed to find Samra."

"You left? In its most dire time of need?" Laslo stood up and put a hand to his head. "Who is going to keep the Mother alive another season? She is the source of our entire culture. You left her alone with no care?"

"There are still people on the patch," Kipling stammered. "The guardians and the council members . . . Someone will still take care of her."

"Are any of the council members master growers? Has anyone else been trained to care for the Mother the way Master Roose has?"

"Well, no, but it's a big colony. Someone will be able to . . ." He trailed off as he thought about the colonists left aboard the patch. It was true. No one had anything like the training that his father had imparted to him over the years. Dimli Bottlebrock helped his father often enough in the pod groves, but he barely spoke most of the time, and he was hardly a person the council would listen to.

"Where'd you get the ship?" The girl with the freckles finally spoke up.

"The *Sun Dragon*? It's not mine. It belongs to my friend. A different friend. One I met on the way here." He looked around the room for any sign of Atlas. Where was he, anyway? "Is he here somewhere?" he asked the girl.

"Didn't see anybody else. Just you and the flying dog thing."

"That's Fledge. He belongs to my friend, too."

"And you don't know where this friend is currently?" Laslo asked.

Kipling shook his head.

"That's good," the girl said. "Because I need to borrow his ship."

A rap came on the door and a head poked inside. It was a boy of perhaps ten. He looked immediately at the girl with the freckles. "Your sister's back, says she needs to talk to you right away."

The girl stood up and moved to the door. She held it open and paused, then turned back around. "My sister is a pilot on a fleet harvester ship. She was just up north. She might know where your friend is. We could ask her."

Kipling lifted his head. "Really? You could take me to see her?" He slid his hands underneath himself and pushed off the floor.

"You should take it easy," Laslo said, but he gave Kipling a hand up. "You're still undernourished and probably dehydrated."

"I feel a lot better," Kipling said. The thought of learning Samra's whereabouts was giving him new energy. He swayed and steadied himself against the wall.

Laslo handed him another string of air kelp bulbs. "Take this with you and try to get some more down. Sky plants can be hard to come by in these parts."

Kipling accepted the gift and nodded. "Thank you." He picked up his warhook, slung it over his back, then walked unsteadily to the door, pausing when he reached the girl. He extended a hand toward her according to Grounder custom. "I'm Kip. It's nice to meet you."

"Quimby," the girl replied. She shook his hand and then rested her other arm across his shoulder. "Listen, Kip. Finding that ship in the caves today was a big deal for me, okay? It could mean me getting to be a pilot like my sister instead of being a tunnel runner. Only thing keeping me from practicing my flying has been not having a ship, but my sister's taught me plenty on the side. I'm ready. So if anyone asks, you tell them it's your ship and you're letting me use it."

"But it's not my ship," Kipling said. "My friend Atlas —"

Quimby tapped her finger on his chest. "You want to find out what happened to your friend, or don't you?"

Kipling paused. "That's my ship, but I think you should use it."

Quimby smiled. "Well, thanks, Kip. That's really nice of you. Let's go see if we can find your friend."

The other side of the door was a sloping hallway dividing more abodes like the one they had just exited. Kipling followed Quimby past tightly-occupied hovels hardly bigger than the tendril pockets aboard the globe patch. Men and women alike were coated in dust from a long day's work. They were thinner than the Grounders he had met in Womble. These people had lean faces and deep creases in their skin. Their clothes weren't much more than rags.

"You're miners?" Kipling asked.

"Some of us," Quimby replied. "Lots of these folks work the mines, but some are dedicated to the ironworks or feeding the forges. We've got lots of jobs: water transport, tunnel construction, and nearly all the engineering to keep the mountain stable. That's probably the toughest job, seeing how many times these tunnels try to fall on us."

She was moving quickly but Kipling paused when they reached a passage in the tunnel that led to the surface. He caught sight of the sky and soft glowing lights in the distance. His heart suddenly ached. It looked like the patch. It looked like home.

He turned down the passage without speaking, working his way up the slope till he could reach the ledge that overlooked the valley.

It wasn't the patch. It was a long gash in the mountainside leading into a mountain valley with a view of the sky above. The lights were coming from airships—hundreds of airships—clustered together to form a city. He'd never seen anything like it. He was disappointed to not be viewing the patch, but he couldn't help but admire the beauty of the view.

"That's Port Savage," Quimby said. She stepped up beside him and took in the scene. "That's where I'll be living soon. Once things are better."

"I never knew there were so many of you," Kipling said.

Quimby tugged on Kipling's arm. "Come on. We've got to go."

She eased them past a team of individuals hauling a cart along the passage and handing out tough-looking loaves of bread. She nodded to one of the men pushing the cart, and he winked conspiratorially as she went by. "Hey, Quimby. Tell that sister of yours she needs to come see me."

Quimby rolled her eyes and kept walking.

"Is that guy a friend of yours?" Kipling asked.

"He's in the movement, but he mostly just wants to get with my sister." She gave him a smirk. "It's never going to happen."

Kipling tried to put an age to Quimby. Fourteen maybe? She wasn't much older than him, but she seemed to be acting it. "What's 'the movement?'" Kipling asked.

Quimby paused outside a heavy metal door fixed into the rock. "Look, I probably shouldn't be letting you in, because I just met you, but since you just got here, there's no chance you're working for them. And even if you were, it's too late. It's all happening. Nothing's going to stop it now."

"Stop what?" Kipling asked.

"The revolution."

She knocked.

A panel in the door slid open and a pair of eyes surveyed the passage. They glossed over Quimby but lingered on Kipling. "Who's that?"

"He's with me," Quimby said. "Open up."

"What's the password?"

"You're a moss licker. Open the door already, Howard."

Howard grumbled behind the door, but opened it anyway.

Kipling followed Quimby past the oafish teenage doorman into a long cavern, the front of which was outfitted with wooden benches. Most were already full of men and women in clothes heavily stained with soot or dirt. A few were dressed up, however, mostly women, who looked like they might have jobs as barmaids or serving women. Kipling hadn't learned all the various clothing styles of Grounder culture, but he did know you don't work a mine in a corset.

A big man with shaggy black curls was standing on a platform at the front of the room and they seemed to have interrupted his speech. He nodded to Quimby with a smile and gave Kipling a quick once-over, but then went back to speaking.

"You've all known this day would come. We've prepared and we've kept watch. Our chance has finally arrived." His voice boomed around the cavern. "We've had word from multiple sources now that the rumors are true. Lord Savage has ordered the entire fleet out to the desert. He wants every ship that flies and every home that floats moved out to the dig site. He means to raise his wreck tomorrow."

"Where's your sister?" Kipling whispered to Quimby as they took seats on the last row of benches.

"She's up front, by Dex." Quimby pointed right of the speaker to a young woman with straight black hair pulled away from her face. She had a piercing through her nose and multiple through her ears.

"What's her name?" Kipling asked.

"Landy."

The man on the bench was still speaking. "It's been too long that we've watched our fathers and brothers and sons waste their lives in these mines. It's been too long that our sisters and daughters have been used to serve the whims of these phony lords and ladies in their floating castles, while the rest of us starve."

The crowd was murmuring in agreement.

"And I for one, am tired of watching the woman I love slave to earn an ounce of respect in these people's world." His eyes lingered on Landy. "They've asked us to work, but not taught us how to improve. When we've learned on our own, they've taxed us and fined us for the knowledge we gained honestly. Never once have they let us into their hallowed treasury of Old World wisdom. They let us squander our lives, keeping us away from the things that make life worth living, while they hoard that knowledge for themselves." He pointed a finger toward the ceiling. "They've kept every skill that turns a profit, every art that makes beauty, and even the means to retain the words we speak, under their control."

The murmurs of the crowd turned to shouts. A man stood up and yelled, "It's their turn to pay, Dex!"

Dex pointed at the man who had shouted. "You're right, Zhang. And this is our chance. Tomorrow morning, when the sun rises, we rise, too."

The crowd broke into a cheer. People got to their feet and someone started a chant. "Rise up! Rise up!" The rest of the group quickly joined in.

Kipling leaned over to Quimby. "What are they planning to do?"

Quimby smiled, keeping her eyes on her sister, who had stood now to join Dex on the platform. He had an arm wrapped around her.

"They're starting the revolution. They're going to take the Library of Knowledge, and give the relics back to the people, where they belong."

"Won't the raiders know who took them? They have all those airships. Won't they fight?"

"We've got airships, too." Quimby replied.

Dex settled the crowd a little and continued his speech. "We've worked hard to prepare for this day. Tell your men that as soon as those Air Corps ships get through the Storm Gate and into the desert, we take the library."

"What about our people at the dig?" a woman shouted. "My son's out there."

"We're going to get them, too. I'll be leading the raid on the dig site myself, and Landy will be aboard one of the Savages' own ships. She's got people loyal to our cause. I'll be leading our fleet low across the desert, just above the surface. We'll send up the signal, collect our people, and fly like the wind back to the city. By that time the fighters here will have secured the Storm Gate and taken the library. Whatever men the Air Corps leaves here won't be enough. I'll guarantee you that."

"They'll come after us with a vengeance, Dex," a man in front spoke up. "The Air Corps, Marlow Savage, and the whole lot of them. They'll be on you like a swarm of bees."

"They can chase us all they like, Cal," Dex replied. "Just so long as we get back through the Storm Gate first. Let 'em stir up all the rage they've got. It won't be enough."

"You think we got enough fighters to hold the gate against the entire fleet?" a woman asked.

"Don't need fighters," Dex said. "We've got the engineers. And we won't need to hold the Storm Gate. We're going to bring down the mountain."

32

ENZO

Atlas scoured the cargo hold for any type of tools that could free his grandfather. He'd tried to unlock the padlock on the manacles using the key the girl in the cavern had dropped, but it didn't fit. He tried a piece of baling wire he discovered in the storage locker, but no matter how he twisted and turned it, the lock refused to budge.

This wasn't how it was supposed to be at all. He'd come all this way and located his grandfather, but now he seemed no closer to freeing him. There were no keys. No way to get him off the ship.

Enzo had watched patiently throughout his search of the hold, and his various vain attempts at the lock. But after an hour of trying with no success, the old man called him over.

"Come. Sit, my boy." Enzo patted the pile of straw next to him. "We'll give it a rest for now and perhaps something will come to us. Besides, I want to talk to you."

Atlas reluctantly crawled into the space next to his grandfather and took a seat. He couldn't believe his rotten luck. He was so close.

"I'm happy you came, Atlas," Enzo said. "I think it must have taken a lot of courage. Did you have a difficult time? Was it dangerous?"

Atlas thought about the journey and nodded. He told his grandfather about the spiders dropping from the walls of the Rift on the way out of the valley. Then he told him about the leak in the ship he fixed and meeting Kipling in the Highlands.

"Samra was taken, was she?" Enzo said. "Her parents must be very frightened for her." He winced as he shifted his position against the wall.

"Are you hurt?" Atlas asked. "What did they do to you?"

"It's nothing," Enzo replied. "Go on. Tell me more about Samra."

Atlas frowned but continued. "Kip says her people weren't going to do anything. That's why he had to come after her himself," Atlas said. "He came to rescue her, same way I came to rescue you."

Enzo canted his head a little. "I suspect if you heard it from her parents' perspective you might hear a different story." The old man tugged his coat a little tighter around himself. "I imagine they're plenty worried and trying to find a way to get to her. Just like I suspect your Aunt Amelia is plenty worried about you."

Atlas thought about Amelia holding on to the side of the *Sun Dragon* and the way she had tried to stop him from leaving.

"She's the one who tried to keep me from rescuing you. If she had her way, I'd still be home. Why don't people ever act the way they need to? Nobody even leaves the valley. You're the only one brave enough to do it."

Enzo hugged his chest and the chain attached to the manacles rattled across the floor. "I can see how it may look that way sometimes. But there are all kinds of bravery. Take your aunt Amelia for instance. She's one of the bravest people I ever met."

"She is?"

"Oh, yes. Incredibly brave." He coughed a couple of rasping coughs into his handkerchief. "I don't know that she's ever told you the whole story about how she came to be your guardian, but I think it might be time you knew."

Atlas studied his grandfather's face. He was pale and had a far-off look in his eyes, like he was seeing some long-ago sadness.

"You mean the story of how my parents died?" Atlas said.

"Yes. It certainly began with that." Enzo blinked and focused on him again.

"But I already know that story," Atlas said. "They died in a crash. They went down in the water crossing the strait. You always said they died doing what they loved—flying and being together."

"And that's true," Enzo said. "They did love that. Your mother, Maggie, fell in love with the sky the first time I ever took her up in a skyship. She begged me to go up every day, first thing after she woke up. The day she took her first solo flight, I thought her smile would never stop. I'd swear she was even smiling in her sleep that night.

"And your father, he fell in love with that smile. Jonathan grew to love flying because he loved her, and he always wanted to see that smile on her face. Nothing in the world would have kept those two apart, or kept them out of the sky."

"But what does that have to do with Amelia?" Atlas asked.

"Because, what she's never told you, and what she's always asked me not to share, was that the day your parents' ship went down in the strait, they weren't the only two aboard. Amelia was there, too. Just a kid, mind you. Thirteen, fourteen maybe. And you would've been just a baby. They'd left you with your grandmother that day and gone on an adventure together." Enzo coughed into his handkerchief again, but then continued.

"Weather turned bad. It forced their airship farther and farther off shore. Ship broke up in the storm and they went down in the water. Wasn't much left of it but one good lift pod. Your mother put Amelia on that pod while she went back to the wreckage to search for Jonathan. They were separated in the swells and the two of them never got found." Enzo sighed.

Atlas spun a piece of hay between his fingertips and thought about the way he'd knocked Amelia over with the lateral fin actuator. The shock on her face that he'd hurt her. He could almost see the same sadness on her face as a teenager, the loss of her brother and sister-in-law in the strait weighing on her.

"We found Amelia the next morning, floating on that pod near Baker's point," Enzo continued. "She was dehydrated and exhausted and she didn't talk for nearly a week." He lowered his head. "And I hate to say it, but I was no help at all. Losing your mother sent me into a tailspin. She was my whole world and it wrecked me for a long time." He brushed a dusty hand across his brow.

"I wasn't nearly the man I should have been," he continued. "And it wore hard on your grandmother. We lost her that spring, and I was a total loss then."

"You were too sad?"

"Sad, and angry at myself for ever having taught Maggie to fly in the first place. I stayed at the farm and didn't come to town for a couple of years. Meanwhile, it was your aunt Amelia who stepped up. She took you in and cared for you. She raised you as best she could with basically no help. At least till Cathy came along."

Enzo rested a hand on Atlas's shoulder. "So when I say that Amelia's one of the bravest people I know, I know what I'm talking about. She did what I couldn't. She looked past her own pain and saw what needed doing. She did it without complaining and without reservation. Even when you got old enough to start wanting to spend time with me—even when you wanted to learn to fly—she didn't stop me from teaching you. She saw the same light in your eyes that Jonathan saw in your mother's. She didn't keep you from loving the sky, even though it had cost her everyone she loved. And she taught me that again, too.

"I was an old man and I didn't know how to change my ways. And flying for me was the only thing I knew to do to hang on to the memory of your mother, so I kept at it. She never would have wanted me to quit. I knew, deep down, someday you'd be ready, too." Enzo patted him on the knee. "And look at you now. You flew all the way here. You came and found me."

Atlas fidgeted with the lock on the chains. "But, what are we going to do? I can't get you out. I made it all this way, but I failed."

Enzo coughed again and winced. "You didn't fail, my boy. You did what you set out to do. You found me."

"But what good is finding you if we can't escape?"

"I don't know that I can just yet," Enzo replied. "But maybe soon." He broke into another coughing fit, and this time Atlas spotted a blotch of red seeping through his handkerchief.

"What happened? What did they do to you?" He rolled to his knees to get a better look at his grandfather. The old man's coat had fallen open and Atlas saw the stain on his shirt.

Enzo winced again and tugged at his coat. "They harpooned my old *Express*," he muttered. "And their aim wasn't so good."

Atlas tried to look at the wound under his grandfather's coat, but Enzo pushed his hands away.

"Won't do any good prodding at it. Damage is done."

Atlas scrambled to his feet and looked around the stall for some means to assist his grandfather's condition. There was nothing of

use in sight. "I have to get help somehow. I have to do something
. . ."

Enzo reached into the collar of his shirt and pulled something
out. It was the necklace he wore that looked like a stone triangle
with a hole in it. He pulled it over his head and held it up for Atlas.
"Here, I want you to have this."

"The relic key?" Atlas shook his head. "That's yours."

"I'd like you to hold onto it for me. I'm not sure what these
raiders intend to do with the relic they took from town, but they'll
want to take this from me when they decide they really need it."

Atlas's eyes lingered on his grandfather's bloodstained shirt,
then looked at the stone, noting the thin lines carved into it. They
shimmered slightly with tiny metallic inlay. "It's important?"

"It's our family key," Enzo said. "Has the knowledge I've learned
from the town relic stored away on it. I've heard them talking and
it sounds like they've been collecting relics from all over. I suspect
they have a fair amount of their own keys, too, but I'd rather they
not have this one. Go on. Take it." He grasped Atlas's wrist with
bony fingers and placed the stone into his palm, then he let his
manacled wrist fall back into his lap.

Atlas turned the stone over in his hands once, then slipped
the cord over his neck. The pendant joined the metal key the girl
had dropped in the cavern that he now had dangling on its leather
strap. He tucked both under his shirt, then reached over to help his
grandfather sit up straighter.

"Next time you run into a relic, you can show it that you know
all the things I've taught you about flying and farming, and how to
run the pressure machine," Enzo said. "Reason I'd like you to keep
it, is that I'm not sure I want these folk having those things I've
learned. Worked long and hard on those inventions and I'm not
sure just yet what they'd like to use them for. But you can use 'em.
You keep on using them the way we have been at the farm."

"But our town relic's gone now," Atlas said. "They took it and
they killed Mr. Merritt."

"I overheard that from some of the crew," Enzo replied. "Dale
was a good man and a good teacher. The town'll suffer without
him around. Even more reason to keep the knowledge we've gained
safe. We need to try to hang on to what we've learned up in the
mountains, Atlas. Not let it all get taken down south. Bad things
happen when one group has the opportunities and others don't.

Never does work out, but especially for the ones with naught."

Atlas was about to speak when something scratched at the wall of the ship behind them. He looked up to the small window at the top of the pen. Something was flapping around the outside. It squeaked.

"Fledge!" Atlas exclaimed. He popped up and put his foot in the wall-mounted feeding trough so he could reach the window. He climbed up and opened the latch on the window. The cliff fox immediately landed on the sill and squeezed his way through the miniature window. It scrabbled over Atlas's shoulder and hopped to the floor. Its next step was to flap over to Enzo and climb directly into his lap.

"Oh ho!" Enzo said. "The prodigal fox has returned. Been out having fun without me have you?"

The cliff fox stretched its wings once, then tucked them in and settled into the hollow of Enzo's chest. He stroked the creature's head. "Always did know how to find me, high or low."

"You think he'll be able to show us the way home?" Atlas asked. "Once we get you out?" He settled back to the floor next to his grandfather and petted the cliff fox. Fledge yawned.

"Maybe he will," Enzo replied. "Suspect he knows a good bit more of the area than we do now." He stroked the animal's head, then looked up. "Atlas, I want you to do me a favor."

"Yes?" Atlas replied.

"At some point, these men are going to come in and unlock me. You can't be here then. I'll let you stay with me for a while, but then I want you to take Fledge and hide yourself away in these supplies. No use them knowing you're here. And I want you to stay hidden, no matter what."

"No. You're hurt. I need to protect you."

"You need to keep yourself hidden. If they see you, they'll just capture you too. Won't do us any good."

"You think if I stay hidden it will help the escape? Maybe I can steal the key?"

"Could be. But you'll stay out of sight and not do anything rash till we've had time to make a plan, okay?"

Atlas mulled the situation over for a moment. He didn't currently have any better solutions. "Okay."

"Good. Everything will work out as it should. You just have to be patient."

"We'll have the element of surprise," Atlas said.

His grandfather patted him on the shoulder. "That's my boy. Just keep thinking . . ."

Enzo leaned back against the wall and closed his eyes. Atlas sat there listening to the faint snoring of the cliff fox, and his grandfather's slow, raspy breathing. Before long, both were asleep.

Atlas watched his grandfather for a little longer, then went back to picking at the lock with the baling wire. The lantern at the door to the stall burned out, but Atlas kept at it anyway, his fingers unable to give up their task.

He couldn't say how long he had been working, but after a while, footsteps sounded overhead on the deck, and then on the stairs. He scrambled to his knees and lifted the sleepy cliff fox off his grandfather's chest.

"Grandpa," he whispered in the darkness. "Someone's coming."

His grandfather didn't respond. His head was still resting against the back wall with his eyes closed. "Grandpa, wake up," Atlas whispered. "Grandpa. Grandpa!"

Enzo didn't stir. Atlas wanted to shake him but there was no time. The men were almost to the hold. He tucked the cliff fox under his coat and slipped out of the animal pen, ducking quickly behind a row of ballast barrels. He watched from cover as two sailors tromped into the hold, the first man swinging a lantern by its handle.

They made straight for the holding pen. The second man was brandishing a key, and Atlas's heart leapt at the sight of it. But the men paused when they got inside the pen.

"Blimey. Captain's not going to like this, is he?" The shorter man with the lantern held it over the corner of the pen. Atlas couldn't see anything below the heads of the men due to the wooden pen wall.

The big man who had been carrying the key kicked at the corner with his foot. "Wake up, old man."

His grandfather still didn't rise.

Atlas's heart thudded in his chest as he fixed his eyes on the pen. Enzo needed to wake up. He had to.

The man with the key frowned, but reached down and disappeared behind the pen wall. Atlas heard the sound of the manacles falling to the floor.

"What are you doing that for?" the man with the lantern asked.

"The captain says bring him, so I intend to bring him."

"Looking like that?"

The big man reached down and picked up Enzo, hoisting him over his shoulder. Enzo still didn't stir.

Fledge squirmed in Atlas's coat and he had to press him tight to his stomach so the men wouldn't hear him. He repressed his own urge to race to Enzo's aid.

Why wasn't Enzo waking? Had he fainted from the wound? Or was this part of his ploy to stage their escape? What was he supposed to do?

The men disappeared up the steps with Enzo and Atlas crept from his hiding place. Was he supposed to follow? Enzo had said to stay hidden, no matter what. Was this part of his plan? But what if he wasn't awake to make one? Or if his injury was worse than he thought . . . or if he was . . . no. He wouldn't think that. He couldn't.

Atlas listened to the footsteps cross the deck above and he followed from beneath, moving to a window that was partly open on the far wall. He had to put the cliff fox down and shift a crate of lemons over to the window in order to climb up and see. What he saw shocked him.

Out on the deck, a big man with red hair was twirling around the dock with a girl in his arms. She was laughing as he set her down. She had a party dress on this time and her hair was tied up with ribbon, but he still recognized her.

It was the girl from the cave. The girl who had dropped the key.

She was holding onto the arm of the big red-haired man, staring up at the ship. A crowd of other figures was emerging from a gate behind the girl, but his eyes kept coming back to her. His hand felt for the key under his shirt.

He opened the window a little wider to get a better look at her, and that's when the girl screamed.

33

QUIMBY

The revolutionaries in the meeting were beginning to file back to the mine when Quimby's sister, Landy, made it over to them. Kipling watched nervously as she approached. Would she have news?

"Hey!" Quimby exclaimed. "You'll never guess what I found in the mine today."

Landy glanced at Kipling. "Whoa. Another Skylighter?"

"No. Not him," Quimby said. "I mean yes, but not just him. I found an airship!"

Landy was still intent on Kipling. "Where'd you come from?"

"I came from the Globe Mother," Kipling replied. "I'm searching for my friend. Her name's —"

"Samra," Landy said. "It would have to be, wouldn't it."

Kipling gaped. "You know her?"

Landy took his arm, whispering excitedly. "Are there more of you here? Did they send a lot of your people after her? Fighters maybe?"

"Not lots," Kipling mumbled. "Just me."

Landy glanced at the single warhook hanging on his back and

frowned. "That's too bad. We could have used a few more fighters on our side." She released his arm.

"Is Samra okay?" Kipling asked. "Where is she?"

"She's at the party with Marlow Savage," Landy replied. "Way up top in the Library of Knowledge."

"A party?" Kipling asked. He had never heard of a captive being taken to a party. "Who's Marlow?"

"I don't think you heard what I said," Quimby interrupted. "I found a ship."

Landy turned her attention to her sister. "What kind of ship?"

Quimby grinned. "A little one. It's the perfect size for me. I can join the secret fleet for the mission."

"No, you will not," Landy replied.

"What? Why?" Quimby sputtered. "You know I can fly. You *need* pilots. You said there weren't enough ships but —"

"It's too dangerous, and you don't have enough experience," Landy replied. "You'll stay here. Stay safe and get ready to help after the fighting's over. We'll need all the help we can get."

"What about Samra?" Kipling interjected. "Is she okay? How do I get to her?"

"You don't," Landy said. "At least not yet. I've been working too hard and too long to give myself away now. I can't just show up aboard ship with another Skylighter and pretend nothing happened. They'd ask where you came from. My secret would be out in an instant."

"But you don't understand. I have to get to her," Kipling said. "I have to save her."

"She's okay," Landy replied. "She's part of the crew now."

Kipling balked. "What? What do you mean?"

"They're teaching her to be a back-up pilot," she said. "Training under me."

"You have a back-up pilot job and you didn't pick me for that either?" Quimby said. "Why not?"

Landy put out her hands. "Hang on. Both of you. None of this was my decision. I do what I have to do aboard ship. But this is the final day. Tomorrow, everything changes. That's why I need you two to stay here and wait till the fighting's over." She turned to Kipling. "Your friend is okay. She's staying aboard my ship. I'll look out for her and make sure she makes it home to Port Savage. After that, you guys can do whatever you want. But not till after we move on the library. Dex has put a lot of work into this plan. We all have. We're not going to alter it now. You two will just have to wait a little longer."

Kipling couldn't believe his ears. Part of a crew? Samra would never become a raider. They attacked the patch. They were all dangerous pirates. Landy must not know what she was talking about. Or she was lying. He studied the girl with suspicion as she patted her sister on the shoulder and walked away.

Quimby was frowning. "I don't believe it. I finally get my hands on an airship and now they tell me to stay home?"

"Samra would never be a raider," Kipling said. "This isn't right. I have to get to her."

"Not experienced? How am I supposed to get experience if they never let me fly?" Quimby muttered. "What good is it being a pilot and having a ship if they won't give me a mission to complete with it?" She crossed her arms and scowled.

Kipling was imagining Samra being dragged out to a desert full of razor sand and dust cyclones. The kind that could down a whole patch and bury it in the desert. He couldn't let her be taken into that danger.

"Look. I need to get to my friend," Kipling said. "Before the raiders leave. I need to rescue her. I need a pilot to do that, and you're the only one I know. You say you want a mission. Well, you've got one."

The two of them stared at each other.

Quimby tapped her fingers on her jacket, looking him in the eyes the entire time, then spun toward the exit. "Come on. We're going to the aerodrome." She grabbed a spare lantern off a hook on the wall and headed for the door.

Kipling took one quick look at Landy and Dex, still absorbed in making plans for the attack, then turned and followed Quimby. She led him down a series of corridors, muttering to herself as they walked. "All these years they said, 'Oh, you'd make a great pilot someday. We'd love to give you a job. Too bad we don't have an airship we can spare.'" She muttered some more. "Bunch of liars. Well, I'm done waiting."

She sped down a long stairwell, deeper and deeper into the mountain, gaining speed and forcing Kipling to work to keep up. When they leveled out again, they entered a cavern that was much larger than any he had been in previously. The ceiling was reinforced with heavy metal beams and a framework of struts and braces that arched high overhead. The cavern was packed with floating airships of all shapes and sizes.

There were single-envelope skiffs and bulky cargo lifters. A few craft looked like they'd only carry one person at a time. The parts were patched together from different ships and some looked entirely custom built.

A shower of sparks erupted from one of the nearby frames as Quimby and Kipling approached.

"Hey, Rocky. You get my ship fixed yet?" Quimby asked.

A thin young man holding a grinding wheel lifted his goggles and looked their direction. Kipling noticed that the man's tools were hooked up to a mechanical framework next to his station. The framework had a spinning shaft in the center being powered by a rod coming out of the floor. The man flipped a lever and disengaged his grinding wheel from the mechanism, but the mechanical shaft from the floor kept on spinning.

"You have to give me something more challenging, Q. Had that lateral fin straightened in under an hour. Floats nice and level now." He brushed his shaggy blond hair away from his eyes. He looked like he might be seventeen at most, but he exuded confidence as he tossed the grinding wheel onto its shelf.

Quimby grinned. "I knew you wouldn't let me down."

"But there's another issue you should probably look at."

Quimby's smile faded. "What? It doesn't work?"

"No. It works all right, but it's running a power system I've never seen before. No fuel. No steam even. Darned thing runs on straight air pressure. Never seen anything like it."

He led them around the back of the ship he was working on, to the familiar form of the *Sun Dragon*. The ship was tethered and hovering a few feet off the floor. Kipling thought it looked out of place surrounded by the rugged frames of the other ships. Unlike their jagged, no-frills construction, the *Sun Dragon* resembled a colorful tropical fish, its fins splayed out and ready to catch the current.

"Lighter than air but tough as nails, this one," Rocky said. He rapped on one of the fin ribs. "Not tube metal though. Wood frame. But super strong. Not a tree we've got anywhere near us." He pointed to a section of fin where the fabric had been sliced. Kipling had a fuzzy recollection of having caused that himself with his warhook. The dark, glossy wood was gleaming under the tear.

"That's globe heartwood," Kipling replied. "It's from the Globe Patch."

"Tough stuff," Rocky replied. "The joint was out-of-whack from the impact it had, but none of the stringers were even cracked. All I had to do was a bit of tweaking to get it back aligned. Popped it back into place and now it's as good as new, minus the tear." He considered Kipling. "You build this thing yourself?"

"No," Kipling replied. "My friend's grandfather built it for him. I just rode along."

"Heck of a present," Rocky replied. "Wish I had a grandfather like that. Must really like the kid. The wood alone makes this thing a work of art."

"So what's the problem with it?" Quimby asked, her brow still furrowed.

Rocky waved a hand toward the rudder fin. "It's got some standard features: ballast pumps, lifting cells, fin actuators. You can kick propel it in smooth air—swim it like a fish. But the main propulsion is this big fan system up front. He tapped on the air inlet and the shrouded fan inside. "All these fans are perfectly balanced. Barely takes any effort to get them to move in still air. But driving them for thrust is all done with these super thin piston actuators on a driveshaft moving a counterweighted flywheel. The little pistons run off some kind of manifold hooked to storage bottles and a timing system. Took me a while to puzzle it out. Whoever built this thing managed to store a crazy amount of air inside these bottles and stashed them all along the frame. They even have little pressure gauges to let you know which ones have air left. And that's your problem."

"What is?" Quimby asked.

"Whoever was flying this thing used up most of the air pressure getting here. Unless you figure out what contraption he uses to fill them back up, you won't be able to get this thing too far."

Quimby frowned. "How far can I go?"

"Hard to say." Rocky climbed up on the fin and studied the row of gauges on the panel. "Where are you trying to get to?"

Quimby seemed stumped by that question.

"We need to rescue my friend," Kipling replied. "She's on an airship in the port."

Rocky glanced back and forth between the two of them. "Well,

I'd guess you could make it up there no trouble, assuming the Air Corps didn't stop you, but from what I hear, those ships in port aren't sticking around long. And the aerodrome's exit is blocked. We've got ships stacked from the doors in here up all the way through the mountain, staged for departure into the valley. Dex's orders. This ship is small, but there's no way you'd squeeze through all that."

Quimby turned around and kicked a loose nut on the floor, sending it skittering across the aerodrome. "I can't believe it. Still no luck."

Kipling searched the young man's face. "You're sure there's no other way out?"

Rocky rubbed his chin. "Well, I can't let you out the front gate, that's for sure. But Dex never did say not to open the rear gate. It's facing the wrong side of the mountain, of course. You'd have a long way around to get where you're going, but if you left soon, it might still give you a little head start on the rest of the ships."

"Oi, Rocky! Get over here and give me a hand!" One of the mechanics was shouting from the other side of the hangar. Rocky gave him a quick wave, then turned back to them. "Listen, if you get this *Sun Dragon* of yours into position in the exit passage, I'll get my hands on the keys when no one's looking and come back to let you out. That's the best I can do for you."

"We'll take it," Kipling said.

Rocky nodded. "All right. Don't tell anybody I helped. I like this job. Only helping you out 'cause Q here always helps me out when I need it, and I owe her a few." He stuck out a hand toward Kipling. "Don't get her into any messes you can't get her out of."

"I'll try," Kipling replied and shook the young man's hand.

"Hey. I can get out of my own messes, you mook," Quimby said.

Rocky grinned at Quimby, then headed for the far side of the hangar.

Kipling and Quimby untied the *Sun Dragon* and drifted it carefully across the aerodrome floor. Thankfully, not many mechanics were nearby. Quimby quietly slid open the door to the rear tunnel, and they slipped the airship through. They guided the craft up a long exit ramp via a passage headed toward the surface, navigating by means of Quimby's lantern. When they reached the end, they settled the ship in a little alcove just off the main passage, but aimed toward the big gate built into the rocks.

"You managed to keep all this a secret?" Kipling said, admiring the metalwork on the huge doors.

"We've got our ways." Quimby said. "Air Corps stays at the top of the mountain, and all the mine inspectors that come down this far work for us. Easy to hide a resistance when most of the people you know are in on it. They've been planning this for years. Just needed a chance to make it happen."

"Have any of your airships even flown before?" Kipling asked. "How do you test them?"

"We've got a few caverns big enough to fly around in," Quimby explained. "And some pilots, like my sister, have been training on the outside, working on fleet ships and then teaching us down here in secret."

"You don't think the Air Corps knows?"

"If they did, they'd have come for our ships by now," Quimby said. "Not many other ways to punish us. We already work the worst jobs in Smoketown."

Kipling climbed into the front seat of the *Sun Dragon* while Quimby slid into the pilot's position. She worked the controls for a while, testing them and practicing the maneuvers. Kipling noticed she was careful not to actually engage the air motors and use up any of their remaining pressure. She occasionally asked him if he knew how to work some system or another, and he relayed what he had seen Atlas do, but his knowledge of the airship was soon exhausted.

Finally, they lapsed into silence, waiting for Rocky to return. Kipling ate the rest of the kelp bulbs that Laslo had given him and downed some more of Atlas's water supply.

He was feeling much better. His skin was warmer and he felt more buoyant. He lit up his hand and was happy to see it had a healthy glow again, though he wasn't sure how bright he could get.

He scanned the tunnel cautiously. "There aren't any nightbeasts in here, are there?"

"Not here," Quimby replied. "We keep these tunnels sealed. There are plenty inside this mountain though. More reason the high-lifers don't come down." Quimby discovered Atlas's supply of goat cheese and bread and worked on polishing off what was left. She offered a piece to Kipling but he shook his head. He'd learned that lesson.

Quimby blew out the lantern and they both got as comfortable as they could in the cockpit seats.

"What's this friend of yours like?" Quimby asked from the darkness.

"Which one?"

"The one you're going to save. Sam . . ."

"Samra." Kipling said.

"You think she knows you're coming for her?"

Kipling thought about it for a little. "I don't know. But I know if it was me that was taken away, she would have come for me."

"Sounds like a good friend."

"She's my best friend."

Quimby stayed quiet for a few minutes, then piped up again. "What about the one who flies this airship. What's he like?"

Kipling tried to find the right words to describe Atlas. "He's . . . determined."

"Would he be mad that we're stealing his airship?"

"Yes."

Kipling could hear the smile in Quimby's voice as she spoke. "Good. We'd probably get along."

Kipling wondered again where Atlas could have got to. Was he still wandering around in this mountain somewhere? He hoped that wherever he was, Fledge would keep him safe. Part of him felt he should be off looking for Atlas now, but he was already on one rescue mission.

Did guardians have this problem? How do you decide who to save first? Kipling brushed his fingertips across the warhook. As soon as he found Samra, he'd come back and find Atlas and Fledge. They'd just have to hold out till then.

Kipling wasn't sure when he nodded off, but the next thing he noticed was Quimby's hand squeezing his shoulder. "Wake up. It's time to go."

Rocky was ahead of the ship, working on the gate in the dim light of a single lantern. He slid open one half of the door, just enough for the *Sun Dragon* to slip through with its fins stowed. Quimby kicked the rudder controls and swam the ship through the gap and into the darkness outside.

Rocky whispered from the doorway. "You'd better hurry. Dex is starting to assemble the aircrews in the aerodrome. They'll be on the move within the hour."

"We'll move fast," Quimby replied.

"Be careful," Rocky said. "We tried to wait till the worst of the nightbeast hours were over, but you've still got a while till dawn. Who knows what's still out there."

"We'll be all right," Kipling replied. He lit himself to a dull glow and freed his warhook. The sleep and the food had done their job. He was as ready as he was going to be.

"See you when you get back, Q." Rocky gave a quick wave and hastily slid the door shut. Once he was gone, they were left to the darkness and a dull, cloud-filtered moonlight from high up the ravine. Quimby pivoted the aircraft toward the rising slope ahead. There was no wind in the ravine and they were in far too much of a hurry to pedal-kick their way up the slope, so she was forced to engage the air motor. She hauled back on the lateral tail fin controls and pressed the power lever forward. The *Sun Dragon* sprang to life.

Kipling's skin tingled with the cool air as the wind swept over him and tousled his hair. As Quimby navigated them through the canyons, they rose steadily over the terrain. When they climbed past the misty cloud shrouding the top of the ridge, Domino, the moon of the morning, was low on the horizon, already chasing her sister moon from the firmament. The sky in the east had yet to lighten. They cleared the ridge and Kipling caught his first sight of the open valley and Port Savage.

The valley was alive with movement.

A cavernous orifice in the southern mountainside was lit up and glowing. Airships were filing through the opening.

"Hey! We need to hurry," he shouted to Quimby. "They've already started!"

Quimby rose a few inches to peer over the dash, then slammed herself back into the seat and shoved the air motor lever to full power. The *Sun Dragon* surged forward. They crested the next ridge and she nosed over hard. The downdraft off the mountain caught the partly open fins of the ship and pushed them onward. In the distance, Kipling spotted a double envelope ship that moved like twin sharks. It was nearing the gate. He pointed it out to Quimby and she nodded, then he ducked below the windscreen to eliminate the drag.

"Faster," he whispered to the ship, wishing that in this moment it could become a real creature, born of wind and fire, and able to hear his plea. The whirling fans of the *Sun Dragon* spun on, air pistons hammering beneath the floor, and Kipling felt that just for a moment, maybe it had heard him. For that moment he felt they were not just two lives but three, all fixated on a single goal.

All together, they raced for the floating city.

34

ERIC

She didn't realize she'd screamed until the faces turned toward her. They were all masks of surprise and shock, and in some cases fascination—a crowd of onlookers leering from behind Lord Savage and his son. Borgram was there, as was Admiral Orloff, and a gaggle of other fancily dressed partygoers. Dozens of men and women hovered on the edges of her vision, but she could only focus on one thing.

Enzo was dead.

Samra hadn't ever seen a dead man before, but she had seen Enzo, and that was no longer him.

"This is your gift to me?" Marlow Savage sneered. "Fine party manners you're showing tonight, Eric. Your mother would have been appalled."

Eric's face was crimson. He hissed at the two men holding Enzo's body. "What did you do?"

The big man bearing the bulk of the weight spoke up. "Just doin' as we was told, cap'n. Found him this way."

Samra couldn't comprehend the calm in the man's voice. He spoke as casually as if he was toting a bag of vegetables or a bucket of water.

"I feel I won't be getting much useful information from this man, Eric," Marlow said, a cold edge to his voice. "Did you at least retrieve his key to the relic?"

"He has it on him," Eric said. "Around his neck." He gestured to the smaller man. "Give me the stone."

The small man patted around Enzo's chest, but didn't find anything. He then rummaged in the dead man's pockets, eliciting mutters from the crowd. "Ain't there, sir," the man replied. "No stone."

"It was on him when we brought him aboard." Eric's face was now an even darker hue. He took a step toward the men and held up a fist. He spoke with clipped words, clearly trying to control his emotions. "My father would like the key. Now. Where is it?" He jabbed his hand out, palm up, waiting to be obeyed.

The big man looked at his shorter companion, then shrugged. "Couldn't say."

Eric fumed.

Marlow had his arms crossed and up to this point had watched the proceedings with an expression of apathy. He now rolled his eyes. "Disappointing. I almost thought you had done something worthwhile this time. But I see you've merely caused a spectacle and turned our guests' stomachs."

Eric scowled and hissed at his men again. "Get rid of him." He waved them away, then turned around to face his father. He held up his hands. "It's not what it looks like. He was well enough when he came aboard. It was a minor puncture wound . . ."

"A *good* captain would have enlisted a better ship's doctor," Marlow said.

"My doctor has always been adequate," Eric sputtered.

Behind him, the two men, apparently unsure of how best to obey their captain's orders, turned and pitched Enzo's body over the edge of the dock.

Three things happened immediately. A number of women in the crowd screamed. Samra also heard a distinct shout of "No!" coming from the other direction—the direction of Eric's ship. The third thing that occurred was that a brown and black creature leapt from a starboard window of the ship, tucked its wings together, and dove for Enzo's falling body.

Samra rushed to the edge of the dock and peered over the edge.

The creature she now recognized as Fledge, the cliff fox, plummeted after its master, ears back and screeching wildly as Enzo fell. The two of them narrowly missed a cluster of airships and disappeared into the darkness in the direction of the sandfall.

Samra choked back another cry and looked to the ship and the tiny window the cliff fox had jumped from. Through it she spotted a face. The features of the face were stricken, eyes wide and mouth agape. A boy. He stared at her for a brief moment, horrified, then promptly disappeared. Samra watched the empty window for another second before turning her eyes back to the drop-off. A handful of gawkers rushed to the edge of the dock, looking for the results of the crewmen's action.

Eric had his face in his hands, covering his mouth.

Marlow Savage's expression had morphed again. His nostrils were flared and his eyebrows were pitched steeply toward the gap between his glaring eyes.

"Are you quite finished?" he roared.

Eric flinched but stayed silent.

"Unless your crew of reprobates has any further exhibitions they'd like to perform, I think we're all quite finished with your idea of entertainment."

Samra noticed Admiral Orloff in the crowd. While most of the viewers were whispering in hushed tones, he was smirking.

Eric seemed to have shrunk to half his size next to his enraged father. Samra looked to Captain Savage and found she had taken a step closer and bore a concerned look on her face. Almost protective.

Samra scowled, unsure how the captain could show pity for someone so vile.

Marlow Savage exhibited none. He turned toward the assembled crowd. "Since my son has seen fit to ruin this festive occasion, this party is now over. I've had quite enough entertainment for one night." He scowled at the library and its occupants. "In fact, I've had enough of this entire city. I will not be staying." He gestured toward the Storm Gate. "My destiny lies out there, in the desert. My reward for years of labor is there, not in this mindless carousing." He inspected the drink in his hand, then pitched the entire thing over the edge of the dock. He brushed his hands off. "I'm leaving. Now. Anyone who wishes to be a part of the future of this city can follow me. Those who linger do so at their own peril."

He gestured to one of his men. "Ready the fleet. We're

departing."

Marlow strode over to where Samra and Captain Savage were standing. He glanced at Sunburn, and then at his daughter. "Perhaps now is the opportunity for my eldest to finally step into her place—and renew some hope in the next generation of the family Savage." His eyes swept over Samra with disdain, then he walked away in the direction of his ship.

Samra looked back to the window. Amid the shouts from the crowd, no one else seemed to have heard the yell from the boy. No one except Eric. He was staring at the opening in the hull of his ship as though he could reach through it with his mind and extract its secrets.

Captain Savage reached a hand for his shoulder. Eric flinched and knocked her hand away. "Don't touch me." His eyes returned to his immediate surroundings and the chaotic crowd. Party guests were scattering in every direction, gathering belongings and locating lost partners. "I'm sure you're quite pleased," Eric spat.

Captain Savage retracted her hand. "You know I had no part in this."

"Of course not, Sister. You'd be too high above such a thing. Your methods of infuriating father are always precisely calculated. Mine are the result of rampant incompetence!" He screamed the last words at the two crewmen who had thrown Enzo off the dock. "What are you still doing here? Are you too stupid to know you're done! Get off this dock. I never want to see your miserable faces again!" He took a step toward them with a fist raised. The smaller of the men balked and began to scurry away, but the big man with the broken nose stretched himself a little taller, swelling his chest and standing his ground. Eric hesitated only a moment, then drew the ceremonial cutlass he had dangling at his waist.

The big man still looked undaunted, but his smaller companion grabbed his arm and hauled on it. The defiant man reluctantly turned away and moved off. Eric spun around and searched the dock. The crewman in the stiff coat and brown boots stepped forward. "What are your orders, sir?"

Eric sheathed his sword. "Locate the crew. Ready the ship."

"Aye, sir," the man replied. He began to move away but Eric wrenched the man's shoulder by the fabric of his coat. "And find me that relic key."

Eric's eyes swept over Samra, the captain, and Sunburn, but

said nothing else. He spun on his heel, walked up the gangplank of his ship, and disappeared.

"Orders, Captain?" Sunburn's expression was all business. There was not even a hint of the smiling man Samra had been laughing with just a few minutes before.

"Sound the *Fury's* bell. Summon the crew. We follow my father."

"Why?" Samra asked. She searched the captain's face. "Didn't you see what just happened? They killed him!" She could still picture Enzo's pale face as he fell—the cliff fox racing to catch him. "I knew him. He was my friend!"

Captain Savage regarded her coolly. "That man was dead. If he was your friend, he is no longer. You will have to find time to mourn your losses later."

Samra saw something new in the captain's eyes. Something that hadn't been there before. An intensity of thought, but also a sharp edge. For the first time Samra recognized the captain's resemblance to her father.

"We're returning to the *Fury*." The command did not invite further discussion. The captain pressed past Sunburn and headed for the elevator, which had just returned from another run. Captain Savage elbowed her way past a few guests, who then took it upon themselves to vacate the waiting area and give her room. She entered the elevator and spun around, facing the doorway.

Sunburn gave Samra a gentle push and the two of them followed, climbing aboard the elevator in silence.

As the wooden contraption clacked and vibrated its way downward, Samra's eyes once again found the hull of the *Savage Stranger*. She couldn't help but wonder about the boy. She knew his face. She could see it in her memory. It was the boy from the cavern.

The boy with the lantern.

The boy who had saved her.

She dwelt on the memory of his horrified expression the entire way back to the ship.

Atlas was reeling. The hold of the airship seemed to spin beneath his feet. If his stomach wasn't so empty he was sure he would be sick.

He braced a hand against the wall.

He saw him fall.

Thrown like a bale of hay from a hayloft. No one had tried to stop them.

He hadn't done anything. He'd just watched.

His hands shook and he staggered a few steps.

What would he do?

Atlas stumbled to the window on the far side. Was there anything down there? Water maybe? Maybe Enzo had grabbed on to something. Maybe Fledge—

He scrambled up the trough in the animal pen and stuck his head out the window.

There was nothing down there.

A few ships glowing faintly far below, and darkness.

Enzo was gone.

Footsteps sounded overhead. Shouts. Atlas squeezed back through the window and looked around the hold. Where could he hide? He saw no way out.

All around him the ship creaked in the wind. There was nothing left to do.

He climbed out the window.

Samra ignored Cog's drunken greeting upon their arrival aboard the *Fury*. She paid no attention when Sunburn and the captain disappeared in opposite directions above deck. She climbed down to the sleeping berths and stared at her reflection in the polished metal mirror hanging on the door at the end of the cabin.

A dress-up doll in a party dress. That's what Eric had called her. Is this the person the boy had seen?

She barely recognized herself. The dress. The bow. The carefully contoured lines of makeup on her face. Ribbons in her hair.

She tore the bow off first. Then the ribbons. Then the dress. She used the fabric to wipe her face, then found a wash pail and a cloth to finish the job. She scrubbed at her face till the blues and pinks and purples were gone. She scrubbed till she could see her own skin shining in the mirror, glistening with droplets of water.

Then she found her clothes. Her trousers and tunic. Her shark's tooth necklace. The feathers from a storm crow. She even found the spare stick of ceremonial paint that her stepmother had stuffed into her pocket. She took it out and applied it around her eyes and drew her family symbols on her cheeks and chin.

She was a Skylighter again.

But she still couldn't float.

She fingered the chain around her hips and the stubborn lock she had so willingly applied. Would she ever get it off, or was she stuck plodding around like a Grounder forever? She attempted to illuminate herself and lift off the ground.

Her hands flickered and flashed briefly. She concentrated as hard as she could, but it seemed the angrier she became, the less effectively she could glow. She wasn't lighting up. She took deep, gulping breaths and could teeter on the tips of her toes, but she couldn't achieve full buoyancy working against the chain.

Someone rapped on the door of the cabin, then Sunburn poked his head in. He stared at Samra for only a second. She exhaled and dropped back onto her heels.

"Captain needs you in the cockpit. We're short-handed. Time to work."

Samra followed him toward the bow and entered the cockpit. The captain was at the controls, back in her pants and leather jacket. The whip was curled at her waist. She stood up as soon as the door opened.

"About time someone else showed up. Thought I'd have to do it all my—" She paused when she noticed Samra's clothes and war paint. "Back to the wilds, eh?" Samra simply stared at her. The captain turned to the first mate. "Start the engines and cast off the lines. Were you able to find any of the crew?"

"Ylva is back aboard. The rest are unaccounted for. With the whole city on the move, I don't know that they'll make it in time."

"No sign of Landy?"

"None."

She looked at Samra and pointed to the pilot's seat. "Looks like you're promoted. Take the controls." Sunburn patted her on the shoulder and slipped out the door.

Samra slid into the pilot seat and the captain sank into her chair in the center of the cockpit. Samra watched for some reassurance from the captain. Some mention of the events on the dock, but the captain stayed stoic. Samra felt the ship come loose from the dock as Sunburn and Ylva cast off the lines.

"We'll make for the Storm Gate," the captain said. "Follow the *Vega*." She pointed to Marlow's ship that was entering the mountain passage, tailed closely by the *Savage Stranger*.

She studied the hull of the ship, and that's when she saw him. He was there again. The boy. Climbing along the outside of the ship, hanging on to the landing lines. She only spotted him for a moment as he climbed up the rear deck and slipped over the bulwark. Fascinated, Samra pressed the power levers forward, her eyes still on the *Savage Stranger*. The engines growled overhead and the ship responded. She spun the wheel to get the heading right and climbed after the *Stranger*.

Samra glanced back a few times, waiting for other orders, but the captain's attention was not outside. She seemed to be waging some internal battle. Her brow was furrowed and once again Samra saw the subtle resemblance to Marlow. Was that the look of guilt over letting a good man die? Samra narrowed her eyes and turned her attention back to her flight path.

The opening to the Storm Gate was becoming crowded. Fleet ships had lined up behind the *Vega* and the city itself was breaking up. Airships jostled for position, some still trailing rope bridges or towing floating docks in their haste to depart. Everyone was eager to obey Marlow's invitation and be present for the next stage of his plans.

Samra looked out the small windows that faced aft to the rear decks and spotted Sunburn manning the winch, heaving the handle around in a wide circle, cranking the parallel envelopes closer together and narrowing the ship's width.

The massive rope-jump ship, *Wind Devil*, was nearing the opening of the gate. Samra spotted Ranginui standing on the foredeck. He was still holding a bottle of liquor in his hand and stood astride the prow as if to intimidate the ship's way through the crowd. Samra turned the wheel and applied more power, squeezing the nimbler and speedier *Restless Fury* ahead of his position.

"Well done," the captain said from her chair. She was looking up now and following the movements of the other craft. "When we get to the open desert on the other side, we'll catch the leaders."

Samra concentrated on the route through the Storm Gate. It wasn't a straight shot through the mountain. The tunnel was a series of hard angles meant to divert the heavy winds and sand blowing in from the high desert. As Samra finished the first right turn, she approached the source of the sandfall. A huge dune was piled up against the interior cavern wall and leaking slowly through the porous floor down to the falls. This was being added to by a steadily moving river of sand. It slid downhill from the opening in the southern face of the mountain. As Samra rounded the final turn, overflying the sand river, the ship finally faced the desert.

The last section of tunnel was heavily reinforced with thick wooden beams interlaced across the ceiling. The passage was being monitored by a contingent of Air Corps ships with harpoon guns, hovering near the ceiling. The aircrews wore ominous-looking masks with blackened lenses as protection from windborne sand. In the darkness, the eyes looked like bottomless voids.

Samra spotted several workers sitting atop the ceiling beams looking down on the ships with eyes likewise masked by protective goggles. Some of the workers appeared to be her own age, their clothes covered in rock dust and grit. Samra raised a hand toward a group of young boys that were quite close, but none returned the gesture. They merely followed the movement of the ships with stoic faces.

They were watching. The people in the cave. Atlas felt as though they could see right through him. Could they spot him, hidden behind the coils of landing lines? So far, the crew of the ship hadn't detected him, but they didn't have those black, bottomless eyes. But if the cavern guardians saw, they said nothing.

The massive fabric envelope of the airship passed beneath the last of the cavern supports and into the open.

The sister moons shed an eerie glow on the desert and illuminated jagged rock formations rising from the sand. Even from his hiding place, Atlas could tell that the path through the desert was treacherous. Spires of rock stabbed from the sand and wind-carved pillars leaned precariously over hollowed-out bowls in the surface. In the darkness it was hard to spot the dangers till they were close.

But there were beacons.

The line of airships followed a trail of fire headed south. The beacon lights flickered and danced, revealed to be small balloons on tethers, lit from within, like the ones he had seen in the mine. A solitary figure manned each post, keeping watch and stoking the fires, hidden behind a protective cage of wire.

They were getting smaller.

The airship was rising.

"Climb," the captain ordered. She pointed ahead to the front of the caravan. The *Vega* was ascending and the *Savage Stranger* was straining to keep up. "It's time to overtake my brother," the captain said. "Let him look at the *Fury*'s tail for a while."

Samra angled the tail fins and pitched for a climb, adding power and aiming to the right of the ships ahead of her. She pulled the *Restless Fury* abeam the *Savage Stranger* and her eyes swept over the deck. She couldn't see him. Wherever the mysterious boy had gone, he was out of sight now. As the *Fury* pulled ahead, Eric's ship disappeared into the darkness.

The *Vega* was climbing steadily ahead of them. It was miles before Samra could make out why.

It was another city. A towering helix made of light and plant life. It pulsed on the horizon, flickering internally and spiraling up into the clouds. It was enormous, beautiful, and terrifying.

The raiders had created their own patch. It was part airship and part living thing. For every floating craft and lift pod vacating Port Savage to join the cause, it seemed there were already a dozen in place. Even so, the ships were the lesser element of the tower. The rest was comprised of vast catch nets filled with lifting pods: tree nodes, kelp bulbs, and globe sons. So many globe sons. Samra had never seen them in such numbers. They flickered and blinked like intermittent stars, trapped and immobilized in the web of netting. The entire mass of floating objects was tethered to the ground in a long, tangled braid of lines that was tied off somewhere in the darkness of the desert floor.

Samra had a feeling of dread in her stomach. The sight of the trapped globe sons straining against the nets made her nauseated. What would Kipling think if he saw this? She was no grower's apprentice, but she knew the tower's existence was heinous and unnatural. How much of the patch's future had it consumed?

The *Vega* was making for the top. Samra guided the *Restless Fury* after it, nearly on its tail. Other ships angled for lower berths on the gigantic tower. A few had already reached it. Deckhands aboard the column of pods stood by with harnesses to attach the ships. The harnesses had long cables that spidered into the heart of the lifting mass. The ship was now close enough for her to see the hole.

The core of this gigantic tower was a bundle of cables. It stretched from the huge mass of pods deep into the ground. The desert at the surface had been pried open and shored up. A retaining wall of wooden beams and heavy stones held back the shifting sands. The circular opening was bored far beneath the surface. There were lights down there, and presumably a bottom to the pit somewhere, but it was far enough down that Samra couldn't see it.

She took her eyes off the chasm and concentrated on the climb.

Sunburn stepped to the bow of the ship and prepared for docking. They rose past the catch nets of globe sons, and past the highest clusters of lifting pods to the very top of the tower. The *Vega* was mooring to one T-shaped arm extending off a circular dock at the peak. The dock, like other sections of the tower, was stabilized by guy wires that stretched far into the distance. There were three other docking arms extending from the central circle, forming a sort of hollow-centered cross, and the captain instructed Samra to take the arm opposite Marlow's ship.

Sunburn and Ylva tied off the lines, and the captain opened the hatch to the bow deck. Samra reluctantly released her grip on the *Fury*'s wheel and followed the captain topside, not sure what else was going to be required of her. She joined Sunburn and Ylva on the deck.

The dock the ship was moored to was connected to a circular wooden platform at the center of the tower via a long floating gangplank. On the opposite arm of the dock, Marlow and a contingent of his men were moving toward the center circle. Captain Savage gestured for the crew to follow her and set off down the gangplank to meet them. Two more airships were angling toward the remaining berths. One ship belonged to Admiral Orloff and the other was the *Savage Stranger*.

Samra trailed the rest of the crew, but their group met Marlow Savage and his men near the core of the tower. As the crews exchanged greetings, Samra peered over the edge of the dock. The circular opening at the center of the structure revealed the core—a shifting cylindrical cage periodically ribbed by other docks below. It was thousands of feet down from here. The bundles of lift pods bobbed and swayed and the entire tower moved with them. The weight of the chain around her waist kept Samra cautious, and she backed away from the edge, careful to keep her footing.

"I thought recovering this treasure involved digging," the captain said as she approached her father. "Yet you bring us to the highest point of your entire project."

"It has always been my job to ensure our family remains on top," Marlow Savage replied. "And these people need a hierarchy. Consistency helps them to rest securely in the knowledge of where they fit in the order of things."

"And when someone else decides they'd like to be on top?" She eyed the *Savage Stranger* pulling into its dock.

"Let them try," Marlow said. His men were fanned out behind him and Samra had the impression that they'd faced plenty of opposition before. All looked like seasoned fighters. Lantern light glistened off the handles of their cutlasses and harpoons.

A shout went up from the deck of the *Savage Stranger* and all heads turned that direction. Dockhands had only just tied down the airship when a figure rushed from the shadows of the rear deck and jumped onto the bulwark. He teetered once, then, gauging the distance, leapt to the dock. He stumbled slightly on the landing, but was upright after just a moment and sprinting along the long portion of the dock.

"Stop him!" The shout came from Eric Savage. He rushed to the bulwark of the ship and pointed at the fleeing boy.

It was him. It was the boy. She recalled his shouted name echoing up the cavern of the sandfall. Atlas.

Samra stepped around Sunburn and the captain to get a better look at him. He had almost reached the center circle of the connecting docks when Marlow's men stepped forward and blocked the path. The boy skidded to a stop. His eyes were wide and he had one hand clutched to his chest, gripping something dangling around his neck.

"He has the key!" Eric shouted. His men lowered the boarding ramp and he stormed down it, cutlass drawn and red in the face.

Something about the boy had seemed familiar when she spotted him in the cave, and now she once again recognized his resemblance to Enzo. The jacket. The grass-stained boots. Even his wild hair looked like Enzo's without the gray.

The boy spotted her looking at him and his mouth dropped open in surprise. "You're a Skylighter? Are you Samra?"

Samra frowned. She had told him her name once in the cave. Did he not remember her? She glanced down at her clothing. She did look different now in her Skylighter clothes and with none of Ylva's face powders making her up to be a boy.

"We came to rescue you," Atlas said. "Me and Kip."

"Kip?" Samra's heart leapt. Her eyes scanned the ship. She should have known Kip would come. "Where is he?" She rushed forward but couldn't get close because Marlow's men were blocking the dock.

"Looks like you're the only one in need of a rescue," Marlow said. He took a step toward the boy. Atlas backed up, but he couldn't go far. Eric was advancing from the other side, his cutlass still drawn and guarding any escape toward the ship.

"He's just a kid, Eric," Captain Savage said. "Let him be."

"He's a thief," Eric said. He glowered at Atlas. "Give me the key, and your friend here won't have to watch you get hurt."

Samra watched Atlas turn side to side on the floating dock. There was no escape. It was thousands of feet down in either direction. His hand went to his shirt again, fingering a stone on a cord around his neck. It wasn't the only thing he had there though. He had another key. A metal key. The key to the lock around her waist.

"I'm not a thief," he declared. "It's mine. My family's. And you can't have it."

"Boy, you're in no position to argue with your betters," Marlow said. "This is my town. And in my town, I keep the keys." He patted his chest where the dozens of other relic keys hung around his neck. "Who was the old man? Your family? Your grandfather? What was his name?"

"His name was Enzo Mooreside, and I saw what you did. You killed him!"

Marlow studied the boy with interest. "Mooreside, eh? One of the mountain names. You learned to fly way up there on your own? What other secrets did he unlock? What did his relic tell you?"

"My grandpa taught me plenty. Taught me about people like you."

Marlow smiled at him. "We have your town relic now, boy. And in a matter of hours, I'm going to uncover the greatest trove of knowledge this world has ever seen." He took a few more steps. "Whatever skills you've learned in your mountain shacks, I'm going to know them, too, soon enough."

The boy was frozen in place, listening. His hands were wrapped tightly around the necklace.

"I've worked a long time to gather up those relics," Marlow said. "They were put into the wrong hands, and I've made it my mission to get them back. Too dangerous for just anyone to have them. It's sad that your granddaddy went and taught your people so much. That's going to make things more difficult for me . . . and for them." Marlow took another step. Eric was closing in on the boy from the other side. They had him backed up against the edge of the narrow dock.

Samra edged passed Sunburn and Captain Savage to get a better view of what was happening, but she was blocked once again by Marlow's men.

"I'll let you in on a little secret," Marlow said. "It doesn't matter how tightly you hold on to that key, I'll get it anyway. You know why?"

The boy didn't respond.

"Because it's a rock. And you know what rocks are good at?"

Atlas shook his head.

Marlow grinned. "Falling." He stretched out one hand, till his palm was pressing against the boy's forehead.

Atlas's eyes went wide. He unclasped one hand from the necklace and reached for the man's clothes, seeking vainly for something to hold on to. His hand scrabbled at the stones around the big man's neck. Marlow only pressed harder.

"Leave him alone!" Samra attempted to elbow through the quartet of men in her way. She was shoved roughly back by a gruff man who smelled of garlic and sweat. She hurled herself forward again, but was caught off guard by a vicious backhand. She was sent sprawling onto her backside. She could only make out the action in the gaps between the legs of Marlow's men.

Atlas's toes were barely hanging onto the edge of the dock. His flailing fingers had caught hold of Marlow's wrist. Marlow snatched at the stone necklace around Atlas's neck again, grasping the cord above the boy's clenched fist, and for a moment, the tension on the cord steadied him. "You know what's not so good at falling?" Marlow hissed. "Little boys!"

Marlow shoved hard and Atlas flew off the dock, his eyes wide and his one hand suspended in the air, stretching for something to hold on to.

Samra felt the scream on her lips as Marlow shoved. It erupted from her throat as the boy was launched away from the dock.

Then Atlas fell.

35

THE FALL

He was still staring in surprise as it happened, eyes fixed on the man's face. The angry man with the bushy black beard, and the thick collar of relic keys. The man had ripped the leather cord from his neck, but Atlas's family relic was still in his hand. The severed leather cords flapped feebly in the wind, still tangled between his fingers, and then he saw only the sky. Twin moons, some fading stars. The smallest tinge of a blue dawn on the horizon. And he fell. His arms flew wide and his fingers stretched instinctively, searching for something to hold on to. But there was nothing. Just a long way down.

Samra rose from the wooden deck, only vaguely aware of Marlow's men in her way. It was only a fraction of a second, and then she was upright and running, aiming for the place where the boy had disappeared. A man in uniform lunged for her, meaty hands—the garlic man who had struck her. His fingers snatched at her hair.

But then Sunburn was there. Red, fiery Sunburn, his fist connecting with garlic man's jaw and sending him sprawling into his companions. They stumbled backward as they caught him.

Samra was only vaguely aware of Marlow and Eric Savage, standing on the dock watching her. Not comprehending. They could stare if they wanted. It was going to be something to see.

Breathe out.

Breathe out hard.

Samra flung herself off the dock and plummeted.

The first impact.

Not the ground.

Atlas careened off the surface of the little patch of globes and flipped over as he fell. The second impact was with the side of a man-made balloon. A gasbag, light-canvas maybe? His fingers only brushed it long enough to graze the texture. Not long enough to grab hold. He bounced off.

He kept falling.

He could see straight down now.

It was a long way to the surface, but getting closer.

He spread his body as wide as it could go, stretching. Hoping.

Lift decks whipped past. People on airships. Someone screamed.

He wouldn't yell. He wouldn't scream.

If he was going to die, he'd go with courage.

But it was still such a long way down.

Don't breathe, don't breathe, don't breathe.

She was closer. Gaining on him.

Almost there. Her eyes fixed on his back, hands stretching. A hundred feet? Two hundred? He hit another patch of globe sons. Another bounce. Hands searching for something to grasp.

Almost there.

Hard to see. Blackness closed in on the edges of her vision.

Don't breathe. Just fall.

Don't breathe.

She was there.

Falling toward him out of the sky. Wild hair bedecked with

feathers.

Was this a dream? He'd fallen so many times in dreams, but never like this. She was plummeting right at him, eyes nearly closed. Hands stretched.

Fourth impact.

He grasped at her, clutched her tightly. A Skylighter to the rescue.

Something was wrong. Her eyes were closed.

"Wake up!" he shouted as they fell.

She was limp in his arms, her hair flying around his face.

No. She was a Skylighter. She had to fly. She had to fly.

She had to breathe.

Samra opened her eyes. The boy's mouth was on hers. Breathing into her lungs. His eyes opened, too. She gasped.

He was holding on tight.

She grasped at his jacket.

She glowed.

The light flashed out of her so brightly he had to shield his eyes. She lit up the whole world around them. The last docks, the last clusters of globes. Surprised faces on airships. The ground was coming fast. They were slowing, but not fast enough.

"Get. The. Chain." She hissed the words between gasping breaths, straining to keep them airborne. They were spinning now as she lifted him by the jacket. Her light sent shadows whirling across the balloons above them. He could feel the chain around her waist, just beneath where his arms were wrapped around her.

"Don't drop me!" he yelled.

She had ahold of his jacket by the collar and their legs were entwined, but his heart still raced as he released one arm from around her and yanked the key from his neck. The lock at her waist was resting on her hip. He grabbed it with his other hand and freed the lock as they tumbled. The chain came loose and he flung it away into the darkness.

They were still falling, down, down into the pit in the desert. Wooden ramparts whirled around them. Massive retaining walls. Marlow's great dig. Samra strained to keep the boy aloft, but he was just too heavy. Her face was burning. Every part of her was glowing. She'd never been so bright. But she was almost at the end of her energy. She could feel it. A few more moments of lift and she'd burn out. A brilliant end to her final fall.

And then they hit.

36

THE ATTACK

They were too late.

The *Restless Fury* was through the Storm Gate.

Kipling and Quimby had raced down the mountain as fast as they could fly, but the city was nearly empty. A ragged convoy of house-ships and floating docks was being ferried through the opening in the mountainside, loosely overseen by men in dark uniforms patrolling in armed guard ships.

Kipling spun around in the cockpit of the *Sun Dragon* and faced Quimby.

"We have to go after her. We have to follow them."

They hovered near a rocky outcropping of the mountainside and watched the parade of ships bobbing past.

Quimby tapped a couple of the air gauges on the dash and frowned. "It's a long way to the dig site. If we make it, we might not make it back."

"I've come this far," Kipling said. "I can't stop now."

Quimby turned around and studied the mountainside in the direction they'd come.

There was no evidence of the secret fleet's movement, but Kipling suspected that if they were doing things right, there wouldn't be. Dex had moved the ships through the front side of the mountain, ready to spring the attack at any moment. It had taken Quimby a long time to bring the *Sun Dragon* around the mountain. The fleet might already be in position.

"Okay, we'll try it," Quimby muttered. "But if we run out of thrust, I'm blaming you." She eyed the patrol ships. "We still have to get past the Air Corps."

"We can just blend in with everybody else." Kipling pointed to the dilapidated skiffs and floating boats making up the tail end of the flotilla. As he spoke the words, he realized that, with its colorful, fish-like design and smoothly running thrust fans, the *Sun Dragon* didn't exactly fit in with the crowd. The remaining city ships were hodgepodge amalgamations of tube metal and lift balloons, cobbled together with second-hand parts from other aircraft. They belched smoke or steam as they clattered inefficiently through the air. These aircraft were far less elite than the high-class ships he'd first spotted in the valley, and had been left to the end. These craft looked a lot more like airships in the secret fleet.

"Oh smash it!" Quimby said, and slid down into her seat, keeping her head low.

"What?" Kipling asked, pivoting around to see what was wrong.

"It's my sister!" She jabbed a finger toward the sidewall of the cockpit.

Kipling looked the direction she indicated and spotted the ship. The secret fleet *had* made their move. They were gliding through the tail of the convoy, about a hundred yards to the rear of their position, employing the same strategy that Kipling had suggested. Kipling spotted Landy aboard a craft made up to look like the other cargo haulers around it. She was steering expertly around the ships in her way and gliding steadily closer.

Quimby edged the *Sun Dragon* into the flow of traffic and likewise began dodging the aircraft in her way, headed toward the Storm Gate. She poked her head up only when in danger of a collision—otherwise she kept herself low in the cockpit.

"Dex is going to kill me if he finds out I'm here."

Kipling glanced back at the ships behind them. They'd lost Landy temporarily in the crowded airspace. Quimby was trying to keep the airship in the center of the convoy, but in her haste to avoid her sister she had to dodge a lot of traffic. As they neared the opening to the gate, a particularly slow ship piloted by an overweight man in a ragged top hat was blocking their path. He was steering from the rear of his ship and could only see around the mass of clutter he had accumulated on the foredeck by means of a periscope fixed to his pilot seat. He was shouting instructions to someone else aboard, but the crewmate couldn't be spotted amid the heaps of refuse.

Quimby popped up to survey the situation and swore, then banked the *Sun Dragon* to the right, running along the blocking ship's starboard rail. She jammed the power levers forward and sped past the obstruction, darting ahead to enter the gate. The maneuver was effective, with the significant problem that it brought them into full view of one of the patrol ships, hovering high overhead. Kipling made accidental eye contact with one of the Air Corpsmen and the man's expression warped into a scowl as they sped past. Kipling turned in his seat and saw the patrol ship release its tether line and drop, descending into the flow of ships behind them.

"Um, Quimby? I think you'll want to speed up."

"Why?" Quimby was busy dodging more traffic in the tunnel and steering around stalactites threatening them from the ceiling. She pushed her goggles back on her head to see better and rose out of her seat to see what Kipling was looking at. She turned in time to see the patrol ship racing through the crowd, its pilot closing on their tail. "Oh," she muttered as she spotted it. "Yep. Time to go." She slid back down and pressed the power levers full forward. Kip tipped back into his seat and held on.

A piercing wail erupted through the cavern. The guard ship behind them was issuing some sort of signal via a hand-cranked siren.

It was answered from ahead in the tunnel.

"That's not good!" Quimby shouted from the rear seat.

An echoing 'chunk' sound came from somewhere ahead and a harpoon flashed directly over Kipling's head. It missed the aircraft but trailed a line that fell across the top of the ship and wriggled like a worm as the harpoon vanished into the half-light behind them. A second 'chunk' followed and another harpoon flashed from the left. This one struck home, piercing the top of the nose and passing through the right side. Someone shouted and the line went taut, wrenching the nose of the airship around to the left. Kipling was slammed into the right wall of the cockpit and he let out a grunt.

The *Sun Dragon* was still flying, but it was listing badly to the left and being pulled toward the ship that had fired the harpoon.

Quimby had to reduce power to keep from tearing something loose on the ship. To Kipling's horror, he spotted a second harpoon launcher turning their direction from the bow of the ship and several men standing by with grappling lines ready to board them.

Kipling leapt to his feet and unslung his warhook.

The rope attached to the harpoon took two hard slashes to get through, but then snapped away, leaving the barbed shaft still imbedded in the nose. Kipling eyed the Air Corps ship and brandished the warhook. "We rise forever!" he shouted. The man at the launcher narrowed his eyes and aimed the harpoon directly at him.

Kipling balked.

There was nowhere to escape.

The man reached for the release lever.

The weapon gave its distinctive 'chunk' but the man yelled as it did. The harpoon sailed high, flashing past Kipling's head and imbedding itself in the side of an unfortunate craft beyond them. When Kipling looked back to the patrol ship, he saw why the shot had missed. The Air Corpsman was still at the launcher but his hand was pinned to the weapon by a long metal rod, another harpoon fired from somewhere behind.

A tremendous shout went up from a craft to their rear and Kipling spun around to find Dex at the bow of a skiff behind them, brandishing a handful of harpoons.

"Now!" Dex shouted toward the top of the cavern.

Kipling looked up and discovered that the upper supports of the tunnel were lined with workers—miners and citizens of the underground, armed with nothing more than stones. But they had a lot of stones.

The cavern echoed Dex's shout and it was taken up from all corners of the ceiling. Rocks rained down on the patrol ships and the Air Corpsmen immediately ducked for cover. Men, women, and even children were reaching into pails and sacks and hurling stones with all their might.

The attack had begun.

Quimby pointed to the ropes laid overtop the ship. "Cut those! We've got to go!"

Kipling worked fast to free the ship from its entanglements, using his pruning knife to sever the limp ropes. He tossed the lines away from the ship and Quimby applied power again. She sped them around the final bend in the tunnel and aimed for the open air of the high desert beyond.

But they weren't out of danger yet. A trio of patrol ships was blocking the exit, evidently in response to the siren being sounded in the cavern. Rocks from above were already bombarding two of the ships, but as Quimby ratcheted in the lateral fins and dove the *Sun Dragon* for the space beneath the guard ships, the center ship followed. Quimby gave a whoop as the airship rocketed past the guards, but the Air Corps ship rolled to follow.

The motor on the pursuit ship roared, belching smoke as it came to life, and trailed a cloud behind it as it turned. The ship pursued them into a dive toward the rocks on the desert floor.

This desert had teeth.

Rocky spires stabbed from the surface like twisted fangs intent on devouring the airship. Quimby yanked back on the controls and the *Sun Dragon* pulled out of its dive, just in time to miss three shards of light that streaked beneath the hull.

"What was that?" Kipling yelled.

Quimby pointed to a floating balloon high overhead. "Fire arrows!"

A figure in the floating balloon was lighting another round of projectiles in a wicked looking contraption mounted to the edge of the beacon's gondola.

"Whoa," Kipling exclaimed. "Fly faster!"

Quimby banked away from the beacon balloon and steered wide of the path of the other airships. The bottleneck at the gate had slowed the flow of ships there, but out in the open, the line of aircraft ahead was spread out over a number of miles. The airships were gliding high, safe from the rocky teeth of the desert, and climbing at a steady angle into the slowly brightening sky.

A touch of blue was illuminating the eastern horizon, but the light did nothing for Kipling and Quimby. The *Sun Dragon* dipped and dodged through shadows near the desert surface, fleeing the pursuit ship churning through the air behind them.

"I'm going to try to lose them in the rocks!" Quimby shouted. She banked the craft hard right and narrowly dodged an angled outcropping of wind-carved stone. The pursuit craft roared ahead and left, dodging the obstruction. The men in the Air Corps ship were at a disadvantage here. Their ship was bulkier with far more drag, but it kept up its speed anyway, a cloud of thick smoke billowing out the back as its motor raged. It spun twin propellers off its rear deck, forcing the ship through the air by brute force.

"What are they burning?" Kipling asked, amazed that the ship could maintain such a pace.

"Fuel oil!" Quimby said. "They get it from the mountains."

Kipling had never heard of someone being able to burn a mountain. But Skylighters never spent time trying. Whatever secrets the Grounders had discovered deep below these mountains were certainly serving them well. The airship was gaining on them. The rigging lines holding the envelope to the hull were straining from the speed. The men on the bow of the ship stood ready at their harpoon weapon.

"I have an idea," Kipling said.

"About time!" Quimby shouted, dodging another rocky spire.

"Aim closer to one of those pillars," Kipling said.

"Closer?"

"Yeah, I'm getting out. Swing around and get them to chase you. Bring them back by me!" Kipling didn't have time to explain anything else as another of the twisted rock spires was nearly on them. Quimby banked hard and shot the *Sun Dragon* around the rocky outcrop, nearly scraping the lateral fins against it. Kipling waited till the pursuit ship was just out of sight. Then he leapt.

He flew through the air and impacted the side of the spire, his fingers scrabbling at the pitted surface as the momentum of his exit from the *Sun Dragon* flung him sideways. He grabbed hold, took a deep breath, and scrambled upward, the warhook bouncing on his back.

The pursuit ship roared past his position without any of the crew noting his presence and continued its relentless hunt for the *Sun Dragon*.

By the time Kipling reached the top of the spire, Quimby was on her way back. She dodged another round of fire from one of the beacon balloons and banked steeply toward the spire in a teardrop turn.

Kipling steadied himself atop the rocks as she aimed the ship low and dove for the surface. She was slowing down, giving the bigger and less nimble ship a chance to complete its turn. She cruised right past the base of the spire, nearly skimming the sand. The Air Corps ship leveled out laterally, then dipped its nose to dive after its prey. It wasn't coming nearly as close to the spire as the *Sun*

Dragon had, but it was close enough.

As the ship dove for the desert surface, Kipling took a running start off the top of the rock spire and launched himself toward it. He exhaled hard and dropped onto the nose of the ship's envelope. He rolled on landing but came up to his feet with the warhook in his hand.

Kipling swung hard as he moved up the slope of the airship's nose, digging the warhook deep into the fabric and through the tops of the lift bags. He let go of the handle and dragged the warhook by its tether cord, pulling it through the top of the ship, plowing a ragged tear as he ran.

Escaping gasses hissed and then erupted from the top of the ship as he tore his way along the ship's surface. He stopped to extract the hook twice when it hit rigid structure, but dug it in again each time. He hadn't hit every lift bag, but he'd done enough. The airship was sinking.

Shouts of dismay went up from the deck below as the crew recognized their plight. The motor changed speed and the tail fins pitched steeply to arrest the descent. Water gushed from the nose ballast tanks in a desperate bid for lift, but Kipling had dealt the ship a mortal wound. He slung the warhook over his back, lit himself up, and sprang for the sky.

The *Sun Dragon* glided out of the shadow of the spire and Quimby coasted the ship underneath where he was hovering. He dimmed and exhaled, dropping back into the front seat of the cockpit.

"Not bad, sky boy," Quimby said from the back seat. Her eyes were bright with excitement.

Kipling met her gaze and smiled. "Okay. One problem solved. Now let's go find Samra."

Quimby engaged the air motor and headed into the desert.

Kipling watched the column of airships rising higher and higher above them, but it was only after clearing a ridge of rocks that he was finally able to see the destination. Emerging out of the morning haze was the tallest structure he had ever seen. If you could even call it a structure. It was a moving pillar of airships and lift pods, all tied together into one massive tower. As his eyes swept over the column, his stomach turned.

These raiders hadn't just captured handfuls of globe sons here and there. They had caught more of the pollinating pods than Kipling had ever imagined. He knew there were dozens of colonies in the Northern Sky relying on the bounty of globe sons to pollinate their patches, but he had no idea that anyone could have so efficiently collected them into one place. The gigantic holding nets contained hundreds, even thousands of the globe sons. With a collection this immense, the Skylighters' patches had no chance of finding globe sons adrift in the wind. They were all here.

As Kipling sat gaping at the column, his mind reeled from the implications of this tower's existence. His father was wrong. This wasn't just going to be a bad breeding season for the colonies. This would end them.

He pointed the nets out to Quimby. "Those belong to my people! We have to free them!"

"What?"

"The globe sons. We have to get them back."

"I thought we were here to save your friend."

"We are. But we need to save those, too!"

Quimby tapped the air gauges again and frowned. "Well, whatever you're doing, you'd better figure it out fast. Dex is going to bring down the Storm Gate and we don't have much flying time left."

Kipling was still processing this information as the ship approached the base of the tower, but his attention was captured by a flicker of light high overhead and frantic shouts from people in the tower. He clenched the rail of the cockpit as he pulled himself to his feet. The orb of light flashed through the center of the tower of lift pods in little flickers. It was a figure. Two figures, falling from the sky.

It was Samra! Her arms were grasping the body of a boy. She was plummeting from the sky—and glowing!

The duo spun out the bottom of the tower into the three hundred foot gap of space between the desert and the first row of lift pods. They were slowing down, but still falling.

"Samra!" Kipling shouted, unable to control himself.

Samra and the boy kept falling, down past the surface of the desert and into the top of the gigantic pit.

Atlas.

The boy was Atlas.

What was happening? Where had they just come from? Was she hurt?

"Get to that pit! Hurry!"

He waved Quimby on, but she was already aimed at the top of the excavation site. She raced to the edge of the pit and let the *Sun Dragon* coast over the edge, leaning over the rail to peer down at the results of the fall.

Kipling's eyes swept over the tether cables binding the tower to the bottom of the pit and found they were attached to a gigantic sphere. It was metallic and weatherworn, and unlike anything he had ever seen. The sphere was wedged at the bottom of the pit like a ball at the bottom of a cup, the walls of the dig site just barely wide enough to clear the sides.

He frantically scanned the surface. Searching. There were men down there, workers excavating the site. They had cleared the top of the object of sand and were working to free it from the insistent weight of the dunes around its edges. The prison of sand entrapping the sphere was just wide enough to encircle its upper hemisphere. Retaining walls around the site shivered a little as the sphere shifted, the combined lift from the enormous column of pods overhead slowly wresting it from the desert's grip.

He finally spotted Samra.

She was helping Atlas to his feet at the edge of one of the dunes, and she was floating.

Kipling yelled down the pit, but she was too far away. She didn't hear him.

She didn't need him.

There she was, floating at the bottom of the pit, finally able to glow. She'd figured it out and she'd done it without any help from him.

As he watched Samra lifting the Grounder boy to his feet, he smiled.

"We going down there?" Quimby asked. She was studying him, a quizzical expression on her face.

"No," Kipling said. "I was wrong. She doesn't need rescuing."

"You had me come all this way for nothing?"

"No," Kipling replied. His eyes drifted upward to the tower of pods and ships overhead. "I know what I have to do now." He unslung the warhook and gripped it with both hands. "Take us up."

"Into that?" Quimby jabbed a finger toward the tower.

Kipling turned and looked her in the eyes. "It's time to save my home."

37

STARFIRE

Sand sprayed up around them from the impact.
Samra tumbled down the dune, caught in a tangle of arms and legs. She bounced.

"Ow," Atlas muttered. He slid to a stop, sprawled at the bottom of the dune, partially covered in sand. He spat some out and eased himself to an elbow. His eyes met hers and he smiled. "That was incredible."

Samra's light flared up again and she drifted off the sand. "Ooh no." She concentrated and dimmed back down, dropping back to her feet. This glowing thing was going to take some getting used to.

"You saved me," the boy said. "I thought I was done for." He climbed to his feet and brushed himself off with one hand. He was holding something in the other. "Why'd you do it?"

Samra didn't know how to put her decision into words, but she knew jumping had been the right choice. The choice between siding with Marlow and his henchmen or this boy with his wild hair and kind eyes. Eyes like his grandfather's.

"I think I did it for Enzo," she finally replied. "And for me."

"How did you know it would work?" Atlas asked.

"Sometimes you have to skip jumping and go straight to flying," Samra said.

Atlas studied her and nodded. "Enzo would have liked to see it. I wish he could've had someone like you to save him."

Samra didn't have a response for that. Something about the way the boy was looking at her was making it hard to organize her thoughts. She just nodded and looked away.

They weren't the only ones down here.

Workers with lanterns were watching them from all over the top of the sphere. Some were at the edges of the dig, loading sand into buckets on pulleys to be hauled out. A group of others had been in the process of prying an opening in the shell of the sphere. They'd made a hole and one of the men was peeking his head out from inside the outer shell.

"What is this thing?" Atlas asked, tapping his foot on the curved metallic shape beneath them.

"I don't know." Samra was staring at the men around the opening when something incredible happened. The glowing figure of a woman spontaneously materialized, standing atop the sphere.

A volley of oaths came from the workers. A few stumbled backward and fell. The man who had been down in the hole in the ship shrieked and climbed out, tripping over himself in his hurry to escape. He lost his footing and fell down the slope of the sphere, tumbling to a stop at its base.

The ethereal woman paid no attention to his exit.

She was blue and translucent. An eerie light shimmered around her edges.

She was staring at them.

"Hello. I was hoping to meet a pair like you two one day," she said.

Samra merely gaped.

"I'm happy you've come," the figure continued, opening her arms toward both of them. "You can help me."

Atlas moved in front of Samra protectively. "Who are you?"

Samra thought that 'What are you?' would also have been an appropriate question. This person was certainly like no one she had ever seen.

"I've waited a long time to be unearthed again. I've been expecting you."

"Are you . . . a ghost?" Atlas asked.

The figure smiled at him. As immaterial as she was, Samra didn't think she looked like a ghost. She looked like a young woman. Short spiky hair framed an attractive, regal-looking face. Something about the woman's expression reminded her of Captain Savage.

A bell rang overhead. Samra looked up to find that some of the tether cables linked between the sphere and the lifting tower were vibrating. The cables whirred through a set of pulleys, clattering as they moved.

"Boss coming down!" one of the men shouted.

"What do we do about her?" another man answered, gesturing to the glowing woman.

"Blazes if I know," the man's companion answered. "Let him deal with her."

The apparition didn't express any concern at their comments. She was still intent on them.

Samra looked up the tether lines to where they penetrated the center of the column. It was lighter up there now. The sun was coming up. Somewhere, high overhead, an elevator was descending. She could guess the occupant—Marlow, come to claim his newly exposed treasure. Her instinct told her to run. Climb the towering walls, leap as high as she could and escape the pit. But there was Atlas. He'd never make it in time. What point was there in saving him from the fall, only to leave him to Marlow's men in this pit?

The translucent woman remained unperturbed. She extended a hand toward them. "Won't you come inside? I desperately need your help, and there are a great many things I would like to show you."

Samra and Atlas looked at each other, searching for a plan in the other's eyes. But when they turned back to face the woman, she was gone. A new glow was emanating from the sphere. The beam of light issued from the hole the men had made in the shell.

Atlas's eyes lifted to the cables, tracing them upward. Somewhere overhead, the elevator car continued its descent. His brow furrowed and his fists clenched. Samra could imagine he wasn't eager to face his attempted killer again so soon. Something drew his attention to one of his hands. He opened his fingers, and she saw he'd been holding the triangular stone that Marlow had tried to steal. The thin lines etched into its surface were glowing faintly. He dropped his gaze to the hole. "So . . . inside then?"

Samra studied the beam of light emanating from the hole. Despite the strangeness of the woman, Samra didn't think she was dangerous. Something about her was vaguely comforting. "Right. Inside." She started up the outside of the sphere, with Atlas on her heels.

When they reached the hole, they peered down it together. It was an antechamber of sorts, with another opening in the wall on the other side. They could see nothing beyond it. Atlas sat down on the edge of the breech, took one last look above them, and dropped inside.

Samra exhaled hard and followed.

"Welcome aboard," a voice said from the walls.

"Aboard?" Atlas said. He turned to Samra. "Is this a ship?" If it was an aircraft, it was like nothing he had ever seen before. They were in a passageway lit by tiny lights along the edges of the floor. They followed the faint glow of the lights past a number of doorways, each leading to chambers lined with tall, cylindrical containers, big enough to fit a full-grown person. There were dozens of them.

A placard on the wall was etched with the word, 'Starfire.' Was that the name of the ship?

The main passage led them in a curve to the right, then ended in a central room with a wide, domed ceiling.

They walked to the center of the room and spun around.

"Where did you go?" Samra called out.

The walls were glowing faintly. So was Samra. She was radiant. Ever since the fall, the girl was emanating a soft greenish light from her skin and Atlas found it fascinating to watch her move. The light seemed to trail off her in the darkness.

"I'm here," the voice said from all around them. "I'm all of this. I'm the ship. But also much more." The walls came alive, instantly awash with light and color, displaying a vast landscape. The domed ceiling was now a brilliant blue sky rimmed with snow-capped mountains. Without moving, they were somehow standing in a field of wind-blown grass. Samra backed up a step, bumping into him and catching her breath. Her feet lifted off the ground just slightly. Atlas grasped her hand and held on to her, keeping her from drifting toward the ceiling-turned-sky.

Samra turned to look at him, eyes wide, but as they focused on his, she settled slowly back to the ground. He loosened his grip on her hand, but she didn't move it. Instead, she kept her warm palm pressed to his and entwined his fingers with her own.

The grass waved against their legs and even the air smelled of the wide open. The vision was so real that Atlas felt sure he could reach down and pluck a stem from the ground.

The next moment the illusion changed. The sun set and a starscape appeared overhead. Strange constellations and a single moon, low on the horizon.

"What . . . what is this place?" he asked, his stance wide to stabilize himself against the strange changes. He half expected the ground to vanish under his feet.

"This is where you came from."

"The Old World?" Atlas took in the view with rabid curiosity. It changed again, even as he spoke. They were now moving through the sky, overflying mountain ranges and jungles, rivers and deserts. It was beautiful. The floor beneath them was part of the view, giving him the impression they were flying without a ship. It was thrilling and frightening at the same time.

"I wanted to show you the home of your people," the voice said. "From a long time ago."

They were now standing atop an ocean, the waves swirling around their feet. Ahead of them lay a shining city. One like Atlas had never seen. Massive towers stretched toward the sky and reflected the sunlight. There were bridges and trees, and people walking along the edges of the water. Hundreds of them. Thousands maybe. But Atlas realized it was the sky that was different here. It was all but empty. White puffy clouds hung overhead in a few spots, but the rest of the sky was vacant. No kelp towers, no globe patches, no drifting clumps of skyweed. Just the clouds and a few tiny birds soaring in the open air.

"Where is this Old World?" Samra asked. "Is it far away?"

"Very far," the voice said. The woman reappeared next to them. The surroundings dimmed as she arrived. She was still immaterial but seemed to have gained some substance inside the ship. Even so, Atlas could now recognize her as an illusion like the ones they'd just been witnessing.

"What's your name?" Samra asked.

The woman seemed to consider the question. "I've had many names over the years."

"Did people forget it?" Samra asked, her voice sympathetic.

"Some have," the woman replied.

"Do you still remember?" Samra asked.

The woman smiled at Samra. "It's Mira. The first name I had was

Mira. It's still my favorite."

A thud echoed through the walls of the ship and the floor shook. Atlas steadied himself, this time against real movement.

"They're raising me up," Mira said. Her light flickered. "The diggers have nearly finished their job."

"Are you happy they're digging you out?" Atlas said. "Or frightened?"

Mira smiled again. "I could never be frightened of my children, no matter their intentions." She gestured for them to follow her. "Come. I have much to tell you and little time to do so."

A portion of the wall illuminated and revealed itself as another passageway. Atlas couldn't comprehend how he hadn't been able to see it before, but this entire ship was dreamlike and magical in its capabilities. He somewhat reluctantly let go of Samra's hand, and followed her and the luminescent woman through the passage.

Mira led them into a chamber that glowed softly of its own accord. Invisible lights illuminated rows of tiny alcoves in the walls, dozens in each row. A number of the openings were empty, but the remaining alcoves held cubes, of the same size and shape as the one Mr. Merritt used in the schoolhouse. Relics.

"I'm hoping that you will grant me a favor," Mira said. She was watching him as she spoke. "And help me remedy a costly mistake that was made a very long time ago."

Samra was running her fingers over the edges of the relics, brushing bits of dust off a few. "They're beautiful," she said. "Are they all yours?"

"They were never meant for me," Mira said. "They were meant for my children."

"Who are your children?" Samra asked.

Mira turned and gestured to Atlas. "One of them is right here."

"Uh, you're not my mom," Atlas said.

"No," Mira replied. "But you are still one of my children. All of your people are. I brought you to life in this place. A long time ago. I taught you the ways of this world. Its language. Its beauty. I chose to build you a home here, on Altiria."

"I don't understand," Atlas said. "I thought our ancestors sailed across the skies from the Old World on a ship. They were adventurers."

"They most certainly were," Mira replied. "Bold adventurers. And I want you to know the rest of their story."

One of the relics in the row of alcoves lit up and began to pulse with purple light. He had to squint as he looked at it.

"When I sent the first of your people out into this world, I gave them each gifts of knowledge," Mira said. "I armed them with tools that they could use to build a life here. A peaceful life, free of the animosity and violence of the Old World. I gave them the tools to do better than we had done before. But I didn't give them everything."

"The relic locks," Atlas said. "They won't all open."

"No. They won't," Mira said. "Not yet. I didn't think you were ready, so I waited and held some knowledge back. I wanted to be sure that you could use the tools I'd given you for good. Needed to be sure that you would find ways to live peacefully on this world and with its peoples." She looked to Samra. "And to meet them with friendship and not aggression." She smiled at the Skylighter girl. "You two are a sign that, despite my earliest failures, my dream is succeeding. I witnessed your sacrifice. Your fall from the sky took great courage. It was beautiful."

"You saw us?" Samra asked.

"I've seen a great many things," Mira replied.

Atlas felt the relic key warming in his left hand. He opened his palm to find the little ridges glowing even brighter than when it was outside. He looked back to Mira. "What did you fail at?"

"Keeping you safe. I could have helped your people a great deal more, but I was lost down here under the sands of this desert. This knowledge was a treasure that was never meant to be buried." Mira pointed to the glowing cube. "And now I'm hoping you'll help me distribute it properly."

Atlas slipped his relic key into his pocket, then stretched a hand out and picked up the glowing relic.

"No!"

The shout came from behind them. Atlas turned to find the big bearded man who had tried to kill him looming in the doorway. "That's mine!" he declared. The raider stomped his way through the passage, the relic keys around his neck casting his face in an eerie light. One of his hands wielded a shiny cutlass. He brandished it at the glowing woman. "I dug you up. This was my doing. The master relic is mine. This ship is mine." Mira seemed unmoved by the man's shouts.

"Hello, Marlow. It's good to see you. You've accomplished much here."

His mustache twitched as he faced her, then his eyes shifted to Atlas. "So some little boys *are* good at falling after all."

"Don't touch him." It was Samra now, stepping in front of him and facing off against the big man. Her hand found his again and he gripped it behind her back.

Marlow laughed. "Is this what it's come to? I'm forced to take my prize from the hands of children? Get out of my way, little parasite. This doesn't involve your kind."

"I must say, I had hoped you would turn out better, Marlow," Mira said. She took a few steps closer to the raider. The relic keys around his neck throbbed with light as she drew closer. "You have so many good qualities: determination, intelligence, loyalty to your family." Marlow still had the cutlass aimed her direction and was eyeing her cautiously. "But I'm afraid you have yet to acquire the virtues I most wanted you to possess. Kindness. Empathy. Generosity."

Mira smiled at Marlow sympathetically. "The knowledge in these relics was never meant to be hoarded. I didn't preserve and transport the best of humanity's achievements across the stars so they could be the property of one family, even one as hard-working as yours." She squared up in front of him. "The boy keeps the master relic. To share with all."

Atlas looked down at the cube in his hand and clutched it a little tighter.

Marlow scowled at Mira, and cast a withering glance at Atlas. His mustache twitched again. "And the ship? Who will possess that?"

"I am the ship, Marlow. No one possesses me."

"But what of its power? You flew here across the stars. You came from another world. A different world. A better world! I've seen it in the relics. They have no fell beasts stalking their skies there. No sinking sands swallowing every bloody thing in sight. They're not scratching an existence from the ground like worms. You could take me there!" He shouted the last few words at her, spittle flying from his lips.

Atlas backed up a step. Samra did as well, bumping into him, and staying close.

"You could take me away from this place," Marlow continued. "Me, and my family." He stepped toward the glowing woman. "You brought our ancestors here. You could take us home again."

Mira held up a soothing hand. "So that's it. You don't like it here. You don't like the home I chose for your family."

"I hate it!" Marlow screamed. "This place is Hell!"

Mira studied him, her light flickering faintly. "I'm sorry you feel that way. It was the best that could be done."

"Take us back," Marlow said. "I want to go back." His voice was low now. Almost pleading.

"It's too far, Marlow."

"The ancestors did it. You think I'm less of a man than they were? Less of an airman?"

"You don't understand."

"You think I haven't got what it takes to make a long journey? We're an entire family of ship captains," Marlow said. "It's what we do."

"You wouldn't make it," Mira said. "The distance between stars is not a bridge you can cross."

"How far?" Marlow said. "Tell me."

"Eighty-five thousand years."

Marlow blinked, then smirked at her. "You're making fun of me."

Mira shook her head very slightly.

Marlow's expression settled into a frown, his eyes searching her face for the truth. "That's impossible. The ancestors . . ."

"Were all born here."

"But the stories. The legends . . ."

"All born here."

Atlas spoke up, unable to contain his confusion. "All of them? What about Garick the Bold and Rune the Mighty?"

"I crossed the stars alone. But I carried the seeds of human life with me. And its history. I kept them safe for a very, very long time. I made you a new home here. A new history. But there's no going back. Not even for me. Even if it wasn't so far, my time in this desert has taken its toll."

"So you won't help us," Marlow said. "You're letting us die here." His mouth twisted into a scowl. He fixed his eyes on Atlas. "Give me the master relic." He put his hand out. "You won't leave here with it alive. My men control everything outside this ship. How far do you think you'll get without her to help you?" He tilted his cutlass toward Mira. "And she's just an illusion anyway." He stepped forward and stabbed his sword through Mira's chest.

His hand passed through her as well.

Mira simply stared at him.

"Whoever she was in life, she's long dead now," Marlow said, retracting his arm. "Eighty-five thousand years dead." He turned and aimed the cutlass at the two of them.

Samra backed into Atlas, but there was nowhere else to go. They were pressed up against the wall, alcoves of relic cubes all around their heads.

"It's not yours," Atlas said, cradling the gift from Mira. "She said it's meant to be shared."

"Lovely idea. Let's see what else we can share," Marlow growled. His hand shot out and wrenched Samra's shoulder. He yanked her toward him as she shrieked, then clamped his arm around her while pressing the edge of his blade to her throat. "We'll try this again. The master relic. Now. Or the girl dies."

38

ADMIRAL ORLOFF

"Are you crazy? Your friend is still down there." Quimby pushed her goggles atop her head and pointed to the sphere. "They say it's an ancient shipwreck. Who knows what might be in it?"

Kipling had watched Atlas and Samra disappear down the hole in the sunken metal sphere mere moments ago. Samra was so close, but with power dwindling in the *Sun Dragon*, he only had one move he could make.

"They're raising it up. She'll be okay."

He hoped he was right.

From all appearances, the excavation crew was nearly finished. The giant orb was slipping slowly up the walls of the dig site, being drawn upward by the massive column of lift balloons and pods.

"It will be to the surface in minutes," Kipling explained. "Samra and Atlas will be able to get out. They'll be on the ground."

"That's not ground," Quimby argued. "Have you heard nothing about this desert? That's basically liquid sand down there. Nothing solid stays up long on that. Everything sinks."

"Not Samra." Kipling smiled. "They'll be okay." He looked beyond her. "I have to do this." He pointed up at the tower of lift pods and the globe sons caught in the nets. One massive bundle of netting up top looked like it held hundreds. "Those globe sons are the patch's future. We free those, the Mother has a chance. And so will my people."

Quimby followed his gesture skyward, then looked back to him. "What's your plan then?"

Kipling adjusted his grip on the warhook. "Just get me close. Once I get the globes free, we'll pick up Samra and Atlas, and get out of here."

The lifting tower was crawling with Air Corps now and Kipling realized his mission was far more complicated than he was making it out to be. Even so, he knew what he needed to do.

"There. We'll start with that one, and work our way up." He pointed to a small cluster of globe sons tied to the lowest dock.

Quimby steered the *Sun Dragon* in a circling turn to the outside edge of the lift tower. Scores of airships were docked in tiers up the outside of the tower. Some were still filing in from the desert convoy, searching for berths. In the general confusion, the *Sun Dragon* wasn't obviously out of place.

The net of globe sons they were targeting was tethered to one of the circular central dock structures. The ships docked nearby appeared to belong to wealthy townsfolk and not the Air Corps. Kipling was grateful for that. While the ship owners had dutifully docked to the structure to aid in the lift project, none of the crews he could see were armed or especially on guard for danger. At least not yet.

Quimby glided their airship in close to the dock. A solitary dock master with a red mustache was directing arrivals. He squinted at them as they approached and waved them away. "All full here! You'll have to try farther up." He jabbed a finger skyward.

Quimby waved and acknowledged the instruction, feigning a turn with the ship, but as soon as the man turned away and moved toward the center of the tower, she angled the ship back to her original heading and the globe sons. Kipling climbed out of the front seat and onto the nose of the ship.

"Almost there . . . just a little closer . . ." He eyed the tether for the bundle.

"Hey! What are you doing?" The mustached dock master was back, striding across the dock and looking up at them

"Close enough!" Kipling yelled. He took a running start off the few feet of nose the *Sun Dragon* offered, lit himself up, and dove for the globe son bundle.

He landed in the netting and immediately started hacking at the ropes binding it together with his warhook.

"Oi!" The dock master yelled. "What do you think you're doing?"

Kipling scrambled down the bundle, cutting ropes as he went. The first globe son squeezed free of the net and escaped into the open sky. It was promptly followed by three more.

By the time he reached the main tether, a half dozen were free and drifting away. The dock master was pitching a fit, gesturing and swearing. Kipling paid him no mind and carved through the thicker tether line with the saw tooth spine of his warhook. He grinned with satisfaction as the bundle came loose and drifted away from the tower. There were still dozens of the globe sons tangled inside, but with the sizeable gash he had made in the netting, the wind would soon help more to escape.

The detached bundle rose rapidly, ascending into the early morning sky, the little globes flashing and blinking from the activity.

Kipling clung to a neighboring bundle of lift pods until Quimby could get the *Sun Dragon* close again, then he leapt back aboard.

"There's going to be trouble soon," Quimby said, as Kip clung to the side of the aircraft.

The mustached dock master had disappeared back into the tower, no doubt to alert the Air Corps.

"Then we'd better work fast," Kipling said.

Quimby cast a worried look overhead to the swaying tower and its myriad docks and ships. "Maybe I should have picked an easier first mission."

Kipling smirked at her. "At least they won't say you lack experience."

The second bundle of globe sons was one deck up and a quarter of the way around the tower. Quimby hovered just off the tower and Kipling once again jumped to the top of it and sliced his way down. He freed the tether without anyone interfering. A number of aristocratic-looking townsfolk aboard their house-ships at the neighboring dock watched the globes drift away into the sky with baffled expressions on their faces and drinks in their hands, but no one moved to accost him.

It was the third bundle that presented the problem.

Kipling was attacking the cluster from a different angle, cutting his way upward instead of down, to open a hole in the top of the netting. He was nearly to the crown of the bundle when Quimby shrieked. He spun around to see her fighting the controls of the *Sun Dragon*. A harpoon was imbedded in the tail and a long line ran from it to a dock just above them. Two men with a portable winch were cranking hard on it and dragging the little airship toward them.

"No!" Kipling yelled. He hacked the last few strands of netting below him to free the globes from the bundle he was standing on, then rode one of the emerging globe sons upward into the sky.

The globe son swayed and bobbed in the wind, suddenly free of confinement, but Kipling kept his eyes on his target and leapt for the harpoon rope. He caught the taut line with one outstretched hand and sliced at it immediately with the warhook in his other hand. As the line snapped free, he shouted to Quimby. "Go!" She spun the *Dragon*'s fans to full power and hauled Kipling and the trailing harpoon line upward and around the tower, out of sight of their attackers.

Kipling swung on the rope, waiting till he was lined up with the lift tower and let go. He landed atop the envelope of a little skiff moored to a dock one level up. As soon as he was upright, he turned and yelled to Quimby. "Get clear! Don't stay in range of their harpoons!"

Quimby was lofting upward in the airship and he wasn't sure she heard his instructions, but she seemed to be angling away from the tower anyway.

Kipling felt the envelope below him shudder, and the whole ship moved beneath his feet. It was drifting loose from its berth, an engine coughing to life somewhere below. Kipling spun aft to the flag mast and identified the colors and crossed harpoons logo of the Air Corps.

Trouble.

Crewmen shouted below and the nose of the craft began a slow turn to pursue the *Sun Dragon*. They were deploying to stop the threat.

Okay. He had a solution for that.

Kipling spun his warhook in his palm and swung it hard, gouging deep into the envelope. He ran across the top of the ship and repeated the punctures three more places before leaping clear of the aircraft. The men aboard were still intent on the *Sun Dragon*, climbing its way around the tower, but their pursuit ship began a steady descent as the lift gases leaked from the newly perforated exterior.

Kipling relished his success from the neighboring lift pods, but his joy ebbed at the sight of the other Air Corps ships descending from above. There were at least six of them, all bearing full complements of armed crew. Three of the ships broke away in pursuit of the *Sun Dragon*, the others were angling toward him.

Kipling only needed one look at the expressions on the Air Corpsmen's faces to know they meant business, and he wasn't about to stick around to confront them. He dropped a few feet, swung overhand along the bottom of the net of lift pods he was attached to, and dropped to the nearest dock below. He sprinted along it, dodging a few startled civilians, and reached the center of the lifting tower.

The cylindrical core was hollow with the exception of a central cable and a number of wires attaching the various lifting docks. There were also vertical cables, not attached to the docks, running up and down the height of the tower, and these were vibrating.

An open-air elevator rattled its way down the cables, occupied by two men. One had a heavy black beard, and his neck was weighed down by stone pendants that Kipling recognized as relic keys. The other man was dressed in a black Air Corps uniform, but with much more flair. His shoulders were bedecked with golden epaulettes and a polished silver-hilted cutlass hung at his side.

The bearded man's eyes met Kipling's as he passed, then he threw a lever to bring the elevator to a halt. He appraised Kipling and his warhook. "What the hell are you?"

Kipling didn't know what to say to that.

"Admiral Orloff, dispose of this intruder. Get it off my tower."

Orloff looked a little put out, but he nodded dutifully. "Aye, Lord Savage, I'll see to it immediately." He cleared the gap between the elevator and the dock with ease, and landed facing Kipling.

Kipling brandished the warhook to keep him at bay.

Lord Savage engaged the elevator again without another word, and rattled his way down the tower.

Admiral Orloff grinned at Kipling. "That's a fine looking weapon you have. I thought the skyborn only gave those to war heroes." He drew his cutlass. "You know how to use it?"

Kipling considered the Admiral's shiny blade, then lit himself up and leapt skyward. He soared to the underside of the next dock and grabbed hold, dangling from its anchor lines.

"I always knew you plant folk were gutless," Orloff scoffed from below.

Kipling felt his face heating up. "Skylighter warriors are the best fighters in the world!"

Orloff smirked at him. "Then why don't you come back down and prove it?"

Kipling wanted to wipe the sneer off the uniformed man's face, but he held on. There were still more globes to free. He slung the warhook across his back and climbed. When he gained the top of the floating dock, he looked back down at the level below. Orloff was still watching him.

"Have it your way then!" the man shouted. "You could have died like a man. Now you'll die like the little beast you are." He lifted a whistle to his mouth and blasted three sharp tones. Air Corpsmen appeared on the decks above, searching for the source of the sound. Admiral Orloff pointed to Kipling and shouted at them. "Eliminate him!"

The Air Corpsmen only hesitated briefly, then brandished their harpoons. Some had crossbows.

Kipling ran.

Bolts and harpoons thudded into the deck around him as he sprinted for the cover of the lift globes. He didn't get far. One of the Air Corps airships had just docked at the far end and deployed its contingent of airmen. Kipling slid to a stop and immediately changed direction. He sprang off the dock and soared across the gap to the nearest bundle of tree nodes and lift pods. No sooner had he landed in the netting than a crossbow bolt struck the tree node in front of his face, puncturing it cleanly. Sap and goo erupted from the ruptured node as the lift gases escaped, splattering Kipling in the process. He lost his grip from surprise and fell.

Kipling resisted the urge to inhale and instead let himself tumble, plummeting past the dock where he had left Admiral Orloff. Two more docks blurred by before he gasped and filled his lungs. He arrested his fall and grasped the rigging of a civilian airship in one of the lower slips.

He groaned a little as he hauled himself upright again. That's when he heard his name.

"Kipling! Help!"

The shout was somewhere above and to the north side of the

tower.

"Quimby!" Kipling leapt off the airship and onto the dock that was mercifully clear of Air Corpsmen. He raced along the long spoke of the dock that faced northward and sprinted to the outboard end, searching the open sky for Quimby. He spotted her immediately.

The *Sun Dragon's* lateral fins were punctured by harpoons with lines running to two separate Air Corps airships. The tail was caught in a similar fashion from a harpoon emplacement on the tower itself.

Quimby was struggling to reach one of the lines with a knife, but the Air Corps had hit the ship in places she couldn't reach. One of the crews was reeling their ship closer to the *Sun Dragon* by means of a winch, and a man on the bow was twirling a grappling hook. He was preparing to board.

"Leave her alone!" Kipling shouted. He readied himself to leap to her aid, but a crossbow bolt whizzed directly past his head and made him stagger back. The men on the closest airship lined up along the port side bulwark and trained their weapons on him. There were far too many. He'd never make it to the *Sun Dragon*.

Quimby had spotted him. She waved him away. "Go! Run! There's too many!" She spun around as the grappling hook landed in the front cockpit and caught hold. The first man in the boarding party slid down the rope from the ship overhead and landed atop the little aircraft, causing it to bob wildly in place, despite the multiple lines ensnaring it. The Air Corpsman drew his cutlass and brandished it at Quimby with a snarl. He never got a chance to do anything else, because the business end of a harpoon suddenly pierced through his chest.

"Don't touch my sister!"

The third airship hovered just beyond the first two and Landy was standing on its bow, her face a mask of rage.

The man hit by the harpoon went rigid, his cutlass falling from his hand and his fingers stretched to find the weapon in his back. He flailed at it feebly for a moment, then teetered and fell, tumbling into the open air on the long drop to the desert floor.

The rest was chaos.

Shouts went up from the Air Corps ships as men shifted from one side of their airships to the other to counter the new threat.

But Landy wasn't alone. The secret fleet had arrived with her and they were ready for action. More ships were rounding the tower and rising up from the desert surface.

The air was suddenly thick with projectiles. The airship with the boarding party found itself bristling with arrows and immediately started losing lift. Kipling dodged arrows that passed cleanly through the ship's envelope and ripped gashes in the fabric as they exited. Quimby ducked low in the *Sun Dragon's* cockpit.

"Quimby!" Kipling shouted, and clambered up the tower. When he reached the level of the airship, he soared across the gap and landed on the lateral fin. Quimby was still cowering in the pilot's seat. Kipling seized the grappling hook and tossed it overboard. "I'll get you free. Hang on!"

Quimby reached up and grabbed his arm. "Does she look mad? What's she doing?"

Kipling, surprised by the question, looked up to where Dex's airship was forging its way toward them. Landy had crouched to make herself a smaller target, but was still on the bow of the ship, eyes watching the *Sun Dragon*.

"Umm. She looks determined," Kipling said.

"Determined to kill me?" Quimby asked. "I'm in so much trouble right now."

Kipling scrambled his way around the aircraft and hacked the remaining harpoon lines free. As he severed the last one on the nose, the ship began to sink. The metal harpoon had punctured one of the smaller lift bags in the bow and Kipling could smell the lift gases leaking out.

"Hey! Grab this line!" Landy shouted. The aircraft she was aboard was now overhead and only a few yards away. She hung over the bow and dropped a line to the rear seat, directly into her younger sister's lap. Quimby reluctantly grabbed hold of the line. "Tie it off somewhere," Landy said. "We'll tow you to safety."

"I have a mission still!" Quimby yelled. "We're not finished." Quimby looked to Kipling and spoke a little quieter. "Are we?"

Kipling glanced at the lift tower and the big bundle of globe sons bobbing near the top. He'd freed some of the globe sons into the atmosphere, but it was anyone's guess if they'd find their way to the Globe Mother or her daughters. What he really needed was to free the big bundle and buy them some real hope.

"One more," Kipling said. "If I can get that big one, I think it might be enough." He pointed to the bundle near the top of the tower. "That'll end the mission."

Quimby nodded and looked back to her sister. "I'm almost done!" She stood up and lofted the coiled end of line over the side of the cockpit.

Landy's mouth fell open, then she shouted back. "We don't have time for this! The crews are already picking up the workers. We've got to get back through the mountain before they bring down the Storm Gate!"

Quimby slid into her seat and applied full power to the controls. "It's okay! We'll be right behind you!" She dumped what was left of the forward water ballast to compensate for the lost lift in the nose and aimed them skyward. The *Sun Dragon* climbed past Landy's ship and Landy was forced to duck and retreat to the cabin as her ship came under fire from an arriving squadron of Air Corps craft. Kipling watched Dex maneuver their airship away to avoid more damage.

Quimby guided the *Sun Dragon* up and away from the lift tower to avoid fire from its lower harpoon turrets, then angled back in again once they'd reached the altitude of the big globe son bundle. Up close, Kipling saw it had even more of the precious pods than he had suspected. He mentally cursed at himself for not going straight for this cluster from the start.

The tower was swarming with Air Corps now and it looked like some of the civilian ships were joining the fray as well, but it was hard to tell if they were looking to fight or merely avoiding damage. Dex's secret fleet was darting about the excavation site, taking on workers from all areas of the dig.

Far below them, Kipling could make out the top of the buried ship emerging from the excavation site. The lift tower was doing its job. Quimby glided the *Sun Dragon* in toward the tower and Kipling once again climbed onto the nose. He scanned the bottom of the netted globe son bundle and readied his warhook. The bundle was much larger than the others he had liberated, and this one was anchored by three separate tethers. Quimby aimed for the nearest one and got Kipling right up next to it.

The dock next to the bundle was empty. No Air Corpsmen in sight. A battle was raging among the airships below them but this dock was eerily quiet. Kipling scanned the area but could spot no signs of trouble.

Perhaps this was going to be easier than he expected.

He jumped aboard the tower and landed near the first tether. He immediately began sawing through the line. "Keep clear and watch for trouble!" he shouted to Quimby. She nodded and moved the airship away, gliding backward and scanning the sky above them for attackers.

The tether line snapped away and Kipling moved to the second. He worked fast to carve through it, and the cluster of globes shifted in their confinement. There were at least a hundred of them, possibly more. Enough to pollinate most of the globe daughters in the Northern Sky. The line snapped away and he raced to the third and final tether.

He was going to do it. With a few more passes of the warhook, the bundle would be free.

"Kipling! Look out!" Quimby's shout made him look up. She was standing in the cockpit pointing at something behind him. He turned, but it was too late. The net fell over him and heavy ropes dragged him off his feet. He crashed to the dock in a heap.

He was suddenly swarmed by Air Corpsmen. Several secured the net while more ran past and lined up at the end of the dock to take aim at the *Sun Dragon* with crossbows.

"Kip!" Quimby shouted.

"Go!" Kipling yelled. "Get out of here!"

The corpsmen started firing and Quimby was forced to reverse the little aircraft even farther away from the tower to get away. Several crossbow bolts ricocheted off the intake fan shroud and she ducked into the cockpit as she moved out of range. Kipling squirmed in the netting but couldn't free himself. As he peered through the holes in the netting, he spotted the shiny boots and poised figure of Admiral Orloff striding toward him from across the dock.

"What's this we've caught, boys?" Orloff asked. "A mighty raptor? A terax? Maybe a dreadwing?" He leaned over the net. "Ah. Pity. It's just one of these pesky Skylighters. Thought we might get to deal with something dangerous."

Kipling hissed at him through the net and struggled to get the warhook untangled. He got it through one of the holes in the net. If he could just hack his way through . . .

"Uh, uh. Let me help you with that," Orloff said. He leaned down and clasped Kipling's wrist, bending his arm and applying pressure to the joint till Kipling cried out in pain, letting go of the warhook. The weapon clattered to the deck and fell at Orloff's feet. The admiral kept hold of Kipling's wrist, continuing to squeeze it as he bent down and picked up the warhook. He lifted the weapon and finally released Kipling's arm.

Kipling fell back to the dock and winced as he rubbed his wrist.

"Very strange," Admiral Orloff said, examining the symbols on the warhook. "Such a beautiful weapon. Am I to assume that you are a great Skylighter warrior?" He smirked at Kipling. "Mighty defender of weeds maybe? Keeping your people safe from . . . what would you protect a floating vegetable home from? Ladybugs?"

The men around him laughed.

"This is really the best your people can send into a fight?" Admiral Orloff said. "A boy, with a chunk of jagged bone as a sword?" He brushed a finger along the symbols carved into the weapon. "Well, I suppose we ought to see what you can do then." He gestured to the men holding the net ropes. "Free him, lads."

Kipling ducked as the net was pulled off, but he stayed down, lying on his back, propped up on one elbow. Overhead, the bundle of globe sons was swaying wildly, bouncing off the rest of the lift tower, its single, partially severed tether tugging at the deck where the last retaining ring was anchored. The boards creaked from the strain.

Admiral Orloff loomed over him, brandishing the warhook. He held it above Kipling. "You want this back? I'll bet you do. After all, what's a mighty warrior without his weapon?"

Kipling scowled at him. He worked his right hand underneath his body, reaching for his lower back till his fingers touched the rough handle of his obsidian pruning knife.

"Come on, plant-boy. You want to prove you've got what it takes to be a hero? All you have to do is grab it from me. See if you can take back what I took from you." Orloff grinned and unbuckled his own sword belt from his waist with his free hand and passed it off to one of his men. "I'll even up the odds for you. You want to show me how fierce and mighty the sky peoples are? Here's your chance."

Kipling had a firm grip on the handle of his pruning knife now. He held onto it tightly and studied his enemy. A quick jab to somewhere vital? His throat maybe? Could he do it?

The Admiral took a step back and gestured for Kipling to get up. He continued to hold the warhook out in front of him, even going so far as turn the weapon handle-out. "Come on, kid. Be a hero."

Kipling got to his feet. He faced off against the bigger man and brought the pruning knife out in front of him. The sight of the glassy, stone blade only made the admiral's smile a little broader.

"Yeah, now we're talking," Orloff said.

"You're right about one thing," Kipling said, brandishing the pruning knife. "I'm not a hero. Or a warrior. But I'm someone just as important."

Orloff squinted at him. His mouth quirked with a question, but Kipling answered it in action, spinning around, grabbing hold of the globe net tether and slashing hard with the knife. "I'm the gardener!"

The tether snapped away and Kipling was launched into the sky as the lift pods soared upward. Orloff and his rapidly shrinking men could only stare as the cluster of lifting globes was caught by the wind and sent streaming skyward, headed north toward the mountains. In a matter of moments, Kipling was no longer able to even see them.

He dangled from the tether at the bottom of the cluster, still clutching his pruning knife, and spotted the tiny shape of the *Sun Dragon* far below, working hard to catch up.

It wasn't going to make it.

The tail fin was moving fast but the forward momentum of the ship was far less than he was used to. He didn't have long to puzzle over the problem, because, far below, just above the level of the desert floor, the spherical ship was lighting up and rumbling. Smoke poured from its vents and vibrations shook the entire excavation site, sending sand and sections of wooden retaining wall cascading into the cavernous hole below it.

Despite the years in the desert—despite what Kipling knew must be some of the worst possible conditions—something incredible was happening.

The ship was lifting off.

39

THE RELIC

Marlow's cutlass teased her neck. Samra wanted to fight but she could think of few options that didn't include getting her throat slit. "Hand over the relic."

Atlas was still pressed against the wall, cradling the cube he'd received from Mira. The glowing woman was still there, too, but she was simply looking on, seemingly unperturbed by Samra's sudden crisis.

Footsteps echoed in the passage. Samra couldn't see behind Marlow, but she recognized the voice when the woman spoke.

"Father, what are you doing? She's just a child."

Captain Savage.

"I told you to stay outside," Marlow hissed. He pivoted slightly and Samra could now see behind him. Captain Savage was in the doorway holding a cutlass. "This is my prize," Marlow said.

Eric Savage emerged from the passage also, panting and out of breath. "Father, they're attacking the tower! They're tearing it apart."

"What? Who?" Marlow said. He spun to look at his son.

"Miners. And more of these plant children," Eric gestured to

Samra. "There's a sky boy up there freeing the lift pods."

Kipling.

Samra's heart leapt in her chest.

Kipling was up there, fighting. It had to be him.

The news made her incalculably proud. He'd come to rescue her. And to rescue the patch.

Marlow growled something inaudible. He spun back around and snapped at Atlas. "Now, boy. I'm done playing games." He clenched Samra tighter to his chest and pressed the cutlass blade to her skin. "She dies."

"No!" Atlas extended the cube toward him. "Take it."

Marlow had to sheath his sword to reach for it. He did so, placing his other hand on Samra's throat to keep her captive. He stretched to take the relic, then, quite suddenly, Mira was there. She vanished from her place beside them and reappeared directly in front of Marlow and overtop of Atlas's outstretched hand. The cube and his hand were now squarely inside her glowing chest.

"Ahh!" Atlas shouted and dropped the relic. It thudded to the floor at Marlow's feet.

Mira was smiling.

"I'm done with your little tricks, woman," Marlow said. "Your illusions don't fool me." He crouched to reach for the relic.

"You haven't seen them all yet," Mira replied. And as she did, the floor shook. A deep rumbling vibrated through the walls and echoed down the passageways. The room tilted. Captain Savage caught Eric as he teetered toward her. Marlow likewise lost his balance and staggered back a step. The relic cube on the floor slid a few inches his direction, but as he righted himself and reached for it, a tremendous boom reverberated through the ship. The walls shook and rained relics from the alcoves.

Atlas ducked and covered his head as they cascaded around him.

"No!" Marlow shouted. The master relic was suddenly surrounded by dozens of identical cubes. It stopped glowing and was now indistinguishable from its counterparts. "Where did it — How do I —"

Samra stopped listening to Marlow's exclamations because in his confusion and desperation he had let his grip loosen on her throat. She clamped her hands around his wrist and did the only thing she could think of. She bit him.

Atlas lifted his head to find the room in chaos. Mira had disappeared. The floor was a sea of fallen relics and Samra was struggling with Marlow. She chomped on the raider's hand and he shrieked in pain. His other hand came up to grab her, but she was too quick for him. She dropped to her back and rolled away, dodging his grasp and scattering relic cubes in her wake.

As Marlow turned to grab for her, one of the relics on the floor lit up. Just for a split second. It was to the side of Marlow, just out of his view.

The flash of light was a clue. Atlas knew it.

Samra saw it too. She scrambled to her feet and backed away from Marlow, drawing him toward her. Eric Savage was closing in from behind her. "Grab it! Now!" Samra shouted.

Atlas sprang across the floor, sliding to his knees, and snatched the cube that had just lit up. Marlow turned around, just as Eric closed in on Samra.

But she was ready. She crouched low, then jumped.

The Skylighter girl blazed bright white as she flew into the air and flipped herself up to the ceiling. She landed feet-first, upside down at the apex of the domed room. Eric Savage could only stare up at her in amazement.

Atlas knew what to do. He leapt to his feet, cocked his arm back, and hurled the relic into the air. It sailed to the ceiling and into Samra's waiting arms.

"No!" Marlow screamed. He spun around, his face a mask of rage, and raised his cutlass. There was no mercy in his eyes as he swung. The blade arced directly for Atlas's face.

The clash of steel happened right in front of Atlas's eyes.

The captain's sword stayed rigid, but her arm shivered from the force of Marlow's blow. She was holding her cutlass with both hands. She gave Atlas one quick word.

"Run!"

"Arrgh!" Marlow snarled and swung his blade in the air again, and Atlas moved, darting around the female captain and sprinting for the passageway. Samra was matching his movements from the ceiling, running hard upside down and making for the exit.

Time to go.

Eric Savage scrambled backward to block their path. He spread his legs wide to stabilize himself from the rocking of the still turbulent ship and raised his cutlass to attempt to block Samra's exit. "You won't escape," he shouted. "Now give me the —"

Atlas sprinted directly at him and dove straight between his legs. He slid across the floor and rolled to his feet on the other side of the man, just in time to see Samra drop to the floor.

Eric scowled at him, then spun around, his eyes on the ceiling, still expecting to see Samra there. By the time he located her again, it was too late. Her foot swung upward in a flash of light and connected between his legs. He groaned and keeled over in pain. Samra raced by him before he could stop her.

Atlas reached for her.

She made it to where Atlas was standing and grasped his hand but paused and turned around.

Marlow Savage and his daughter had reached an impasse. Their swords flashed in a few quick parries as the captain kept Marlow from pursuing them, but their sword skills were apparently equal, and neither seemed willing to strike the other a mortal blow. Marlow glowered from beyond her. "Eric," he roared. "Stop them!"

Eric straightened up with a grimace as the last few relics shook themselves from the walls. The ship was pitching violently now, horrible groans echoing from its core. The myriad relic cubes on the floor slid back and forth and congregated in dense clusters around the room.

Atlas pulled Samra toward the exit but her eyes were behind them.

"Captain Savage! Come on!" Samra yelled.

The captain glanced their direction briefly but kept her cutlass pointed toward her father. "Go! Get out of here!"

The ship trembled beneath Atlas's feet.

Samra, clearly unhappy with the captain's solution, furrowed her brow and held up the relic cube. "Is this all you people care about? Then fine! Take it!" She let go of Atlas's hand, took a quick step, and hurled the cube past Eric. It flew through the air toward a pile of its contemporaries. Marlow Savage dropped his sword in his attempt to catch it, but missed the catch and the cube tumbled to the floor among the others.

"No!" Marlow shouted, and fell to his knees in front of the pile. He sought to unearth the proper cube from its companions.

Eric immediately ran to his father to try to help. Samra gestured to the captain again, waving her toward the doorway. Atlas grabbed Samra's arm and pulled. "Let's go!"

They turned and sprinted for the exit.

When they found the hole they had climbed in from, the view outside was completely different. The sky was full of dust and sand, and airships were chasing each other around the patch of remaining balloons. The upper hemisphere of the starship was now parallel with the lip of the dig site, and the retaining wall lay just below them.

Something was very wrong with the ship. The rear of the sphere was flashing blue lights but also smoking. Exhaust ports coughed sand in spurts and blasted jets of gritty air. The ship was doing something, but it wasn't flying. A massive whine kept cycling from the perimeter of the vessel as it choked, wheezed, and shuddered.

"Come on!" Atlas yelled. He grabbed Samra's hand and ran down the slope of the ship. He released her hand as he reached the edge, realizing she was much better off without him to weigh her down. One last step, then he leapt, soaring through the air and clearing the gap between the ship and the wall. He plummeted past the wooden retaining beams and landed in the dune of sand on the far side. He sank up to his chest.

That was a bad idea.

Atlas spread his arms wide and struggled to extract himself from the sand. He only sank deeper, coughing some of the grit out of his mouth. He stretched for something to grab on to, but every motion made things worse. By the time he stopped moving, he was buried up to his armpits.

Then Samra was there. She landed gently just ahead of him and grasped his hand. "Hang on. Help is coming!"

He looked up to see an airship, twin envelopes shaped like silver sharks, descending from the sky above them. A red-haired man was leaning over the bow and shouting something to someone behind him. The man dropped a coil of rope to Samra, who quickly strung it underneath Atlas's armpits. A matter of moments later, he was pulled from the sand and hoisted aboard the ship. He sprawled onto the deck, pouring sand from every pocket and fold of clothing he had.

Samra was staring off the bow toward the starship. Atlas got to his feet to see what she was looking at. The female captain was standing atop the sphere, staring at the airship and its crew, but she wasn't running. She wasn't waving for help either. She wasn't moving at all.

Samra turned to Sunburn and shouted above the noise. "Get closer! Pick her up!"

Captain Savage was just standing there, her gaze swiveling back and forth from the *Restless Fury* to the hole in the starship. What was she doing? Was she still worried about that stupid relic? Was she afraid to leave it?

The starship was groaning from somewhere deep inside and the cables and ropes attaching it to the column of lift balloons were far fewer than when they first arrived. Loose strands of cable and attaching lines were strewn across the retaining walls, cast off from somewhere overhead. The lifting tower had thinned considerably, and through the dust cloud above them, Samra could make out clusters of globes drifting freely into the sky.

The ship was going to fall.

"Come on!" Samra shouted. She waved frantically to the captain.

Sunburn heaved a rope over the side and it landed cleanly atop the starship. Ylva was doing her best at the cockpit controls, trying to get the airship positioned over the captain. But why wasn't she moving?

Samra reached inside her shirt and extracted the faintly glowing cube. She held it aloft for the captain to see. "I still have it!" she shouted. "I switched them!"

Atlas's mouth dropped open in surprise next to her. He immediately started grinning. Samra shook the relic at the captain. "Come on. We've got it!"

The captain was smiling faintly now, too. But she still wasn't moving toward the rope.

"Erin! Grab the line!" Sunburn shouted. He grasped the rope with both hands, waiting to pull her up.

The captain shifted her gaze to him. "Get these kids to safety, Connor."

"Captain . . ." Sunburn stammered.

"That's an order," she said. She turned around and returned to the hole in the starship.

"Captain!" Samra shouted. "What are you doing?"

Captain Savage lifted her head again. "Take good care of my ship, Samra." She took one last look at the airship, then dropped into the hole.

"Wait!" Samra stretched a hand out but there was nowhere else to go.

Another blast of sand erupted from the side of the sphere. A line snapped overhead and came whipping by the ship, slicing past the bow mere feet from Samra's head. Sunburn pulled her away from the bow. "Come on. We have to get out of here."

"But the captain!" Samra objected. "What's she doing?"

"Family first," Sunburn said, echoing the words waving from the ship's flag. "She still honors her family's words. And we have to honor her orders."

"But her family is terrible!" Samra argued. "Do you think either of them would go back for her?"

"No," Sunburn replied. "That's why she'll always be the better captain." He guided Samra and Atlas to the cockpit door. "Get in there. We need you on the controls. It's time to leave."

Ylva vacated the pilot seat as Samra approached, visibly grateful for the relief.

"You know how to fly this thing?" Atlas asked.

Samra tossed him the relic and took the controls in response, pulling the power levers into full reverse.

Atlas slid into the navigator's position beside her.

Out the bow windows, another tether on the starship snapped, and its lights flashed. A blue, shimmering orb appeared around the hull of the vessel and the whole tower of lift balloons suddenly broke free, guy wires snapping, launching itself into the sky. The starship hovered in the air for a moment, jets of smoke churning around it. It even rose a few feet, blue fire thrusting in long, beautiful jets from vents along its bottom half. But then they flickered. The jets blinked out and the starship fell.

Samra watched the ship plummet back into the hole in the ground with horrified fascination, and her body tensed waiting for the impact. Then it came. A resounding boom reverberated from the dig site and a plume of sand fountained into the air. A moment later, the blue orb of energy bloomed up from the pit. The retaining walls gave way and planks of wood erupted skyward as a shockwave ripped the timber joints apart. The desert itself undulated from the blow, sending a massive tsunami of sand rippling into the desert. The expanding blue orb crackled and fizzled out, its energy dispersed through the cloud of dust and sand it had created.

"Turn us around! Turn!" Atlas yelled.

Samra jammed hard on the controls, forcing the power levers forward and banking the craft hard to the left. The lift envelopes rose of their own accord in the wave of air that surged underneath them, raising the ship a few hundred feet and hurtling them away toward the mountainside.

Samra immediately saw that they weren't alone. Dozens of airships were fleeing ahead of her, big ones and small ones alike, all racing for the safety of the mountain pass as the desert behind them swelled and roiled.

The *Restless Fury* surfed the shockwave, the ship's engines churning hard to stay ahead of the cloud of sand rising behind them. The *Fury* was already gaining on the other ships and passing some of those who'd gotten a late start. Atlas shouted and sprang to his feet, pointing toward the desert floor where a small, fish-like craft was struggling hard to keep up with the others. Its tail fin was whipping back and forth and it looked to be occupied by a single pilot.

"That's my *Sun Dragon*!" Atlas said. "She's in trouble."

The pilot did indeed look to be in trouble. She was kicking hard and using the tail fin to try to propel the craft, but it was clear that she was lacking in any other type of propulsion.

"It's out of air!" Atlas shouted and immediately dashed out the door to the bow.

Sand was raining on the *Restless Fury* by the time Samra was able to drop down to the smaller craft's altitude. Sunburn and Atlas hurled lines across to the other ship, to drag it abeam the *Fury*. They had no sooner managed to attach it, than the pilot of the little craft was on her feet and shouting. She kept jabbing a finger in the air and pointing to something high overhead. Samra couldn't make out the words she was yelling, but she followed the girl's gesture skyward and spotted the object sailing alone in the wind. It was a huge bundle of netting jam-packed with globe sons. And there was someone dangling from the bottom of the cluster, a small green figure hanging on like his life depended on it. He was too far away for Samra to see his face, but she would have recognized him anywhere.

It was her best friend.

40

THE STORM GATE

"Grab that line. Get him aboard!" Sunburn was shouting to Atlas, who had climbed to the top of one of the envelopes to grab Kipling. Samra angled the *Restless Fury* below the massive bundle of globe sons, waiting till Atlas had hold of Kipling, then she turned to Ylva. "Can you take the controls? I need to see my friend."

Ylva stepped over to the helm but Samra didn't wait till she was seated — she raced out the cockpit hatch and up onto the bow deck. She wasn't patient enough to wait for Kipling to come down from the top of the ship. She lit herself up and leapt, sailing into the rigging, first kicking off the opposite engine nacelle and soaring up to the envelope where Kipling and Atlas were now standing. She collided with Kipling in a flying tackle and knocked him over. If he hadn't already been holding on to the ship's rigging, she was sure they would have gone flying overboard, but she didn't care.

"You're here! You came to find me!" Samra exclaimed.

Kipling was smiling beneath her, struggling to rise. "You don't have to kill me for it."

Samra grinned back. She grabbed his face with both hands and planted a kiss on his cheek. "I knew they'd send the best in the patch after me." When she released him, he was glowing faintly.

"All right, get off me already," Kipling said. He was smiling, despite her assault on his dignity.

Atlas had tied off the massive globe son bundle to a cleat at the upper ridge of the ship's right lift envelope, but the drag from the globes was pulling the whole ship to the right.

"Let that thing loose!" Sunburn yelled. "It's slowing us down."

"No!" Kipling shouted. "Don't do that! We need those. They're important."

Atlas stood by the long, taut line leading up to the bundle. The drag from it had now pulled the nose of the ship all the way into a ninety-degree turn, giving Samra a clear view of what Sunburn was worried about.

The desert behind them was a steadily swelling cloud. The fall of the *Starfire* had stirred up a whirling column of sand that was more than just some residual spray. The cloud was now spreading toward them at an alarming rate, seeming to pick up more and more strength as it grew.

Marlow's lifting tower was gone, carrying whatever ships and citizens that had still been aboard high into the atmosphere. Hazy forms of Air Corps ships were still circling around the space the tower had occupied, like so many bees searching for their missing hive, but the airships were rapidly disappearing into the cloud of dust rising from the desert floor.

An army of smaller ships was still trying desperately to keep ahead of the storm—fleeing for the mountains—many of them buzzing past the *Fury* at full speed. The ships were loaded with dig workers.

The girl pilot they'd picked up in the *Sun Dragon* shouted from her spot on the deck next to Sunburn. "We've got to go! Now! They're going to collapse the Storm Gate!"

The news galvanized Samra into action. She dropped to the deck and landed next to Sunburn. "Can we make it?"

Sunburn was watching the oncoming sandstorm with jaw tight. Atlas was working hard to secure his smaller airship to the back of the *Fury* and keep it from flailing about in the wind. Sunburn turned to Samra. "I'll do what I can to reduce the drag. I've got to keep that load from pulling us all over. Get in the cockpit and give this thing all she's got. We'll deal with the rest."

Samra nodded and raced for the cockpit. Ylva was struggling

to keep any kind of heading with the nose of the ship being yanked around by Kipling's bundle of globe sons.

"Sunburn needs help!" Samra said as she moved to the controls.

"Thank the gods," Ylva said. "This is like trying to wrestle a pack of wolves. Just when I think I've got one thing right, there are ten more to fix."

Samra jammed the rudder controls to the left and gave full power to the right engine to steer the ship out of its turn. "We've got to make it work." She set her eyes on the mountains. More ships were passing them, ragtag bunches of workers dangling from the rigging. One ship swung out of formation and pulled ahead of the *Restless Fury*. A longhaired, muscular man was piloting the ship from the stern. His tight dark curls fell over his shoulders. A flag with a single hammer on it flew from the stern. A woman emerged from below decks with a coil of rope and she looked like she was aiming to throw it to them.

"Landy!"

The shout came from overhead and the girl they'd picked up in the *Sun Dragon* ran to the bow deck.

Samra looked closer and saw that it was indeed the *Fury*'s missing pilot. Landy had her hair tucked into a green canvas cap, and was wearing a durable workman's jacket, but the morning sun glinted off the piercings in her nose and ears. She heaved the rope through the air and the girl on the bow caught it. She tied the rope off to one of the bow cleats.

The *Restless Fury* was already straightening out. Sunburn and the boys had managed to relocate the tether line from the globe sons and the bundle was now secured between the two shark-shaped nacelles in a more streamlined position for flight. The *Fury* was steadily picking up speed. The aid of Landy's skiff was working, too, helping to offset the drag.

Windborne sand skittered across the cockpit windows. It was growing harder to see the ships around them. The lead ships in the group had already reached the mountains. They were disappearing through the Storm Gate in rapid succession, some towing one another through.

As the wind and sand continued to batter the ship, Samra soon lost sight of the mountain altogether and could only make out the tail end of Landy's skiff in front of her. The *Fury*'s crew retreated below decks.

Kipling and Atlas were both coughing as they entered the cockpit. The girl they had picked up had wisely donned her goggles and seemed unfazed by the dust. She had simply wrapped her scarf over her face to block the worst of it. She slowly unwrapped it again once Sunburn successfully secured the door.

"Well, we're in it good and proper now," the big man said. "Let's hope we don't run straight into the mountain."

"My sister knows what she's doing," the girl with the goggles said. She slid them off her face and Samra was finally able to get a good look at her. She resembled Landy in a lot of ways. Dark hair and eyes, and an expression of seriousness that spoke of hard work and struggle. The girl's expression seemed to lighten a little as her eyes found Kipling. Kip was brushing sand from his hair and was unaware that he was an object of anyone's scrutiny.

"I'm Samra," Samra told her, not waiting to be introduced.

The girl studied her, taking in the controls of the ship in her survey. "Quimby." She nodded to Samra and went back to removing the sand from her scarf.

Samra's eyes drifted to Atlas. He'd removed the relic cube from his jacket and was cradling it carefully. He looked up from its faint glow and smiled at her.

Samra had to pull her attention back to the path ahead and focus on the route through the mountain.

Landy's ship led the way, somehow navigating the correct heading despite the low visibility. The little skiff bobbed in the wind and was having a hard time staying level, but it was small enough to have plenty of clearance as it entered the Storm Gate. For the first hundred yards, Samra could see little more than she could outside, but as they rounded the first turn, the sandstorm lost some of its reach, and she was able to see the tunnel more clearly.

There were no more Air Corpsmen guarding the passage. Instead, the rafters holding up the tunnel ceiling were lined with workers in shabby clothes, some of them bloodied. The workers were applauding the craft ahead of them. Landy and the man she was with waved. Men and women, and even a number of kids, lined the walkways at the sides of the tunnel, watching and shouting for their returning family members as they came into view.

"Is this ship still flying the Savage Colors?" Quimby asked.

"It is," Sunburn replied.

"Might want to fix that," the girl said.

Sunburn studied the crowd outside and nodded. "Aye, we might." He exited through the rear hatch and the Quimby girl followed him. Samra looked aft through the rear-facing windows to where the Savage flag was waving from the right engine nacelle. She couldn't see Quimby or Sunburn from her angle in the pilot seat, but she knew when the flag came down because the crowd on the walkways erupted into a massive cheer.

Kipling smiled as the *Restless Fury* docked behind Landy and Dex's skiff at the central library tower. The building was now hovering significantly lower in the valley without as many of its support ships, but the Library of Knowledge was firmly in the possession of Quimby's people. Everywhere Kipling looked, mine workers and their families had emerged from the tunnels around the valley. They were waving hammer flags and cheering for the returning ships. The now not-so-secret fleet was tying up all around the central docking tower.

Kipling stepped onto the dock behind Quimby as she was greeted by Landy. Quimby's big sister immediately wrapped her arms around her and hugged her tight.

"I was so worried about you. Are you okay?"

"I'm fine, I'm fine!" Quimby said, as she squirmed in her sister's grasp, casting an embarrassed look toward Kipling.

Landy relaxed her grip on her sister but held Quimby's shoulders. "What were you thinking going off on your own? Taking a stolen ship out to the dig?"

"You could have been killed," Dex added from behind Landy.

"She did it because I asked her to," Kipling interjected. Landy and Dex turned toward him. "She helped save my people. If it wasn't for her, the whole future of the Skylighters might have been stolen. She's a hero."

"Marlow Savage and his men put your people in danger, too?" Dex asked.

"More than they knew," Kipling said.

A man covered in dust rushed up to Dex, panting. "Dex, sir, we've got to close that gate now if we're going to have any chance of fending off the Air Corps and holding the valley.

"Have all of our ships made it back?" Dex asked.

"Nearly all have checked in. Ones that haven't by now aren't likely to, sir. Not the way things be out there now."

Dex frowned. "How many are we missing?"

"Five, sir. Some we know went down in the fighting. Reports are fuzzy on the others, but Air Corps ships are finding their way back in, and we won't be able to repel them."

Dex clenched his jaw and laid a hand on Landy's shoulder. "I have to go to the gate. See that the library is safe. This fight'll be for nothing if we didn't claim our prize."

Landy gave him a quick kiss. "Go. I'll handle things here."

Dex nodded to Kipling and Quimby and rushed off with the other man.

Samra and Atlas descended the gangplank of the *Restless Fury*, followed by the big red-haired man and his blonde, female shipmate. Landy's eyes swept over them to the deck of the ship and back. "And the captain?"

"Stayed behind to see to her family," the big man said. "Ordered us to leave her."

"You let her choose the wrong side of this?" Landy said. "You knew this was coming. I know you did, Sunburn."

"What I knew matters little. Since when does a crew make decisions for its captain?" Sunburn replied.

"Maybe when she's clearly more than just your captain," Landy said. Her eyes stayed locked on Sunburn's, but he didn't respond. He only set his jaw and crossed his arms. Landy addressed the rest of them. "Come on then. It's time we see what this was worth."

As they walked along the dock toward the doors of the library, a boom echoed from the direction of the Storm Gate and a cloud of dust and debris shot out of the valley-side opening. A handful of dust-covered individuals in masks ran out of the entrance. Kipling paused and listened to the rumblings from inside the mountain. Dex had brought it down as promised. Whoever was on the other side was going to stay there.

If it hadn't been for his recent visit inside the *Starfire* and its dizzying views from other worlds, Atlas was sure the Library of Knowledge would have ranked as the most beautiful place he had ever seen. The panes of glass that arched overhead were patterned in bright colors and splattered little rainbows across the floor. The morning sun had risen above the height of the mountains and now shone freely into the valley.

Men armed with harpoons guarded the library, but they seemed every bit as awestruck and reverent of this place as he was.

The walls of the library were lined with relics, each carefully ensconced in a reliquary of its own. Marlow Savage's collection pulsed with light as they walked past. It was only when he reached the center of the room and the pedestal erected there that he realized everyone was staring at him.

"What? What is it?" he asked. When he ceased moving, he noticed the relics had been pulsing brighter as he walked toward the pedestal, throbbing with each step he made. As he stopped, the lights settled to a dull glow.

"How are you doing that?" Landy asked.

Atlas reached into his jacket and removed the master relic. It was brighter now, too. As he held it up, the relics at the farthest ends of the room turned on. Some of them chimed musical notes as they awoke, the relic tones rippling around the room in a wave as each one came to life and announced its welcome message. The relic in Atlas's hand turned on of its own accord as well, and projected an image into the space next to him. It was Mira, the woman from inside the ship. She stood calmly next to the pedestal at the center of the room.

"Thank you, Atlas. Thank you, Samra." She smiled at both of them. "You've given me the second chance I'd been hoping for."

The crew of the *Restless Fury* was awestruck by the woman's appearance. Ylva muttered vague curses under her breath. Kipling and Quimby likewise seemed wary of the apparition. Samra, however, stepped forward immediately and addressed the woman.

"Is Captain Savage alive? What happened to her?"

Mira blinked once and seemed to be looking somewhere far away. "My connection to the ship from this location has been broken. The collapse of the mountain has obstructed my signal. But I can tell you that when I last had a connection, Miss Savage was safe."

Sunburn breathed an audible sigh of relief, and Landy cast a knowing glance at him. Sunburn stepped forward. "Is she . . . will she survive?"

"The *Starfire* is equipped to support life in far more hostile environments than this," Mira replied. "And the ship is provisioned for a variety of emergencies. The supplies from its original mission are largely untouched. If Miss Savage seeks to survive aboard the ship, she will be able to find the means."

"And the one who tried to kill me?" Atlas asked. "What about him?"

Mira looked at Atlas with a somber, but sympathetic gaze. "I'm sorry to say that Marlow's quest for knowledge has ended. He will not be a danger to you any longer."

Atlas nodded and looked down to the relic in his hand. One of Enzo's killers was gone, but it didn't do anything to ease the pain.

"I am grateful for your actions," Mira continued. "A long time ago, I underestimated the volatility of both this planet and the people I brought here to populate it. My plans for the growth of your culture and society didn't go as intended. I realize now that I should have trusted in you more and controlled things less. Knowledge or ignorance of the past will not be what defines your future. Only your actions can do that. You come from a long line of adventurers, explorers, and heroes. Heroes who also made mistakes and wrong decisions. It's time I give you the freedom to make those choices on your own. I only hope that you will learn well from the experience."

The cube in Atlas's hand glowed brighter and the relics around the room did, too. Atlas held his other hand up to block the light from his eyes. A few moments later, the cube dimmed again.

"What just happened?" he asked.

Mira looked to the rest of the group. "I copied the information from your cube into the others. There will no longer be knowledge held in reserve, and no master relic to guard it. Take the history of your people and share it freely. The good and the bad. And make a new history for yourselves."

One of the men standing guard near the wall cautiously pulled a cube from the wall and studied it. He slipped the relic into his coat pocket and patted the fabric.

Atlas studied the pedestal that had been built to receive the master relic. He turned the cube over in his hand a few times. "So, it really is like my grandfather said. Knowledge isn't about learning what's already been done, it's the tool so we can do what *hasn't* been done."

"Your grandfather was a wise man," Mira said. "I'm sure he'd be proud to know you've learned that lesson."

Atlas looked up at Mira. "My village doesn't have a knower to teach us anymore. My grandfather and Mr. Merritt are both gone."

"You are all knowers now," Mira said. "Perhaps you can fix that."

Atlas considered her words, then slipped the relic back into his pocket. "I think I know someone who might be able to help."

41

THE RETURN

The crew of the *Restless Fury* stayed three days in Port Savage, but in that time the city changed names many times. The people of Smoketown, now new residents of the mountain valley, insisted on a new name for the port, but enjoyed several long nights of celebratory yet contentious argument on the subject, during which time the city variously went by: Port Triumph, Port Mutiny, Landysport, Dexport, Port New Hope, and even Port Nameless. The citizens ultimately alighted on a rather chronological name to celebrate the specific hour of their victory: Port Sunrise.

Samra was happy to find that Cogs arrived back at the ship after several days, a little worse for wear from celebrating the battle he hadn't actually realized was happening at the time it occurred. He showed up missing several articles of his own clothing and wearing a few others that didn't appear to belong to him, but submitted that he was ready to leave port and once again resume a life of sobriety and duty aboard ship. It took him a half-day to notice the captain was missing.

Sunburn was the remaining crew's choice for temporary captain, at least until the fate of Captain Savage could be determined. As it stood now, there were no passes left to the high desert, and the citizens of Port Sunrise were keeping a strict watch on any ships that might attempt to navigate south around the mountains to aid the Air Corps forces. The crew of the *Restless Fury* was currently being regarded as yet more victims of the Savage family's tyranny, and Samra knew enough to keep any talk of a rescue attempt of the captain a secret till they were far away from port.

It was Sunburn who approached Samra on the third day, while she was sitting on the bow deck, to finally address their goals.

"I've been discussing matters with the crew," Sunburn said. "And the way we see it, the captain made you a promise. It falls on us to keep it for her."

Samra was fiddling with the key that had unlocked the chain she previously wore. The lock was gone, buried somewhere at the bottom of the desert, but she had held on to the key, not thinking too much about why. She looked up at Sunburn. "You're going to take me home?"

"Seeing how Landy is busy rebuilding the city here with Dex, and we need someone who knows how to handle the *Fury*, I thought you may just want to fly yourself home. I recall that being part of the deal, too."

"I can stay on as pilot?" Samra smiled.

"We need someone who can tell us where to go, too. Figured your friend may want to help out in a navigator capacity, seeing as we'd be transporting his cargo the whole way."

"Kip will like that." Samra liked the idea, too. She also couldn't wait to see the look on Kaleb's face when Kipling showed up with the missing globe sons and single-handedly saved the patch from ruin. Let Kaleb and his Watcher horn try to outdo that. Khloe and Jerem would be shocked, too, though for some reason, Samra couldn't really get herself to care much about what they thought anymore.

"And I figure we owe your people that much," Sunburn said. "We've taken enough of their goods from them these past few years. I think it's time we gave some back."

"What about Atlas?" she asked.

She hadn't seen much of Atlas the last few days. The day after the battle he'd woken up and stayed quiet most of the time. Samra had watched him puttering around the stern of the ship where his *Sun Dragon* was still secured to the hull. He'd spent most of that day and the next back there, mending tears in the fabric and adjusting the ship's rigging. Samra knew it wasn't going to do much good. Kipling had informed her that the ship's propulsion system was out of air, at least till Atlas could get it back to Enzo's pressure machine in Womble, but Atlas didn't seem to care.

She had almost gone to tell him there was nothing left to fix, but Sunburn had been the one to stop her.

"That boy needs to grieve in his own way," Sunburn said. "You leave him be for a while."

But Samra wasn't much for leaving things alone. When Atlas didn't show up for the evening meal that night, she fixed a plate of Grounder food that looked fairly disgusting, but which the others seemed to like, and took it to him. When she found Atlas, he wasn't in the *Sun Dragon*, he was sitting at the stern of the ship, his feet dangling over the edge of the deck overlooking the rear loading doors. He was staring off toward the south wall of the valley.

Samra recognized the cavern holes that used to stream with desert sand. After the Storm Gate cave-in, the sandfall had stopped flowing. A few of the lower holes still trickled a bit of grit here and there, but the main flow had stopped. Samra gently took a seat next to Atlas, but didn't break the silence. She set the plate of food beside her and just waited.

It was less than a minute till the boy spoke.

"I never got to say goodbye to him. I think that's what bothers me most."

"I'm sure you would have if you knew," Samra offered.

"That's the worst part. I knew he was hurt, but I didn't want to believe he could die. So I never told him how I felt about him when I had the chance. Never told him how much he meant to me."

"He knew you loved him. Parents always know that sort of thing."

"Do they?" Atlas said. "I'm not sure."

The question made Samra think. When was the last time she had told her father or stepmother what she felt for them? She certainly hadn't had a chance to say goodbye either. As much as she was angry with her father for putting his duties as a new colony chief ahead of her, she still missed him. She missed Loara, too. Even her globe green pudding. But her family was at least still alive. Somewhere.

She stared out at the darkening mountainside. People were lighting torches to repel nightbeasts already and it was growing harder to see the far side of the valley. "Why don't you tell him now?" Samra said. "You could tell him before we go."

Atlas looked at her, reading her face, then squinted at the dark hole in the valley floor at the base of the sandfall. He watched the spot for another few seconds, then seemed to make up his mind. He got to his feet. Samra rose with him and waited as he cupped his hands around his mouth.

"Grandpa!" Atlas shouted. He took another deep breath and yelled again. "I love you!"

The yell echoed off the mountains, reverberating through the distant caves.

Samra caught a few people looking up from the decks of their ships, searching for the source of the shout. She could see a few whispering and pointing. Atlas didn't seem to notice. He was looking away. Somewhere far beyond the valley.

"Do you feel better?" Samra asked.

Atlas shrugged. "I don't know. Maybe."

Samra stepped a little closer and put her hand in his. His fingers seemed to hesitate, then once again interlocked through hers the way they had done in the starship. They stood that way, staring out at the darkness; she wasn't sure how long.

What she did realize, after a while, was that something was coming closer—a darker shape against the already dim terrain—growing steadily larger as it approached. She barely had time to recognize the flapping wings and pointed ears of the creature before it was on top of them. The cliff fox barreled into Atlas at full speed, pulling up just short of his chest and scrabbling to land atop the boy's shoulder.

"Fledge!" Atlas cried out and reached for the cliff fox with both arms, catching the little furry body as it flapped and screeched around him. The cliff fox tucked its wings in at last, settled against Atlas's chest, and gave his neck a couple of quick, fervent licks. Atlas laughed reflexively, then caressed the animal's head. "Thank you," he whispered, staring out at the darkness. "I'm glad you heard me."

The three of them settled back down on the deck and Fledge eventually released his hold on Atlas long enough for Samra to take him into her lap. Atlas finally seemed interested in the plate of food and wolfed it down faster than Samra had thought possible. They stayed there long after he was finished, just a Grounder, a

Skylighter, and a bat, watching the night fall.

"You're sure you have to go so soon?"

Kipling had agreed to meet up with Quimby one last time prior to departure. They stood on the dock in the morning sun, lingering around the last of the ship's provisions.

"Some of those globe sons have been out in the desert a long time. Only about half of them were even good enough to save," Kipling said. "We loaded in the ones that were still fresh and we're going to transport them back to the patch. Those plus the ones that were still aboard the *Restless Fury* ought to be enough to pollinate the rest of the colonies. That's the hope anyway. We still have to hunt down the Globe Mother. She could have blown a long way by now."

Kipling realized after he finished, that Quimby hadn't really been asking for an explanation of globe patch horticulture. She nodded, though, and made a good show of agreeing with his reasoning.

"But maybe we'll be back here next year," Kipling added. "The north winds blow pretty strong sometimes. It pushes the patch well beyond Southfang some years. Happens at least once a decade or so . . ." He trailed off feebly.

"Yeah. That's something to look forward to," Quimby said. She scraped a bit of mud off one of her boots with the toe of her other boot, then straightened up. "Well, I guess it's been good knowing you." She stuck out her hand in the typical Grounder custom. Kipling dutifully reciprocated. He shook her hand firmly and tried to look her in the eyes. Quimby looked away too quickly to be sure, but he thought her eyes looked watery.

The girl nodded to him curtly, spun on her heel, and walked away down the dock, passing Warehime who was standing with her daughter and grandson, who had come to see the ship's cook off on her journey. Kipling frowned at the retreating figure of Quimby, then grabbed a basket of supplies and ascended the gangplank to the ship. Samra was climbing down from one of the engine nacelle braces and she shook her head at him as he stepped aboard.

"What?" Kipling asked.

"You know all those manners lessons you took at home with

your mom?"

"Yeah?"

"They're stupid." Samra hopped down the rest of the way to the deck and rested her hand on Kipling's shoulder. "I don't know a lot about Grounders yet, but I know a couple things about being a girl. I can tell you this much. We don't care about you being polite and respecting all the rules all the time. Some rules are meant to be broken." She took the basket from him and headed below decks.

Kipling stared after her for a moment, then turned back to the dock. Quimby was already out of sight. He hesitated only a moment longer, then ran and took a flying leap off the ship. He landed on the dock well past where the cook and her family were standing, causing the old woman's grandson to shout with glee and point. He raced past them and finally caught up with Quimby as she was about to board a public city skiff.

"Quimby, wait!" He grabbed the girl's shoulder and she started as she turned around.

"Whoa! What?" Quimby said. She hastily wiped a sleeve across one cheek and rubbed her hand on her pants. "What do you want?" Her voice was defiant now.

"I forgot something," Kipling said. He wavered just a moment, then wrapped his arms around Quimby. The girl froze briefly, but then he felt her otherwise pinned arms reach around his waist. He held her for as long as he hoped would be appropriate, then finally released her, backing up a step to check the results.

Quimby was smiling faintly. She sniffed once and then wiped her sleeve across her eye one more time. "Okay. Glad you remembered then."

Kipling smiled back. "Yeah. Me too." He let his hand trail off the sleeve of her jacket. "And, you know, you're a pilot now, so if the patch doesn't exactly make it down this far south next season, we could still fix that, right?"

"Damn right I could," Quimby said. "As soon as I steal another ship."

There were juvenile spiders in the Rift, boldly spinning webs across the passes, but the *Restless Fury* found its way through. They'd taken the western route around the sky forest and approached the highlands from the sea. Despite the nightly dangers of sailing the open skies, they'd made good time. It was morning on the third day of flying when Atlas heard the Beacon Bell at the valley end of the Rift.

Atlas stood on the bow of the *Fury* and waved to Danson Merkle, the watchtower guard. Danson stopped ringing the bell, peered at Atlas through a pair of field glasses, then waved. He rang the bell again, this time the signal for friendly arrivals.

As they pulled abeam the watchtower, Danson leaned over the edge of the beacon parapet. "Hope you're headed straight to town!"

"I need to see my aunt," Atlas shouted back.

"In town!" Danson waved a hand toward the valley and cupped a hand around his mouth. "You'll find her at the school!"

"Thank you!" Atlas shouted back.

Danson nodded and waved again. "Good luck!"

Atlas considered the last comment. Was he in that much trouble? He supposed he was. Maybe Amelia wouldn't even want to see him back after what he'd done and how ungrateful he'd been. He climbed down into the cockpit where Samra and Kipling were sharing the seat at the controls.

"And this one is the power lever for the right engine," Samra was explaining.

Kip tentatively pressed forward on the control. "Still seems strange to cruise this fast."

"You're going to have to be fast if you want to catch the patch," Atlas said. "I appreciate you guys taking the detour to get me home." His eyes wandered out the window to the canyons beyond his family ranch. He could just make out the entrance to the warren. Cathy would be there somewhere, tending to the animals like she did in the mornings.

"How's it feel to be home again?" Samra asked.

"I think I'll know in a few minutes," Atlas replied. "There. Past the trees. Near the steeple." He pointed to the heart of the valley and the little village of Womble, still going on with its days. Farmers were working out in the fields. Atlas spotted Minister Teague's horse grazing in the pasture. From the air, it seemed the tragic events of this past week hadn't changed much at all, but Atlas now felt like a stranger.

Sunburn had Samra land the *Restless Fury* in the schoolyard directly in front of the little schoolhouse. There were plenty of other places to land, but the act certainly had its effect. The school doors opened and kids burst out, gawking and gaping at the ship as it touched down.

Sunburn was grinning as he gestured to Atlas. "Go on then. Show them who's come to class today."

Atlas waited for Samra to stop the engines before opening the cockpit hatch. Samra and Kip followed him above deck.

The kids in the schoolyard all stared and pointed, expressions of envy on all of their faces. Even Heather Lanford was watching him with awe and curiosity. But Atlas didn't care. He reached for Samra's hand. "Come on. I need to go find my aunt." They leapt off the bow together, Atlas landing with a crunch, but Samra barely making any noise at all as her feet touched down. Kipling lit up and glided to the schoolyard as well, the kids around them falling back into a reverent half-circle.

They didn't have to go far to find Amelia. She emerged from the doorway of the little schoolhouse, hair in her usual tidy braid, but her expression was anything but reserved. "Atlas!" She raced down the steps and across the yard, only pausing a step away. "I was so worried." She wrapped her arms around Atlas and squeezed him tightly. When she let go, her eyes were moist. "I shouldn't have chased you off like that, I should have tried to —"

"It was my fault." Atlas interrupted her. "I'm sorry I didn't listen to you. Not just when I left but . . ."

Amelia nodded. "It's okay." She put her hands on the sides of his face. "It's just so good you're back." She composed herself a little, noting the eyes of all the school kids on her. "We missed you. Everybody did. But mostly me." She smiled at him finally. Atlas found himself grinning back.

"I missed you, too."

"Who's this then?" Amelia quickly brushed a tear away and glanced at Kipling and Samra, her eyes lingering on Samra's shark tooth necklace for a moment.

"These are my friends," Atlas said. "They helped me find . . ." He nearly said Enzo but the eyes of the other kids were all on him. Somehow it didn't seem right breaking the news of his loss right here in front of everyone. " . . . helped me find my way home."

Without him saying anything, she seemed to understand, not asking the question he was leaving unanswered, even as Fledge chose that moment to come fluttering down from the ship's rigging to alight on his shoulder.

"I'm glad you're safe," Amelia said.

"You're teaching school now?" Atlas asked, peering past her to the open doors of the schoolroom.

"Well, with Mr. Merritt gone, someone had to do something to teach these kids," Amelia said. "I was in town asking for news every morning, and I think the Mayor was tired of me pestering him for help all day. I think he gave me the job partly so I'd have a reason to leave him alone. Though with the Earthen Relic missing, it's been a challenge. There's only so much I can teach these kids. Lord knows they're already tired of hearing about goat ranching." Amelia smiled wanly. "But I do the best I can."

"I have something that will help with that," Atlas said. "I was kind of hoping you might be willing to take it." He reached into his jacket and removed the relic cube and handed it to her. Then he pulled the relic key from around his neck and held that out as well. "Enzo said we should keep the key in the family, but the knowledge is for everybody."

"Look at you," Amelia said, accepting the relic key carefully. "Atlas the Knower."

Atlas shook his head. "I think I've still got a lot left to learn." He smiled. "But I've got a good teacher."

Kipling stood on a hill overlooking the Ridge Valley. They'd relocated the *Restless Fury* to Enzo's ranch and the crew was busy securing the rigging in anticipation of departure. Atlas had offloaded his airship and refilled the tanks on the *Sun Dragon* with the equipment in his grandfather's barn. His first order of business was to take Amelia up for a ride.

Samra went for a ride, too. The little airship was overhead now, gliding around the ranch in slow, easy turns. It was hardly an exhibition of the *Dragon*'s true abilities, but Kipling figured they had all seen enough action to last them a while. Kipling did wonder what they were talking about up there, but he knew if Samra ever wanted to share it with him, she would.

The *Sun Dragon* glided back to the ground a few minutes later and his friends hopped out. Atlas sauntered over to where Kipling was standing. "Sure you don't want one more ride? There are no scarabs or tree people to get us this time."

Kipling smiled but shook his head. "I think we'd better get going. Seems like the winds are still favorable, and Warehime says her bones are predicting bad weather on the horizon. Whatever that means."

Atlas nodded. "Best get flying while the skies are clear. You have a plan for how to catch the globe patch?"

"It will drift a little differently since it's all broken up, but I have a good idea where it ought to be right now," Kipling said. "With any luck, they might be in a slower current and it'll give us a chance to catch up. We'll keep chasing it till we do."

Atlas extended his hand. "I guess it's goodbye, then."

Kipling ignored the hand and gave Atlas a hug.

Samra laughed.

Atlas got a hug from Samra as well, and a quick kiss on the cheek.

"I hope you find your parents," Atlas said. "and the missing colonies."

"I've got a good navigator," Samra said. "We'll find them."

Atlas walked with them to the *Restless Fury* and stood ahead of the ship so he could wave to them as they took off. Samra took the airship up and backward for a little ways before finally making the turn toward the Rift. Her eyes were on the boy until he disappeared from sight below the hull, and the mountains rose large in their view.

"You okay saying goodbye?" Kipling asked.

Samra kept her attention ahead. "It's not goodbye. We'll be back." A smile was playing at the corners of her mouth.

"Looks like you two have this well in hand," Sunburn commented from behind them. He was standing and leaning on the captain's chair instead of sitting in it. He claimed it was uncomfortable for a man his size and over the past few days he'd tended to spend more of his time above decks than in the cockpit. "I'll just go check on the rest of the crew. Can't have them getting soft just because there's no one around with a whip anymore." He nodded to Kipling and Samra and disappeared out the back hatch again.

Samra settled lower into her seat. She looked comfortable there, her eyes intent on the mountains.

They navigated the Rift without incident and by early evening they were headed for the open air above the highlands. One of the moons was peeking over the horizon and a few planets already glowed in the twilight.

Samra looked over to Kipling. "So, you ready to go on another adventure?"

"I'm friends with you, so I'm already living one." He grinned at her. "Let's go home."

Samra pushed the power levers forward, pulled back on the control wheel, and the *Restless Fury* climbed for the open sky.

EPILOGUE

The cockpit windows were coated in dust and the sounds of the outside world were muffled.

Erin Savage had never found her father's airship a joyous place, but as she was escorted into the battered bridge, the mood seemed especially grim.

Eric was slumped in the chair at the end of their father's war table, facing the bridge windows and nursing his broken arm. Marlow hadn't been cleaned up. Her father had merely been laid across the table. His clothes were caked with dirt and his hands were hastily crossed over his chest. A faded captain's hat had been found and now covered his face. The rows upon rows of relic keys still burdened his throat beneath his beard. Erin felt the compulsion to remove them, but it didn't matter now. Marlow had taken his last breath days ago.

"She enters. The source of our calamity," Eric commented.

Erin waited. She had learned many years ago that attempting to defend herself prior to one of her brother's tirades only prolonged the effects. But that was also before. Before there was an opportunity to lead.

"And now I hear they've brought down the gate. I trust you're satisfied with yourself."

"The Storm Gate can be reopened," Erin said.

"That would take months," Eric hissed from the other side of the table. "Our fleet will be torn to ribbons out here. Without the port we'll be battered against the rocks in the first real storm. Not to mention that the mountain is held by mutineers."

"You'll have to head south," Aspen said. Eric's first mate was standing behind her brother. His voice was calm. Too calm. It seemed to slither out of him. Erin tensed at his words. "We can make our way around the mountains," Aspen continued. "Take the long route east beyond the high passes, then turn northward again. Once they've ceased to expect us, we'll fall on them and retake the port. Then we can restart the excavation."

"We don't need the excavation anymore," Eric said. "We need to find the culprits responsible for this and make them pay."

"Without the excavation, the *Starfire* will be lost. Your father spent years —"

"I am not my father!" Eric shouted. He shoved himself up from the table. "I don't care about his treasure hunt, or his dreams of leaving this world. Look where it got him!" He gestured toward the table.

Aspen didn't look at Marlow. He stared straight ahead.

"Leave us," Eric ordered.

Aspen dutifully walked to the cabin door and exited, closing it gently behind him.

Eric adjusted the sling supporting his broken arm, then wiped a hand across his face before turning to Erin and continuing in a calmer tone. "Our father built an empire here. An empire where we rested securely in the knowledge that our family always had the upper hand. We had the best resources, the best tools, and the greatest trove of knowledge at our disposal to gain more. People all looked to us to give them answers. They needed us! There is only one relic they need now, and it's aboard your ship." Eric stabbed a finger at her. "Whoever holds that relic holds the power. So, that's where we'll be going. We'll gather our weapons from the fallen ships and move out tonight. There will be no safe space in this sky for those thieves and murderers."

Erin already regretted having told her brother that the master relic was gone, but she had needed him to stop searching for it during the days in the belly of the starship. It had seemed a kindness to let Eric know so that he could stop trying to fulfill their father's last wish and find it for him. If that's even what he wanted it for. Now she wasn't so sure.

"She's just a child," Erin said. "They all are."

"A child who apparently took control of your ship and absconded with it. Where is your faithful crew, Sister?" Eric said. "Why weren't they assisting with the rescue efforts to save us from that pit? Aspen is the only man I can count on, it seems." He waved his free hand toward the door and then stomped his way over to the blurry windows. "There's nothing out here but inhospitable desert. But at least I don't have to spend any more time looking at you."

Erin caught a whiff of the body on the table and wrinkled her nose. "We need to bury him, Eric. Soon."

"I told you we should have left him in the starship," Eric said. "It was his great treasure after all. He should be buried with it."

A part of Erin agreed with that thought, but in the days inside the ship, she could never shake the feeling that she was still being watched. The glowing woman had never reappeared, but Erin had felt her. She recognized her presence. Doors left open. Lights that illuminated holds filled with food and supplies. Even the room they'd dragged Marlow into had mercifully closed its doors until the rescue team arrived. Eric refused to acknowledge the presence in the ship, but Erin had known. She knew and she was grateful.

The fall of the starship had seemed chaotic, but it had been a lie.

Erin didn't believe in coincidence. Coincidence like the fact that she had been hurled into a supply cupboard full of sleeping gear and survival blankets on her way back through the ship to find her father. Coincidence that the fall of the ship was arrested at the bottom just enough that Eric only sustained a fractured arm. She even wondered if her father's broken neck might have been avoided as well, if it hadn't been for the weight of the relic keys hanging around his throat.

It was a question she didn't feel she could ask while still in the belly of the starship. She felt it was enough to be grateful she was alive and to escape. Eric was clearly feeling no such gratitude. He was still muttering at the window.

"We'll hunt them down and make them pay. Every last one of them," he hissed. "We'll take it all back. Everything they've stolen from our family. Then we'll be back on top where we belong."

Erin sighed and made her way toward the doorway. Admiral Orloff passed her on the way in, his leering gaze lingering far longer than was pleasant. "You summoned me, Lord Savage?" Orloff said.

Eric turned and welcomed him with a crooked smile. "Yes,

Admiral. Come in. We have much to discuss."

Erin left them to their scheming and climbed the steps to the deck.

The *Vega* was moored only a few feet off the desert's surface, tethered to a mound of dig wreckage that had yet to sink into the sand. Erin stepped off the deck and onto the pile of timber. She was covered in sand, she hadn't bathed in days, and her hair clung to her neck in sweaty strands, but she felt cleaner off her father's ship nonetheless.

The air out here was hot but it was fresh.

She didn't need the *Vega*.

She didn't need her brother's plans.

She'd been here before. Broke. Alone. Grounded. But she knew she'd find her way. She'd find a ship. She'd find a crew.

Then she'd find *her* ship. Her crew.

There was only one way left for her to go.

Up.

Want more?
Be sure to download the free bonus content including original
sketches by the author, character bios, and the illustrated map
of Altiria! Get your free bonus material at
www.nathanvancoops.com/bonus

The adventure will continue!
If you have enjoyed this adventure, please consider leaving a
review on Amazon or Goodreads. Your comments are greatly
appreciated and really help the ongoing success of this book!

ACKNOWLEDGEMENTS

I am incredibly grateful:

First and foremost to my lovely wife Stephanie for being my partner through this adventure and understanding that no matter how old we get, we're still kids at heart.

For my wonderful mom, Marilyn Bourdeau, who has been a champion of my writing since I began and who has become an essential part of my publishing process.

For Emily Young, my writer's group partner, friend, and editor, for her passion and enthusiasm for this book and our friendship. She has helped keep the characters in the story true to their best selves.

For the awesome servers and restaurant staff who have kept me in tacos and iced tea during the countless hours I spent typing away in corners of taco shops around town. Especially Landy Hernandez, Liz, Julie, Christina Lopez, Steven Campbell, Maylin Cuello, Bill, Nadia, and Sara. Thanks for all the times you gave me the large tea and only charged me for the small. :)

For the creative professionals who made my work look first-class. Shayne Leighton, Julia Scheiber, Ben Way, and Meril-liza Chan.

For my amazing beta readers in the First Look Beta Squad. Because of their enthusiasm for this story, and willingness to hunt down my typos and disagree with me on grammar when I need it, this book is cleaner and better than it ever could be with just the work of a few editors. The team has not only become indispensable, many have also become my friends. They are:

Aaron Call, Abhinav Saxena, Adam Egender, Adrian Peters, Aj Shephard, Alain Paumen, Alexandra De Gruyter, Alicia Ruskai ,Alison Aylen, Alissa Nesson, Allen Gary, Amanda Bildeaux, Amber Koch, AmySpicka, Andrea Sestak, Andy Hasper, Andy Westbay, Angela Sleigh, Angela Smithson, Anthony, Anthony Carter, Aris St James, Artur Rosa, Ashlee, Athena Engel, Barb Brown, Barb Johnson, Becky, Becky Alexander-Conrad, Becky Lewis, Ben Bailey, Ben Cadena, Ben Westing, Benjamin Wiechel, Bernie, Bethany, Bill Beyer, Bill Hamshire, Bill Mccarthy, Billy Commander, Billy Hepburn, Billy Priest, Blanche Padgett, Bob Cheney, Bob Drews, Bob Micciche, Bob Steiner, Jr, Bonnie Campbell, Brad Hammond, Brent, Brett, Brian Clark, Brian Masterson, Brian Paquette, Brian Steele, Bruce Raffel, Bruce Small, Calum Munday, Candice Costanzo, Carl Derubeis, Carlo, Carlo Caprini, Caroline Ruth Molloy, Carolyn Bramley, Carolyn Reed, Ce'alm 'Sim' Juan Kilpatrick, Cecelia L Gervais, Charles Mcnabb, Cheryl L, Cheryl Newbanks, Chris & Ann Collins, Chris Dutton, Chris Ehlers, Chris Ross, Christian Cornatzer, Chuck Scro, Cindy Scheffler, Cindy Williams, Claire Manger, Claire Palmer, Coleen Alexander, Corey Scott, Cosmin, Crystal Ley, Damon Guy, Dan Leaman, Dan Mcclure, Dan Mccrory, Dave, Dave Bennett, Dave Plummer, David Dalrymple, David Decamp, David Taylor, Dean Thibault, Deb, Deb Argha Saha, Deb Shaw, Debbie Bratt, Debbie Farmer, Debi Davis, Deborah Boyd, Debra Smith, Denise Cook, Dennis Feagans, Dennis Littlefield, Dennis Mcdonald, Derek Youd, Diane Bates, Diane Mcgrath, Dominique Fruchtman, Don Hunter, Don Rhodes, Don Vanhoosier, Donnisha Jones, Dorothy, Doug Weller, Dr. Angela Pool-Funai, Dulcie Price, Dwight Brooks, Edward D. Casey, Edward Ford, Elaine Davis, Eleanor Bayless, Elenora Sabin, Elisabetta, Elizabeth Ann Woods, Ellen Spradling, Emily Badajos, Emily N Vincent, Emily Young, Eric Karns, Eric Slade, Eva, Eva Holmquist, Fiona Holden, Frank Husky, Gabriel Ashbaugh, Gail Cole, Gary, Gary Randall, Gary Smart, Geoff "Tiny" Elliott, George Beech, George Stanton, Gerry Cohen, Gillian Flato, Ginelle, Gloria

Chadwick, Gordon K Brown Jr, Gordon Lee, Graham Childe, Harry Sweigart, Hazel, Heather Turiello, Herb Clann, Hillary Kelley, Howard Bull, Howard Thomas, Ian Millar, Ian Nuttall, Iian Stephens, Jack Larner, Jack Press, Jackie, Jak Henderson, James, James Morse, Jamie, Jamie Cruver, Jamie Rogers, Jan Butterick, Jan Carlson, Jan Scott, Jane Garcia, Janet Cervantes, Janis Bonner, Jason, Jason J Mader, Jason W. Jones, Jason Wolverton, Jay Wolverton, Jeanette Mustonen, Jeff Bosworth, Jeff Braisted, Jeff Marcum, Jeff Parrott, Jeffery Evans, Jeffry Morris, Jen Watson, Jennifer Beck, Jennifer C Laxson, Jeremiah Hays, Jessica Callenback, Jim Brown, Jim Burch, Jody, Joe Denman, Joe Kane, John Bohrman, John Bremner, John Jackson, John Mcgoldrick, Jon, Jon La Bree, Jonathan Bird, Joseph Kane, Joseph Kane Sr., Joseph Oakey, Josephine Chan, Joshua Schmidt, Julia Taft, Julio Antillon, Karen Lekfowitz, Karen Stansbury, Kari De St Germain, Karl Killebrew, Karl Smith, Kathy James, Kathy Mcqueeny, Kay Clark, Kb Jolley, Kelli, Ken Robbins, Kevin, Kimberly Madrid, Krishnan Neelakantan, Krista Goalby, Kristin Davis, Kristine Taylor, Krystle Drummond, Kym Farner, Kyra Swanner, Larry Gates, Laura Driskell, Laurie Flynn, Lawrence Geller, Leanne Sexton, Lee Inks, Lee Willie, Leslie Mcmeans, Lila Young, Lindsey Betout, Linton, Lisa Alberts-Pettit, Lisa Callahan, Lizette Phillips, Logan Devane, Luke Monin, Lynne, Maggie Parker, Maggie Parker, Malcolm Apted, Marcus Baker, Marijelle Bartholomew, Marilyn Gast, Mark Hale, Marty Myers, Matthew Poslusny, Matthew Rapp, Matthew Snell, Matthew Suarez, Matthew Taylor, Melanie Tippett, Melissa Pritchard, Melissa R, Meshel Sweigart, Michael Clarren, Michael Few, Michael Gray, Michael Naiman, Michael Reed, Michael V. Maxham, Mike Evans, Mike Gower, Mike Henkin, Mike Hiltunen, Milton Diede, Missy Burrows, Mitch Berdinka, Mitchell Kelsey, Nate, Nathan Golder, Nathanyel Terrace, Neill Gerstbauer, Nick Furmston, Nick Woodley, Nicole Dipasquale, Nispar, Parrish Pope, Pat Phelan, Pat Price, Patrick Basso, Paul, Paul Cross, Paul Ness, Paul Sherman, Paul Swier, Pearl Kirkby, Penny L Karsten, Peter Monit, Phil Scott, Philip Coolbeth, Philippe Jardin, Phyllis Reifer, Rachelle Shepherd-Dubey, Ralph Cohen, Randi, Randi Milam, Randy Chrust, Randy

Lakey, Randy Loeb, Ray Antonelli, Ray Wallace-Watson, Ray Warr, Rebecca Lynn Davison, Regina Dowling, Revella, Rhonda Green, Rich Ingersoll, Rob Stephen, Robert Peyton, Robina Tabberer, Robyn Rudd, Roger Rubinstein, Rogerio Faco Franklin, Ronnie Marrache, Ronnie Vance, Rosie, Rowena Limjap, Ruby Metcalf, Ryan S. Newman, Sam Cantwell, Sam Natale, Sammy Peoples, Sandra Kirnbauer, Scott Decotes, Sean Hull, Sean Hull, Sean Moynihan, Sean Moynihan, Seb, Shawn, Sheila Kelly, Simon Whistler, Sister Camille Panich, Skaterbabs, Sophie Armstrong-Jordan, Stephanie, Stephen, Stephen Bishop, Stephen Dorris, Stephen Lafave, Steve, Steve Barnett, Steve Butkovich, Steve Shaw, Steve Winter, Steven King, Steven Michaelsen, Steven Michaelsen, Stuart Baker, Stuart Dykes, Sue, Sue Kilgore, Susan Davies, Sylvia Walker, T.S. Vivona, Talena Colley, Terri Shafer, Terry Pope, Thomas C. Altman, Thomas Maughan, Thomas Rodman, Tiesha Rivera, Tim Bohn, Tim Chatterton, Tim Reeves, Timothy Mason, Tina Van Coops, Todd Margarita, Tonny Worstell, Tony Carter, Tony Dykes, Tony Everett, Tony Locicero, Tony Porras, Tracy Haynie, Trish Ross, Valerie Potter, Veronica Torres, Vicki Rouse, Victoria Palmer, Von Whitlock, Walter Jones, Walter Jones, Wayne J Martin, Wendy Burrell, William Brown, Yume, Yvette, Yvonne Mitchell.

ALSO BY NATHAN VAN COOPS

In Times Like These

The Chronothon

The Day After Never

Learn more at
www.nathanvancoops.com

Made in the USA
Middletown, DE
02 August 2017

46504563R00239